THE

ROUGH

AND THE

SMOOTH

To Hilary + Peter,
with every good wish
for your Australian friend,
Mary.

Mary L. Roberts.

Mary Nelse Roberts

First published in 1998 by Mary Roberts
Victoria Downs, Morven, Qld 4468.
© Mary Roberts

National Library of Australia
Cataloguing-in-Publication data

      Roberts, Mary, 1933– .
      The rough and the smooth.

      ISBN 0 9585888 0 5.

      I. Title.

      A823.3

Designed and typeset by Sun Photoset Pty Ltd, Brisbane
Cover design by Icon Design, Brisbane
Edited by New Word Order, Brisbane
Photographs supplied by Boosie Crighton
Printed and bound by Watson Ferguson & Co., Brisbane

OTHER TITLES BY THE SAME AUTHOR:
Uncle Peter.
Morven, 100 years.

Author's Notes

The whole aim in writing this story has been to record our way of life, our culture, as I see it. When I am away from home, so many people ask me what it is like to live in the bush. I believe I have been privileged to know this life so well. This novel is an attempt to tell the world how it is to live out here.

What better way to introduce it to the world than through the Great South-West Regional Cultural Summit? My thanks to the committee for their faith in me that this book would be worthy of a place at the summit.

There is also need to acknowledge a debt of gratitude to the Regional Arts Development Fund, through the Murweh Shire Council, for sponsoring this book. It is expensive to publish and their help has made it possible to produce the book for sale at a reasonable cost. This is important if it is to reach the reading public. Thank you, RADF committee.

A very big thanks to Suzanne Oxford from New Word Order. There is absolutely no doubt that her help has resulted in making it a more professional book. It has been a pleasure to work with Suzanne.

Kylie Smith, Helen Balmain and Sally Gorman have each contributed to the text in their respective areas of expertise and for that help I am most grateful.

Quite a few people have typed the manuscript for me as it has progressed over the years and thank you to all of you. Without exception, everyone has been helpful and encouraging.

Lastly and probably most importantly, thanks to all my friends and acquaintances from a lifetime spent out here. These are the people who have been the raw material for the book, whose story I want to tell. The characters in the novel are completely fictitious. No character is based upon anyone I know. On the other hand, it is a true story in that the things that happen to them – nearly every single incident – is something I've seen or heard around me. So likenesses are inevitable, but unintentional. No character is taken from real life but is an amalgamation and blend of several personality types and characteristic opinions.

I truly admire and love the people I know out here. I love their spirit. They are hardworking and full of grit, determination and humour. Australia itself will be the loser if it allows the people of the west to be sacrificed to economic rationalism or short-sighted expediency in any other matter.

Chapter 1

It was just breaking daylight when the two motorbikes crossed the creek and came out of the shadows of the trees. In the early light, the riders could see quite clearly the figure of a tiny woman standing on the top step of the cottage that was beside the road just a little further down the track. With unspoken agreement, they moved across.

The first bike pulled up with a bit of a flourish. Good looking and charming Tony MacFarlane smiled at the small, spare old lady, confident of a welcome. "G'day Mrs Alsop," he said, grinning up at her. "How're you going?"

The old lady glared. "None the better for your asking," she replied curtly.

Taken aback, Tony just blinked at her.

The second bike pulled to a stop a bit more sedately, but equally ready with a friendly greeting. "You're up early after the party, Mrs Alsop," the rider said. "It's good to see you looking so chipper."

The old lady snapped. "It's a pity I can't say the same about you, Charles Carmody." She waved her hand at them dismissively. "Be on with your job. Get your cattle and get out of here."

Charles was as surprised as Tony. "'Struth, Mrs Alsop, what's the matter?" he asked. "What's the problem?"

She was ready enough to tell them. "I was late last night, as you know, and when I got home your wretched cattle had knocked down my fence," she said in an accusing tone. "And they must have been covered with lice, too, because they'd rubbed themselves on all my precious new trees. Advanced trees that I'd just paid a fortune for at the nursery. And they had the whole lot broken to the ground."

She swept her hand around dramatically at what they now realised was a pretty devastated garden and indicated the broken little saplings that were lying every which way on the grass. "And,"

1

she continued, "one of them must have rubbed himself against a tap and turned it on and it's drained my high tank. So now I don't have any water."

They were beginning to get the picture, but she hadn't finished with them yet.

"Out the back, near the septic tank, they'd been fighting out there and at least one bullock has been through the sullage pit and broken it in." She was fairly steaming. "The place is a total disaster, thanks to you and your cattle."

Tony edged in a few cautious words. "Geez, I am sorry," he said apologetically. "How could we expect anything like this to happen?"

Charles added, "Look, we have to go on and muster these cattle now, but we'll come back and do something as soon as we can."

Mrs Alsop was determined to have the last say. "Save yourselves the trouble. I'd be better off without you. Your parents were my friends, fine people, but you're nothing but irresponsible ratbags. Always rushing off here and there, never attending to your places. Nothing done properly. Whatever happened to good, old-fashioned, hard work, I don't know."

She turned to go inside, but carried on. "No dedication to the job any more. No-one does things properly. I don't know what the world is coming to. But, I suppose, if you haven't got it, you can't produce it."

"That's rather hard, Mrs Alsop," muttered the irrepressible Tony as they started up their bikes again and without any discussion went to work.

Charles and Tony had worked together often enough to become a good team. Since they'd only pulled up to speak to old Ethel Alsop as a courtesy when they saw her standing there, they went on to muster the cattle as planned.

Tony had one hundred and fifty bullocks in this paddock. Charles had helped him to bring them in to truck away to sale a week ago, but a passing storm had made the ground too wet for the trucks to get in to load.

Luckily for Tony, Joe McMahon – who owned Juno Station, this property right beside the little centre of Juno – was generous and often helped his friends and neighbours out when they were caught by rain. Not that it happened often, because it was rare that plans were changed on account of rain. He'd told Tony it was OK to let the bullocks go in the paddock until it was dry enough to load them.

Mrs Alsop was Joe's aunt, and she now lived in this cottage in the bottom corner of the paddock not far from town and the yards and loading ramp. It was an old cottage and had been done up for her – but it looked like the fence still needed a bit of work done to it.

"Mrs Alsop's comments were a bit tough," Charles mused to himself as he and Tony rode away. Then he grinned as he wondered what his employees in Brisbane, who thought he was a bit of a martinet, would have thought about seeing him put on the carpet by such a tiny, irate, old lady. He wondered just how much damage the cattle had really done and if it could be put to rights fairly easily. He'd have to see what system Joe had for pumping water and if they could be any help. "Can't do much about the trees, though," he thought.

They'd known Mrs Alsop all their lives. She had always been known to speak her mind, but it did seem as though she had a case today.

They spread out and got to work. The cattle hadn't been there long and it was only a holding paddock, really, so it didn't take the two experienced stockmen long to get them together and into the yards. The trucks weren't coming until the next morning, but they'd started early in case they ran into any trouble. They certainly hadn't anticipated running into trouble with Mrs Alsop.

Tony was obviously still thinking about the tongue-lashing they'd copped. "What do you think, Charlie?" he asked. "Have the cattle really done much serious damage to the old girl's place? Silly old bat. You'd think it was our fault! The fence must have been rotten or something."

"Whatever the reason, Tony, I think we'd better work out a plan of action to try to settle things down," Charles replied. "Things aren't too good back there, you know. We don't want to spoil an old friendship."

"Good, old-fashioned, hard work," Tony mimicked her voice. "I didn't know people actually said that any more. Doesn't she live in the real world?"

A bit quick-tempered by nature, Tony started getting aggrieved. "We bloody well never stop working and what's more, everyone knows good, old-fashioned work on our places is never enough any more."

Charles agreed, really, but tried to placate his mate. "Give the old girl a go, Tony," he said. "She knows it well enough. She blew her stack because she's upset and cross, but underneath she understands."

"Bloody hell! Understands, you say?" Tony was really starting to fire up. "How the hell does anyone understand just what another person has to do? Who really knows what you've done, Charlie boy? Your old man would be out on his ear if it wasn't for your money and organisation. Who knows about that?" He broke off, smiled ruefully and finished under his breath, "Or about me for that matter."

Charles caught the last bit. "And that's for sure," he thought. "I certainly don't know or understand just what you're up to, my friend, and I've lived next to you all my life." Charles had a few ideas about Tony's affairs – but only a handful of half-formed ideas and no facts. For all of his charm, Tony was not the type to let on much about his life.

Meanwhile, Tony was still going off about Mrs Alsop. "Everybody is in trouble making their places pay, but if anyone is a bit imaginative and tries to do something else to make money, everyone knocks them. 'It's all right for them,' they say, 'But if they had my troubles..!' Bloody hell, we've all got our troubles these days. The government makes sure of that."

Charles was getting bored with his rhetoric. "Aw, come off it, Tony," he said. "We'd better go over and see what we can do to put the place in order."

Tony quietened down a bit. "Actually, I guess we should see what we can do to help." He thought for a moment. "She wouldn't really have been like that if it wasn't serious. I guess I'd better dig out the sullage pit and see what I can do about the fence."

Then Tony started organising Charles. "You're a whole lot smarter than I am, so you see if you can fix old Ethel's computer. I heard it died the other day. It'd be a real help if you could get it going before you go. After all, you're the electronics man." He grinned. "There has to be some reward for doing well at school. I get the digging and you get the easy job."

Charles shook his head at his mate wonderingly. "How the devil do you know about her computer?"

Tony looked smug. "There have to be some rewards for just hanging around at the pub, Charlie boy," he said. "A fellow can't

4

drink much any more, but he can talk to everyone who comes in. I know all the gossip. Actually, Bill-Bob's been trying to fix her computer for a while – but he's a bit long in the tooth now and doesn't understand this new technology. If it was anything mechanical now, it'd be a different story."

Charles nodded. He had a soft spot for his old mate Bill-Bob, who worked with him and his father on their place, Carmody Plains. "If he can't find anything mechanical wrong, well, there is nothing mechanical wrong," he agreed.

Tony kick-started his bike. "In Mrs Alsop's case, you'd better reach into your bag of tricks," he said. "At least it's easier work fiddling with a few wires than digging out a trench."

The two took off.

When they got back to the house, Tony turned on the charm to sweet-talk Mrs Alsop before she could turn them away. "Look, we're here to help, if you'll let us," he said placatingly. "I'll fix up that septic drainage and Charles here is good with computers and he'll have a look at that one of yours."

Being Tony, he couldn't resist a slight joke. "This is where his good education comes in handy," he said, winking at the old lady. "He gets the easy job."

Mrs Alsop was not amused. Reluctantly agreeing, she made it clear it was against her better judgment. Her expression clearly said she didn't think the men would be of any use to her – and that Tony was surely too flippant to be productive.

Tony proved her wrong within minutes. For all of his flippancy, he was a damn good worker. He started in with a will, digging out the drainage pit.

For his part, Charles tried to be quiet and unobtrusive to avoid causing the old lady any more distress. She was crotchety, all right, but he was perceptive enough to realise that it was being upset over the damage that was causing her to be so uptight. He wanted to fix things if he could. He'd already made up his mind he'd have a talk to Joe to see if he needed any help to pump up some water. For now, though, he could help Mrs Alsop with her computer.

"Now show me where you keep your PC and tell me what's been the trouble," he said quietly.

But Mrs Alsop was not completely won over. She looked doubtfully at Charles. "I'm not quite sure I should let you touch it, even though Bill-Bob says you're a wizard with these things," she said. "I'd take his opinion on most things, you know – but in your case, Charles Carmody, I think he's a bit prejudiced. For some reason, you can do no wrong in his eyes." She reluctantly led him through the hallway to the office where the computer was. "I'll just reserve my judgment. In the meantime, I suppose it'll do no harm to let you look at it."

Charles thought it was a good thing he hadn't expected any great appreciation for his offer. The old lady couldn't have been more off-putting. The fact his old friend had given him such a wrap-up took the harshness from her words.

Mrs Alsop was explaining how her computer crashed. "The computer has always worked well, but then one day I rearranged my office completely and the computer hasn't worked since. I moved it, I didn't drop it – although I nearly did, so it got a bit of a jolt – and now it just sits there, with the green light showing but a blank screen."

They were in the office now and Charles sat down at the PC and turned it on. Sure enough, it started to boot but then it just hung. As the old lady had explained, the green light was showing but the screen was dead. Charles carefully disconnected the keyboard, screen and mouse, and opened the box. A quick inspection showed the motherboard had been jolted a bit and wasn't seated properly. He reseated it, thoroughly checked the connections and before long had the computer hooked up again. He hit the on switch and this time the computer rebooted successfully through to the sign-on screen.

Despite herself, Mrs Alsop was impressed. She hadn't really had any confidence that he'd be able to do anything and here it was working again in such a short time.

Charles stood up from the desk. "There you go, Mrs Alsop, I think you'll find that's okay now. Shouldn't be any more trouble, but if there is, just call me. I'm going away for a while – I have to see to some business in Melbourne – but after that we'll be shearing and I'll definitely be back then. In the meantime, we'd better put a barb around your fence to stop any more trouble."

He went out to see how Tony was coping.

By the time they left, Mrs Alsop was practically beaming. "You two aren't so bad after all," she conceded. "I'm sorry I was so upset. You'd think that by now I would have learned to take the rough with the smooth and not put on a turn when something goes wrong. Bill-Bob just might have been right about you after all."

Having done what they could, the two were feeling pretty pleased with themselves when they stopped off for a drink or two at the pub before pushing off home.

Old Dan Flannigan was the only other person at the bar. A big, bulky, old bloke with a bushy beard, he spoke with a bit of a stutter. His dirty shirt didn't quite meet his trousers at the back, which sat down low on his hips. It didn't meet over his ample beer gut, either.

"G'day Dan," Charles greeted him.

"G'day f-fellas," he said, glancing up. "How've you been?"

He was just turning back to his drink when a thought struck him and he turned to the two men. "You know, I've been looking for someone like you fellas. How'd you go lending me fifty quid?"

Neither Charles nor Tony were terribly interested in helping old Dan. He was a good enough bloke when he wasn't on the grog, but to lend him money when he'd already started drinking..?

Undeterred by their lack of interest, Dan made a determined effort to get them on side. "G'on," he said. "Give us fifty quid, will you? One of you must be able to lend a bloke fifty quid."

Finally, Charles took pity on him. "What do you want it for, Dan?" he asked warily.

Dan eagerly started to explain, "I need it to get a permit to take me old truck out to..."

But Tony interrupted, a bit exasperated. "Cut it out, Dan. It's Sandy's day off. You'll have it spent long before the police station opens and you can get your permit."

Dan looked shocked at the idea. "No, no, fellas, he's waiting for me to come down and pay him."

Charles agreed with Tony. "Not today he won't be, Dan."

"Yeah, fair dinkum," Dan was getting desperate. "He knows I need a permit and he's waiting. Go on, Charles. Lend us fifty quid. You're g-going to be shearing soon and you'll be w-wanting an extra ringer. You can take it out of me wages then."

"Who says I'm that desperate, Dan?" Charles tried to look annoyed, then sighed. "You blasted old rogue. A man needs his head read even listening to you."

Charles turned to the man behind the bar. "Can you give him the fifty quid, Arry, and chalk it up to me?"

Arry turned to the till. "If you want to, Charles, no skin off my nose. There's one born every moment, you know."

But Dan didn't just take the money and go. He stood waiting at the counter.

Arry looked at him. "Anything else I can do for you, Dan?"

Dan nodded. "A square bear mate'll do me fine," he said.

Arry reached for the square-shaped Bundy rum bottle with the polar bear on its label.

The bartender didn't have to say 'I told you so' to Charles as he passed him. He just rolled his eyes.

The door opened and a short, stocky, fair-haired man walked into the bar.

"G'day Bruce," Tony called out to him. "What are you doing in here at this time of day?"

Bruce walked over to join them. "Geez, I'm glad to see you blokes," he said. "I've been trying to get you both on the two-way, but neither of you were answering."

Charles looked concerned. "What up, mate?"

"I've just shot the biggest pig I've ever seen," he replied. "It's a bloody beauty. I didn't even know it was on the place. You'll never believe it until you see it."

Tony and Charles exchanged glances. It wasn't like Bruce to rave on like this without a good reason, but everyone had heard big pig stories before.

"I wanted one of you blokes to come and give me a hand to load him, but now I've got you both together that's even better," Bruce continued. "We could actually need the three of us to load him and get him into the chilling box in town. They're paying pretty well for them now."

Not convinced, Tony tried to get out of it.

"Fair go, Bruce, you don't expect us to come all the way out to your place now, do you?" he asked. "We're busy drinking."

Bruce was insistent. "You've gotta come, I'm telling you. It's a bloody beauty. It'd be worth a good two days' wages at least."

Usually quiet, Bruce wouldn't shut up about his pig. When the others realised he genuinely wanted them to come out and help him load his wretched pig, they finished their drinks and piled into his Toyota with him and they were off.

Bruce told them the story as he drove. "I was out in this doing a water run," he said. "As I came up to that gate that's just near that patch of scrub in Box Flat, I saw a mob of pigs take off. Right into the scrub they went. I thought one looked pretty big but I didn't get a good look at it. I thought they'd be too far away to worry about."

He was really warming to his subject. "By the time I'd opened and shut the gate, Nut – you know my good black dog?"

The others nodded, thinking it was better to let him rave on and get over it.

"He took off into the scrub where the pigs had gone," Bruce continued. "It was too thick to see much and I thought it was a waste of time to go after them, but I called Nut and he wouldn't come. I couldn't even see him, either, but I could hear him barking. 'Damn dog', I thought. 'Come here, you useless mongrel'. I wanted to get on and get a few more paddocks checked. 'Get over here', I called again – but he stayed where he was, barking."

Bruce shifted up a gear, still talking. "I was getting wild, I can tell you. I was calling Nut every name under the sun. I didn't really think he had anything worthwhile bailed up, but I had to get him back. So I turned off the car and got out to get him. I tell you what, it was lucky I took my gun with me."

As Bruce's captive audience, Charles and Tony exchanged another glance of disbelief, but still said nothing.

Bruce continued. "I went over after him as casual as you like, although I was irritated as hell that he was wasting my time – thought he had a sucker or something. And I'm still yelling at him: 'Get over here, you bloody, useless, mongrel of a dog'. And then: 'Oh, good dog, good dog'. Nut had this bloody, great pig bailed up. While I was there, the pig had a go at him and Nut snapped back. So I just got a lean on a tree and waited until Nut was clear and *bam!* Got him! Wow, what a pig! You fellas won't believe the size of him."

Arriving at the spot, Bruce was right. All of his raving couldn't prepare them for the size of the hulking great beast which lay in its dead glory where Bruce had shot it.

"That is a big pig," Charles agreed. "Probably go one hundred kilograms."

Tony walked around the beast, shaking his head at the size of it. "Bigger, I reckon."

Bruce interrupted their estimates, focusing them on the task at hand. "I've been trying to work out how to get him up on the back

9

of the Toyota," he said. "I thought maybe we could use the Toyota to pull him up onto a tree a bit so we can get it back under him."

The three, working together, did just that. They tied him onto the top rail at the back of the cabin of the Toyota with a truckies' knot and pulled him up as high as they could get him, and then just swung him back onto the tray.

When they got him to town, Jim, the fellow at the pig box, was equally surprised. "Christ!" he exclaimed. "That's a big pig!"

Realising his scales wouldn't cope with the size of the pig – Jim's scales only went to a hundred kilograms – the four of them trekked out to the nearest woolshed and put the pig on the wool scales. The beast went a massive one hundred and thirty-three kilos. Then it took the four of them to put it on the hook in the cool room.

The three friends were pleased with that job and went on back to the pub, talking animatedly about the pig and other exploits they'd shared.

When they swung into the cool of the bar to have a well-earned drink, the only other person in there again was old Dan.

He tried to bite them again, too, but they fobbed him off and started to talk together.

"You know, Bruce, we've just had a run-in with old Ethel Alsop," Charles informed him.

"Fair dinkum?"

"My oath!"

Bruce laughed as he thought of a couple of times when he'd been on the receiving end of Mrs Alsop's anger. "She can be sharp when she wants to." Then he frowned and said, "What was the problem? I thought she was reconciled to losing her place. Poor old girl. She was telling Aunt Bessie the other day that she's free of worry now for the first time for at least thirty years."

Old Dan called out, "Sharp-tongued old bitch. She makes trouble, that one."

Bruce glanced at him, but ignored the interruption. "You know, all the time she was trying desperately to keep the place going, I don't think she could've always been sure of getting a decent feed. Now she's sold the place, paid her debts and she thinks she's in clover. The government wouldn't give her a cent when she needed it, even though she was contributing to the economy. Now she's got nothing to look after but herself. Her nephew gives her a house to live in and the government gives her a pension."

He turned to Charles. "Why didn't you buy her place? It would have made a good addition to Carmody Plains."

Charles shook his head and replied with vehemence, "You're joking – why the hell would I throw good money away? I'm definitely not in a build-up mood. After Dad goes, I'm not even sure I'll keep the place I've got – if I've still got it after all these land claims. Can't sell the place out from under Dad, but it's a bloody white elephant as far as I'm concerned."

Tony was thoughtful. "Crikey, another one doing a runner."

Bruce looked saddened, but not surprised. "That'd be a pity," he said. "Your family's been here as long as anybody. Are you just going to let them push you off?"

Charles's assessment was truthful but blunt. "Well, I'm not married, nor likely to be, so there's no son to pass it on to. Why let it eat up money for ever, just in case it all comes good? Neither side of this country's government looks like trying to organise the economy to help the man on the land, regardless of the fact that every other developed country in the world does. This country has a cultural cringe and can't bear to think it's beholden to primary industry. Call it a 'hayseed economy' – even though it's a major force in the nation's balance of payments."

Warming to his subject, Charles went on. "While they had Ethel Alsop on Curlew, the government made money out of her, even if she was losing money every year. The shearers were paid and they paid taxes. The truckies were paid and their taxes went into the coffers and her little bit of wool went to keep the storemen and packers and agents and others in work and paying taxes, too. Then the wool sold overseas to help the national debt. Now her block is added to old Jim's next door and they'll run no extra sheep while things are as they are. It's only an insurance policy for them and it's contributing absolutely nothing to the economy."

Bruce nodded. "Well, at least it hasn't been bought out by bloody overseas investors who just leave it empty and going to rack and ruin like the place next door to us. It's an absolute haven for feral animals and noxious weeds and erosion. I wonder how many parliamentarians know or even care how much of our land is going this way, much less the ordinary man in the street."

They all sat a moment in silence and contemplated their beers.

"And now with the native title debate, we don't even know who'll own the land in twenty years' time," Bruce added.

Tony's contribution was melancholy. "Haven't you blokes learned anything? Nothing makes sense. Life's meaningless. Governments are crazy."

Changing the subject, he added, "Getting back to Ethel Alsop. She says she wants to surf the internet. Can you set her up to do that out here, Charles?"

"Sure, there's no worries about that," his friend replied.

Like many of his generation, Charles had left the land for a while to study at university. A computer science degree, studied in Sydney, had been his ticket to the outside world. Natural entrepreneurial sense and a commitment to hard work saw him start and steadily build a computer software development company during the technology boom. Now, a decade later, the company spanned three Australian capital cities. With enough management staff to take over the reins, Charles was able to regularly return to Carmody Plains and help out his ageing father.

Bruce, who wasn't at all computer literate, was all the same curious about the internet. "How much extra stuff do you have to get?" he asked Charles.

"Not much." Charles drained his beer, and was away on his pet subject. "With a modem on your computer you can access the line with no trouble. Well, the computer's not the trouble. It's the phones being on the digital radio concentrator system and solar-powered batteries that causes the problems."

The other two nodded.

"We had a lot of trouble at Carmody Plains not long ago, but that was when there was a spell of cloudy weather and the batteries had no charge," Charles continued. "Now that a few of us have made enough fuss to get Telstra to leave those damn padlocks off the batteries and we can recharge them ourselves when we have to, it makes it pretty reliable. Not foolproof of course, but pretty good. Hardly any different from using a computer in a city now."

Bruce looked impressed. "Geez, I didn't know that."

Tony didn't. "Well, you've over-estimated my interest, mate. A simple 'not much' would have done. You'd think you were a bloody politician, the way you go on." He finished his drink.

The door swung open and they all looked around as Sandy, the local police constable, came in.

"G'day Sandy, how y'goin?" Tony greeted him.

Sandy nodded. "G'day fellas."

Then, spotting Dan, his attitude changed. "I might have known this is where I'd find you, you thankless old rogue. Wasting a fellow's time and thinking nothing of it." The constable was really cheesed off. "What the hell are you doing here while I waste my time in and out of the office all day waiting for you?"

Dan was self-righteous. "G-give a fella a fair go, Sandy! I-I was just trying to borrow the money!"

"A fair go!" Sandy was outraged.

The other fellows realised Dan must have been in the pub the whole day. They couldn't resist trying to stir Sandy even more. "Come on, Sandy, give the fellow a fair go. You can see he's just been busy..."

Sandy turned on them. "You lot butt out. Busy! He rings me on my day off to get a permit to use an unlicensed vehicle. I tell him to give me half an hour."

"Half an hour!" The others burst out laughing.

"Half an hour I said," Sandy fumed. "And then I hung around my office like a fool waiting for him."

Dan looked sheepish. "I-I was just coming over to see you, Sandy."

"Yeah, like hell!" Sandy retorted. "You've missed your chance today, Dan. You missed it a long time ago. I was just coming in for a few beers myself."

"B-but what about my truck? H-how'm I gonna drive it?" Dan looked aghast.

Sandy smiled and sat himself down at the bar. "That's not my problem any more. I've waited long enough, and now I'm going to have a drink. You'll just have to wait until the next lot of office hours."

None too steady, Dan lumbered out of the bar muttering to himself, "It's all right for you lazy bastards, but some of us have work to do."

"See ya, Dan." Sandy was already into his first beer.

The bartender, Arry, was a tall, fine-looking fellow. Watching Dan work his way out of the pub with difficulty, Arry ran his hand across his thick, swept-back grey hair and looked around at the small group. "Anyone want to hear a story about old Dan?"

Well-known for spinning a yarn, Arry could tell the most preposterous stories and always give them a personal touch. It was good for business – it kept the customers happy.

13

"What's the story, Arry?" Tony egged the barman on.

Arry glanced over, and then launched into it.

"Well, it was just the other day – the day it stormed, it was – that this city fella came in. Friend of Joe McMahon's, he was. Fred someone. Flash cove, but he was OK. Well, old Dan, he came in and, feeling a bit aggro, he started taking the mickey out of this Fred."

He paused and said, "Can I fill your glasses, fellas?"

They nodded, not wanting to interrupt the flow of the story. Arry went on as he worked.

"Every drink Fred ordered, old Dan would say, 'I-I'll have the same'. Finally, it got on Fred's goat, it did. Dan went out for a leak and Fred had enough of him and said to me, 'The next drink I order will be a cocktail and you damn well put a rotten egg with his drink to stop this blasted game of his'.

"I thought I'd play along and when Dan came back I said to Fred, 'Ready for another drink? What'll it be this time?'

"'Well', he said, looking thoughtful, 'I'll have a cocktail'. Sure enough, Dan, he piped up with 'I-I'll have the same'. So I went outside to make them up, came back with the two drinks in cocktail glasses and put them on the bar.

"This Flash Fred sipped his drink slowly and watched old Dan out of the corner of his eye. Dan picked his up, smirked a bit at the fancy glass, then tossed his head back and swallowed it.

"'Christ', he said, without even a falter when the taste got through. 'What was that?'

"'That's a cocktail', Fred told him.

"Anyway, Dan shuddered a bit and blinked and then he said, slowly again in that way of his, 'He might have c-cocked his tail in yours, mate, but he b-bloody well shit in mine'."

They all shouted with laughter.

"Good one, Arry, you spin a good yarn," Charles said.

"It's the truth," Arry said gravely, collecting their glasses. "True as I'm standing here."

Sandy laughed. "Aw, yeah, Arry, and we believe you, too!"

"You tell a good story anyway, mate, I'll give you that," Bruce added.

Charles turned to him. "Listen, getting down to the truth," he said. "How's old Sam?"

"Not too good," was the reply. "They think he'll be OK though. He'll be in Brisbane for a few weeks having radium treatment."

"Poor old bastard," Tony said. "He's such a good old bloke. He did a lot for us when we were growing up. All those years of trying to turn us all into a polocrosse team! He did a good job too, I reckon. Cancer is a rotten business."

Then he turned to Charles. "I saw Bill-Bob in here as usual last Saturday and he said your father's slowing down a bit."

Charles looked a bit grim. "Yeah, the old man's not too good. We really need to get someone reliable permanently at home now. They say it's hard to get a job. Well, it's bloody hard to get someone good to work for you, too. There's a lot of no-hopers about. That last yobbo we had walked off with no notice and we're shearing in a few weeks. Bloody good riddance, too."

He shook his head when Arry gestured towards his glass. "I'm trying to get someone well recommended this time. With any luck, we'll have a bloke here before shearing." Charles smiled. "Even if I do have a contract with Dan."

He stood and told the men he had to get going. Then he added, "Bill-Bob's a good old stick, but there's definitely something wrong with him lately. He gets breathless too quickly to be OK."

He lost his thoughtful manner and went on briskly, "Well, I don't know about you fellows but I can't stay here yarning." He mimicked old Dan. "Some of us have work to do." He picked up his hat. "See you chaps later. I'm off to the big smoke for a couple of weeks and I'll see you when I get back."

Chapter 2

Charles was up and away early the next morning. Tom, his father, saw him off and went back inside to clean up the kitchen.

Bill-Bob came out of his quarters nearby and sat on the verandah step, a mug of tea in his hands. It was a beautiful morning. If it were not going to rain, he thought, he might as well enjoy what life was offering – and it was indeed a glorious morning.

The first crimson glow had faded and there was that soft, pearly glow that preceded the second blaze of colour before the golden rim of the sun appeared to form a stark, pure, perfect circle. Today, there would be no 'trailing clouds of glory' in the clear sky. The whole blazing ball of the sun would appear within seconds, dazzling and blinding in its splendour. In fact, if he blinked or lost concentration for just a second, he'd miss the moment.

He knew precisely where the sun would rise today, between which trees it would appear. It was one of his daily treats to watch the sun rise every morning, to watch its measured journey towards the north each winter and back towards the south in the summer.

Too many people denied themselves the daily miracles of sunrise and sunset, he mused. The ancients knew and appreciated it. Myths and stories abound in all cultures that try to explain the chatoyant beauty of dawn and dusk. Bill-Bob thought of Aurora, and rolled the sound around in his head. Aurora, the Roman goddess of dawn – she would find her horses a handful this morning, he thought. There would be no obstacles in their way today.

And what about that nonsense of who told the ancients, like the builders of Stonehenge or the Incas or the Egyptians, all the astronomical details? It didn't take aliens to do that. All they had to do was look to the heavens.

Sure enough, the crescent of gold came up precisely where Bill-Bob was looking and within seconds the blaze of light was too intense. But he had caught the moment and knew to the millimetre how far back to the south to expect it tomorrow.

He loved the sunrise, however it happened. He enjoyed the days when heavy clouds would have spectacular effects, with dark crimson and deep grey with ripples of golden highlights, and the muted effects of other days with soft greys, pinks and whites. When days were dusty, the sun came up as a blood-red ball and he could watch it rise without the shining splendour hurting his eyes.

Somehow days like today seemed to be the best. Stark reality, with no trimmings. The day had dawned and the sun was in the sky. He was quite oblivious to the fact that nearly every day he decided he liked that day's offering the best.

The birds of the bush attended the awakening ceremony as well. As usual, the kookaburras were the first to be heard, laughing in the opalescent predawn light. The galahs had been chattering for some time in the trees further up the hill where they had slept for the night but now were raucous in their screeching as they came turning and wheeling in their flocks to the trees around the water. A lone magpie in a tree nearby greeted the day, proclaiming his territory to the world. Another answered from across the flat stating his claim to his patch in liquid, melodious notes.

A willy wagtail had been busy announcing *sweet pretty creature* on and off all night in the moonlight and felt the need to have his say in the affairs of the morning as well. There was the bell-like flap of top-knot pigeons' wings, as well as the coarse *ark-ark-ark* from the crows, and a raspy *tweet* here and there from a pee-wee or two.

Bill-Bob felt sorry for anyone who had to go indoors or, God help them, underground today – or any day for that matter. Most of his friends and acquaintances would think he was less than a full quid or that he kept kangaroos in his attic, he thought to himself. That is, if they knew what he was doing.

But he was sure he was the only sane one out of the bunch. Perhaps someone else had found a really good life, but Bill-Bob was convinced the vast majority of people were victims of modern civilisation, full of distortion and delusion. They had been fooled into thinking more was better, squandering the only real values in life while hiding behind elaborate possessions and masks. All of them were on a make-believe trip while real life passed them by. Bill-Bob was sure they stuffed their minds with ideology to avoid having to create their own ideas, and lived by popular catch phrases instead of relying on thinking for themselves.

He had no desire to rejoin their numbers. Imagine living in an expensive house designed to cut out the beauty of the awakening day? Imagine living a life that cut out real experiences – and then having to manufacture experiences to get a kick out of life? Crazy.

He'd finished his tea and set about his basic tasks to keep himself and his spartan camp, as he thought of it, clean and decent. He had few possessions and each that he had was kept in its place. It was almost an obsession, except for his newest possession – his spray for angina. He never knew where to put the wretched thing. And when he found a place, he never remembered where that place was.

"Maybe it's a Freudian slip of dislike," he mused to himself as he set off up the hill to the workshop. Maybe he didn't want to think he could get sick and need to depend on other people. The thought terrified him. God forbid he should go to hospital or live in a nursing home.

Bill-Bob liked the walk up to his workshop in the early morning. He'd been at Carmody Plains long enough to feel a real part of the place and to know what Tom had in mind for the day and how to go about it. Admittedly, he sometimes found that walk up in the mornings a bit difficult. Today was bad.

By the time Bill-Bob had reached the grid and the lawn at the back of the homestead, his chest was ready to bust. His heart felt as though it had grown huge and there was no room in his chest to breathe. Grey-faced, he lowered himself onto the grass and leaned his back against the big tree. His whole attention taken up with the sheer effort of breathing, he groaned when he realised he'd left his angina spray back at his camp.

Gradually, though, his breathing improved and after a bit he pushed himself up to his feet and started to make his way across to the shed where he usually worked. "Come on, Robert, get yourself going," he told himself sternly as he saw Tom Carmody come out of the house.

"G'day Bill-Bob," Tom greeted him. "'Struth! What's the matter with you?"

"Bloody nothing." Bill-Bob tried to look as though nothing had happened. "Can't a man be a bit late in the morning without you making an issue of it?"

Tom knew better than to comment on the obvious – how grey his old mate looked, and how he was having trouble walking properly. He'd only get his head bitten off for his trouble. Bloody fool of a man if he wouldn't take care of himself. Still, it was his life and Tom knew how fiercely Bill-Bob resented any interference. Even so, he quickly revised his plans for the day as he squatted down with Bill-Bob at the doorway of the shed.

As Charles had already left, he'd intended to get Bill-Bob to help him get started cleaning out the shearing shed and quarters, but hastily changed his mind. "Well, you'd better get on and check over the vehicles and machinery," he started. "Got to make sure they're right before shearing starts. Can't afford any hold-ups once the activity gets under way. Don't want to be giving Charles a chance to say that the place goes to pot without him here."

But Bill-Bob wasn't fooled by Tom. He knew – and he knew that Tom knew – that there was nothing that needed doing with the vehicles, but he was grateful to Tom for his tact, all the same. He wasn't going to show it, though. He wasn't a bloody child to be pandered to. Admittedly, he didn't feel up to cleaning the sheds today, which he was pretty sure should be on the day's agenda.

"Right-oh," Bill-Bob agreed, his breathing slowly easing back to normal. "Should be finished here by lunch time and perhaps we can get stuck into the sheds this arvo."

That would give him time to feel a bit better.

So the two old-timers at Carmody Plains organised their day acknowledging in their actions that the time had come in their lives to make allowances for their failings – but never admitting it in words. After all, neither of them had the slightest wish to do anything else with their lives and they were committed to their lifestyle.

They also knew they were only there by the grace of Charles and his company, and that they were costing him dearly. Even if there was money to be made in the bush again one day, the money the place was worth could return substantial dividends invested in his other pursuits.

Just as firmly, they also both believed they were doing Charles a favour by enforcing his links with the land. Both held there was an honesty and integrity about work on the land that could only benefit the boy, as they thought of him. Charles's welfare was as close to their hearts as their own contentment.

In the meantime, they knew they were safe and that he would never let them down. Charles was completely committed to keeping them there whatever it cost him financially and they were grateful, even if words of gratitude – in the best tradition of Australian males – could never be expressed.

You'd never get a better bloke or son than Charles, even if he wasn't given to pretty speeches. For that matter, neither of them were either.

Chapter 3

Charles stood dressed in a tailored suit in the front garden of a house in Mosman and looked out at Sydney Harbour.

As always, the view was magnificent. Lush, green trees and the water sparkling in the sunlight made a stark contrast from the grey-greens and red ochre of the dry west. Australia was unbelievably beautiful, he thought, from this wonderful coastline all the way to the outback. He was conscious of how lucky he was to know both places so well.

This house and garden overlooking the harbour inlet was the home of his maternal grandfather and he'd spent much of his boyhood here. His father had remarried after his mother's death, and he'd spent a good bit of his time here with his grandparents rather than going home to the rows he had always had with his stepmother. He thought of all that had happened – so much water under the bridge. He laughed to himself at the analogy. What a comparison to make while looking at Sydney Harbour!

At the moment, Charles was trying hard to get over his impatience with his cousin, Julie, before he went inside to see his grandfather. Julie's little daughter, Belinda, had been lying sobbing on the grass when he'd arrived. She was broken-hearted because her mother had told her that her Daddy was leaving because he didn't love her any more – and that he had a new family and a new little girl to love.

Charles was really disgusted with his cousin for being so cruel and thoughtless. "Really," he thought, "she's been the same over-emotional fool all her life."

Julie and Charles had both grown up spending much of their time with their grandparents. Both only children, they'd built up a rivalry usually found only between siblings. Quietly superior, Charles disdainfully thought of his cousin as selfish and unkind.

After sending a still-hiccupping Belinda around the back of the house to find the housekeeper, Charles had stood for a minute in the garden to cool his temper before climbing the stairs of the lovely old Sydney house to where he knew he would meet his cousin.

The wide stone steps were flanked with graceful urns overflowing with greenery and the stained glass panels in the massive cedar door were magnificent, but Charles saw none of it. He'd been in and out of the house many times over the years, and in many different moods – but he'd never been more exasperated than he was at the moment.

Charles prided himself on being calm and collected in all circumstances – but if anyone got under his skin, it was Julie.

As he crossed the verandah, he could hear her talking and complaining. "Damn fool," Charles muttered under his breath. "No sense, no guts, no gumption."

If he knew Julie, she'd be getting at Grandy now, making him miserable as well. Didn't she realise other people had a life to lead? Grandy wasn't a young man, and it was time he had a bit of peace and quiet from his troublesome family.

Despite his best intentions, he'd made himself really angry by the time he'd entered the drawing room, although he knew it was hardly the time or place to pick a fight with Julie. He virtuously thought he had himself well in hand. Blinded by his own judgmental air, he had no idea how much his 'holier than thou' attitude to Julie contributed to their arguments.

He shook hands with his grandfather.

"Hello, my boy," the elderly man greeted him warmly. "Good to see you."

He nodded to his cousin, who peevishly said, "Charles, of all people – what are you doing here? I wanted a quiet talk with Grandfather."

Charles's good intentions vanished and sarcasm escaped. "And welcome to you too, Julie. How are things with you? Everything's going well, I hope."

Grandfather interrupted. "Goodness, Julie, at least be civil to Charles for a moment or two. Your problems are not going to be solved overnight and you should have the manners to be polite."

Julie glared. "That's right, everything else has to stop the moment Wonder Boy walks in. God knows that he's the only one of us you really have time for."

Ignoring her outburst, the old man continued talking to his grandson. "It is good to see you, Charles, but we thought you were still in Melbourne."

Charles sat down opposite his grandfather. "Things were fixed there earlier than I'd expected, so I thought I'd stop off here and see you and Penny before I go home."

"Penny's out but you're just in time for a cup of tea with us." Grandfather looked to Julie, who was still scowling. "Julie can get you another cup, can't you, dear?"

Her fury worsened. "Oh, of course," she snapped. "Anything for Wonder Boy. Now he's here everything else stops."

Grandfather gently replied, "Come now, m'dear, you're a bit upset and feeling a bit tetchy. It's really only a basic civility after all and we'll have plenty of time later to discuss your problems."

Julie stood up slowly and left the room with a withering look at Charles, which he ignored, and started to talk to his grandfather about his business trip to Melbourne. Alan Carpenter had lent him his starting capital and had been his business mentor in his early days when he first saw opportunities in the computer field. The old man was still intensely interested in details of Charles's activities, and his grandson's business success always gave him a great deal of pleasure.

Life at their grandparents' home was always a reasonably formal affair and long habit and respect made the two cousins try to keep their feelings to themselves. Despite their good intentions, their tea together was an uneasy time at best – neither could resist a dig at the other. They were acting more like two naughty children sparring than as adults, and finally their grandfather became fed up with them and told them so. "I really am surprised and disappointed the two of you are behaving in this fashion," he said. "Surely two mature adults can have a social discourse without bickering like children. I'm ashamed of you."

Julie rushed in. "Now, Grandfather, that's unfair," she said. "Even with all my problems you know I was quite calm before Charles came in and ruined everything. He's always got to be considered first before anyone else." Her voice caught a bit. "Besides, I'm finding it really hard to concentrate with my whole life collapsing around me."

Charles said evenly, "What's your problem, Julie, anyway, that you're being so melodramatic about?"

Julie blazed. "Only my husband walking out and leaving me. Andrew, taking off with his secretary, that's all. His secretary! She was a poor pathetic widow with a little girl, I thought, but she

23

schemed and connived until she got him right where she wanted him. She's not pretty, she's not clever, but she deceived me all right. She's devious."

Charles matched fire with fire. "Is that why you told that poor defenceless child of yours that her father didn't love her?" he accused her. "You heartless devil. Wouldn't it be bad enough for Belinda that her father is leaving home without your telling her he doesn't love her any more? It probably breaks his heart to leave her when it's you that he needs to get away from. Who wouldn't want to get away from all your self-pity and melodrama?"

Julie sneered. "Listen to Mr Marriage Counsellor himself. You'd know all about it, of course. What are you? Thirty-five? Thirty-six? And you've never even had the guts to get married. Scared as hell of women. You and your silly father have no more sense than you could put in an eye dropper and you've got the hide to tell me what's the matter with my marriage. How dare you judge me!"

Charles prided himself on keeping calm, even in an overwrought situation. Dryly, he merely replied, "Julie, your behaviour makes me realise what I've been missing. It must be marvellous to have a marriage like yours."

Charles knew he would be better out of the way. There was no use upsetting his grandfather. Julie could do that well enough on her own. He turned to the old man, who was watching them both exasperatedly. "If you'll excuse me, Grandfather, I'll go now and come back to see you next time I'm down. I don't want to upset you and it's obvious Julie hasn't got enough sense to talk rationally with me here. I might be sorry for her if I hadn't seen how upset she's made her own daughter."

Julie was really furious. "You try having children of your own before you tell others what to do. You make a fuss of children, oh yes – but always someone else's."

Their argument stayed with Charles as he walked to his car.

"No wonder I never got on well with Julie," he thought. "She's just so selfish and silly." It didn't occur to him that he was habitually less than tactful with her either.

But her comment about him being scared of women had hit its mark. It riled him. He wasn't scared of women, he told himself. Just sensible. He'd seen all the trouble bad marriages could bring and heaven knows it didn't even need a marriage for a woman to be trouble.

His grandmother's attitude to life hadn't helped as he'd been growing up, either.

Grandmother Carpenter was a controlling woman. She bitterly resented the fact that two of her children, Robert and Nancy, had slipped the leash and gone bush. She told Robert and told Robert that he wouldn't make a go of it out there. As a result, he disappeared from their life altogether, and she'd never forgiven the bush for that.

Nancy married that man Tom Carmody, even though she'd begged her not to. Begged her, ordered her, demanded, she stay at home. Nancy died from an ectopic pregnancy. Grandmother Carpenter was always quite sure she would not have died if she'd been anywhere civilised. Everyone could assure her all they wanted that it could have happened anywhere. She knew it would not have happened if Nancy had been where she belonged – in Sydney with her. It was a classic case of 'I have made up my mind – don't confuse me with the facts'.

So Grandmother Carpenter hated the bush, and all that was in it. And that included his father. It didn't make it easy for Charles to love her as much as he loved his grandfather, who was more accepting. Charles even suspected that Grandfather was in touch with Robert now and then, but that was his vague suspicion, not a confirmed fact.

That was all in the past and on the other hand Julie didn't know everything. She didn't know about Angela.

Finally, after years of disastrous women who seemed to have abounded in his life, Charles had found a woman he would be willing to marry. Tall, beautiful, blonde, with honey-coloured skin. Bright, intelligent, loving. Quiet and reserved, not a bit emotional and not a bit like Julie. Angela was truly cool, calm and collected.

They'd been together for a few months now, and he was getting very used to having her to come home to. In fact, he had a good mind to ask her to marry him when he got back to Brisbane.

Charles warmed to the idea. That'd set Julie on her ear.

Thinking about Angela and their life together occupied Charles's thoughts from Mosman to Sydney airport, to the car rental desk, departures and the Golden Wing lounge. Even the seventy minute flight to Brisbane – a time usually spent on company matters – passed in a blur as he contemplated Angela.

It was a good thing, he thought, that she hadn't accompanied him to Melbourne and Sydney. He couldn't remember why Angela said she couldn't come, but he hadn't really minded. He much preferred to fly solo when he was constantly at dinner meetings, business breakfasts and on the move. He was working to a time limit, too – with shearing at Carmody Plains, and then the new man arriving out there. With Dad a bit shaky, Charles wanted to spend a fair bit of time out in the bush.

His life was truly split between country and city. In fact, he never could decide if he was a country boy or a city businessman at heart. Maybe he didn't have to. His life was very well organised, and he never really needed to choose. He had the best of both worlds. His base in Brisbane made it easy to make trips to Sydney and Melbourne or to the West.

Charles's thoughts turned to Angela again. He was pleased Angela hadn't had to witness that particular encounter with his family. Nor did he want to subject himself to a well-meaning inquisition: 'Who is the girl?' 'Are you serious at last?' He'd suffered through those questions enough times. Heaven knows, his wealth had attracted enough willing partners over the years.

For once though, he thought he'd found the answer. Angela was a woman he could imagine spending his life with.

Now that he'd decided to ask Angela to marry him, Charles was plagued by indecision. Strangely enough, he wasn't positive Angela wanted to marry him. Certainly, they hadn't discussed it directly.

Part of him was still anxious, though. Charles knew what he wanted – but what about Angela? There were times he was sure she was keen to be married, and other times she seemed a bit distant. Maybe, he thought, Angela had felt he was unable to commit.

That was it. Charles straightened, relieved. Well, Angela was in for a pleasant surprise. He'd ask her to marry him tonight when he got back to their apartment in Brisbane.

Staring into the hotel fridge's minibar, Charles drew out a handful of tiny spirits bottles.

Throwing them and himself on the bed, he cracked one open and raised it to the ceiling derisively. "To Angela," he declared, already a little under the weather. "May she rot in hell."

Earlier that night, he'd pulled up outside their apartment with an arm full of roses and a heart filled with expectation.

Things did not turn out as he hoped.

Charles knew he was an astute business man. He knew it was his talent and wily business sense that had created his present wealth. He knew he commanded his employees' respect and his competitors' awe.

At school, he had led. At Carmody Plains, he belonged with his father and Bill-Bob. He adored his grandfather. He loved his grandmother, although they'd never been close since she'd made it clear she couldn't accept anything to do with the bush, including his father.

But looking back on the wreckage of his relationships with women, aided by the clarity of bourbon, Charles knew he'd missed something.

He'd always had such high ideals and always found women wanting. Too emotional, or too flighty, or too selfish. And too conniving and too demanding. God, had he been taken for a ride by a few over the years.

His plans to change all of that tonight hadn't even left the ground.

It had been getting late when he finally arrived at their apartment. He knew Angela would be in bed.

He'd suspected that all right – but not that Angela would be in his bed with another man.

Haggard and hung over, it was six o'clock when Charles awoke from a fitful sleep. Devastated but in control, Charles was determined to bank down his anger, bank down his feelings. Other people might rant and rave and lose perspective, but Charles was still in control. He knew one thing, though. Hell would freeze over before he'd let another woman into his life.

Not that the pain of his betrayal had gone – that was like a toothache. Sharp and constant. He could deal with it, and focus his mind on the immediate issue of getting his life in order. He rang and organised breakfast, showered, shaved, ate his breakfast when it arrived, dressed and went straight to his office in Eagle Street in the city.

He ripped through the morning's agenda like a dynamo. Not that his personal assistant, John, nor any of his staff could tell anything was wrong. They were well used to him appearing suddenly with a mind full of plans.

He was preparing to leave the office for Carmody Plains when there was a quiet knock on his door. The girl from the front office opened the door and stood hesitantly. She was a new employee and shy of the head of the company that she didn't really know.

"Mr Carmody, sir, there is a Mr Tony MacFarlane asking for you at reception. Do I say you are available or not?"

For a moment, Charles's decisiveness slipped. For an entire morning, he'd managed to successfully cut off all thought and feeling, and keep it subdued under his business personality. His problems were a dull, persistent ache he didn't want anyone to get close enough to see. But maybe Tony would be just what he needed. He was a real fireball and always caught up in something or other which, God knows, was usually dramatic enough. He'd probably be good company. Just what he needed.

He nodded at the girl. "Yes – tell him I'll only be a moment or two here if he'd be good enough to wait and I'll be right out."

He turned back to his PA, who had been patiently waiting. "Well John, I think we've got most things straightened out here now. Do you have any other questions?"

John consulted his notes. "No, Charles, I think you're free to go to Carmody Plains. I was a bit concerned about you leaving when we've been having the phone and fax problems with Juno, but I've been in touch with your father and we've both hassled Telstra, so I think that's all straightened out now. And I'll email you this report when I'm done." He indicated the pile of papers on the desk.

"Fine." Packing his briefcase, Charles paused, then turned again to John. "Oh, by the way, would you please arrange to sell my unit on Hamilton Hill? I no longer require it and you can make all those arrangements with Marty Pearson, the manager of the building. I was going to see him today but you can fix it instead. The title is with my solicitor and here are the keys. There is one other person with a set of keys. There should be no trouble there, but if there is I give you full authority to use every process of law to put it all in order."

That done, he went out to meet Tony, who was sitting in reception looking bored and flicking through a magazine.

"It's good to see you, mate," Charles greeted him. "Sorry to keep you waiting. What're your plans for today? I'm sorry to say I'm leaving on the plane this afternoon. There will be time to have a meal together first."

"No worries, mate, no worries," Tony replied. "I've been down and bought myself a really beaut set of wheels that I'm taking home. Your Dad said you'd be coming home soon and I wondered if you'd like to come out and do some low flying in a really good vehicle instead of the staid old Flight West. It's downstairs, if you want to have a look."

Typical of Tony to do something extravagant, Charles thought. But where did he get the money for another new car? Charles hurriedly scanned his plans and thought he could just as easily change his arrangements to go with Tony. He could count on Tony to keep things lively and Charles would be able to push his worries behind him and let them slowly fade. Angela was still an ache somewhere in the back of his mind, but nothing he couldn't cope with.

Moments later, Charles looked with amazement at the sleek black Porsche Carrera Tony indicated in the carpark. Tony had certainly made good his claim about his new set of wheels.

"Wow," Charles said in awe, as Tony stood relishing the moment. "Holy moly, what a beauty!" He walked around it slowly, noting the curves, the spoiler, the luxury interior. Then he stood back and took it all in. For the moment he couldn't even speak. Tony grinned. He was delighted with the effect the car was having on his friend.

Every young man's dream is to own an elite sports car but to most young men that's all it ever is – a dream. No man ever gets so old that he can't remember the thrill of such a machine. Charles was certainly not that old.

He finally voiced his opinion. "This is one hot machine," Charles said, shaking his head. "Is it turbo charged?"

Tony grinned again, hardly able to contain his enthusiasm. "Yeah, it goes like a rocket – it's a real beast. Hop in and I'll show you what it can do."

They climbed in. The machine roared throatily as Tony turned the engine over, then edged forward and sped out of the parking lot, tyres squealing.

"Check it out when we get to the lights," Tony instructed Charles. What a feeling, just knowing he had all that power there under the bonnet waiting for his command. With just one light touch on the accelerator, he could jump from the start and was away. There was all the power he'd ever need.

"Sit back, mate, and watch this beast go. No worries if it's got the power or not – you know you've got it there. Pretty good feeling too, I reckon."

Stopped at their first red light, Tony sat with eager anticipation as they waited for it to turn green. He couldn't resist revving it up and he revelled in the experience of power. When the moment came, the car shot forward and across the intersection like a bullet. Tony was in another world, totally absorbed in the sensation of the handle and the power of his machine.

Within minutes, they were on the freeway and Tony let 'er rip. "Just wait until I get on the open highway, and then she'll really open up," he said, basking in Charles's admiration of the car.

Charles for his part was absorbed as well, experiencing the power and performance of the car and watching his friend's total concentration in the joy of driving his new acquisition. He was also wondering how soon before he could ask to take over the wheel. He was itching to have a go at the controls and see for himself how it felt to be in control of such a machine.

But he knew he'd have to let Tony satisfy his own delight and exuberance and show off its accomplishments before he'd be happy to relinquish control and let his friend experience it for himself. It was a long drive home and Charles knew his turn would come. He stifled any impatience and let its owner glory in the moment.

The car ate up the kilometres in no time at all. Charles had time to let his mind wander from the glory of the machine itself to how his friend had found the money to pay for it.

Charles loved motor cars as much as the next man, and now and then Tony made him rue the fact he'd always gone for practicality and comfort rather than the more flamboyant style of a sports car. Not that he had a slouch of a car – a Jaguar, after all – but it lacked the sheer exuberance of this car. He'd chosen a precision-built, comfortable, long-range touring car that handled well and he had his business to pay for that.

But what the hell was Tony using for payment? He just hoped his friend was not getting himself too deeply into debt. He desperately hoped Tony had found an opal mine or been left a legacy and was not just borrowing on the equity of his property. Once he would have been sure Tony had matters under control. For all his flamboyant bravado, Tony always used to have his head firmly screwed on. But lately he'd seemed a bit irresponsible, even out of control – living his life at a frenetic pace.

Charles couldn't resist asking. "This is magnificent, but blimey, Tony, you've got me beat. You must have paid an arm and a leg for it. What are you doing, mate? You've always been reckless, but not crazy. Times are bad and..."

Tony interrupted good-naturedly. "Belt up, Charles. Life is short and I'm going to see that it's sweet. People can be careful too much. I know what I want and how to get it. There's only me, and believe me I can afford these toys."

He pulled to a stop at a set of lights and revved the engine impatiently.

With a slight edge to his voice, he continued. "Your job is to help me enjoy them, not preach at me," he said. "I've been to hell and back, and life holds no terrors for me now. I've earned my freedom, freedom to enjoy things like these and without that feeling, I wouldn't want to live."

He added decisively, "Besides, there's nothing and no-one to live for."

Charles didn't answer for a moment, knowing it was better not to get Tony started on that tragic topic. But he did wonder if he was hearing his mate say something that was really worrying. He was just going to say more when the moment passed.

Tony's attention had shifted and he was saying excitedly, "See that fellow over there crossing the road, that big square fellow, block head and built like a brick dunny? Well, doesn't he remind you of that big, beefy, young ag student you had out there on work experience once?"

Charles looked across casually. He was wondering if Tony was just deliberately changing the subject. Then he saw the fellow he was pointing to, and gave a bit of a chuckle as he remembered.

"That bloke who was a weightlifter and footballer for the high school. The one who thought he knew the lot?"

"Yeah, that's him." Tony laughed, remembering.

Charles continued. "You said, 'Let's take this fellow down a peg or two and see if he'll fall for that lift-yourself-in-a-bucket routine that we did before with another loud-mouthed know-it-all'. I thought he was too smart to fall for that one."

Tony joined in. "You were always hard to get going, but you were pretty good at it once I got you revved up."

31

Charles was enjoying recalling their silly escapade. "More fool me – but God, it was funny, wasn't it? I said I'd give it a go but only if you'd help me. Help me! You were more useless than a pocket in a singlet. You just couldn't keep a straight face for any time at all."

Tony laughed. "Yeah, yeah – but I was good to start with. He just looked so silly as it went along. We waited until smoko the next day and then you quietly broached the subject. Remember? I remember it so clearly."

Charles pictured the scene. "I was all serious and innocent-like, wasn't I? 'Can you still lift yourself in a bucket, Tony?' And you said, 'Oh, my back is a bit crook at the moment, but I could do it eighteen months ago and I'm sure I'll be able to do it when my back gets a bit better'."

"We had him," Tony said, dropping down a gear and revving the engine to overtake a slow semi on the open road. "The young chap swallowed the bait. 'That's impossible', he told us, 'nobody could lift themselves in a bucket'."

Charles joined in. "That's right, and I was still being all serious. 'Oh yes, they can', I told him. 'Not many people can, of course, only a very few. You've got to be really strong to lift your own weight or more'. And the kid couldn't help himself! He started flexing his muscles and telling us he could lift his own weight!"

They were both laughing out loud now. Tony was a reprobate but he was damn good company, Charles thought. It was wonderful to be back laughing and joking about these silly things they'd done in the past. And if he didn't watch out, he'd be doing them again if he let Tony con him into any more of his hair-brained schemes.

Tony went on. "Remember the bloody great big bucket you went and got? And the young chap climbed into it, put both feet firmly in, picked up the handle and tried to lift it. He was strong, I'll give him that. Just a bit thick. He pulled and pulled on the handle. He nearly tore it to pieces."

"That's right," Charles said. "Then I told him, 'Hold it, mate. The ceiling of the shed is too low in here and you could easily bang your head if you suddenly lift up. Come outside where you've got plenty of room'."

"And after another terrific tussle you advised him to..." Tony could hardly get the words out because he was laughing so much.

"To jump, to break the friction! Can't you just see him now crashing to the ground with his feet still in the bloody bucket?" Tears were streaming down Tony's face.

Charles nodded. "Yeah and by that time, you – who had promised to help me by keeping a straight face – you were lying sobbing on the ground with laughter. But luckily the boy was trying so damned hard he didn't see your antics and I had to just keep telling him he'd nearly done it."

Tony fairly howled. "He just kept on frantically trying and trying and nearly killed himself, while you said quietly, 'You'll soon get the knack, mate'."

"Yeah, great help you were," Charles hassled his mate, laughing. "You were just jelly on the ground, and then you sat up with your face streaming and said, 'You were suckered, mate. It's just not possible'."

The two friends enjoyed their laughter. They had played some terrible tricks on many people over the years when they weren't busy trying to catch each other.

Charles thought of some of his city acquaintances – both friends and adversaries. They had quiet dinners or lunches together talking business, or played golf or squash or went out on each other's boats. They didn't try to take the mickey out of anyone and everyone around them. They took out their aggression in the power play of their work.

"Give me the bush any day," Charles thought to himself, "just taking the mickey instead of board room manoeuvres and deadly one-upmanship on the golf course."

Tony was off again on another reminiscence and the time passed pleasantly and quickly.

Outside Toowoomba, Tony casually said to Charles, "Like to take the wheel for a while?"

Charles's eyes lit up. At last! Now it was his turn. He grinned at Tony. "Is the Pope a Catholic?"

"This car is pure delight," Charles thought as he got the feel of the gears. "And it handles like oiled silk." Even though the bitumen had a few potholes and bumps over the culverts, it travelled like a beauty.

"Geez, you could get some speeding tickets with this one," he commented to Tony, a bit jealous.

Tony dozed a bit as Charles concentrated on the long stretch ahead of him. Within a few hours, they drove into Miles.

Spotting the last roadhouse before the bridge, Charles roused his mate. "Time for a bite to eat?"

Tony stretched. "Yeah, let's wet the whistle, mate," he answered.

Charles slowed down and prepared to turn, then had to stop in the middle of the road to let a road train pass. As the road cleared, he noticed with displeasure a coach disgorging passengers. It was the last thing he wanted to see. The roadhouse would be full of people – half of them nitwits who didn't even know what they wanted and would keep changing their minds and wasting everyone's time.

If Charles were on his own, he knew he would have gone on again immediately. It was another one hundred and fifty kilometres to Roma, and Charles knew Tony would enjoy all the people admiring his car. They'd better have a break. He turned in.

Cautiously edging the car into the roadhouse, he couldn't help but notice a girl standing on the raised edge of the garden. Perched for all the world as if she was on a pedestal, she was statuesque, tall, red-headed and dressed as if she was going to a party, not standing at a roadhouse in the bush. She wore a full billowing skirt and a large hat, plus dainty sandals. She took Charles's breath away.

"What the hell would a girl like that be doing just standing there, making no effort to flock in like a mob of sheep like everyone else?" Charles couldn't help wondering to himself. Then he caught himself. "Women like that take your mind off the job," he told himself severely. He would have like to have driven around to the right into the full shade to be served, but he was distracted and pulled in to the left of the bowsers.

As Charles turned off the ignition, the woman commanded his attention again. "God, she's lovely to look at," Charles thought idly. "And here I am with only Tony for company. How would I like to be in a car like this with her beside me." Then Angela sprang to mind and his mood darkened. "She's probably as treacherous as all women, silly bitch. She's just standing there flaunting herself," he told himself. Tony was oblivious to Charles's wonderings, and he'd climbed out to to refill the car's petrol tank.

But Charles's mind was still focused in another direction. "Women are only trouble," he instructed himself. "She'd probably be willing to sleep with anyone with a big enough bank account." Despite his best intentions, his heart still pumped a bit faster.

"Bloody women!" Charles muttered to himself. "Can't live with them and can't live without them."

He decided then and there he wasn't going to be dictated to by a randy set of genes. He was completely taken by surprise at his own fury when Tony said in an undertone, "Geez, cop the redhead. What do you reckon it would take to get into her pants tonight?"

Instant aggression surged through him. A lifetime of controlled feelings stood him in good stead and he was shocked at his urge to lash out and flatten Tony. Charles felt his adrenaline surge and his fists clench – and when the moment passed, couldn't believe it had happened. He'd wanted to protect this girl – someone he'd only just seen and never met, and, after all, Tony's comments just echoed his own thoughts.

Something about that woman really got under his skin, and Charles Carmody was not a man who wanted anything to do with women, thank you very much.

Chapter 4

As soon as the coach pulled into the roadhouse at Miles, Kendal jumped off. After being stuck on the bus for hours, she was dying to stretch her legs and get a breath of fresh air. The long trip had taken away her appetite, and she wasn't keen to swap the confines of a crowded bus for an equally crowded roadhouse cafe. Besides, she'd befriended a frail elderly couple on the bus who had needed their granddaughter's help to board the bus. Kendal thought she'd wait until everyone else had left the bus and then check the Carsons were OK.

The only shade close by was a small patch under the Mobil sign and to fit in it she had to stand up on the cement edge of the garden. From there she could watch both the coach and the activity going on around her. There was plenty to see because the roadhouse was busy and she thought it would probably be a bit of a battle to get any food in a hurry. The more she thought about it, the more she realised her elderly friends would need a hand in there.

Looking around, Kendal examined her surroundings. The town they'd driven into wasn't genuine outback, but it was a long way out of the city. The air was dry and the trees were grey-green and, despite the exhaust fumes and the oil and petrol smells of the roadhouse, there was a definite feel of a small country town.

The roadhouse itself was busy. Sharing the main road with the usual semis and road trains were cars of every description, especially utes and four-wheel drives. But the most eye-catching of them all was a black Porsche that seemed to appear from nowhere and deftly slid in and glided to a halt at the petrol bowser. The sun roof was down and the two men inside were quite stunning. As they stood up, Kendal saw one was tall, a bit angular, but dark and elegant, and wearing a crisp linen shirt. The other was a real Adonis. A regular Greek god of a man. Tall and well-built with a bright, laughing face, his smile was dazzling and his hair dark and curly. He was dressed in fairly loud rodeo-style clothes.

Looking from one to the other of the men, she in turn saw their eyes turn to her a few times. She heard a couple of girls who'd followed her off the bus comment on these fellows – and receive a couple of covert looks from the driver and his mate.

"It's a case of girls watching boys watching girls," Kendal thought, amused.

So it was no hardship just to wait. The fascinating sport of people-watching made the time pass quickly.

Kendal was worth looking at, too. She was a tall girl, well built, and she loved beautiful clothes. In fact, fashion was probably going to be her career and she enjoyed dressing for a particular look. Since tomorrow she was going to start work as a jillaroo with a daily uniform of jeans, work shirts and boots, she'd decided she'd celebrate her last day of freedom by wearing a feminine dress that skimmed her figure and a large, shady hat that covered her red-gold, shoulder-length hair. The effect was stunning, if you liked a woman who looked like a woman instead of a skeleton.

A roadhouse attendant was still filling the Porsche with petrol and checking its oil. Time and time again, Kendal felt her eyes go back to the elegant driver and his laughing Adonis friend. The Adonis was stunning, but strangely, he wasn't the one who drew her attention. The driver was looking at her too, and now and then their eyes met. Kendal couldn't believe it. There were plenty of men coming in and out of the roadhouse. Why did this man draw her attention and not the others? She was irritated with herself and, irrationally, also with him.

More than occupied checking out the Porsche driver, Kendal didn't notice the Carsons starting to disembark until the bus driver helped them down the stairs. She hurried over to see if they needed a hand.

Mr Carson walked with a stick and, sore and stiff from sitting so long, leaned heavily on his wife's arm. Mrs Carson, a sweet-natured, white-haired lady, was grateful for Kendal's offer to help.

"Oh, that's so kind of you, dearie," Mrs Carson beamed. "I'd love to pop in to have a comfort stop straight away if you'd just help John to go in and sit down somewhere."

So Kendal escorted John Carson to the tables inside, discovering he was a bright, talkative, old gentleman.

"I am ready for a break," he said, "And I do like a cup of tea. Elsie is a great one for tea, too. The cup that cheers, we always say."

Kendal offered to get the tea, and asked him if he wanted anything to eat as well.

"We don't need much to eat, the two of us," he replied. "A few sandwiches – ham and tomato would be nice. Yes, ham and tomato sandwiches would be just the job."

He chatted brightly to her while she got him settled comfortably. Soon Elsie joined them, and Kendal offered, "You sit down, too, or stretch your legs, and I'll order for you. Your husband just wants tea and sandwiches. Is that what you'd like?"

Elsie lowered herself onto the seat beside her husband. "Thank you, dear. Ask for a pot, if you could. I don't want just a cup if I can help it. I like to pour my own. I know just how John likes it. John likes ham and tomato sandwiches. I tell him ham is no good for him, but he does like it."

Kendal smiled to herself as she walked over to the counter to place their order. "I'd love to be with someone long enough to know them that well," she mused.

Waiting for the order, Kendal's thoughts turned to how lucky she was to be returning to her home country. She'd grown up in the far outback of western Queensland, and was returning as a favour to her brother, Kenrick. She only hoped that, under the circumstances, she was doing the right thing. It was really her brother who had answered the advertisement for a jackaroo on a sheep property, but at the last minute he badly twisted his leg. It had seemed a pretty minor injury, but then Dr Wilson – an old friend of the family – told him he had a torn meniscus, a cartilage in the knee joint, and he had to stay off his feet for at least two weeks.

"Come off it, doctor," Kenrick had complained. "There's no way I can do that. It's not too bad. Can't you just strap it up and give me a few pain killers for a while?"

Doc Wilson had shaken his head. "Take my advice, young man, and it will be as good as new," he'd promised. "But if you're not careful of it you could have real trouble, and regret it for the rest of your life."

The diagnosis had been a real blow to Kenrick's plans. After searching long and hard for a really good job, this one seemed perfect. The owner had wanted someone who knew what he was doing with both sheep and cattle, preferably someone who had grown up on the land. Also, they were needing help – the man who had been running the place had left suddenly, just weeks before shearing. If Kenrick did well at the job and impressed Mr Carmody with his ability, he could well find himself running the property one day.

By a stroke of good luck, Kendal was available to help when Kenrick had his accident. After school, she had gone on to design studies and for the last two years had been working for a great company. She was struggling with the idea of playing it safe and getting another job, or taking the risk and going out on her own. She was having trouble making up her mind and thought a complete break away might be good for her, as well as helping Kenrick.

"What if I go in your place, Rick?" she offered. "We were brought up doing the same things together and Dad always said I could handle the stock well. It's a while since I've done any work like that, but I could manage for a short time." Her arguments were persuasive. "The original advertisement said jillaroo or jackaroo, and so the only difference is they are getting a jillaroo with a little experience instead of the jackaroo with a lot of experience they expected. I can do the work, and it will keep the job open, and they won't be let down at the last moment."

"Are you sure you don't mind, Sis?" He was keen, but didn't want to take advantage of her good nature.

Kendal had no hesitation. "No problem, Rick. Actually, I'd love to get back to the bush for a while."

They didn't often talk about their disappointment – that losing their father had also meant losing their property. Their mother had struggled on for a while after he died but, with the two children away at boarding school, she just couldn't cope. The place wasn't even making enough to employ a man without going further into debt. Andrea MacKenzie reluctantly decided that there was no way she could keep the place going without her husband. She would have loved to have kept it long enough for Rick to grow up and take over, but lots of young people didn't even want to return to the land any more and she wanted him to be completely free to choose his own path.

So, now Kendal was on her way and the only real problem was that they couldn't get hold of Mr Carmody to tell him about the change in plans. They tried to phone him, but after constantly getting no answer, they called Telstra only to discover there was a fault on the line. They tried again this morning before the coach left, but still there was no answer. So Kendal found herself on her way to a new job, in slightly difficult circumstances. She knew she could handle stock – but she did hope Mum or Rick could warn Mr Carmody before she arrived.

"Ham and tomato sandwiches for three and a pot of tea?" called the girl at the counter. Kendal collected the order, paid her and carried it into the the dining room where the Carsons were sitting.

As Kendal approached the Carsons, she saw John accidentally knock his walking stick under the chair. So, placing the tray on the table, she leaned in behind the elderly man to pick the stick up, holding onto the back of his chair for balance.

Just then the two men from the Porsche walked in the door. Kendal felt a shock of excitement pass through her when the driver again looked right at her. Feeling the intensity of his gaze, Kendal sensed it was no casual glance. "Was he looking for me?" she wondered.

The more she tried to look away, the more she found her gaze drawn to him. Never had she felt such a physical reaction from just looking at an attractive man. She'd had a few boyfriends in her time, but her reaction to this Porsche driver was totally different. There was something much deeper than mere physical attraction that she felt for this man. Something deep down in her being reacted to his presence. Was she just imagining that she felt it was reciprocated and that there was mutual attraction between them? Was this what people meant by 'their eyes met across a crowded room'? Kendal decided she didn't like it. It was overwhelming and frightening in its intensity. Not to mention the fact she was embarrassed and she was sure the whole room could see her blushing face.

Struggling with her inner turmoil and desperately trying to act calm and unconcerned, Kendal jumped when someone said directly behind her, "Well, if it isn't True Blue!"

She turned to see a solid young man, dressed in a typical western Queensland outfit of moleskin trousers, double-pocketed shirt, wide felt hat and elastic-sided boots. For a moment she just looked at him blankly.

He was taken aback. "Hey, you are Kendal MacKenzie, aren't you?"

She racked her mind for a name. He did look familiar.

"I'm David Courtney," he explained. "I was at school with Kenrick – your brother, Rick. We played in the same football team. I remember meeting you often when you came to our matches. You're not as easy to forget as I am, apparently."

The few clues helped his identity fall into place, and Kendal was pleased to meet a friendly face – even if he did call her True Blue. She cringed at the old nickname her family gave her for her flaming red hair.

They soon fell into a lively conversation about mutual friends.

"Are you on the bus – going west?" David asked.

"Yes," Kendal replied. "I'm going to Juno."

David was keen for company, especially a pretty girl, and he offered her a lift. "I'm going as far as Roma, and then I turn north. But I can give you a lift that far. Come with me to Roma, and you can get on the bus again there."

Kendal thought it would make a bit of a break. "Why not?" she thought, and then made her way over to where the coach driver was standing. But the driver was a stickler for rules, and didn't appreciate her announcing that she was going to get a lift with a friend before rejoining the bus at Roma.

Loudly and ungraciously, and embarrassing Kendal in front of the rest of the diner in the process, the bus driver warned her he wouldn't wait for her. "If you're not there on time, I'll go on without you. I'm not going to wait around for you and get behind with my schedule."

Kendal felt like a school kid again, who'd been told off by the bossy bus driver. The drivers might have had to keep the students in order, but she was an adult now and it was none of his business if she wanted a lift with a friend. So, with a feigned nonchalant air, she bade farewell to the Carsons, collected her sandwiches and made a regal exit with David.

Climbing into David's Commodore, Kendal spotted the Porsche again and felt a little embarrassed that the attractive man had witnessed her encounter with the bus driver. She wondered about the car and its occupants, and wondered if their paths would cross again. "Not very likely," she told herself, as David pulled out of the roadhouse and onto the road. But never before had a brief encounter made such a deep impression on her.

Kendal shook herself out of her reverie and pulled herself into the present, trying to concentrate on what David was saying.

Attractive as David undoubtedly was, there was no great spark between them – just a comfortable rapport and they enjoyed their time together.

The Commodore beat the bus into Roma by a long shot, giving Kendal and David enough time to go into Kooka's takeaway for a drink and she bought a packet of barley sugar. The big plate glass windows gave the two a good vantage point to spot the coach while they drank their Cokes.

There were children playing in the playground outside, and they made Kendal wonder what the family would be like that she would live with. Jackaroos or jillaroos usually lived in the house with the family they were working for, although sometimes there were separate quarters. Kendal hadn't heard anything about the set-up at Carmody Plains and she wondered if there was a wife and a family of young children. She liked children. Whoever was there didn't really matter that much for her, because she wouldn't be staying long. All the same, she couldn't help wondering about where she was going, and what possibilities lay ahead.

As the coach pulled in, she said goodbye to David and thanked him for the lift. It certainly made a break in the long day on the bus. Kendal knew the Carsons were getting off in Roma, so she went across to the bus to help collect all of their things. The children who had been playing on the jungle gym and the slippery slide turned out to be family. She watched as they ran excitedly to their grandparents. The children's parents followed after them, and helped the Carsons from the bus.

Kendal noticed one of the other bus passengers – a pretty young woman with a halo of fair curls, studying the family scene intently. She looked interested, but also a bit worried and lost.

In her usual kindly way, and thinking she might need a friend to talk to, Kendal walked across to her. "Those children look pleased to see their grandparents, don't they?" she commented.

Smiling nervously, the girl agreed. "Yes, they do." Then she went on. "Actually, I'm going to a job to look after some children and I was standing here wondering how they will like me. I'm starting to get quite worried about it. I knew it would be a long way away from Brisbane, but I didn't really expect it to be all so far away and so empty."

Unconsciously wringing her hands, the young woman went on. "Quite frankly, I'm scared. It all sounded great when I was at home

42

– you know, to come into the outback and look after some little children without their Mum – but I didn't know it would be like this."

Kendal felt sorry for her. "My name's Kendal," she said, "and I'm going out to a job, too. I'm going as a jillaroo though, but I'm also wondering what my job and the family will be like." She offered the girl a barley sugar.

"At least I'm lucky," Kendal continued, "I lived out west all my life except for the past few years, so I know a bit about what life's like out here." She motioned towards the bus. "Listen, the bus is getting a few more spare seats and I know that the seat opposite where I was sitting will be empty, so if we get on and take them now, we'll be able to sit together and talk."

Her companion looked instantly relieved. "That would be super, Kendal. I was getting a bit lonely and I'd love someone to talk to. My name's Thea and I'm going to a place called Juno. They told me there would be a boy on the bus going to the same place as I am, but I can't see anyone that could be the one they were talking about."

The bus was only stopping long enough to unload and to pick up passengers, so Kendal hurried Thea onto the bus and to the row of seats where she and the Carsons had been.

Once they'd made themselves comfortable, Kendal told her she was headed for Juno, too. "I must be the young man you're expecting," she explained. "My brother Rick was going to come out today, not me, and we hadn't actually told anyone about the change because it all happened so quickly. Now tell me all about your arrangements and what you're doing."

Thea was only too pleased to have someone to talk to. "Well, I did a teaching course, because Mum thought I'd be good at it. But somehow I wasn't terribly happy working in a school. There are some lovely children, but some of them are just so rude. I needed a break, and Mum thought I might enjoy working in the country, so we bought a copy of *Country Life* and looked up the jobs section. Mum thought this sounded like a good job and we rang them up and here I am on my way."

Kendal thought to herself that Thea's mum seemed to have made all of the decisions in her daughter's life.

Thea was still describing her circumstances. "I thought it sounded so good while I was home. I'm going to look after two little girls named Carla and Kirsty for a Mr Bruce Thompson. Their mother's not there. I don't know if she's dead or divorced or what. They had a girl helping but she had to leave for family reasons and now their father needs someone else."

She was busy pleating the material in her skirt as she spoke. She looked at Kendal. "I don't have to do all the work. He has a married man on the property and his wife comes to help in the house a bit but doesn't want to be there all the time. He has an old auntie who lives there too, but he needs someone young to be with the two little girls all the time. Carla is only three and Kirsty is five. She'll start school next year – she's in preschool now. If they like me and I'm happy, I can be her governess next year."

She looked down and started to pleat the material in her skirt again. "But I didn't know it would be all so far away and so empty, and I think I'm frightened. It's a long way from home."

Kendal looked at the pretty little Thea and felt half sorry for her and half exasperated. She really did go on a bit – and perhaps needed to grow up a bit before she took on such a job. "On the other hand, she's not all that young," Kendal thought, "so maybe she'd be better off away from her mother for a while."

As the girls talked, they discovered they'd both be staying at the Charleville Motel overnight before finding out how to go further west the next day. Thea told Kendal she'd been told her new boss, Mr Thompson, would pick her up with the new jackaroo for Carmody Plains and drive them to Juno the next day.

The long, empty stretches of road were clearly starting to bother Thea. "There are no houses here at all," she said, a little worried. "There are no people, no houses, no animals – just empty land."

Kendal disagreed. "Not really," she said, "if you watch as we go along, you'll see a road turning off every now and then. That road will lead into a homestead. It might be a big place with a few people working there, or it might just be a cottage on a smaller property. But everywhere, every now and then, there will be a homestead a few miles in." She pointed. "See that sign that shows a mother and child?" She turned to Thea to make sure she was watching. "That sign that looks like a children's crossing sign in Brisbane is where a mother and her children will wait to catch the school bus each morning. Then the mother comes back in the afternoon and waits there to pick the children up off the bus. If you watch very carefully, near some of the signs you'll sometimes see a

44

couple of bikes beside the road where older children have ridden down to the bus on their own."

"But they're not locked up," Thea said in surprise. "Do they just leave them there in the open?"

Kendal shook her head. "They don't need to hide the bikes because no-one takes someone else's bike out here, or not very often, at least. Besides, they're harder to see from a car than up high in a bus like this. Keep an eye out and you might see some." She smiled encouragingly. "There are lots of signs of people if you know what to look for. There mightn't be that many people about, compared to a city, but there are quite a few, really. When you get to know the people in the district, you'll find you'll meet up with them quite often."

Thea wasn't all that impressed. She had other problems, too. "Well, if the people live at the end of those dirt roads, where are all the animals?" she asked. "I thought I'd see cattle and horses and white, woolly sheep. No wonder they say our native animals are at risk – our kangaroos, our emus and our koalas. Where are they? This is just empty land. All those trees before and now big empty plains. There's no sign of life anywhere."

Kendal nodded at the window. "There are some sheep, and over there, a few cattle."

"I've seen a few," Thea acknowledged. "Just a few dirty sheep but not many, and even I know there must be more than that or people would have nothing to live on. We're going further and further into nowhere with nothing," she lamented.

Kendal had known a few city girls who just never took to country life, but continued her orientation lesson to try to cheer her up. You never know which ones would settle in well and which ones would always hate it. "Come on, it's not as bad as you think," she said. "The sheep aren't all white and woolly like cotton wool, because they get the dust from the paddocks on the tips of their wool as it grows and so they end up the same colour as the ground. And the reason you don't see a lot of sheep together is that out here you need about four acres for one sheep. So the paddocks are pretty big and the sheep are not spread about evenly. They will have a couple of hundred in a thousand-acre paddock and the sheep move about in a mob – so a lot of the paddock looks empty."

"Why such a big paddock?" Thea said wonderingly.

Kendal explained, "It all comes down to rainfall. If you have enough rain or enough water to irrigate pastures, you can put the same couple of hundred in a ten-acre paddock – in fact, a nice green paddock with clean white sheep that you can see. This is just different, that's all. Where you're going they need even more room – probably ten acres for one sheep – so the paddocks are bigger again."

Thea hunched her shoulders and looked down again. "I can't bear to think about it," she said, half to herself. She eventually pulled herself together and watched out of the window again. After a while, she exclaimed animatedly, "Oh look, look over there, a few emus! Don't they look funny running like that." She was quite animated for a moment. Then her resolve faltered, and she said, depressed, "There's not very many of them and I haven't even seen a live kangaroo yet – only dead ones on the road."

Kendal tried to reassure her. "And you probably won't see them," she said, "kangaroos don't move about much in the day time. They're very well camouflaged. They just look like a bit of old tree or something lying down. When it gets to just about sundown and on into the evening, you'll see some for sure. In fact, no-one on the road wants to see them because we're all scared of hitting them. Sometimes they just jump right into the cars and you can't help hitting them."

"Well, why don't people stop?" Thea wanted to know.

Kendal felt her patience wearing a little thin. "You don't see them in time and, damn it all Thea, you can see how far it is to get anywhere. If you drive too slowly you'll never get to where you're going. Besides, going slowly doesn't always help. It is still dangerous. Some people believe the faster you go the less chance you have of hitting a roo." She had another thought. "But you haven't got much chance of seeing a koala. They were once plentiful out here, but now they're quite rare. They aren't often on the highway and if they were you'd never pick them out. They are really hard to see in the treetops and anyone who knows they have a colony of koalas feels they are extremely privileged and quite possessive of them. There are a few idiots about who try to catch them or worse, so no-one makes it obvious where they are."

Thea tucked one leg up underneath her to get more comfortable. "It's all very strange; not at all what I expected," she said. "Did you see that place called Muckadilla? I was looking on the map before I came, and I thought it was marked as a town. But there was a motel and a service station and nothing else."

Kendal laughed. "Muckadilla is a town, in a way," she explained. "People all gather there for functions. There's a school there, too. It may be a little centre, but it does bring people together. There may not be many people, Thea, but there are some and they are all very friendly. You said that you will have Bruce Thompson, his two little girls and his aunt on his property. Then you mentioned a married man and his wife – and even if there is no-one else there, you'll meet up with other people every now and then. I suppose it's different from a lot of people being just outside your front door, but it's a lovely way of life when you get used to it. Everyone works hard but everyone looks after everyone else. No-one ignores you when you do go out, like in the city."

The two girls passed the rest of the journey to Charleville chatting about their backgrounds and their expectations for their new jobs. But when at last the coach pulled up at the motel in Charleville, the girls were relieved to get out and stretch their legs.

The manager of the motel was even more relieved to see two girls chatting together and to discover there was no young man to accommodate.

"Oh great!" she said, "I'd been told there was a young man and a young woman coming on the bus tonight, but I have an extra couple who want a room. If you two are friends and don't mind sharing a room, I can give the couple that other room. I was going to ask one of the other blokes if he would take the young fella, but now I won't have to put anyone in with a stranger."

The girls looked at each other and then nodded happily. "That will be quite OK," Kendal told the manager.

Later, Thea confided she was quite pleased to share Kendal's room. "I probably would have been scared again on my own," she said. "I haven't often been on my own and it is really quite scary coming all the way out here and getting out in the dark."

After all her years of travelling long distances to school and back on the bus – accompanied by other school children who were also used to the idea – Kendal tried hard to see the experience through Thea's eyes. She really quite liked Thea, but thought she seemed far too dependent to be very happy out in the bush. Still, Kendal kept telling her good things about country life, and hoped Thea would be happy.

The manager had told Thea that Mr Thompson wouldn't arrive to pick them up until ten o'clock the next morning, so the girls decided to sleep in and have breakfast late. It was their last day before work, and they realised late starts with breakfast delivered would be a luxury after a few days on the job. They filled out their breakfast order together, and Kendal took it over to the office.

She'd just delivered them when she heard a loud shriek that seemed to be coming from their unit. Running across to their room, she wondered what was happening to Thea. Meanwhile, a few people appeared at the doors of a couple of other units. Two young men came out of the unit next to theirs and went straight in the door Kendal had left open. She was hard on their heels.

Thea was sitting on the end of the double bed, white with fright and shaking.

"Whatever's the matter, Thea?" Kendal asked, concerned.

Thea shivered. "Oh my God!" she gasped. "There's a spider. It fell on me. The biggest, hairiest spider I've ever seen in my life." She pointed to the bathroom. "It's in there." She gave a great shudder as the two men moved towards the bathroom.

Kendal gave her friend a comforting hug. "It's probably just a huntsman," she said. "They're huge and hairy, but quite harmless. You'll be OK."

Thea's expression plainly said she thought Kendal was out of her mind, and she shrank back terrified as the two young men came out of the bathroom with the spider on a towel. It was alive and moving now and then, and they were trying to jiggle the towel to keep it from falling off or running up their arms before they could get it out the door.

"Kill it, kill it!" Thea pleaded. Even Kendal gave a bit of a squeal as the spider dropped to the floor, but she rushed over to help the men shepherd the creature out the door. They were laughing and jostling each other as they eventually persuaded the poor, long-suffering spider that it was safer outside.

With the spider dispatched and Thea's fright out of the way, they could introduce themselves. Their rescuers told the girls they were Jim and Tom, and were in the district studying Pacific locusts.

As they stopped their fooling around, Kendal noticed that a car had pulled up under the awning beside the motel office – and that it was none other than the black Porsche she'd seen earlier in the day. Her eyes flew to the driver and yes, it was her stranger and he was looking at her. Unfortunately, he seemed to be thoroughly disapproving of what he saw.

Kendal thrust out her chin stubbornly. "Damn you," she thought, as she saw the car reverse out. "I suppose you'd manage to move a spider with no fuss at all. It would be all done in one clean movement and the spider wouldn't dare move until it was where it was put." Well, she'd enjoyed the laughter and the jostle and the tangling of arms and legs. The Porsche driver might have some magic about him, but he needn't look disapprovingly at her.

The fellows, obviously wanting an invitation to come in, said they had to help calm Thea and trooped back into the girls' unit. They made cups of coffee, and tried to convince Thea that huntsman spiders were all harmless. But, not too keen to have a late night, Kendal firmly but pleasantly turned the men out before too long. It had been a long and tiring day.

The room the girls shared could accommodate a family and Kendal took the double bed and Thea slept in the single bed. There wasn't much unpacking to do.

Seeing the Porsche and its passengers again had set Kendal to thinking about the driver. She wondered as she stretched out on the bed just what it would be like to share a bed every night with a partner. She knew it was the particular encounter that day with her stranger that made her so conscious of such things. He really did fill her mind in a way no-one else ever had.

Never one to daydream much about marriage, Kendal found herself wondering what it would be like to be with someone who made your pulse race. "There are definitely possibilities about it that are infinitely attractive," she thought to herself as she drifted off to sleep. "Maybe there are things worth losing your independence for." She sighed. Why did this one man make her feel this way? She hadn't even met him.

Chapter 5

The next morning dawned clear in the little outback town of Charleville. It was possible to feel the stillness, amid the bright light, and smell the dust and the trees. It was even a different sensation to breathe the air out here in the arid dryness. Kendal was conscious that her senses were aware that she was a long way from the coast of her timeless country.

Despite their best intentions to sleep in, the girls were too excited to stay in bed, so they dressed for the day's travel – Thea in pretty clothes and Kendal in more practical navy pants and a shirt – and explored around the motel.

All the rooms had been full and, although a couple of travellers had pulled out at daybreak, most of the cars were still there when the girls first went outside to look around. There were quite a few four-wheel drive vehicles in the carpark. Some looked as though they had tourists aboard, while some obviously belonged to locals in town on business.

In the room next door was a lively three-year-old girl, Tammy, who was busy trying to play with the motel cat while her parents were packing the car. Tammy would catch up with the cat and try to pick it up with both arms around its stomach. But Tammy was no match for the wily puss, which resolutely kept its feet on the ground and would seem to get longer and longer, like a cat in a cartoon, as the child struggled to lift it.

Thinking the cat might soon get sick of the game and scratch the child, Kendal crossed over to Tammy to talk to her. "Here, Tammy," she said to the child, "just pat that cat. He doesn't want to be picked up."

An elderly man came out of a nearby door and looked around with appreciation. "Another beautiful, fine day, girls," he said as he brought a suitcase out to his four-wheel drive. "A lovely day for adventure in the west."

"Yes, isn't it," Thea agreed.

Kendal looked at his basic vehicle and became concerned. "You're not going west from here, are you? Not like that?"

The elderly man reassured her. "No, we're not going further west; we're going north up the highway. We're not going out to that desert country. We've read all about it and we're not keen to go into those dangerous, out-of-the-way places. We just want to see the west and get the feel of the bush in a bit of comfort. A lot of our friends think we're adventurous enough coming out here, and along the highway to the Stockman's Hall of Fame at Longreach."

When he went back in to his room, Thea asked Kendal curiously, "Why did you worry about him? How did you know he was a tourist and not a local?"

Kendal thought about how to explain her instinct. "Well, no-one local would say 'another fine day' in all sincerity," she said. "Too many days are a fine day out here, so everyone looks for a few clouds and wonders if it will build up to rain. Someone might say 'it's a nice day' if it's not too hot or too windy or too cold in the winter, but no-one who lives here ever says 'It's another fine day' – except facetiously when they're really fed up with waiting for rain. He had a four-wheel drive, which made it look as if he might be going camping, and that can be dangerous further west from here if you haven't got extra water, food, tyres and petrol, and probably a two-way radio at least."

"I don't think I'll ever feel as if I belong," Thea said worriedly. "There's just too much I don't know."

Kendal laughed. "Goodness! It doesn't matter if you didn't know that. You won't be going out on your own and most things are common sense, really. As you live here you'll soon pick it all up. Everyone is friendly and you'll feel okay, I'm sure. You'll never have to set out for anywhere without knowing exactly what you need to take."

Thea looked a little doubtful, but agreed with Kendal. "You're right on one count – everyone is friendly enough anyway," she said.

As the morning progressed, most of the people packed up and left on their way. The girls said goodbye to Tammy and her family, and later on to the elderly man and his wife who were looking forward to getting to the Stockman's Hall of Fame.

By ten o'clock there were only a few cars left and one was the one next door to them from the Department of Primary Industries.

It belonged to the two young men, Jim and Tom. They'd already told the girls they were waiting for a fax to be sent to them before they went out for the day. The men were working on a few figures and writing up their work from the previous days. Jim had just gone out to the car when a rather battered station wagon pulled in.

The driver got out, stretched, and seeing no-one in the office walked over and said, "G'day mate" to the research officer. "Keeping dry?"

Jim replied, "Yes, but the report this morning said there was a front coming through and there is a slight haze on the horizon out there to the north. It might build up into something."

The driver nodded. "You might be right. Well, we could do with it." He put out his hand. "Thompson's the name," he said. "I'm looking for a young girl, Thea Moreton, and a jackaroo, Kenrick MacKenzie. Seen anyone who might be them?"

The girls could clearly hear this exchange from their unit. Kendal giggled a bit as Thea's eyes widened in amazement at how accurate Kendal had been while she was listening to this typical exchange of greeting in the west.

Thea went out to meet her new employer. "I'm Thea," she said shyly.

Bruce smiled warmly. "Hello there, Thea, and welcome to the west. I hope you'll be very happy with us. "Well, let's get your things." He nodded to Kendal as she came out of the unit. "There is a young man I'm supposed to pick up as well. Do you know where Kenrick MacKenzie is? He was meant to be staying here last night, too."

Kendal stepped forward and said confidently, "Actually I'm Kendal MacKenzie and I came instead of my brother Kenrick."

Bruce looked stunned for a moment and then he smiled slightly and said, "Do the Carmodys know you are coming?"

Kendal was a bit annoyed at his obvious surprise and she started to defend herself. "No, they don't know of our change of plans, but I can't see why you are quite so surprised. Lots of girls work as jillaroos and plenty of girls train at the Longreach Pastoral College. I'm not trained but I grew up out here and I can be useful."

"Well, you don't have to explain yourself to me," Bruce said easily, "and I can't leave you here. But it would be interesting to be there when you get to the house tonight!"

Kendal wondered what Bruce's cryptic comment meant and had an uneasy twinge, but decided to forget it. Bruce and Thea were starting to collect the suitcases to put them in the car, and so she shrugged her shoulders and went after them.

Their luggage fitted in the boot and Bruce opened the front door for Thea and Kendal hopped into the back. They quickly drove through the main part of town, across the Warrego on the double bridges and then turned left onto the Quilpie road, a beautiful new highway that cut through mulga scrub nearly all the way.

It wasn't long before Bruce and Thea were chatting away quite happily. He found it was her first time for a trip out here and he took over Kendal's role from yesterday, talking about various things of interest as they went. It was only a couple of hours and the time passed quite quickly until they came to the last little step-down before Quilpie.

For a moment they had an almost bird's eye view of the country ahead. From this vantage point they could see the clear, blue, cloudless sky and the land lying flat and covered with low scrub right to the horizon. The land looked like it went on for ever and ever.

"Not too far to Quilpie now," Bruce said reassuringly. He glanced at Thea. "This probably seems as if it's going on forever to you."

Thea said nothing, but her expression gave her feelings away.

"A few people feel that way," Bruce said. "You know, the other day a fellow was coming out to Quilpie – a fellow who was selling something at the flower show. He must have felt it was a long, long way I guess, because when he got to Quilpie he walked in to the post office and said, 'I'm glad to be here at last, but tell me, how much further do you have to go before you fall off the edge of the world?'" Bruce laughed, and Kendal joined in.

Thea smiled politely, but she wasn't so sure it was a joke. She was wondering pretty much the same thing herself. The car sped quickly down the hill and they were back on the flat again towards the Bulloo River and into Quilpie.

Pulling to a stop, Bruce asked the girls if they would mind filling in a bit of time there as he had a bit of business to do with a few people. He showed them where they could go for a meal and said, if they didn't mind, he'd leave them to their own devices and meet them again at three o'clock.

Quilpie is a small town by any standards, but it is on the edge of one of Australia's great gem fields. Opals are found in many places in the surrounding country, and so quite a few of the shops were trying to tempt the tourist trade. Kendal had seen it all before, but she never tired of looking at opal. She knew Thea would love the opal altar at the Catholic church.

She was right. Thea loved it and spent a fair while in the church just looking at the altar. She'd only seen opals in ordinary jewellery shops in the city, not as decorations, so she was fascinated.

As they went around, Kendal met a few people she'd known well when she lived out west and had a great old chat to some friends. Joe Randle, one of the boys who used to play polocrosse with Kenrick and Kendal, was one of the first to meet her.

"Kendal, great to see you back," he greeted her. "What are you doing? Visiting friends?"

Kendal shook her head. "No, I'm just going to Carmody Plains to help out for a while."

Joe laughed. "Carmody Plains? You're going to Carmody Plains? What a turn-up this will be for the books!"

Kendal became easily annoyed if she thought someone was doubting her ability to work. "Come off it," she said, "what's the big deal? Don't you think I can handle the job?" She looked angry. "Don't tell me you turned out to be a chauvinist, too."

Joe held his hands up as if surrendering. "Calm down, old girl, don't bite my head off," he said. "I was just surprised, that's all. Anyway, what's Rick up to these days – and, more importantly, who's your pretty friend?"

Kendal introduced Thea to Joe, and after his reaction, she made sure she didn't mention her plans to anyone else. If anyone asked her, she just turned it away and talked about Kenrick coming out to Carmody Plains soon, or Thea going to Kalanoa with Bruce Thompson.

But she did ask Mrs Kelly, an old friend of her mother's, when she bumped into her in the cafe, if she knew anything about the Carmodys from Carmody Plains.

"Haven't thought about them for ages," Mrs Kelly replied. "I don't really know them all that well, my dear. I don't know if old Tom is still there or that boy of his, Charles. I haven't heard if Charles is married or not. No, I can't tell you much about them. Why, my dear?"

Kendal avoided completely answering the question. "Well, Rick is going to work out here in a few weeks' time."

"Oh, he'll be fine," Mrs Kelly said reassuringly. "I'm sure they're very good people. I've never heard a word against them. Old Tom Carmody went to school with one of my cousins. Haven't seen him about lately, though."

Before long, it was time to meet Bruce. Thea hesitated as they went to get in the car. She dearly wanted to sit in the front near Bruce again, but she didn't want to look pushy. Kendal saw her confusion and stepped quite definitely to the back door, saying, "You hop in the front, Thea. Bruce can show you the sights and I can doze off in peace."

"Enjoy your time in Quilpie, girls?" Bruce inquired, as they settled themselves in the car. They assured him they had and he started up for the drive home. It wasn't long before Bruce was in full swing, talking to Thea again. This was his home territory and he had an interested audience. "This is where you really start to drive," he told them. "Coming out this far the roads are major highways. That new bit from Charleville to Quilpie is pretty good, isn't it? But from here on, you don't just hop in your car and go. You have to know a bit about it and keep your mind on the job all the time. It's certainly not a time to let your mind wander."

As they travelled out of town, the road narrowed to barely more than one car width. "This old road was built after the war some time. It was a great wonder then, I can tell you. It was what they called a beef development road and went from Windorah to Quilpie. It was a bloody marvel – the only bit of bitumen between home and Dalby." He laughed ruefully. "All these new roads make it look pretty ordinary now, though."

After the sameness before, this country was quite interesting and attractive. There was quite a bit of vegetation about and the road was winding through some water channels. At one point, the road actually appeared to be in between two little dry creeks, one on either side of the road. Bruce started to talk about it. "This bit of road we're on now is pretty dangerous, really. It crosses a lot of water course country. You know, opinion is still divided about what should have been done about the road. You can always stir up a pretty lively argument if you feel like a bit of fun. A lot of the old hands think it should have gone a lot further north. Others disagree and have their own theories about how it should have been handled. Anyway, what we've ended up with is quite tricky – it winds in and out and you can't always see too well ahead." He turned to Thea and said earnestly, "Remember this if you come into Quilpie some time. It can be tricky if you're not aware. You really have to stay constantly alert and scan through the trees ahead for any sign of movement. You'd be a sorry mess if you met a semi with three dogs around some of these corners."

Thea asked what seemed the obvious question. "If it is so dangerous, why don't they change it and build a new one?"

Bruce shrugged and said one word. "Money." Then he went on. "There's so much competition for money for roads and this would be a big job. And as I've said, there is no agreement on what would be the best thing to fix the problem, anyway."

Past the water course country, Bruce indicated the outside plains. "Most of the country here is very lightly stocked indeed, because with so little rain, there's not much feed. It gradually changes into the desert country further out."

Thea said woefully, "I hate to tell you, but it almost looks like desert to me now. I didn't know it would all be so red. There's red sand or red stones beside the road all the time. Sometimes there are little trees and sometimes not, but the ground is always red."

Bruce agreed. "There is a bit of other country about, but you're right, Thea, it is mostly red. You get used to it and don't think about it, I guess."

Conversation wasn't all that difficult to conduct from the back but most of the talking was still between Bruce and Thea together in the front. They had a few more kilometres to drive yet and Kendal was happy that Thea would probably be feeling quite comfortable with Bruce by the time they met up with the Carmodys in Juno and they went their different ways. Close together in this sort of country can be very far apart. Kendal had become quite fond of Thea and hoped she would be happy in the isolation of the great outback. A lot depended upon your companions, and Bruce and Thea seemed quite compatible already.

Left to her own thoughts, Kendal wondered to herself what her time at Carmody Plains would be like. Before her father had died, her family had lived south-west from Quilpie, south from Eromanga. Juno was away to the north-west of Quilpie, and Kendal was fascinated by the subtle differences in landscape as they drove along.

The trio had one more stop to make, when Bruce dropped off some parts he'd picked up in town for a friend. So it was just on dark when they drove into Juno.

Juno was a typically small, outback centre with the usual wide streets, few shade trees, post office and, of course, an old wooden hotel.

Kendal pointed out to Thea that all these settlements in the outback were built with their few buildings spaced across a wide expanse of street. "It's not just because they have all the room in the world out here, it's because that is the distance it took for a bullock team to turn around in the old days. They were built to suit them."

However, the days of horses and bullock teams were long gone and as Bruce, with Thea and Kendal, pulled into town, there was a Ford Falcon and a Toyota Land Cruiser parked in the main street.

Two men, one quite young and the other obviously older, were standing yarning together, leaning on the bonnet of the Land Cruiser. They were both waiting for Bruce Thompson to arrive. Young John McMahon had been letting Tom Carmody know how anxious he was about his father's best dog, Flint.

"I was just so glad when Ethel told me that Bruce was going through Charleville," he said. "Miss Thompson passed the message on for me to ask him to call in at the vet. I'm really sweating on it. Dad's away and I just couldn't stand anything happening to Flint while I'm in charge. Dad wouldn't blame me so much, but I'd blame myself. The dog's pretty crook, but the vet said it should be OK if I can get this stuff she's sending into him tonight."

As they saw the station wagon coming, the young man said, "This will be them now. I'll just grab it and go. I want to get a dose into the poor old fellow as soon as possible."

Bruce parked the car and got out of the vehicle, stretching his cramped muscles. Then he reached into the back to take out a small poly foam cooler. He held it out as John walked over to take it eagerly.

"Thanks, mate, I owe you one," he said. "I'm really glad to have that."

Bruce said pleasantly, "No problems, John. Did you get onto the vet?"

"Yes," John replied. "We had a talk and she gave me all the instructions. Sorry to rush off but this is urgent."

He nodded to the other passengers and to old Tom and couldn't get his vehicle on the move quickly enough.

The girls hardly had a glimpse of John, but they watched the older man walk across to them. He was tall and looked a typical country gentleman. His skin was like tanned leather and his face had deep creases running down, rather than wrinkles. But he had kind blue eyes and an air of quietness and decency about him that made you feel he was a man to be trusted.

He put out his hand to Bruce. "G'day Bruce, have a good trip?"

"Not bad, not bad," Bruce replied.

"Young John was certainly sweating on that delivery," Tom said, and then his interest turned to the two girls. "Who have you got here, Bruce, and what have you done with the young lad Kenrick MacKenzie?"

Bruce motioned towards Thea. "Well, Tom, this is Thea Moreton who is here to help me with my young nippers."

Tom took off his hat, revealing a distinguished head of grey hair, and nodded pleasantly to Thea. His gaze moved to Kendal with polite interest.

"And," Bruce continued, "this is Kendal MacKenzie who came out instead of her brother Kenrick."

Tom Carmody stood stock still for quite a few seconds. His eyes never left Kendal but they widened in surprise and then seemed to sparkle in merriment. "Well, what do you know?" he replied. "How about that? Well, never mind." He put out his hand to her. "How do you do, my dear – Kendal, did you say it was? I'm sure we'll hear the full story in due course."

Kendal shook his hand and he turned to Bruce, "Well, Bruce, I won't hold you up – you must be wanting to get on home to your little girls. Come along, my dear, we'll get your things out of the station wagon and we'll be off."

Tom didn't give anyone else time to say anything. Kendal bade a quick farewell to Thea and Bruce, and climbed into the Land Cruiser for the last stretch of the journey to Carmody Plains. Tom seemed very interested in hearing all about Kendal and her plans and how it was that Kendal had arrived instead of Kenrick, or Rick as she usually called him. He was most supportive, and said he was sure they would all be very happy with the arrangement. Now and then he looked at her with a little bit of a worry in his eyes, but Kendal was so busy looking around that she didn't notice. By now it was so dark that Kendal couldn't see the country they were passing through very well. She could only see bits and pieces outlined in the headlights and she was watching carefully not to miss what there was to be seen.

They drove over several grids and then came to double swing gates in sandy country. Then on again they drove through taller trees until they came to another gate. As Kendal got out to open the iron gate she could just make out a group of buildings to the right, and on the left there was the sheen of the moonlight on a large stretch of water. It was bordered on the far side with big old water gums outlined against the skyline and Kendal felt the beauty of the country as they were going past. These buildings would later prove to be the shearers' quarters and they drove past these and up to the house. She liked what she had seen and felt comfortable that this would be her home for the next few weeks.

As with most country houses, they drove around to the back. Many beautiful Australian gum trees stood out in the headlights of the Toyota. "Here we are, then," Tom said, and he picked up her case while she collected her other things. There was no sign of anyone else about at the moment – only an old dog who didn't get up, but lifted his head and thumped his tail as they passed.

Tom led the way into the kitchen. "I expect you'd like a cup of tea and something to eat before turning in," he said to Kendal, who was hungry and quite ready for a cuppa. The kitchen was spotlessly clean – almost clinical – without a single thing out of place. No clutter, but no real character to it either. "Not like most country kitchens," Kendal thought to herself, a little curious.

She felt a natural urge to help, but not knowing where things were she felt she was a bit slow in helping Tom to get the things out for tea. While he filled the electric kettle and flicked the switch, Kendal could see the tea canister clearly on a ledge above. As she reached for it, so did Tom. She moved away, but in doing so knocked the pepper pot down and pepper fell straight into her face.

Coughing and spluttering, Kendal's eyes started to smart and water. "What a way to start!" she managed to say to Tom, while feeling dreadfully embarrassed at her blunder.

"Are you OK?" Tom was terribly kind, passing her a large handkerchief and trying to pat her on the back to stop her coughing.

"What exactly is going on in here?" Cold, clipped words cut through Kendal's discomfort and their very unexpectedness caused her to start in surprise. Even more surprising was the speaker – her tall, dark Porsche driver who had fascinated her at Miles. But one look at his furious face convinced Kendal there would be no daydreams now – but why he was so angry was more than she could imagine.

"Good heavens, Charles, you did give us a fright!" Tom said.

"I can see that I was interrupting something," the younger man said, his anger not abating, "but I really am at a loss to know exactly what it is that I'm interrupting. You go into town to pick up a jackaroo – and I come home to find you've got your arm around one of the most accomplished little flirts I've ever seen! Dad, will you never learn? A girl with a sob story is your only downfall. We've agreed we won't have women on the place and here you are with this little tramp already sobbing in your arms! What is going on?"

"What is going on, indeed!" Kendal thought to herself. Staring at the two, she was horrified and amazed at Charles's reaction. Why did he talk to his father like that – and react so angrily to his father helping her? "Something really strange is going on here," she decided.

"What's wrong?" Kendal demanded of Charles, but at the same time Tom said, "Charles, you really don't understand what's going on."

Charles turned to his father. "No, Dad, it's you that never understands what is going on until you're in over your head. But I would like to know where you've left Kenrick MacKenzie and what this girl is doing here."

Kendal felt it was time to stand up for herself. Ignoring Charles's scowl, she said, "My name is Kendal MacKenzie and I've come instead of my brother Kenrick. Rick hurt his leg badly and the doctor told him he couldn't work for a couple of weeks – and so I've come in his place to help you out. We tried calling to let you know, but there was a fault on the line." She tried hard to look more friendly than she felt towards this growling, angry man. "You did advertise for a jackaroo or jillaroo. You've just got a jillaroo for a while instead of a jackaroo."

"Oh no, I haven't," Charles retorted. "You'll have to stay here tonight, obviously enough, but first thing in the morning it's back to town with you. All the designing charm in the world will not make me change my mind. I distinctly told the agency to make sure we didn't get a girl. The Trades Practices Act says I have to advertise for a jackaroo or jillaroo – but there is no way a girl will ever get a job on Carmody Plains while I'm here." Then he added, "And you're the last person I'd ever let on this property."

Kendal couldn't believe her ears. That it was necessary to advertise like that hadn't entered her head and she had thought she would have been just as welcome as a man – or, at the very least, judged on her own merits. She was tired, upset, embarrassed and quite bewildered by the undercurrents in the household, but there was no way she was going to let this objectionable man be so rude to her.

"How dare you speak to me like that!" She was outraged. If she was going to be sent home the next day, she decided she'd go fighting. "That's twice now you've said I'm no good, and you've never even spoken to me before in your life. How did I know you didn't want a girl when you advertised for one? If it was by law you did that, then by law I'll stay here! You can't discriminate against me like that! Anyway, what right do you have to make judgments against me when you've never seen me before?"

"I've seen all of you that I ever want to see, and if it's a fight you want, young lady, you've chosen the wrong man. You can come along to your room now, but you're leaving first thing in the morning."

Tom clearly had endured enough of his son's ranting. "Come now, Charles, I do think you're being a little harsh and rude to young Kendal here. She strikes me as a pleasant girl and I'm sure it was an honest mistake that she made. She thought she was helping us out."

Charles sighed. "Dad, any woman with a sad tale to tell can pull the wool over your eyes. You're the most kind-hearted man in the world, as we've found to our cost more than once. We've agreed to have no women, and believe me, I've seen women like this," he pointed to Kendal, "in action. As soon as her type sees a man, she's all over him like a rash. I mean, look – she couldn't have been in the house more than a minute or so, and already she was crying in your arms. She's a predator, Dad. Be warned."

Charles spoke over Tom's protestations. "I don't want to know what happened," he said. "I saw it for myself." He motioned for Kendal to follow him. "Come along, and I'll show you your room for the one and only night you'll be staying here. And you can save your breath in trying to talk to me because I'm not interested."

61

He picked up her suitcase and walked off and Kendal had no option but to look desperately at Tom and then to hurry off after this electric, extraordinary man before he disappeared into the dark with her suitcase. He walked straight along the back verandah, with Kendal hot on his heels, and nodded to one room as they passed. "Bathroom in there, and be careful with the water," he said, and as they crossed the big open breezeway, stopped at the first door and told Kendal she'd find a bed made up in there.

Charles put down her suitcase at the doorway and suddenly turned to leave, bumping into Kendal, who had been following him closely. Oops. She was about to apologise, when the intense look on his face stopped her in her tracks.

Suddenly, before she could respond or pull away, Charles bent down and kissed her full on the mouth. Momentarily disoriented and thoroughly confused by his behaviour, Kendal started to pull away. Then, to her own surprise, she found herself responding.

They stood for a moment locked in their embrace. Slowly, Charles drew away. He moved his hands to her shoulders and looked straight into her face.

He looked upset. Then his face hardened again. "Yes," he said, "one touch and you really are anyone's." Then he turned on his heel and disappeared across the verandah into the main part of the house.

Chapter 6

"What the hell is going on out here?" Kendal was fuming at Charles's treatment of her. Confusion over his behaviour had turned into anger. "What gives him the right to treat me like that!"

Kendal found her reaction to him equally as annoying as his behaviour. "How could I have found someone like him the least bit attractive?" she asked herself angrily. "The sooner I get out of here the better." As she unpacked her suitcase to get her nightclothes and toiletries, she couldn't help going over and over the night's events. She was sure she was too stirred up to rest, but she was young and healthy and she soon fell into a deep sleep.

Towards morning, she started to toss and turn, and the sounds of the Australian bush began seeping into her subconscious and brought her dreams of her childhood. The willy wagtail had been chanting *sweet pretty creature* since the early hours of the morning. Then with the first light there was the beautiful dawn chorus of birds in the bush. Kookaburras were laughing down by the water, and magpies were in the trees quite close by, along with galahs by the hundreds and the bell-like sounds of top-knot pigeons flying. Something was missing. "What was it?" Kendal thought to herself sleepily. "No roosters crowing, that was it. Why no roosters? Didn't they have chooks here? Everybody had chooks, didn't they?"

The bird calls brought back memories of her early childhood. As much as she would have liked to stay in bed and remember old times, she realised the last thing she needed was to feel like a vulnerable child. Recalling the previous night, it was imperative she marshall all of her resources to be practical, efficient and capable at this job.

The good rest had brought clarity to her thoughts, and Kendal arose for the day's work determined to make good her intention of helping out both Rick and Tom Carmody. "As for that other objectionable individual," she decided, "he is not going to sway me one way or the other." Kendal knew she could do a good job helping at shearing time, and she decided then and there she wouldn't let any man stop her.

Whatever he had thought of her last night, she knew exactly what she needed today to look presentable as a jillaroo. She quickly braided her hair to keep it neat and tidy under the wide-brimmed Akubra she'd be wearing in the sun, and she wore jeans and a pale blue work shirt with double pockets that she'd borrowed from Rick. The pockets held her notebook and pencil so she wouldn't fail to keep tally of numbers and notes of things through the day. She pulled on the expensive riding boots she'd had since she was a schoolgirl, but they still fitted well and they were just right for work.

Secure in the knowledge that she was dressed for the job, she stepped onto the breezeway and walked toward the kitchen. The old dog – an ancient black and tan kelpie –was lying down beside the verandah just where he'd been last night. He was dozing and didn't look up at her at all. Kendal would have liked to pat him but now wasn't the time for that.

Only a few decades ago, the homestead kitchen would have had a wood stove, with someone allocated to building a cheerful fire in the morning. But the Carmodys' kitchen was well and truly modern. Kendal could smell food, and the kettle was hot to the touch, so she guessed someone had been in the kitchen before her. Hunting around – and remembering with a pang of embarrassment her episode with the pepper pot – she quickly found bread.

Just as she was searching for the toaster, Tom Carmody walked in. "Goodness, girlie," he greeted her, "you don't have to do that – your breakfast is in the oven." He looked at her approvingly. "You look ready for work, but very fresh and pretty. No trouble waking up?"

Kendal smiled. Tom appeared to be a pleasant man, she thought. "Thanks, Mr Carmody," she said out loud. "I slept well and I never have any trouble starting the day early."

"You had better call me Tom," he replied. He looked around as if for someone, and then continued. "I had a talk to Charles last night and I feel sure the two of you will work something out," he confided. "We need help right now and you're on the spot. Better eat your breakfast now and you'll be ready when he comes in."

Before she had finished her breakfast, Charles walked in. She noticed his quick glance taking in her appearance. She knew that even if his eyes did widen in appreciation of what he saw, there was no way his pride would let him admit any satisfaction.

"Well now," Charles said in a slightly condescending tone. "Dad says I should at least talk to you. So would you be good enough to explain to what I owe this extraordinary situation? I engage a young man with good references and the highest commendation to come to start work on our property in the hope that he will be one day suitable to appoint as manager. And what do I find? Here, a few days until shearing when every sheep on the place has to be moved, I find instead a glamorous hussy. You look as if you think you're some sort of model. Completely and utterly useless for what I have in mind. If this is some sort of a joke, I am not amused." Then he added, as if pleased with his own fair-mindedness, "Now I am willing to hear your story."

Kendal listened to his diatribe, her mind racing, and thought "Big of you" at his willingness to listen. She'd come out to Carmody Plains thinking she was doing these people a favour, as well as her brother. She knew shearing was the busiest time of the year on any sheep property and she was equally well aware how difficult it would be without proper labour. Fine, she wasn't Kenrick. But she knew more than most newcomers because she'd grown up in the same south-west corner of Queensland. Sure, she'd come out to help her brother keep his job – but she'd also realised what a spot the Carmodys would have been in without anyone helping out. Contract musters can be hard to get at a moment's notice.

Normally a friendly and placid person, she wondered at how this Charles Carmody had managed to get under her skin. She was attractive and used to men being friendly to her – yet this man seemed to have some sort of confusing electric effect on her. Attraction and repulsion darted at cross-purposes around them. It was as if each time they looked at each other, the electricity in the air practically crackled.

She knew why she was at Carmody Plains – but why this conflict between them? Part of her wanted to tell him to go to hell, and the other wanted to kiss him. For an independent woman, the situation was uncomfortable.

Pulling herself together and conscious that Charles was staring at her, waiting for an answer, Kendal realised she definitely would do neither of those things. Instead, she tried to reasonably explain the obvious.

"It's all very simple really and if you'll stop to listen long enough, I'll explain," she said, and began to outline the course of events that had led her to Carmody Plains – and concluded with the pepper pot disaster.

If she had expected him to be apologetic for his antagonistic attitude and his jumping to conclusions, she would have been disappointed. Then again, by now she realised she had no idea what to expect from this man. They continued talking, and by the end of their conversation had reached a wary truce.

Charles made it apparent he wasn't grateful for Kendal coming to his rescue. Only the fact that she thought she'd like to help Rick keep his job made her agree to stay, under sufferance. "Though why Rick would want to work for him, I wouldn't know," she thought to herself.

Charles was concluding, rather ungraciously, "Goodness knows how much use you'll be, but you may as well come along and I'll show you around."

Leaving Tom to clean up the kitchen on his own, Kendal followed Charles out the kitchen door. The old dog got up very stiffly, shook himself and came slowly over to Charles. Charles's expression softened and he took a moment to fondle the old fellow's ears before continuing briskly on his way across the lawn and past some sheds and outbuildings. Two other dogs, both younger black and tan kelpies, fell in behind them.

Kendal could see the usual meat house, hay shed, petrol drums and vehicles that were an essential part of every station set-up. There was no sign of the black Porsche, although the Land Cruiser was there, along with a battered Holden ute and several agricultural motor bikes.

Charles led her to the bikes. "I hope you're good on one of these," he said. "This is no time to just look decorative. I need you to be useful. We've got a lot of stock to move."

With her eyes blazing but voice steady, Kendal said quietly, "I'm quite used to handling sheep with a motor bike and I can draft and do the yard work and penning up. There is no need to act as if I'm some sort of imposition. I came to help and I assure you I wouldn't have come if I didn't think I could do the job. After all, it's only for a week or two."

"You'll have to keep your bike in good order," Charles continued as if he hadn't heard her. "You'll find it ready for you now. Bill-Bob always keeps the machinery in perfect order and I'll expect you to do the same."

Thankful the bike was a model she had ridden before, and feeling fairly confident that she'd be able to manage the first part of her job, Kendal kicked the bike into a start and listened to it idle for a minute. She tried the gears and slowly started. So far, so good.

* * * * *

Bill-Bob had made sure he was up at the shed early that day. Charles was home, the new boy had arrived and the mustering for shearing was about to start. Charles might have something he'd like to arrange with Bill-Bob even though they'd talked at length when he had arrived yesterday. Anyway, Bill-Bob liked to keep a pretty good eye on all that was happening even though he made it his business to appear not to be interested in anything but his own work.

He loved machinery and all the station vehicles were in excellent order – and what's more, pottering about in the sheds all the time on the hill at the back of the homestead gave him a pretty good vantage point to suss out the lie of the land and to see what was happening. Today, with a new bloke starting at Carmody Plains, it was the perfect way to get a good look as soon as possible.

"Yep," he said to himself, wiping his hands on an oily rag. "Any minute now Charles should be bringing the new bloke, Kenrick MacKenzie, out to get his bike and other gear ready for the day."

But when he saw the two figures come from the verandah and across the lawn towards the shed, Bill-Bob's jaw dropped. "What is this now?" he muttered to himself. As the figures disappeared from view through the trees, Bill-Bob wondered if he'd been seeing things. He could have sworn the young fella was a girl, the way he was walking.

Bill-Bob put his head down to his work and concentrated on tightening the chain and checking the sprockets. He heard Charles tell his companion not to look decorative. Then he heard what was definitely a girl answer.

"Well, stone the crows," Bill-Bob thought, suddenly realising that there really was a woman at Carmody Plains. "It just shows it pays to keep an open mind in life." Keeping at his work, Bill-Bob wondered at the change of situation. The last thing he would have suspected would be a girl going out to do the mustering for shearing. Women had caused a lot of trouble at Carmody Plains, and Bill-Bob knew that Charles had decided that he'd never have a woman on the place again. In fact, everyone knew what Charles thought – it was common knowledge across the district.

"Good thing I'm a sticky beak," Bill-Bob thought to himself, satisfied. "Otherwise I'd never have been able to take it in my stride when I met her." Bill-Bob prided himself on acting as if nothing fazed him. But a woman at Carmody Plains? Wonders would never cease.

He heard Charles saying, "You'll have to keep your bike in good order. You'll find it ready for you now. Bill-Bob always keeps the machinery in perfect order and I expect you to do the same."

"Fair enough," thought Bill-Bob. He did keep the machinery in good order and he didn't mind having it acknowledged. A bike was kicked into action.

The two-way receiver started to crackle.

Bill-Bob could clearly hear Tony's voice come through. "Y'there, Charles, got a copy? I'm flying over your bore now. If you're not there, I'll land at the boundary gate."

There was a pause, and then Bill-Bob heard Charles's reply. "Right, Tony. We're ready to leave the homestead now. So why don't you fly around and look in the channels, and I'll call you when we get there."

On the other side of the shed, Charles turned to Kendal.

"Now girl, this is where we start," he instructed her. "Follow me out to the paddock and we'll see what he's found. My guess is that the sheep will be making their way up to the ridge this morning. The wind is starting to blow from that way and they always walk into the wind. If we're quick and lucky, they'll still be spread out on the plain and we'll catch them there." Half to himself, he finished, "Surely something has to be going my way."

He whistled his dogs. They jumped up on his bike behind him and Charles rode purposefully down the road.

Chapter 7

Thea's reception at Kalanoa was a very different experience from Kendal's at Carmody Plains. Then again, it was a very different establishment.

On their way out from Juno, Bruce described the people she would meet when they arrived. His Aunt Bessie, Bessie Thompson, lived in the house and he was sure Thea would get along with her really well.

"She's a dear," Bruce said lovingly. "She knows how she wants things done but she's very motherly and kind. She's never unreasonable and I'm sure you'll get on well together."

Thea inquired about his little girls, thinking she'd start to get to know them through their father's eyes.

Bruce was obviously the proud papa. "I can't really tell you objectively about my little girls, Thea. You'll just have to see for yourself. Naturally enough, I think they are the most wonderful little people who ever lived."

Thea felt sure she'd love them when she knew them. After all, Bruce was just so nice himself she was sure his children would be OK, too.

Bruce continued describing Kalanoa. "Then," he said, "there's Sam and Clara. They live in a cottage a bit away from the house. They're a great couple. Sam is a dry old stick but he's a great bloke. He puts himself down a lot, but he's such a reliable old cove. His wife Clara fights his battles for him – she's a bit rough at times but a real battler. The only thing she's scared of is snakes. And you can't knock Sam, not when she's around. Sam is the shining light in her life. You're sure to meet them tomorrow, because they both help out a lot about the place."

When they arrived at the house, Thea was the centre of a great welcome. The dogs barked, the lights went on and the plump, pleasant figure of Aunt Bessie was out to meet them. She was full of questions, firing them all at once and not really waiting for any answers. "Well now, did you have a good trip? Welcome, my dear, welcome. Did you get all the jobs done, Bruce?" She fussed about. "It's a pleasant evening, isn't it? Not too hot at all yet. Your name's Thea, isn't it? You want us to call you Thea, don't you, not Miss Moreton?"

Thea finally got a chance to answer. "Oh yes, please call me Thea."

They came into a large breezeway and the little girls were waiting there for them. They stood back and stared at Thea as she came in with their Aunt Bessie, who said, "This is Thea, girls. Say hello to her."

Kirsty and Carla gave hesitant little smiles, not sure at first what to make of this new person who was coming into their household. Their eyes kept sliding back to the door to see when Bruce would arrive. As soon as he appeared they rushed to him, squealing, "Daddy, Daddy!" Bruce put Thea's bags on the ground, and gathered the girls in his arms to cuddle them while they bombarded him with questions.

Meanwhile, Bessie took Thea to the second room on the right of the large breezeway and said, "This will be your room, dear. I hope you'll find everything you need here." She indicated a door opposite. "The bathroom is just across the way." She bustled into the room and smoothed the bed down. "Just put your things down over there and we'll go on into the kitchen. Bruce will put your suitcases in your room when the children get over their welcome and they'll join us." She bustled out and went on down a wide passage.

Thea followed her, her eyes trying to take in everything around her. The house seemed large. It had high ceilings and was built in tongue and groove timber. There were pictures and photos and maps and interesting things all over the walls that Thea was dying to stop and look at, but she had to keep Aunt Bessie in sight to make sure she got to the right room.

Arriving at the kitchen, there were more questions fired at her – "How do you like your tea? You do like tea, don't you? What would you like to eat? There's bread and butter of course, and some biscuits and cake. But would you like something more solid?"

Bruce had come in behind them now, a little girl on each side of him and each one firmly holding one of his hands. He received the same loving questions.

"What would you like to eat, Bruce? I've got shepherd's pie I can heat up in the microwave, or something light?"

Bruce turned to Thea. "Are you okay? Not too tired?" She smiled a little and nodded. "Are you hungry?"

As they ate, they talked. Bessie asked Bruce if he'd received all the messages and been able to do all of the jobs. Bruce assured her that he had and talked about the journey. They included Thea in their discussions and she felt grateful for their acceptance and welcome. It was all so strange and unfamiliar, but at least Bessie and Bruce made her feel at home.

Finally, they cleaned up their dishes. Bessie announced it was time for bed. "You put those children of yours to bed, Bruce, and I'll see that Thea's all right."

Bruce bade her a good night, but the little girls really stole Thea's heart. Having somewhat thawed out, they each came over to Thea and put up their faces to be kissed, saying "Goodnight, Thea". Thea dutifully kissed them, and they took their father's hands and left the room. Bessie pointed to a tap low down beside the door. "This is the only rain water tap. We use it for drinking. The water in the bathroom is river water and a bit discoloured. We have a plentiful supply at the moment – so it will be all right to have a bath now or in the morning." Thea was glad Kendal had warned her or she might have been a bit upset when she saw it. She was a bit put out that there were little lizards running all over the walls catching insects, but bravely decided to hope the lizards would eat spiders.

Bruce and the girls slept not far from the kitchen, but Bessie's room seemed to be beside Thea's. Unpacking her night gear and getting ready for bed, Thea felt relieved she wasn't too far away in a corner of the house on her own.

Finally ready, Thea turned out the light and looked out the window, to where the garden was illuminated and pretty in the bright moonlight. "Almost storybook romantic," Thea thought, satisfied. Some of the trees had leaves that picked up the moonlight and they were luminous and beautiful. There were darker shapes and shades that made interesting patterns in the peaceful surroundings. She went to bed feeling that, although there were so many strange things around her and she was so far away from home, she would be happy here where she'd been made to feel so welcome.

Some hours later, Thea awoke and lay rigid in fright. The darkness around her was more than she could believe. The absolute blackness was something she had never experienced before and if she survived the night, God help her, she would make sure she never experienced it again. Just seconds before, there had been a blood-curdling scream somewhere close to her. She had been awakened from deep sleep by this nightmarish screech and then there was no sound and no sight at all.

All of Thea's brave resolutions left her at once. She panicked. "Why did I ever agree to come out here?" she thought to herself. She opened and shut her eyes a few times. There was no difference whatever whether they were open or shut – just blackness. Nowhere she'd ever been was as black as this. There had always been light from a street light, a neighbour's light, passing headlights in the street, even the light from the electronic clock and video that glowed quite brightly in what she'd always thought of as the dark before.

Oh, dear God, this was frightening. No sound, no sight and the memory of that awful sound. Trying to take control of her quivering emotions, Thea tried to convince herself she'd dreamed it. So she shut her eyes and thought she'd try to go back to sleep. A scampering sound above her made eyes fly wide open, as if she could see what it was. Was it just a possum in the ceiling? Or maybe something worse?

Then she heard it again – another scream in the night! Then there was another sound she didn't recognise and again more silence. With nowhere to go and no idea of what to do, Thea was paralysed with fear in her own bed. She pulled the bed clothes over her head and tried to calm herself. Then all she could hear was her hammering heart beat. She was sure whoever – or whatever – was outside could hear it.

Then another thought struck her. She remembered she'd read that animals smell fear. Could any animal outside get inside the house, she wondered, and smell her? All pleasant feelings about Kalanoa disappeared with her bravery. She wished with all her heart she'd never come here.

It had all been so different when she had arrived. She'd been made so welcome. The children were lovely and she thought she would be able to be great friends with them. They'd had such a pleasant evening together and bustling Bessie had come with her to her room to see that she had everything. She'd felt so happy and welcome. The moonlight had made the country look peaceful and romantic.

Any excitement she had felt about teaching the girls with the help of the School of the Air had disappeared. The dark around her was so thick and black, she put out her hand, almost expecting to feel velvet.

She couldn't escape, so Thea decided to think about something else. "Don't get too frightened," she told herself sternly. "Think of something else. Think of Bruce."

Bruce. Bruce was just wonderful. What a wonderful person he was. So kind and considerate and good to be with. She'd love to think she could have a husband like Bruce one day – but deep down she thought no-one like that would be interested in someone ordinary like her.

Besides, she knew now she could never live here. She was far too scared. Whatever dreadful thing had happened to make someone scream like that would be too much for her. Now she thought she might survive the night, she decided to pack and leave tomorrow morning if possible. She wouldn't have another night like this one – not for anything or anyone.

It seemed only moments later Bruce was saying loudly and cheerfully, "Hey, sleepyhead – do you like a cup of tea in the morning? I've just taken one in to Aunt Bessie and, if you'd like to come on out, there's plenty in the pot in the kitchen.

Thea was overcome with confusion; the fear of the night was still clear in her mind. Bruce was acting as if nothing had happened when something dreadful must have happened. She quickly dressed and hurried to the kitchen. She was still a bit shocked and unhappy, but didn't know what to say, when he inquired, "Sleep well?"

Thea shook her head, wondering where to start. She felt so foolish saying she'd been terrified in the night, but it was the truth.

Bruce must have noticed the look on her face, because he said, "Hey, what's the matter? Did you have a bad night?"

Biting her lip and determined not to cry, Thea choked out the bare details of the night. The more kind and caring he was, the more Thea told him. "Oh, Bruce, I heard the most dreadful screams I've ever heard in my whole life last night. What on earth happened? And when I woke up it was pitch black. So awful and so scary."

Bruce held his cup in one hand and leaned against the doorway. "You know, Thea, you probably only heard an owl."

Thea was aghast at the suggestion. "No, Bruce, an owl goes *whoo-whoo*. This was someone or some animal screaming. They were being badly hurt." She was about to suggest they search outside, when Bruce continued.

"I think you must have learned about owls from English story books," he said gently. "The owls out here make lots of different noises. You know, we've had a couple of barking owls around here lately, and I think I can remember one screaming last night. They usually make a barking sound like a dog – *wook-wook, wook-wook*. They even make dog-like growling noises. But occasionally – not often, but you certainly remember the first time you hear it – they let out an appalling high-pitched scream. Now that we're talking about it, I'm pretty sure I can remember one last night."

As Bruce talked, Thea started to feel comforted.

He continued, "When you're used to those sounds, you just identify them and forget them if there's nothing you have to do about it. Just turn over and go back to sleep. I could bet that's what disturbed you. The first time you hear them can be pretty terrifying. They scream out like a soul in torment but they are quite harmless. No more trouble than that magpie out there." He indicated a magpie that they could see on a branch out the window. "She's trouble enough for worms and the odd insect and the owl is trouble for the odd small animal, but neither of them will hurt you."

Full of enthusiasm for his subject, Bruce said, "Come over here and I'll show you some of our regulars." Together, they stood quietly at the window and watched and listened.

Thea was delighted when a couple of little wrens hopped busily into view. He identified a couple of parrots for her and then said, "The galahs will be wheeling around pretty soon now. If you had gone on to Carmody Plains with Kendal last night you'd be hearing plenty of galahs by now. They're on a bit of a ridge and the galahs rest in the trees behind them at night. Then they make such a commotion just after dawn each day. We probably have more varieties of birds down here on the plain, near the creeks, but not the sheer numbers of galahs."

He listened again. "There's a top-knot pigeon and a willy wagtail." Thea was fascinated by now with what he was saying. She'd never really thought about birds much before. Bruce went on, "There can be all sorts of odd noises until you learn to identify them – but don't worry, nothing will hurt you. The only thing to worry about is if you hear water running when you shouldn't. Water is precious out here and if you hear water running over, that's a priority."

Bruce straightened, and changed the subject. "Well, I'd better get on with the chores. The kids will be up soon and Aunt Bessie will have finished her tea and be out to get breakfast in no time."

As Bruce walked away, Thea realised she'd allowed herself to be lulled into a sense of security. Her mother had always made most of the decisions in her life, and Thea had been happy that way. Now, she realised she'd found a man whom she could trust. Bruce was knowledgable and wonderful, not to mention good-looking and gentle.

Thea walked back to her room, preoccupied with thoughts of Bruce. If Bruce said everything was okay, then sure enough it would be okay. After all, it's hard to remember the fears of the night when you're standing in bright sunlight.

Chapter 8

Kendal's first day at Carmody Plains was long and exhausting. She had expected it would be tough getting back to hard physical work but hadn't realised just how tough it was going to be. Charles, she'd noted, was in no mood to be chivalrous and make allowances that she was out of condition, that she was a girl or anything else. So if she wanted to stand on her dignity and demand equal rights, by God, she'd get them. Equal rights for a long, hard, day's work. Even if that meant a tiring day's work for anyone used to doing such work day in and day out – and absolute torture for anyone not in condition.

As they left the homestead, Charles led the way and Kendal just followed along. He wasn't in an expansive mood, to say the least, so he didn't try to explain where they were going, or point out anything of interest. She just had to manage as best she could.

Tony was already out at Top Creek. He'd found a big mob of sheep on the plain near the gate and, as expected, they were walking with their noses into the wind and making for the ridges.

Tony relished working with the gyrocopter. Some people thought of them as suicide machines because they were for all the world like riding a motorbike in the air. The gyro had no cover but was a wonderful sensation to fly. Tony knew people who had flown all sorts of expensive planes and helicopters and were rapt when they first tried a gyro. The tiny helicopter-type machine was a wonderful ag aircraft and a joy to use for working with the stock.

He got busy with the job of turning the sheep back onto the plain, using a siren mounted on the front of the gyro. Flying down low in front of the stock, he blasted the horn, sending them turning and scattering back the way they had come. Another trick he loved was to go up to about three hundred feet right in front of the sheep, and then cut the motor. The gyro would go into a vertical descent and at about fifty feet he'd pump the throttle and turn the ignition – and nine times out of ten, it would backfire a beauty. The frightened sheep would wheel around and go in the direction he wanted them to go.

As Charles and Kendal arrived at the gate, Tony flew overhead and radioed them. "There's a big mob of sheep on the plain that keeps moving up towards the ridge," he said. "If you move up there smartly you should catch them before they get into the rough country."

"Great," Charles said, "that's what I expected. You go along the fence there, Kendal. Don't leave the fence and I'll push the sheep over to you."

Tony heard Charles over the two-way and was surprised to hear what sounded like a woman's voice answer "Right". Tony was instantly curious. "Surely Kendal's a woman's name," he thought to himself as he hovered above. "What's going on here?"

He called down to Charles. "I'll leave you with that mob now," he said. "I pushed them back a couple of times to keep them out on the plain while you were coming out. I'll go over the ridge now and see what I can find."

Thinking about Charles's partner, Tony thought he'd first come in for a closer look. So he made a long sweep down, getting lower and lower. But as he came closer to the ground, the draft from the gyro stirred up a cloud of dust and grit.

"Blast," thought Tony, "just my luck that they were in a dusty spot near the gate. Now I can't see anything."

Charles was quickly on the two-way. "Bloody clown!" he said to Tony. "For God's sake, find something better to do than bomb us!"

Tony knew he'd have to leave his curiosity until later and took off over the hill.

The paddock the trio were working in was fairly big – roughly about fourteen thousand acres. The plan was to move all the sheep from the bigger paddocks out the back of the place to the smaller paddocks closer to the shed. These paddocks – only about four or five thousand acres – would keep the sheep in closer and make them easier to manage when shearing started. They couldn't bring all of the sheep into the shed at once because the large numbers would eat out the grass around the shed, leaving nothing to feed them. Sheep used to grazing in paddocks couldn't do well being suddenly swapped to artificial feed, even if the grazier could afford it, so the stockmen had to be careful to choose wise strategies.

Like most properties, Carmody Plains tried to organise its shearing well, according to where the feed was best and where storms had fallen. Running a place well or badly could mean the difference between keeping your head above water or not – or lately, losing a bit of money or a lot.

Charles knew Carmody Plains well and wasn't afraid to take infinite pains to do a good job. He'd talked over his plans with his father and together they'd decided on the best course of action. When he was younger, Tom had made all the decisions but gradually the decision-making had fallen to Charles as he tried to take the burden from his father.

Bringing the sheep in was almost second nature for Charles, and so he allowed his thoughts to wander a little while he worked. Foremost in his thoughts was his father, whose health problems were starting to concern Charles. "Same with Bill-Bob," Charles mused, picturing the ageing men in his mind. Charles was committed to keeping his father happily living at Carmody Plains but, really, it was just one worry after another. Like every other wool property it cost money just to run the sheep and have them shorn, but also it was hard to get decent help. The right sort of people just weren't being attracted to a life that promised very little hope of a return.

"And so you end up with someone like Kendal MacKenzie," Charles thought wryly. He wondered what her brother's story was. He had hoped Rick could be the sort of bloke he could leave with Tom and Bill-Bob. But now, with his scheming sister riding around his paddocks instead, he didn't know what the outcome would be. He knew one thing, though. Kendal had met her match. "I'll give her a day like she's never had and, with a bit of luck, she'll quit," he thought determinedly.

Oblivious to what was going on in Charles's head, Kendal was valiantly trying to concentrate on doing a good job. She found it easy enough to get back into the rhythm of working with the stock – not pushing too fast and keeping them going in what she devotedly hoped was the right direction. To her relief, she discovered she'd retained her intuitive stock sense and could anticipate when some of the mob were restless and could break away.

In fact, Kendal thought she actually could have enjoyed herself, except that as the hours passed she became progressively more sore from the constant bump-bump of the motorbike. That and the constant concern of whether she was doing an all right job for her difficult boss.

Tony, for his part, did his work well but was surveying the scene below with interest. Tony hadn't been Charles's best friend and neighbour for so long now that he wasn't able to judge his mood pretty well. Charles was apt to get a bit short when he was put out. He was a blasted perfectionist and always wanted everything spot-on and worried away at a problem if things weren't quite right. And, judging by Charles's tone, Tony was pretty sure things weren't quite right just now.

Obviously this new man situation wasn't all Charles had hoped. Tony knew Charles's concerns about his father and about old Bill-Bob. With Charles away so much, there had been so many problems with finding the right staff. "If I've judged Charles right, it looks like this fellow isn't right, either," Tony thought to himself as he swooped and hovered. Then he remembered his suspicions about the new fellow's gender. "Could he really be a she?" he wondered, then laughed. "That'd be a turn-up for the books!"

Watching Charles below, Tony decided he'd swing by and stir his mate up a bit again. After all, they had just about all the sheep as far as he could see, and they weren't far from the gate with the mob. His work was finished and they'd probably stop for lunch once they were through the gate. Curious about Charles's offsider – who, from Tony's perspective, had done a pretty good job that morning – Tony decided to join them for dinner camp.

"That's about it, I think, Charles," he called, but his voice was distorted with static.

"Sorry, I didn't get that," Charles replied. "You think we've got them all?"

"That's a roger," Tony said. Then he added, "You going to stop for dinner camp when you get them through the gate?"

"Yep," Charles replied. "Thanks, Tony. See you."

Tony grinned, thinking of Charles's reaction. "You sure will. I'll come down and join you."

Charles grimaced. "Blasted Tony!" he thought. He should have expected his friend would drop by to see who was with him. Normally he'd fly home to get on with his own work, but Tony always liked to know what was going on.

Charles and Kendal pushed the mob through the gate and then Charles pulled up near Kendal to say, "We'll go over into the shade of those gidgee trees over there and have our lunch".

Exhausted after five hours' hard labour, Kendal could hardly wait. Still, they'd got the sheep and as far as she could tell she hadn't made any blues. She was pretty sure it had all gone quite well – Charles wouldn't have hesitated to tell her if it hadn't. Testing her muscles slightly, Kendal knew full well she wouldn't be able to move properly when she got off. By this stage, though, she didn't care. She just hoped it didn't hurt too much. It did.

Up in the air, Tony was preparing to put on a show. He took the gyro up to about a thousand feet and then idled his motor right back. Then he turned the power off – cutting all noise except the swish of the rotor – and pulled the stick back to lose air speed. The gyro fell to about 300 feet, before Tony started to nose it over to take the craft practically to their feet.

His landing was spectacular. The wheels of the gyro had gidgee leaves caught around them and when Tony climbed out, he had a small gidgee branch in his mouth, no less. He'd picked it up when he'd been trying to chase a few sheep out of the clump of trees. The onlookers didn't know whether he'd been hit in the face, or he'd broken it off and put it in his mouth. Whatever it was, it was flamboyant and typical of Tony.

As he took off his helmet and turned around, he and Kendal were equally amazed. "He's that devastatingly handsome man from the roadhouse," Kendal thought, while Tony smiled to himself, "Well, well, well, the beauty from the highway".

Charles, somewhat exasperated, watched them recognise each other. Tony was the first to recover. "Well," he said, "you're a pleasant surprise. Lovely ladies aren't thick on the ground around here. Wonders will never cease." He made an elaborate bow. "I'm Tony MacFarlane, your next door neighbour."

Kendal was just about to answer when Charles interrupted with, "This is Kendal MacKenzie. Her brother Rick was supposed to come, but Kendal came instead."

"Well, we may as well make the best of such a happy circumstance," Tony replied. He sat on a log and patted the spot beside him. "Sit down here, Kendal, and tell me the story."

In an icy tone, Charles said, "Tony, this is not a social occasion as you seem determined to make it. Kendal is here to work and we've still got a busy day ahead of us even if you have nothing to do."

Tony was not at all intimidated. "Get real, Charles. We've just got all the sheep, for God's sake, and we can have a bit of time off for lunch. Go back to your hollow log."

That night, Kendal was really stiff, tired and sore. In fact, she couldn't remember a time when she'd felt worse. Actually, probably no-one in the history of the whole world had ever felt worse, she decided. Every bone in her body was sore from being jolted all day on the bike. Her seat was sore from constantly bumping on the bike. Inside her thumb was sore from the throttle. Her legs were scratched, and a couple of times sticks had come up and banged her shin. "Sticks?" Kendal thought incredulously. "Great big logs more like it." She had blisters on her hands from gripping the handles and wind-burn on her face. She'd kept her hat on so she couldn't have third degree sunburn, but it felt like it. She was so dried out that she'd still be thirsty if she drank a gallon of water. And if Charles happened to ask her how she was – which she very much doubted – she'd force a smile on her face and reply, "I'm fine, thanks. No problems".

What she really wanted to do was to soak in a bath or stand under a shower for a couple of hours. She knew from experience that her sort of thirst could only be slaked by the skin soaking up moisture – not just by pouring it down her throat. Then she wanted to cover herself in healing oils and creams and be left alone to sleep for a week.

But she would have a quick shower, dress and force herself to have an evening meal, even if it killed her. Kendal was not going to admit any weakness, however bad she felt. But first, she would allow herself the indulgence of washing her hair. She had to feel a bit human again.

Somehow, Kendal got through the evening. Charles didn't bother to ask her how she was. Tom did, but Kendal didn't get much satisfaction from lying through her teeth to him as she wasn't even sure Charles was listening. If she'd been sure he couldn't hear her she would have been more honest with Tom and admitted she was desperately tired – but with even the possibility of Charles hearing, she wasn't going to admit anything. Anyway, the way it was, if she'd opened up the flood gates to say how awful she felt she might never have stopped.

When she was able to escape to her room she just wanted to flop on the bed, but force of habit made Kendal change from her clothes into her nightie and clean her teeth. For a brief moment, she savoured the comfort of stretching out and feeling the softness of her bed. Then, she was out cold. Dead to the world in a deep, dreamless sleep.

Kendal would have been really surprised to know Charles came to her door that night and looked in to check she was all right before he went to bed himself. She would have been even more surprised to know what Charles was thinking. In fact, Charles was really impressed with the way Kendal had tackled the day's work.

He'd started the day determined to give no quarter and to treat her no differently from the experienced young man he had expected. They'd done a full day's work. He had known she'd be soft and that the work all day on a bike would be exhausting, but that's what he'd planned. He'd been angry that so many of his plans had been upset. Plus, she'd unsettled him. So he'd started out determined to show her she couldn't cope and to get rid of her.

Instead of that, as the day progressed, Charles had been the one who changed. He couldn't help but be impressed with her sheer determination not to let anything beat her. Practically out on her feet, Kendal had made no protest and had actively participated and, what's more, thought about what she was doing, right to the end of the day. It was then Charles decided he'd call a truce. Hardly that, since war hadn't been declared, but Charles decided he'd back off and let her settle in more gradually. "After all, if she's that gutsy, her brother is probably worth waiting for," he'd concluded.

That evening, Charles spent a good deal of time on the phone. None of the usual contract musterers were available at short notice, but Bruce could give him some time and old Dan Flannigan could come for a few days. Bruce, of course, was as good as you'd get anywhere. Dan was pretty good too, as long as they kept him off the grog and managed to stay on the windward side. That would be OK for a few days. Just long enough, with Tony's help, to get all the sheep out of the back country and all the really long, continuous days' mustering out of the way.

Charles decided a bit of bike work each day would get Kendal hardened up – and, besides, there were plenty of other jobs she could do. Of course, it was a bit of a waste of time showing her the run of the place if she wouldn't be there long, but he hadn't reached his age without realising things rarely went exactly as expected. Then again, he'd been worrying about Tom and Bill-Bob. Maybe now he had help to get the larger paddocks mustered, Kendal would be free to help the two ageing men with their jobs. Maybe it was all for the best.

Morning came all too soon. Despite feeling saddle-sore and weary, Kendal's youth and grim determination worked wonders to help her present a brave face to the world. She arrived at breakfast in good time, not caring what she looked like or what sort of impression she was making. She just desperately needed the ability to keep going. She really wasn't looking forward to the bike.

As she'd dreaded, the morning started out on the bike again. Then Charles happened to ask her to get back to the house. "We're close to South Pines here and I'm going over to see Tony," he told her. "I can't get him on the two-way, but I can hear his 'dozer going and I want to catch up with him. They rang last night to say most of the shearing gear has arrived in town, so you'd better take the one-tonner and pick it up, will you? Check with Tom, he'll give you all the details."

Kendal couldn't believe her luck as she travelled back to the house. "Thank you, God," she said, half-devoutly. "Thank you, God, for small mercies." It was bliss to sit in the comparative comfort of the truck, and not endure the bump-bump of the bike.

Kept busy preparing for shearing for the rest of the day, Kendal never once suspected Charles was reorganising his plans to make things easier for her.

Bill-Bob had kept the maintenance up and most of the mechanical equipment hardly needed any work. Still, he checked everything meticulously – the engine at the shearing shed, all the overhead gear, the pump in the sheep yards, the dipping gear. Everything was overhauled and checked and nothing left to chance. Kendal worked with him, learned a lot and enjoyed it.

Besides that, all the yards had to be checked. The fences, the latches on the gates and the catching pens attracted particular attention. The troughs in and around the yard were also cleaned out and Kendal knew that closer to shearing starting, the yards would be watered to stop the dust, so hoses had to be in place.

The shearers' quarters, too, were thoroughly cleaned and checked out to make sure everything was up to scratch. They had to make sure insect protection was in order on the verandahs, so they checked out the wire screens, and they also checked that the required number of mattresses, pillows and chairs were in place. Bits of gear could go missing between each year's shearing for all sorts of reasons. People stayed for a while in the quarters during the year, while others borrowed things. So Charles and Tom always made sure things were in order a couple of weeks before shearing and everything was fixed up before the bulk of the stock work began.

Kendal figured her role at Carmody Plains was simply to defeat Murphy's Law. After all, it's one of life's ironies that the busier you are, the less time there is to check – and then more things go wrong. Like Murphy: If anything can go wrong, it will and at the worst possible moment.

She was quite enjoying herself; she expected the busyness. The household itself was a novelty to her. She had never been in an all-male household before and it was quite an experience. She was used to the banter and the joking that went on in the shearing shed over the years as she was growing up, and the same sort of thing occurred among her brother's friends. But she'd always been one of the family before – and here she was the odd one out in a very different atmosphere from anything else she'd ever experienced. It was a bit like being one of the first lone women in a shearing team.

She had no way of knowing the men were modifying their language in front of her. She felt they all talked quite freely and certainly they talked about a great number of topics. She was surprised at how much they talked about local affairs. Dare she think of it as gossip? They talked about everything, everybody and each other. And always, with Tony around, there was never a dull moment.

They were all particularly interested in Bill-Bob and a certain Ethel Alsop. Obviously no-one discussed this in front of Bill-Bob, and she noticed Tony and Bruce discussed it together, but never in front of Charles. When she asked them about this, Tony explained, "Charles is a loyal friend and he gets stroppy if anyone discusses what he considers Bill-Bob's personal business," he said. "That's OK. He wouldn't let anyone pry into our affairs, either."

Kendal noticed the men never tired of trying to fathom the relationship between Bill-Bob and Ethel Alsop. She learned that everyone agreed, every Saturday without fail, Bill-Bob went into Juno to the pub. He didn't drink much but sat in the pub and listened to all the talk but talked little himself. He also went to the library. Bill-Bob had practically no possessions and kept no books but he did borrow heavily from the library. Ethel ran the library, had done for years. And every Saturday night Bill-Bob went to Ethel's house for the evening meal. But – and this was where opinion differed – were they having it on? Kendal soon learned this was the point of everyone's interest.

Tony, for his part, was certain they were. Bruce thought they were just friends. Ethel was a friend of his aunt's and he couldn't imagine her doing something that was so out of character with respectable people from her generation.

Tony was characteristically blunt in his assessment of Bruce's idea. "It has been in character in all generations," he laughed. "That's how the generations keep coming, you bloody twit!"

Dan also had a contribution to make to this conversation. "I-I wouldn't sleep with that Ethel Alsop if her b-b-backside was studded with diamonds," he declared. "The skinny, sharp-tongued b-bitch. What you need is a r-real woman like my Daisy. She's a r-real beauty, my Daisy."

The others looked at each other with their eyes rolling. That successfully finalised that subject for the night. Dan and Daisy might both have been real beauties once, but now their only beauty lay in the eyes of the beholder. Yet throw off at each other as their friends and neighbours would, innate decency stopped them from saying what they might think of Daisy. Dan was a dirty, disreputable, old cove but his pride in his family was legendary.

Kendal made several trips to Juno during the next couple of days, picking up supplies and equipment. The road was quite good and she started to get to know its twists and turns. There was one particular section of the road that crossed a black soil plain. It must have been pretty boggy in wet weather, because it had been built up with gravel to about a metre above the surrounding country. It was only the width of one vehicle, just the two tyre tracks, and it was very rough. The black soil, on the other hand, made an excellent smooth road in dry weather. Naturally enough, the people using the road had made a track going off to the side of the built-up road and that was used most of the time. Usually that track ran quite close to the main built-up road but sometimes it went way out to avoid a particular problem. It went off to the right going from Carmody Plains, came back to the built-up road to cross a grid about ten miles out of town, and then went on again on the left. Mostly it went through plain country where you could see the open flat land in all directions.

There were just a couple of patches of scrubby ridge. One in particular was a bit tricky, where both road and the track turned quite abruptly and took a change of direction. After going almost due south from Carmody Plains, the road swung around here to the west towards Juno. There was a very pretty creek crossing, with quite a few channels, and the road wandered about through rocks and sand with lots of different trees and grasses. Although this was in sandy country, Kendal wondered how it would be in the wet. So many roads became impassable in the wet and years ago everyone just had to stay home. Now some properties had light aircraft and even hovercraft so that they could move around in all conditions.

None of this was her problem, anyway. She was only here a little while, and it was a much better job driving in and out to Juno in the air conditioned vehicle, than bumping around the paddock on a motor bike in the heat and dirt and flies. She had no complaints. The Toyota had a radio and she listened to that as she drove.

The road was all hers. It went to Carmody Plains and on to South Pines and there was only Tony there regularly. Then it went on to wild ridgy cattle country where no-one lived. The country only ran about one snake to the acre. It was checked by the owners flying around the waters once a week or so and they only came in to muster once or twice a year, so no-one else used the road much.

One time coming out of Juno, she met a vehicle at the creek crossing. There was plenty of room to move and she pulled over to let them pass. She gave a wave but they pulled up to talk. They were a couple of young fellows who had been out camping and shooting. They looked pretty wild and dirty, with a few days' growth on their faces, and wearing the clothes they'd slept in, but they were happy and enthusiastic about their trip.

Another time, again coming out of Juno, she had an experience that really terrified her.

She was travelling comfortably along the side track that was running right beside the built-up road, listening to the radio. She was casually approaching the turn at the timbered corner when she suddenly saw, right in front of her, a great big semi trailer coming straight at her.

Her heart stopped beating and she couldn't breathe. The instinctive thing to do was to immediately swing hard to the left, but alarm bells rang in her brain. She couldn't see properly – was the truck on the built-up road or on the side track? Track and road were so close together at this stage she couldn't tell.

She couldn't move right. There were too many trees. If she moved to the left, that would take her onto the built-up road, and if he was on the built-up road, he'd plough right through her. If she stayed where she was and he was on the side track, they'd collide there instead. It was all happening so quickly. A decision had to be made.

She stayed on her side track and the semi rumbled past on her left along the built-up road. In a flash the crisis was over, as quickly as it had started. They had avoided a complete smash-up. It was only by the grace of God. Certainly not by any skill of hers – nor by the semi driver.

Sickened by the near-miss, Kendal felt quite light-headed. She pulled over for a moment to get over her shock but that didn't work. She felt agitated, restless, and couldn't sit still so she slowly started driving again. Once around the corner, she was travelling across an open plain, with full visibility in all directions. She could hardly believe what had happened to her. She was sure her heart had stopped beating for a moment, but now her pulse was racing and her breath was coming in little shudders as though she'd been crying. It really had been a near-miss. She had known it was a sharp corner but hadn't realised how blind a corner it actually was.

Driving home very slowly, still feeling very upset, Kendal decided she wouldn't tell the others, or they'd think she'd been day-dreaming or was exaggerating.

Bill-Bob was at the shed ready to help unload the stuff she'd brought out and Bruce and Charles arrived by chance as she pulled up. White-faced and shaken, Kendal couldn't help herself. She blurted out to them all of what had happened. In her distress, she forgot that she wasn't going to admit to any weakness in front of Charles that he could attribute to her as a hysterical female.

The others were completely understanding. Instead of scorn from Charles, she got nothing but concern. They took her up to the house and made her a cup of tea with lots of sugar.

Keen to let Kendal know she'd handled the situation well, the men started talking about accidents and how easy it was to have them out in the bush.

Charles told her that only the other day, travelling on one of the station roads, he'd come up over a rise and hadn't seen Dan approaching. "Luckily, Dan was going slowly, otherwise we would have had a head-on," Charles said. "I've lived on this place for thirty-odd years and I didn't know it was such a blind spot."

Bruce agreed. "You know just the other day on the news there was a story about two young blokes killed in a bike collision on a back road," he said. "It's always a tragedy, but it's inevitable on these bush roads. There's so many miles and so few vehicles that you could go for years and not even know some spots were dangerous – until you met someone in the wrong place unexpectedly."

Listening to them talk made Kendal feel better.

Intent on calming herself down, she hadn't noticed the men exchanging a few questioning glances and a few considered nods of the head. Eventually, by common consent, they decided to tell her.

Charles began. "Whatever you do, don't talk about this in front of Tony," he said to Kendal.

"Tony had a dreadful experience at the very same spot," Bruce explained. "A few years ago Tony and his fiancee Elspeth went into Juno one Friday night for a polocrosse weekend. Did you know he'd been engaged?" Kendal shook her head. "He was, you know. Anyway, his parents happened to be leaving on the Monday morning for a trip. It started to rain through the night, and Tony decided that if he didn't want to be caught in town, he'd better get his horses home before the road got too slippery. Plus, he was wanting to get his parents away before the roads got too bad."

Kendal was interested. Tony's actions made sense.

"So Tony woke Elspeth and told her what he'd decided," Charles continued. "She understood and they quickly dressed and loaded the horses and set out for South Pines. From what we've heard, his parents must have been half awake all night, too, wondering what the rain would do. Apparently they got up early as well and packed their things so they could get past the worst of the roads before the rain really set in."

Charles looked concernedly at Kendal, who was sitting down and looking a bit stricken. "Is it all right for me to go on?" he asked Kendal. She nodded, and he continued.

"Just before daybreak, because the black soil was slippery, Tony was on the built-up road driving east along the first bit of road towards home. Even though it was overcast and showering, the light was glaring and rotten to drive in. It would have been right in his eyes along there. Anyway, unfortunately, his parents coming from South Pines were also travelling on the built-up road. At that corner that you were at today, Kendal, they couldn't see each other coming and they hit. Head-on."

The rest of the details swam in Kendal's mind as she tried to comprehend the tragedy that had befallen Tony. Tony alone had survived the crash. Badly hurt, he was recovering in hospital when he was charged with dangerous driving. The local police had already investigated the accident and decided Tony was innocent – but it turned out Elspeth's parents needed to blame someone. They lashed out in grief and frustration, and made so much fuss that charges were laid.

Smashed up and in a fog of grief, Tony had no idea he had to vigorously defend himself against the charges. The blend of a slightly dishonest police officer misrepresenting the facts and an aggressive prosecutor earned him eighteen months in jail for dangerous driving causing death.

Local feeling, naturally, was that Tony was terribly badly treated. In fact, the district was horrified to learn the legal system and justice were not the same thing. What happened to Tony was not what they'd imagined justice to be. Anyone knowing all the facts knew the accident was not Tony's fault. But three people were dead. Only one person was alive and Elspeth's parents needed to make that person pay.

Devastated by his loss and almost beyond the point of caring what happened to him, Tony had assumed, in his innocence, that the police and the courts would work together to establish the truth. What he and his friends didn't realise was that it was the prosecution's job to win the case. Little details like the truth can become a casualty, and slightly distorted evidence a weapon.

For his inexperience and grief, Tony paid a terrible price. So did everyone else in his community. They all learned there were times a good lawyer was needed.

Tony was released from prison after serving nine months, but everyone agreed he just wasn't the same. He still laughed and joked and could turn on the ready charm, but something was different. Something essential in the old Tony was missing.

Tony also had an obsession with preserving his memories of his parents. He still lived in the cottage that had been done up for him and Elspeth, and he tended his parents' old house like a shrine. He didn't worry about the garden around his own house, but he kept the garden at his parents' house in elaborate order. They'd been keen gardeners, and Tony seemed determined to keep their spirit alive. It was more than that, though. No-one, but no-one, could enter the house or garden, except Tony. They thought it wasn't a healthy attitude, but they figured he'd get over it in time.

In a strange way, hearing of Tony's loss helped Kendal to realise how lucky she was and put her accident into perspective. She got over her shock and bounced back.

Tony's plight was never far from her mind, and she thought it helped her understand him better. In fact, as the days went on she got to know them all a bit better. Bill-Bob said very little, Dan said only a little more. Tom loved a yarn and really enjoyed having the house full of people. Bruce was quiet and sensible and he enjoyed a good yarn as well. Charles was completely comfortable with all these people but not one to chatter unnecessarily, and Tony was always irrepressible.

Kendal did her work as well as she could and she spent the time listening to, and enjoying, all the talk around her. Despite relaxing into her role at Carmody Plains, Kendal knew she had to tread warily. They had all been kind to her so far – except for Charles's initial greeting – but she knew that she wouldn't get away with stepping out of line. Two major rules were at play: Never rise to a bait and never try to be a smart aleck. They'd cut her down to size if she started to get out of line. Luckily, she'd had lots of practice as she was growing up.

Sometimes she worked with Bill-Bob. He hardly spoke unless it was necessary and it became a game with her to get him to say anything at all. He knew his job thoroughly and she enjoyed working with him. He was a perfectionist but he made it seem easy. So Kendal learned a lot about engines and vehicles from him, even if she couldn't get much more out of him.

Working with Tom was different. He tended to ramble on quite a lot. He told her stories about incidents that had happened about the place and people he'd had on the property over the years, and little bits about the people of the district.

Tony, Bruce and Dan were usually out in the rest of the back country, moving the sheep in closer, so she didn't often work with them. Sometimes they were together, though, for dinner camp, and, of course, for dinner at night.

One day when Charles had gone over to South Pines to see Tony, he had found him pushing up the bank at the back of an earth tank with his 'dozer. He was pulled over when Charles got there.

"He's probably stopped to roll a smoke," Charles thought. Certainly with his ear muffs on and the 'dozer motor going, Tony wouldn't have heard him arrive.

Charles knew a good opportunity when he saw one. "Well now," he thought good-naturedly, "here's my chance to get even with him for being such a busybody about Kendal. If I don't go around to the front, he won't see me and I'll just give him a boost to get his heart pumping properly."

So he carefully climbed up behind Tony, who was quietly licking the paper on a freshly-rolled smoke. Charles grabbed him and yelled, "Gotcha!"

It worked.

Tony nearly jumped out of his skin. He threw his arms out, the cigarette disappeared forever and his heart rate broke records for a few seconds.

"You bloody, rotten bastard!" he said when he'd recovered somewhat. "I'll get you for this!" They laughed together for a minute or two and then Charles asked Tony if he could work a few more days.

"Bloody man should let you rot," Tony retorted, but they both knew it was only talk and Tony would come. Actually, nothing would stop Tony coming. He was plotting revenge in his heart and he also wanted a ringside seat to watch how Charles and Kendal got on. He'd do a bit of stirring there, he'd bet his bottom dollar. Yes, he'd be very pleased to be at Carmody Plains now and then and see what he could do to help.

It was only the second day he was there when he saw a chance to get even with Charles.

The one-tonner had been playing up when Charles had taken it out into the paddock. Bill-Bob had it in the workshop now to pinpoint the trouble. They were sure it was an electrical fault of some sort, but the two men didn't know if it was the alternator or the battery.

When Tony arrived, the bonnet was up and Bill-Bob and Charles had their heads in under the bonnet working. They decided to put in a new battery to see if that was the trouble. They were busy tightening the terminals and didn't notice Tony silently wriggle his way from underneath the back of the vehicle until he was right underneath where they were working.

Tony grinned and started puffing away on a cigarette. A fine wisp of smoke curled up around the motor. A few more puffs and there was a definite column of smoke.

"Hell!" said Charles, frantically trying to pull the terminals off to stop the short he thought was down there somewhere. One of the terminals came off in a rush and he hit the back of his knuckles on the bonnet and took some skin off. He stood there cursing.

Bill-Bob was more cagey and was still peering down at the motor, trying to fathom what might be wrong, when he saw Tony's face looking up at him. Tony winked at him.

"Bloody young fool, wasting a fellow's time like that," Bill-Bob growled, but he couldn't help smiling to himself at their nonsense.

Tony and Charles continued to amuse themselves every chance they got. Their silly tricks only took a bit of time off the working day, but gave them a lot of fun.

Tony still felt he hadn't evened up the score properly and he had an old beer can full of sump oil he wanted to put under the bonnet of Charles's vehicle. When the time was right, he planned to put a small hole in the bottom of the can, and when Charles saw the oil slowly leaking out he'd have a heart starter, all right. It was a bit tricky to get the exact moment though, because he didn't want to worry Tom or Bill-Bob any more than he had to. Never mind, that moment would come eventually, if he was prepared to bide his time.

While Tony didn't try to take the mickey out of Bill-Bob or Tom, he did spend a bit of time trying to wind up old Dan. Dan had a record of having a go at anyone, especially a cocky when he got a chance. Dan was playing it cagey and wouldn't rise to the bait, try as Tony would. Tony would sometimes race past him and put his foot down and deliberately spray gravel and sand all over him. One time he raced ahead and hid in a thick patch of scrub and when Dan came along, he raced out and threw his hat at him and yelled. He knew he shouldn't have given the old man such a fright, but he couldn't help himself.

When old Dan got upset, he would simply utter, "G-g-good on you, g-good on you" and continue to go along quietly. Try as he could Tony just couldn't get him stirred. What he didn't know was that Dan was just biding his time.

One day when Dan and Tony came back from work, Charles was setting up a ladder to get a couple of old branches down from one of the trees at the back of the house. He was concerned they could be dangerous in the big winds common in a summer storm. They stopped to yarn, checking up on what he was doing, when the phone rang and Charles was called inside. It was all there ready to go and Tony could see the job wouldn't take long, so he took the chainsaw and said to old Dan, "Here, Dan, hold the ladder steady and I'll go up and cut it down."

Dan held the ladder for Tony. Tony climbed up and put the chainsaw carefully in a fork of the tree and then swung himself up to the branch. He turned around still hanging on, and moved carefully to get the chainsaw, giving his full attention to the job. It was a bit tricky and he had to hang on well. While he was so occupied, Dan just as carefully took the ladder and put it against the trunk of another tree a little bit out of sight and then disappeared inside for lunch. He was taking off his boots when Tom, who was in the kitchen, heard him and said, "Oh, you're back, Dan. Where's Tony?"

Dan scratched his beard and said casually, "H-he's just hanging around out there s-somewhere."

One night they were all laughing about something and that started them talking about the Australian sense of humour.

"Lots of people don't understand the way we all laugh when things go wrong," Tom said. Tony, who had joined them that night for dinner, disagreed. "Aw, I dunno. What about the pie in the face or the slip on a banana skin routines? I reckon it's pretty average humour anywhere."

Tom nodded. "Yep, but we take it further than other people. Most people still feel we're pretty funny the way we laugh at ourselves and our mates. My opinion is that life is pretty tough and we have to either laugh or cry – and what's the good of crying? It's bloody hot. So what? It's hot for everyone so there's nothing to be gained by moaning. So we make a joke of it if we can. It's a relief thing, too. Someone looks as if they're in trouble, and if turns out OK, it's such a relief you laugh."

He paused, polished his glasses, and continued. "I remember this one young fellow who came out here years ago – we were cutting scrub in the '65 drought. I said to his mother, 'He'll be going straight out onto a chainsaw, you know'. 'Oh, that's all right,' she said, 'he's a big strong boy'. Well, he wasn't big and he wasn't strong. We were cutting into thick scrub and he cut about ten trees and they were all hung up on each other. Finally, he cut the key tree and they all came down on top of him and drove him into the ground.

Kendal drew in her breath sharply at the image.

"They were trees about that big," Tom continued, forming a circle about four or five inches wide with his hands. "Of course, we were pretty concerned and we raced in and pulled him out. We found that he didn't have a broken skull or other broken bones. He was breathing OK and not bleeding to death and we were so relieved, I can tell you. He looked pretty awful though. He did have a bit of blood running down his face and in his hair and everywhere these sticks had hit him. So what did we do? We started laughing! Bernie and I started to laugh. All the way home in the Land Rover he kept saying, 'You bloody bastards! I can't see how it's funny!' Then he'd say, 'You've got a weird sense of humour', and course that would make us laugh even more. Anyway, he went right off his head. It took him ages to get over us laughing at him. He just couldn't figure it out. All I know is that, in his case, we started laughing when we realised he wasn't dead or badly injured. It was just pure relief."

It was only the next day that there was an event that Tony didn't find at all amusing.

He told them the story as soon as he got in. He was quite distressed. "An old man emu nearly got me this morning," he said. "It all happened so quick. One minute you're just cruising along looking around keeping an eye on things and next thing there's a bloody emu lining you up." He shuddered at the thought of it. "I was riding along a fence line when I saw this bloody big emu behind a clump of sandlewood. There he was sitting there -- the great big bastard! Head up, alert, probably listening to me coming.

He stood up and all his feathers along his neck flared out and that's when I spotted his chicks around his feet. They were only little fellows about six inches high."

Kendal noticed Tony was really reliving the incident. His breathing was fast and his hands were going ten to the dozen demonstrating and gesturing.

"Anyway, he put his head down and charged," Tony said. "He came right at me! I didn't know what to do. I was going too fast to turn around and go back. I clicked it down a gear and just went for it. I went as close to the fence as I dared and he only just missed me! I could see his head. You know how they flatten right out as they're coming at ya. His bloody great beak only just missed me by a whisker. I could feel the bloody thing practically. I nearly screwed the throttle clean off the motor bike." He gave an exaggerated sigh and rolled his expressive eyes. "Would have been a bloody mess if he'd hit me." Then he said reflectively, more to himself than his audience, "Imagine being trampled to death by a bloody emu. What a way to go! How bloody embarrassing. There have to be better ways to die than that."

Charles was saying, "Gee, that's unusual. They usually only charge for about ten metres and then veer off."

"Well, this was only about ten to fifteen metres off the fence line," Tony explained.

"You were invading his territory, mate," Charles commented.

Tony laughed wryly. "Well, I won't again if I can help it, I can tell you!"

Kendal was fascinated by the fact that Tony seemed to be infinitely more worried by the embarrassment and the indignity of being trampled to death by an emu, than the thought of death itself. What a funny reaction! She wondered if anyone else had caught Tony's strange response.

Meanwhile, Charles was getting uptight about a kangaroo that kept coming onto the little patch of lawn at the back of the house. He grumbled every morning when they went out and saw the grass pulled up all over the place and littered with roo droppings.

"Don't get so upset about it, boy," Tom said. "It's not worth it and it's not doing any real harm."

"Bloody thing wrecks what lawn we've got," Charles complained. "He can go out and forage for himself. Pity Snap wasn't still here – the roo wouldn't come so close to that dog."

Kendal couldn't help herself. "What makes you so mad about the roo, Charles? Tom doesn't seem to mind."

"Bloody creature!" Charles exploded. "There's very little that's decent around here now. We used to have such a lovely garden and gradually we've had to let it go. I'd like to get it in order for Dad, but it's too much work to do to keep it up with no help when I'm not here. A bit of green and order around the house makes it decent for a fellow to come back to after a day's work. It's dry and hot in the paddocks and you see so much you can't control and can't help. It's a great help for your health even if you can come home to a spot that is green and shady and well kept. It gives you heart – a retreat. I hate to see this little sanctuary for Dad ruined by that bloody animal."

Kendal could see his point. "They do make a mess of things, all right. It's a pity they always pull the grass up and leave it all around and don't just eat what they need and go."

"Bloody thing will go all right if I can help it." Charles wasn't going to be pacified.

"What are you going to do?" Kendal asked.

"I'll tie the dogs up over by the grid," Charles planned. "That's where it's coming in and out I think. That silly bloody Rusty yapping would keep anything away."

It worked. For a few nights, no roo. Then again one morning the lawn was a complete mess scattered with tufts of grass and small brown blobs everywhere.

"Look at that!" Charles was dismayed. "Bloody thing must have worked out that the dogs were tied up and gone around them. I'll take the gun and shoot the bastard. I'm not going to let it beat me."

"Aw, come on Charles, that's a bit extreme," Kendal said, feeling a bit protective of the visitor.

"Well, lady, you tell me what you'd do?" Charles demanded. "It's getting drier and drier in the paddock – it won't just go away now. We're watering the lawn and working just for him."

Kendal didn't really have an answer. She would have just put up with it. Tom would have just put up with it. The little patch of grass was being ruined and it was obviously driving Charles to distraction.

Charles didn't forget. He got his gun out that night and put the box of cartridges beside it on the table after their evening meal. Kendal could see he was full of purpose and she had a heavy heart.

Roos were being shot all the time in the paddocks because they were so thick and ate what grass there was, but it saddened her to think their nightly visitor had to go.

She went to bed but thought she wouldn't be able to sleep because she was expecting at any minute to hear a shot. In fact, she slept well – but the roo mustn't have come, because she didn't hear a shot all night. Even if Charles had missed, she should have heard the shot.

At breakfast she said to a tired-looking Charles, "Didn't the roo turn up last night?"

Charles answered in an offhanded sort of way, "Yeah, he came in."

Kendal was curious, although a bit wary of questioning Charles too far. "What happened? Why didn't you shoot it?"

Charles was diffident in a way Kendal had never seen him before, almost as if he were ashamed of himself. "Well, if you must know, I didn't have the heart to shoot the bastard when it came to the crunch. Poor bloody thing. It must be pretty game or pretty sick to come so close to the house and brave the dogs. It's battling life out here as we all are. I just couldn't pull the trigger."

As if he'd revealed too much, he was suddenly full of purpose again. He got to his feet saying, "And now, if you're quite ready, we've got work to do. Unless you want to sit here chattering all day."

Kendal knew better than to make any comment at all. Obviously Charles thought it was sentimental weakness to spare the life of the roo but Kendal admired him tremendously. Underneath the rather abrupt exterior he sometimes assumed, she was pleased to know he had a soft heart.

The dog he called 'silly bloody Rusty' was another case in point. He put up with such a lot of trouble from Rusty just because he was so full of life.

It occurred to Kendal that Charles was quite a fine man.

Chapter 9

With all the activity and the fellows around her, Kendal decided she was really enjoying her time at Carmody Plains. She'd been so busy and so exhausted and there had been so much going on that she'd almost forgotten the beginning. She hadn't even told her family about the rotten start because by the time she'd had a chance to talk to them in depth, Charles was acting quite pleasantly towards her. There was one thing she was a bit puzzled about, though. She wasn't sure really why they needed someone to take over when Charles was such a good manager. Maybe he had other interests. Still, that wasn't really her worry and she'd be gone soon enough. Any day now they'd hear from Rick that he was on his way.

But it didn't work out that way. One evening after Charles had gone into the office to take a phone call, he came back and said to Kendal, "Your brother's knee is still playing up. He's going to have an operation."

Kendal was concerned and hurried to the phone. Rick explained his leg was getting worse and that he'd been sent to a specialist. That doctor had told him he needed an arthroscopy of the knee done to repair the damage. A simple procedure, he'd said, and not a big reconstruction job, but he would not be able to work for another month.

Kendal said all the right things to Rick about taking care of his knee, spoke briefly to her mother and then went back to face Charles. But as she came back to the kitchen, he stood up and said, "We'll talk about this in the morning", and walked out of the room.

Kendal never really knew what Charles thought about the situation. Any anger, disappointment, or maybe pleasure he felt, was hidden from her. By next morning he was completely matter of fact. Would she like to stay to help them through shearing? She didn't dare to ask if she was really wanted or was there under sufferance, and simply answered "Yes". She'd been wondering all night what she'd say if Charles did ask her. Her own plans could wait, there was no deadlines there. It was just her reaction to Charles. One moment she thought she'd tell him to take a running jump and the next she virtuously thought she should help Rick and stay. But when it came to the crunch, she agreed because she wanted to stay.

The next days at Carmody Plains went really quickly for Kendal.

Bruce and Dan had both gone home. Tom had been kind to her from the moment she'd arrived so it was very easy to fit in with him. Charles wasn't too bad either, really. It was the way he made her feel. He had a funny attitude to her at times but lots of little things kept happening to make her realise that he was a very kind person underneath his stern exterior. He was inclined to keep a good eye on his father and to see that he wasn't called upon to work out in the paddocks in the heat for too long at a time. He took every chance he could to suggest that Tom went back to the house and he'd come and get him when they got busy again.

Bill-Bob did very little work outside on the place at all. He stayed around the sheds and the vehicles. The charming Tony still helped out now and then, sometimes with the gyro, sometimes on a bike, but only when they were pushed.

So she worked with Charles most of the time and they worked together well. The stock were organised and Kendal found it easy to understand what Charles wanted done. Somehow they clicked and they made a good team. His paddock management was great, and by the time shearing actually started they could keep the sheep up to the shearers and take the shorn sheep away with a minimum of fuss, and she was relieved they'd established such an easy working relationship.

Occasionally, if there was a pause in the work, when she'd just pushed sheep up into a forcing yard, closed the gate and looked up to see whether to go up to help draft or to move back to bring up more sheep, she would catch sight of Charles, not as a working companion, but as the virile, magnetic man that he was. She'd feel her pulse race and her body almost go to liquid. Goodness, what an effect this man could have upon her!

She usually cut a lunch to take with her wherever she was, so she could have it quickly at whatever time fitted in with what they were doing. Often enough during smoko or dinner breaks at the shed, she ate with the shearers. All shearers kept very precise working hours and her work didn't always fit in to their times, but she tried to be there as often as she could and so she got to know all the members of the team quite well.

Working with a team like that, Kendal knew better than to have a thin skin. There was always a great deal of banter and joking going on, but she'd been in and out of shearing sheds all of her life and knew what to expect.

Like the average Australian outback worker, the shearers worked hard, played hard and had no time for pretence or a 'man who blows'. They shared the Aussie characteristic of cutting a mate down to size, loved taking the mickey out of him and had a tremendous ability to tell great tales and relate enormous fabrications with a perfectly straight face.

One of the new young shed hands, Steve, proved to be a prime candidate for the team when they went into town one night. No matter what everyone else had done, Steve had done it a little better, faster or longer. So Stumpy, the contractor, asked him if he could run. "Of course," Steve replied, a little indignant, and by his stories you would think he'd run the Boston Marathon.

Stumpy's grinned widened as the night progressed. He could sense a victory. So he bet Steve a bottle of rum against a week's wages that he could not out-run him. All the team jumped into the troopy and headed back to the shed. When they were about five miles from the shed, they put them both out to run. Steve took off like a rocket and Stumpy just ran along for a little while until the rouseabout was out of sight. Then Stumpy jumped back into the troopy and began to drink the bottle of rum that he had not yet won.

They followed the young lad, and every so often Stumpy would jump out of the vehicle and run along beside, and then let him go and then jump back into the vehicle. When the rousey would see Stumpy running beside him, he'd run faster and each time he would get so hot he'd take off a few more of his clothes. By the time they got back to the shed, Stumpy had finished the bottle of rum and was still able to beat the rousey over the finish line. By this time, the poor bloke was down to running along in a pair of underpants and nothing else.

The rest of the team thought it was a fair enough way to treat a loud-mouthed know-it-all. In fact, it'd help him really – good for his poor, swollen head. They were pretty sure they had an ideal candidate for the lift-yourself-in-the-bucket routine, too. That would brighten up the odd dull moment.

The classer of the team was a young woman, Donna Turner. That would have been unheard of once, but was now only slightly unusual. Curious about her experience, Kendal asked Donna how she got along.

"When I first started working in the sheds, there were not a lot of other women working in the industry and there were even fewer women woolclassers," Donna said.

"Did you have any trouble?" Kendal wanted to know.

"A lot of the graziers and most of the wool advisers would come into the shed and shake the hand of the male wool roller on the other side of the table, assuming that he was the woolclasser," Donna said. "Then they usually didn't know whether to shake my hand or kiss me. I would have to take the initiative, stick out my hand to shake, to make them acknowledge me. I had to be more on the ball than male classers, because when you're a woman doing a man's job, they're always looking for you to make a mistake."

"What about the team, though?" Kendal asked, thinking of the shearing teams she'd met over the years. "I bet they weren't all pleased to see you?"

Donna laughed. "You can bet your boots! I had many confrontations with male shed staff. I suppose they felt threatened by a woman being in a power role. But after having proved myself as a classer, I found the second year much easier. It was pretty good, really. I found that the graziers would ask for advice about their wool and that they had faith in the decisions I made when classing."

The cook in the shed was a female, too. Years ago, it was always an all-male team. Women cooks were the first of the changes quite a few years ago. This particular girl, Sheila Manning, was tiny and fresh out of the city – but in every other way she was quite, quite different from Thea Morton. She was very aware, quite sharp and could hold her own in most situations. She was there with them one time when Donna was telling Kendal about some of the things the blokes in the team had done to her.

"Since I was a little girl, I've always been prone to kidney attacks or urinary tract infections," Donna said. "On one occasion, when I'd gotten one at work, I had to keep running across to the toilet during the shearing run. After lunch the problem hadn't improved and when I ran across to the toilet, I sat down and discovered I'd sat on a seat covered in vegemite. I'd been caught a beauty."

Kendal shook her head sympathetically, knowing what was coming next.

Donna continued. "When I walked out of the toilet, all the shearers were hanging out of the shed, laughing their heads off."

"The bastards," said Sheila.

Donna went on. "Instead of cleaning off the seat, I decided I'd leave it there and let someone else get caught. But when I went to bed that night, vegemite on the toilet seat was the last thing on my mind – and guess what? I got caught again! But don't worry, it soon became pretty clear who had done this little deed. As they say, every dog has his day. I returned the compliment by putting treacle in their Red Wings and on the seat of their motor bikes. It was too dark to see and they were too drunk to know – so they got caught out. Only they didn't seem to see the funny side to it at all. Funny that!"

"Good one, Donna!" Sheila exclaimed. "That'll teach the bastards. But what are Red Wings?"

"They're boots," Kendal answered.

"They're a brand of working boots most of the blokes wear," Donna added.

"It looks as though I'll have to watch my step," Sheila mused. "They've all been pretty good to me so far. My only real worry is that the damn stove keeps going out and someone pinches my matches. I'm pretty sure I know who it is but it's a damn nuisance. I think it's that great big bloke who does the pressing."

Kendal had an idea for how Sheila could get her own back on the presser, but thought she'd rather not involve Donna. Donna had a responsible job in the shed and she didn't want to get her mixed up in deliberately causing a hold-up.

So it was a little while later when she asked, "Are you sure it's the presser who pinches your matches?"

"It sure is," said Sheila. "I've had a go at him but he only says, 'So sue me' or something and takes another box as he goes out. He's a bit big to attack outright."

"Well," said Kendal, "his work depends as much on little things called bale fasteners as yours does on matches. One time when you bring smoko over and I'm there I'll show you where they are. If they disappear he can't get on with his job at all. They hold the bale he is pressing together and without them he's stymied. He won't be able to do a thing until he's found them. That'll teach the big boy a lesson."

Sheila smiled. She thought she might just about be able to handle that.

Changing the subject, Kendal looked ruefully at her hands and enviously at Donna, who had rejoined them. "Working with the wool all the time keeps your hands in good nick," she said. "Look at mine." She held them out to show the cuts, scratches and a few broken blisters.

Sheila sympathised. "I can't imagine doing what you do – it's bad enough the number of blisters and cuts I get from the hot stove and knives."

The three girls often talked about the blokes around them. Donna and Sheila both thought Stumpy was a good contractor and that he organised the team well. Donna thought this from a fair bit of experience in sheds, and Sheila as a newcomer.

Tony MacFarlane often came up for a bit of mention with the girls. Kendal and Donna both suspected Sheila was more than a tad interested in Tony – and why shouldn't she be? He was the best looking guy in the district.

They also talked about Bill-Bob. Donna, who'd seen him about town over the years, had a bit of a soft spot for the old man. She knew all about the talk in town about his exact relationship with Ethel Alsop and was a bit indignant. "Those busy bodies should just mind their own business," she told Sheila and Kendal. The fact that she was gossiping to have brought it up completely escaped her.

Sheila was interested but, as she didn't know Ethel, she was more intrigued with his nickname. Bill-Bob was a weird name really. Everyone still called her Sheila and she wondered if she stayed any time whether she would end up with a nickname, too. She wondered how Bill-Bob had got this name and she'd been asking the blokes in the team. Most of the fellows hadn't known.

"Search me, he's always been Bill-Bob" said Curly.

"Wouldn't have a clue," Stumpy said, helpfully.

But Jacko, one of the older members of the team, actually could remember when Bill-Bob came to Quilpie. Thirty years ago or more it must have been, he reckoned. He knew the story and told her.

"Bill-Bob was a Bob, not a Bill," Jacko said. "And he started with a shearing team. For some reason, the contractor at the time –

old Leo Atkinson it was then – just couldn't remember to call him Bob. He always said 'Hey, Bill'. Bob would quietly say 'Bob' — and so it went on. Every time Leo said 'Bill', Bob said 'Bob'. It didn't take the fellows long to catch on to Bill-Bob as his name. Funny how you just accept it after a while and forget he ever had any other name."

But more than all the nonsense and fooling around that went on, Sheila loved to sit around and hear the team yarn about their experiences over the years. Kendal loved it, too.

One day it was cloudy. It looked very heavy and as if it would storm any minute. As usual, it didn't rain, but the talk turned to the days when it did and the floods came.

Stumpy started the tale. "We were shearing at two places when the 1990 floods hit Quilpie. One of the teams was doing some crutching and cleaning up fly ready for shearing while the other was doing the general shearing on the neighbouring property, which was owned by the same company."

One of the boys Kendal knew best, Curly, continued. "That's right. We were rained out. There had been heavy rain the previous night and the rivers had already been running for the last couple days."

Donna was a regular member of the team and she took over. "Yeah, remember, it was decided that they'd shear the sheep on the neighbouring property, so I had to go over and class the wool. The contractor, Stumpy here, told me I'd only be there for the rest of the day, so I only took one clean set of clothes and my dog across to the shed.

"It was only possible to get to the other shed by four wheeler and boat. We were situated between the Bulloo and one of the main channels of the Bulloo so there was a lot of water flowing around, and most of the smaller channels were running bankers. At times, going through the channels was really scary. The water was up to the seat on the four wheeler and it was being pulled about in the current.

"We finally made it to the main channel, where they boated me across. We were still able to get across to the other shed by four wheel drive – but what was to be for one day turned into five weeks. Which meant I had to wear whatever clothes I could get me hands on and I cut a fine figure in a pair of dungarees and a Jacky Howe."

They all added their bits and pieces and the story unfolded.

Jacko remembered, "Some of the other team got across the river but the rest of them got stuck there for a week. The river came up to the floor boards of the quarters and the men could row from the quarters to the shearing shed. We finished as many of the sheep in the shed as we could. In the end, there was nowhere to put any more wet fleeces so we stopped shearing.

"Over the next few weeks, it rained on and off. It would just look like clearing, but by that afternoon it would be raining again. We shore as many sheep as we could, mainly to try and keep the fly out of them, but I don't think we ever did a full day's shearing in the whole time we were there."

Curly broke in. "There were three and a half thousand sheep caught on an island – remember that island? It was cut off by a channel which ran about five hundred metres behind the shed. The fly was getting so bad that it was decided that we'd set up a makeshift shed on the island to try and crutch as many of the fly-blown sheep as possible."

Jacko nodded his agreement. "Christ, yes, it was cold. It was the beginning of winter and the water was terribly cold. It was up to the chest on most of the men and in the middle the current was quite strong. We made a raft out of two forty-four gallon drums and an old door to get the shearing gear across.

"The shearing shed was two portable shearing stands which were motor driven, and they were strapped to a piece of wood between two mulga trees. We used tarps for the shearing board and made the yards out of chicken wire.

"The crutching on Mosquito Island, which was what we had called it, went on for about a week. So each morning we would all brave the water to get there, and it was a wonder that we didn't all end up with pneumonia.

"It was a very slow process and the sheep seemed to be dying quicker than we could get them crutched. So we decided we'd go to a neighbouring property and pick up a portable dip to try and stop the fly.

"We put the dip on the raft and put the dogs in the dip and headed across the channel. Only half-way across, the dip capsized, taking the dogs with it. It was a mad panic for a while, but the dogs eventually surfaced and we were able to get the dip back on the raft and to the other side. But the dogs were more than happy to swim the rest of the way."

Kendal was amazed listening to it. She figured for once they were all telling the truth.

Stumpy remembered another saga in the tale. "Do you remember on the way home the grazier's son staked himself on a stump under the water and the men had to carry him the rest of the way home? That was no mean feat – I reckon he weighed about seventeen stone."

Donna was talking again. "By the end of about the second week we were nearly completely out of food, other than potatoes, flour and mutton. The men had found some emu eggs when they were out mustering so we made good use of them."

Curly lit a cigarette and after a long draw said, "A helicopter was flown out to do food drops along the river and to pick up a pregnant lady from down the river. When it landed at the shed, we hit the chopper like a pack of wild dogs going in for the kill. But it wasn't food we were after, it was smokes.

"In the next couple of days, the first of the big army helicopters arrived. We thought that all our Christmases had come at once when they unloaded this large black object which we thought was an inflatable boat, but it turned out to be a net to carry the portable yards across to the island to do the dipping in."

That started Stumpy off again. "The Chinook took the yards and a few of the guys over to the island where they set up the yards. The trailer came in very handy as well. We hooked it up behind the tractor so we didn't have to walk from the channel to the yards, which were a good couple of kilometres from the river.

"We had to do all the mustering on foot and sometimes the sheep weren't too obliging, they'd break the yards and we'd have to start all over again. Barney was the man in charge of the cooking while on the island – actually, he basically thought he was in charge of everything. He was fairly harmless and we all got a laugh out of some of his antics.

"He was a bloody good cook, though. He fed us on damper baked in the coals and legs of mutton which were placed into a hole in the ground and had hot coal put over them. And 'til this day I have still not tasted meat as good."

Curly laughed and added, "Barney was generally a man of a great many words, but the day he filled his water esky out of the drums – which he thought had clean water in them but in fact had already been mixed with sheep dip – he had very little to say. In fact, if it had been anyone else they would be dead for sure, but not Barney. He was too tough to let a gut full of sheep dip kill him."

Stumpy interrupted to reclaim control of his story. "After about a week, the channel had gone down enough upstream to try to get the sheep across. They picked a place which had a rocky bottom so they wouldn't get the sheep too muddy while they were crossing. It was about, oh, seventy yards wide and thigh-deep in the middle. We tied sheep to trees and formed a big circle around the back of them to try to push them across, but they refused to see things our way. It was hard to keep the sheep together and they'd only go across in ones and twos, which wasn't getting us anywhere. The sheep were starting to go into the mud and tempers were starting to rage. In the end the cookie yelled, 'Let them go. Who cares how they get across, as long as they make it to the other side'.

"So half of us got into the water to stop the sheep from being swept down river, and the rest of us kept pushing the sheep across. After five hours we managed to get all the sheep across and we only lost half a dozen of them – and they were already badly fly-blown to begin with."

Later, Stumpy told Kendal the floods were the beginning of hard times for many people. Some places lost up to a couple of thousand sheep. Elsewhere, the rain caused discolouration. And everywhere, the flies were terrible. Add to that the falling wool prices, and a lot of graziers were forced to let their level of flock management fall. "Very few growers did any culling or classing over the next five years," he said. "Some even let go of lice management and didn't dip or spray. They're paying for that now."

A few of the team occasionally had a go at Kendal, but she didn't rise to their bait and deftly turned their teasing away. She'd quietly earned their respect. One of them tried to talk her into joining them in town for a few drinks. "You've been here a few weeks now and you've never been into town. What's the matter, don't you like us fellows?"

Curly came to her rescue. "Come off it now you blokes, fair go – you know she only arrived just before shearing. She couldn't ask for time off and a vehicle to take her to town. If she did, you'd all be saying she was a girl and couldn't take hard work – that she'd had special consideration or something."

Kendal stepped in. "Thanks for defending me, Curly. Actually, we have got a quiet weekend coming up, I think," she crossed her fingers and held them up, "I hope. We have all the sheep from the back country in close now, or will have when Tom and Charles get in tonight. Once we get this mob away and in their paddock tonight we can take it a bit easier for a day or two. But I won't be going to town – a good quiet day is all I'm looking forward to. That and catching up on a few things. At the moment I've got to get this mob branded before I take it out."

"He's a bit hard on you, isn't he?" Curly asked. "We've always heard he won't have women on the place," his eyes ran over her suggestively, "and you look like a girl to me."

Ignoring his last comment, Kendal defended her boss, "He's okay, fellas. I like to try to do a good job. My brother Kenrick is coming out soon to take over from me. The last thing I want is for anyone to say a girl can't do the job."

Another of the team called out, "We don't want a bloke to come. There's plenty of them around. Why don't you stay, Kendal?"

She laughed and left them to their work.

That afternoon, her tasks kept her around the shed. She was penning up and counting out and branding as they went. This was the last mob of wethers, so there was to be a cut-out tonight. Tom was out with Charles checking the waters and fences and making sure there were no stragglers in the country where they would be taken.

Because of the cut-out, the shearers were finished before the usual 5.30pm knock-off time. A few of the younger boys, who'd been teasing Kendal the most, decided to stay behind for a while and help her with the last of the branding.

"That'll get you through this lot a bit quicker," Curly said. "You'll get back to the house earlier."

The shearers were always in a hurry to get back to town on a Friday afternoon. The usual stopping place was the local pub and the boys said, "Well, we're real sorry you can't come with us, Kendal – we wouldn't mind havin' you around."

Kendal enjoyed the back-handed compliment. "Well, thanks for helping me boys, anyway. I'll catch up with you one day."

At this stage, someone produced an esky with some cold stubbies of beer and opened one each and passed them around, saying, "Here, have one with us before we go."

Kendal thought a cold beer would go down very well. "Well, just one because you've all been such good blokes. Thanks a lot for helping, fellas."

Curly started to sing, "I love to have a drink with Duncan... 'cause Duncan's my mate!"

Looking forward to the weekend off, they were soon all singing, getting more and more rowdy and starting to clown around. The two on each side of Kendal had their arms around her and were looking at her laughing and singing loudly a new version, "...and Kendal's my mate", when a piercing whistle broke through their song.

Charles had arrived and was irate. "What the bloody hell is going on here? I should have known better than to let you stay, Kendal."

He gestured to the shearers. "You fellows might have finished for the weekend, but let me tell you, we've far from finished." Then Kendal copped the full force of his wrath. "What in hell's name do you think you are up to, Kendal, drinking and singing and carrying on as if you had nothing to do? I particularly told you that you had to be as quick as you could with these sheep. You know they have a long way to go and they won't travel well after dark – even if I wanted you out working in the dark. As for the rest of you, you boys get off to town."

The shearers scattered. Kendal stayed on the job. Charles took over and organised the sheep. Tom had gone on back to the house, so Kendal and Charles were forced to work together – but mechanically, like clockwork. Kendal felt numb about it all. Whatever reason he had to dislike her before would be more than reinforced now. It had all been so innocent, really.

The boys had been helping and she hadn't been behind because of the few minutes' singing and only one stubby of beer. But, to be fair, she had to admit it did look bad. Charles couldn't know the boys had been helping and had no way of knowing how long they had been drinking.

What a miserable thing to have happened and to have wrecked their good relationship.

Chapter 10

The next day was Saturday, and indeed, after all the drama, the sheep were out of the yards and there was time for a very welcome sleep-in. There were a few little jobs to be done down at the yards but, on the whole, things were well in hand. Thank heavens there was time to take things a little more slowly for the weekend.

Kendal's mind was buzzing, though, as she dressed and tidied her room. Sick of being on tenterhooks, she was determined to have it out with Charles. Why did he always think the worst of her?

All last night, he'd acted cold and withdrawn again, and finally she'd had enough. She would make him see that the boys in the shed were only teasing and that she wasn't the scatty little flirt he thought she was. Who did he think she was anyway?

She sat down on the edge of her bed, sighing. She had to admit it. He had her in a whirl. He was affecting her in a way no-one else ever had. She was too vulnerable to him blowing hot and cold to her and she didn't like being affected like this. He definitely was an enigma – one minute a good companion, and then the next saying all sorts of cruel things to her.

Well, she'd had enough worrying. She decided she'd try not to think about him. After all, she wasn't going to be there forever. She was sure Kenrick would settle in all right – and at least he wouldn't have to suffer the deep undercurrent of ill feeling Kendal felt from Charles.

It was only a matter of days before Kenrick would arrive, according to his last phone call. "The doctor says I'll probably be there by the end of next week," he said when he rang during the week. "Thanks for holding the fort, Sis, but soon you'll be able to get on with your own life."

Strangely, that thought didn't make her happy. Somehow, as fed up and all that she was, she didn't really want to be away from all this.

With conflicting thoughts still chasing round and round in her head, Kendal finally smoothed down the quilt on her bed, had a brief check of her reflection in the mirror and went out to face the day.

As she walked across the breezeway and the back verandah on the way to the kitchen, she looked up at all the lovely big gum trees in the back garden. She caught her breath with excitement as she remembered a similar sight while she was mustering yesterday morning. Instead of all of her rehearsed phrases of reproach, she burst into the kitchen and exclaimed to Charles and Tom, "You'll never guess what I saw yesterday!" She didn't give them time to answer. "A koala! It was in the trees along the creek at the back of the Stony Creek paddock. Somehow, with all the drama," she managed a look at Charles, who ignored it, "I forgot to tell you last night."

Tom was immediately interested. "That's good news, Kendal. Was it only one or did you see a few? Were there a lot of their trees about? Would there be likely to be more?"

But then it happened again. Charles killed the moment by saying, "Don't you tell all those young rouseabouts mates of yours about this, they're just the type to think it's smart to shoot them or catch one for a pet or something."

Her earlier resolve instantly reignited, Kendal was up in arms.

"Damn you, Charles," she fired off. "You never give me credit for an ounce of sense. I know better than to shoot my mouth off about a koala and those boys were only being friendly. Which is more than I can say for you."

Tom, as usual, was the one to try to settle things down.

"Come on, Charles. I don't know just what was going on at the shed last night, but I do know she has enough sense not to tell all and sundry where to find a koala."

Charles was more interested in the personal matter and said in a conciliatory manner, "I suppose I did overreact at the shed last night. I was about to suggest, before all the fireworks started here, that we should take a run out there and see if there are a few about, or just the one."

Tom said he was too busy, but encouraged Charles and Kendal to go for a look.

Not one to hold a grudge, even though she had plenty of things to say to Charles, Kendal decided to leave well enough alone for the time being. Going to look for the koala was exactly what she'd thought she'd like to do when she saw it yesterday. She'd been behind a few stragglers that she was trying to push into the mob and there hadn't been time to stop to have a good look. She'd thought then that she'd come back the first chance she got and have a good look around. If Charles would be civil to her, it would be great to go together and she knew that his few words were as close as he would ever come to an apology.

"With all this mustering on bikes, the horses are needing exercise," Charles was saying. "We'll get the chores done and then take lunch out the back and move around quietly on the horses. The bikes are fine to get the work done, but a day like this would be better on the horses. If you can ride, Kendal?"

"Sure thing," she responded, "we had horses at home when I was a kid."

"What do you think, Dad?" Charles looked inquiringly at his father. "Who should I give to Kendal? Do you think that bay mare Dancer would suit her? Or would Cinderella be more suitable?"

"I'd give her Dancer if I were you and it would be a good thing if you rode Sideon," Tom replied. "He hasn't had a workout for some time and if you ever want him for polocrosse again you'd better give him some work."

Charles went out to run in the horses and Tom helped Kendal put together sandwiches, tea and sugar and showed her where she would find some saddle bags and quart-pots. She collected her hat and went down to the yards in time to help groom and saddle up her mount.

They rode along in relative harmony, not needing to speak. Kendal thought how lovely it all was. "It's a pity," she mused to herself, "how the Australian outback can be empty and threatening to those who don't know and understand it but it is such a wonderful place if you are observant and tune in to the world around you."

It was so much better on the horses than on the bike. The horses disturbed a few animals, but nothing like the bike. If you go quietly, it's always possible to hear and see something. The quiet stillness of the outback has its own sights and sounds. The harsh *ark-ark* of a crow in the distance, the peculiar whistle of a Major Mitchell cockatoo. Flocks of galahs wheeling together, turning from soft grey to pink and back to grey. Occasionally a little quail is flushed out of the grass, or a flight of green budgerigars flashes past and is gone in an instant, and there are always goannas and other lizards. She loved the lizards. Some just freeze, absolutely still, making it hard to tell if what you're looking at is a piece of bark or something alive. If they think danger is too close, they run like a flash towards a patch of fallen timber and immediately become invisible again. Long-legged goannas can move like lightning and usually dart up a tree. The slow-moving stumpy tail or scaly-back looks for all the world like a miniature escapee from Jurassic Park. It freezes, too, when it's frightened, but just turns and opens its mouth and hisses if you get too close. It's too slow to dart anywhere and relies on looking fierce.

Occasionally the riders would disturb a few kangaroos lying about under the trees and they would see them hopping off into the distance. An old man emu with last year's chicks all nearly as big as himself stalked past and hardly turned a head in their direction.

It was quite a good season and there was plenty of seed about. Despite being late in spring, there were still a few wild flowers about – paper daisies here, a flowering hop bush there.

After riding for a couple of hours they came to the dry creek bed they were looking for and followed it along.

"It was somewhere around here," Kendal said, scanning the area. "I remember the way the creek divided around that bit in the middle there – that must be an island when the creek is running. I reckon it was in one of these blue gums around here."

Charles responded, "Let's get off here and walk along the creek bed. We'll see more clearly into the trees from down there."

With all the blue gums and bull oaks growing along the side of the dry creek bed, there was no problem finding a strong branch to tie the horses. They both stood still, looking into the trees around them and then they scrambled lower to the dry sandy creek bed scanning the branches around them as they went.

They spent quite a while looking around. Kendal's eye was caught by a few birds and a couple of dark patches on the trees that turned out to be just that, just dark patches on the trees.

Then Charles called, "Kendal, I've got one! Look over there, a little to the right of that broken branch."

Kendal looked up where he was pointing but couldn't see anything. Charles stood behind her and put his left hand on her shoulder and pointed with his right hand across her right shoulder to a little dark spot. Following his hand she finally made out the shape and then she laughed.

113

"Hey, will you look at that! It's a mother with a baby. I'm glad she's so hard to see. I hope no eagles see her from on top. Isn't she lovely?" With eyes alight, she turned around to face him. "Thanks. That's excellent. I'm glad we found one at least. And one with a passenger."

Charles had stopped looking at the koala and was now looking directly at her. There was no mistaking the look in his eyes. Kendal felt sick with anticipation and beside herself with excitement and a thousand emotions in between when he very slowly put a hand on her face, caressed it, then put his arms around her and drew her to him.

Like a bird fascinated by a snake, she found herself paralysed by the moment. Emotions rushed unheeded through her head and ended with a single thought – what about how he'd treated her after the last time he'd kissed her? But heart ruled over logic, she lifted her face and he gently kissed her.

At last, Charles released her and seemed for a moment to be just as confused as she was. Then he quite visibly gave his head a little shake and said, "We'd better collect some firewood and put the quart-pots on for dinner camp. We can look around a bit more while they boil." He added conversationally, "At least these dry creek beds are a great place for a fire. We don't have to clear anything because there's nothing to burn."

A bit dazed from the embrace – and stymied by her reaction to him – Kendal felt like she was operating in a fog. She was glad he suggested collecting wood or she felt she would have stood on the one spot for ever.

The spell broken, the two quite companionably collected wood and leaves and soon had a fire going with their quart-pots placed among the flames to come to the boil. As they moved about, they searched the tree tops and found two more koalas. Kendal made a point of not going near Charles and he made no effort to come close again.

It wasn't a big colony, but they were happy that there were some koalas about and expected there were a few more about they had missed. They were so damned hard to see. There were any number of dry channels about in this country and there could be small groups all over the place.

They sat away from the fire a bit, leaning against an exposed tree root in the shade. They talked a bit, but not much. There was lots of life all around them vying for their attention. A grasshopper and some sort of buzzing insect were nearby, as were the ever-present flies and ants of the Australian picnic, but they weren't too bad. There was a patch of blue verbena with a host of tiny blue butterflies and, besides the elusive koalas, there were magpies calling, the sound of a crow as it flew over, little lizards scurrying around and any number of birds and animals going about their daily lives.

Despite not fully comprehending the underlying currents between them, Kendal felt companionable and comfortable with Charles. She knew he was appreciating the quiet time in the bush without all the bustle of work, too. Motor bikes might get things done more quickly, sure, but they robbed workers of time to think or appreciate the world around them. As a result, even though most station folk used bikes, most still loved their horses – both for heavy, wet weather when bikes would get bogged and simply for the great creatures they were.

The fire was burning down low now. Charles had picked up a small broken branch and was slowly pulling off the half-dead leaves and throwing them onto the glowing coals that were all that was left of their camp fire. They spluttered and burned. Some shot up a bright flame and some turned slowly inwards, getting smaller and smaller as they shrivelled up in the heat. The smell of burning gum leaves was pungent like a heavy incense.

Kendal watched Charles's hands and thought how strong and yet how sensitive they looked. He had a couple of small scratches and one quite severe cut across one knuckle, and yet they didn't look tough like the hands of most station workers. Her beloved father's hands had been rough and calloused – almost as gnarled as Tom's – but Charles's hands were supple and strong without looking weathered.

Even just looking at his hands brought unbidden thoughts to her mind. Like what it would be like to have his hands touch her.

Kendal decided to concentrate on finding something safe to talk about.

"This part of the creek bed is sandy and the creek seems to be sandy all over. Why do you call the paddock Stony Creek?" she asked Charles, grateful for a question to pose.

Charles replied, "Sounds funny, I suppose, but that's not the idea at all. There are three paddocks that this creek runs through and this one has that rocky outcrop across the southern corner and most of the paddock is stony. The next paddock is all plain and the other paddock goes up the foothills a bit and so we have Top Creek, Plain Creek and Stony Creek paddocks, but it's the same sandy creek bed. It was all one big Creek Paddock once, but we split it up to make it more manageable a few years ago."

Kendal thought how well the property was organised. Moving stock was as simple as possible at Carmody Plains, and had taken a lot of good planning with fence lines. She wondered if it was Charles's idea or Tom's legacy.

But Charles interrupted her reverie. "It's great to be able to sit here quietly and enjoy this, but we'd better get on home. It'll be dark before we get back if we leave it too late. I'll saddle the horses again if you put sand on the fire. There's a bower bird's playground not far from number two bore that I'll show you as we go past. I haven't had a look in it for years, but there might be something interesting in it."

Kendal stood up and slowly went over to the ashes of their fire and with her foot, well shod in her old elastic-sided riding boots, slowly pushed up the sand around the ashes to make sure no spark could be fanned and blown out by the wind. She made doubly sure it was safe. After all, the last thing they wanted after specially coming out to look at the koalas was to set alight their trees and burn them.

The mechanical task gave her a chance to wonder what on earth was going on between her and Charles. His anger and his passion, his gentleness and his iciness, his cruelty and kindness – everything about him was a mystery, and she had to keep a firm hold on her senses to stay balanced.

His kiss this afternoon had been so gentle, yet her response had been so immediate and strong. They had had a wonderful afternoon together. They obviously suited each other's mood perfectly, finding joy in simple pleasures. The afternoon had been heightened by their physical awareness of each other. For Kendal's part, she was alive with sensuality in a way she'd never known before. It was extreme and it was undeniable, but she had no idea how it was going to work in with her relationship with Charles.

Then there was his reaction to ponder. Why hadn't he kissed her again? He must have found her attractive and he seemed to enjoy the kiss, but why no more? They'd shared a wonderful afternoon, but it had raised more questions than answers.

There wasn't time for too much introspection with Charles around. "Hurry up, slow coach, that fire is buried so deeply that if an archaeologist found it in years to come he'd think it was used by stone age men."

With a laugh, Kendal realised she'd been slowly scooping more and more sand into a mound over the spot where the fire had been. She ran up the steep creek bank to where Charles had both the horses. He handed her her reins and watched her mount before swinging up into the saddle himself.

Then just before he turned to ride off he leaned across and gave her a little posy of white everlasting daisies. Kendal was surprised and delighted. She opened her eyes wide in surprise and they sparkled in pleasure. Who would have thought the chauvinist Charles would pick her some daisies? But Charles wheeled and cantered away, giving her no time to thank him.

Her words of thanks died on her lips and she shook her bridle and gave Dancer a gentle kick and cantered along behind Charles and Sideon.

It didn't take long before they were at the gate near the number two bore and after Charles had dismounted to open it and let her through, he led her on foot to a little clump of sandalwood trees. Kendal dismounted and, close to where he was crouching, discovered the collection of bits and pieces in tunnels in the grass that made up the bower bird's playground.

It had been years since Kendal had seen a playground and she was enchanted with it. The two of them knelt on hands and knees examining the area, being careful not to touch it.

There was always a chance that something interesting would be found around a playground, but even it there wasn't, it was wonderful to see how the birds built their passages, tunnelling through the grass and filling it with collected things.

Kendal marvelled aloud at the birds' inventiveness. "Isn't it amazing what you find in those playgrounds? What's the best thing you've ever found, Charles?"

"One day when I was a kid we found a ladies' watch," Charles replied. "It was old and scratched and didn't go, but it was fun to find. Sometimes we've found rings from soft drink cans and bottle tops, things like that. Mostly, though, it's just been old bones and shiny stones."

Kendal nodded. "One day we found a ring. Again, it wasn't valuable, but it makes you wonder who lost it and when and what the whole story was. It's quite exciting to find something of a personal nature."

Kendal slowly stood up and Charles did too. She looked straight at him, and he met her glance. "Thanks, Charles, for showing me that. It's great to see and they're so darn hard to find if you don't know where they are." She made a rueful face. "And when you're mustering there is never time to stop and look, even if you do think you see one."

Charles smiled. "I'm glad you like it. You're fun to show things to. Your eyes shine like a child's when you see something that interests you."

He suddenly pulled her close again so that she was pressed tightly against him, and kissed her quickly and hard. "You don't feel like a child, though," he said gruffly, then he let her go abruptly and quickly swung into the saddle and cantered off.

Kendal dressed carefully that evening. She'd been wearing work clothes each day since she'd arrived at Carmody Plains and when she showered in the evening she'd changed into fairly simple clothes. She'd always been clean and practical, suitable for a working week, but tonight she felt like looking pretty. They'd arrived back early enough for her to spend a good, long time doing her hair and her nails and her makeup. She was extra conscious of her own hands. They were starting to show signs of the hard work, but a little sugar and lemon juice cleaned them up. With a good soak and plenty of cream, they looked cared for again. She decided on one of her prettiest dresses, a heavy white cotton one made to just skim her figure. She felt good as she smoothed it down over her hips and looked at herself in the mirror. The dress showed off her figure which she knew was full but wasn't bad. Her mass of auburn hair fell around her shoulders, and a dash of her favourite perfume finished her preparations. Kendal was quite big, but in this frock she looked as fragile and feminine as she could and that was how she wanted to look tonight. She was really feeling happy and relaxed as she left her room.

Tom was in the kitchen when she went to find a little vase for her beautiful daisies. She could have used anything, really, because they were everlasting flowers, but she thought she'd like to put them on the dressing table in her room.

Tom whistled his appreciation when she walked in. "And don't you look attractive tonight!" he commented. "We'd better look in the cupboard for the good silver and crystal to do justice to you for dinner. You've had a good day, I should think – there's a special look about you. Charles says you found a few koalas. It's great to think they are building up in numbers again."

Hunting around in the back of the cupboards, Kendal replied, "Yeah, there would probably be quite a few along the creek, we think. And yes, it was a great afternoon. I've enjoyed the sheep work and being busy, but today was a wonderful change. Just to be able to look around and enjoy the bush was great. And now I've come home and spent ages in the bathroom, I feel a new woman."

Finally, Kendal found a pottery jar in the back of the bachelors' cupboard and said, "Do you mind if I take this over to my room, Tom? I've got a few little paper daisies I'd like to put in it."

"Sure, Kendal, it isn't doing much in there by itself."

As Kendal passed the dining room on her way back along the verandah she couldn't help overhearing Charles on the telephone. "... And make it a really superb bouquet of white orchids and send it to Miss Penelope Carpenter. Nothing flashy, just quality. Don't worry about the cost. Put on the card, 'Special flowers for a really special lady'. Now, the address is..."

Kendal didn't wait to hear any more. Disgusted and distressed, she ran to her room and threw the vase on the bed. What was the point of arranging a bunch of wild flowers when the same man who gave them was on the phone ordering beautiful flowers for someone else?

Kendal didn't know if she was more hurt or angry. Was it hurt pride or a matter of the heart? Whatever it was, she felt miserable, bleak, cold and bitter. They'd had such a special afternoon together and now here he was ordering flowers to be sent to some other woman. Damn him to hell. She'd show him the afternoon meant nothing to her, either. There was no way he was going to know the pain and rejection she felt. All his tenderness and kindness meant nothing. If he thought of her at all, it must only be as a child. After all, hadn't he said, 'Your eyes shine like a child's'? That's what he said, so he gave her a bunch of wild flowers. His real thoughts were with some other woman who rated orchids. Kendal was wild. She'd show him she was no child, and she didn't care a fig about him.

She swept her hand around her hair and piled it up on her head. She was used to doing this but some sort of desperation added a certain surety to her hands and she secured the roll with a jewelled clasp. She added glittering earrings and in those two small moves changed her looks from a warm, vibrant woman to one with a more sophisticated image, who had eyes that were hard and brilliant with unshed tears.

She would be damned if she'd let him know she cared and she gathered all her pride around her and swept out confidently. Anger and pride would keep the tears unshed until she was back in her room again on her own.

Tom and Charles were in deep discussion as she walked defiantly into the room. Tom looked at her in amazement. He clearly couldn't believe the change in her. Charles looked up at her in what she would have otherwise thought was a very special way, and said, "Dad and I are just choosing a wine to go with our meal. We don't have a lot of choice, but we've got some quite good ones put away. It's been a while since we've thought of having wine with a meal. Having a woman around must be good for us."

Kendal was not about to be drawn in. If she hadn't been warned by that darned phone call, she would have jumped in. She would have been all starry-eyed and enthusiastic about choosing a wine for a party evening and he would have been patronising and thought she was like a child. Well, acting cold and reserved gave her no pleasure but it was the only way she could get through the evening.

She didn't want to be rude to Tom, so the best she could manage was offhanded coldness. "Whatever you like, Charles," she said. "I'm sure it makes no difference to me."

Charles's eyes narrowed and he seemed to stiffen a little. Tom simply looked bewildered, looking from Charles to Kendal and trying to fathom the undercurrents.

Throughout the night, Charles tried repeatedly to get Kendal to relax, but there was no way she was going to let her guard down. She was frigidly polite – even to poor Tom. She couldn't trust herself to relax at all. And, in fact, the more Charles tried, the more upset Kendal got and the more brittle she seemed.

So the evening that had held so much promise turned into what seemed to Kendal to be a game of charades. Everyone pretended and acted a part. But no-one guessed the question, much less the answer.

120

Chapter 11

Kendal was relieved to have another day's reprieve from work. So she collected some of her sewing and went out early into the old garden at the front of the house. She'd been past there and the cursory look had made her want to investigate further.

There hadn't been much time for a really good look around anywhere at all since she'd been at Carmody Plains. The working days had been long – away early in the morning and back after dark. This weekend was quiet and today she had nothing to do until the late afternoon, when they would bring in the sheep that were in the paddock close to the shed ready for the regular early start on Monday morning. Hand sewing was a soothing occupation for her. And at this particular point of her life, Kendal felt she needed all the comfort she could get.

She was pretty sure she'd be undisturbed because no-one ever went around to what used to be the front of the house. Everyone usually drove around to what had once been definitely the back of the house and was now used as the entrance. It led straight onto a verandah that went to the kitchen and laundry. There, the grass was well watered and planted with many Australian native trees, giving shade and character to the area. There were a few geraniums with bright red flowers along the edge of the verandah and, apart from that and the hedge of blue-flowered plumbago, there were no flowers.

Kendal wandered down the side of the house around to what must have once been a very attractive front garden. It was obviously a long time since anyone had tended this part, but the outline of the garden was still quite clear. A path, paved with flat stones but now overgrown with grass and weeds, led in from a garden gate that was hanging crookedly on a broken hinge. An old gnarled rose grew over an archway and it was huge, wild and straggly, obviously not pruned for many a long year. There were garden beds built up in stonework going away from the path but they only held a few hardy weeds now. Kendal could see that there was a bank with steps going down to what must have been a tennis court at some other time.

Kendal found a spot that was well shaded, settled herself and looked around. This once well-loved garden that was now neglected and unloved suited her mood. She felt neglected and unloved and she was wallowing in a fit of the dismals and nostalgia. She sat and sewed and, as her hands wove the needle deftly in and out, she let her mind wander.

She wondered what had become of their own old garden that her mother had tended so carefully. Most families in the bush dedicated a lot of effort to their gardens, toiling unimaginably in the harsh climate to create a tiny oasis. But it was worth it. Coming in exhausted after a day spent in dry, dusty paddocks to a patch of cool, green garden was a tonic and worth struggling to achieve.

Kendal could remember stories of her mother – how one of her friends, Margaret, always asked politely when she rang up, 'How are the children?' and next question was, inevitably, 'How is the garden?' Her mother insisted that Margaret always asked. She had made a point of watching for it. Only once, in all the time she knew her, when Margaret was in a great hurry, did she miss the question.

Kendal wondered if the new owners had let her mother's garden go to ruin like the way Charles and Tom had ignored their front garden. Anyway, why did Charles and Tom live the way they did? She knew every family was different and every property had its own story, and wondered what the story was here. She'd been so busy with the drama of shearing and the effort of physical work – not to mention figuring out her own relationship with Charles – that she hadn't really spent much time wondering why these two men lived as they did. Why did Charles want a manager anyway? He was capable and all he needed was a bit of help. There was probably not really much need for Kenrick to come out here.

There were always men, and women too, who were bits of hermits and liked to live on their own. Some let their places become derelict because they wouldn't have help to fix them up. Kendal knew there were people like that everywhere, not only in the bush. Funny thing was, Tom didn't really fit that pattern and Charles certainly didn't. Tom was friendly and cheerful and, although Charles was a loner in some ways, he was no recluse.

Carmody Plains was all a mystery, she decided. Soon she'd be finishing up here, and she thought she'd tell Kenrick not to come. He was finally due to come out at the end of next week but she couldn't see much point. Charles didn't need a manager and Rick would end up a jackaroo forever.

She watched a black and white butterfly fly past and go lazily from one wild flower to the next. There were masses of the tiny blue-grey butterflies again on another patch of the wild purple verbena. There was much more of that purple stuff around than when she was a child. Was it a wild flower or a weed? It looked a bit like Patterson's Curse. She wondered if it could be a problem weed, too.

A little brown pardalote was flying about picking up bits and pieces, calling *witt-witt* now and then, sometimes with a charming little echo. Kendal thought he was probably gathering bedding for his nest as he picked up and discarded various pieces of dry grass. When he finally chose one, she watched him carefully as he flew away, keen to see where he might be building his nest.

She was quite distressed when she saw him fly into the downpipe coming from the roof of what looked like an old garden shed. The pipe came straight down from the guttering and then turned a ninety degree angle away from the building. It made a nice little tunnel and she knew he'd be building in the cavity the angle provided.

"You silly little twit of a bird," Kendal thought. "One good fall of rain and you'll be washed out, and all your family with you. Why don't you dig a tunnel in that bank like pardalotes are supposed to do, or in the creek, or find a small hollow in a tree?" Then she reconsidered. "Actually, it's probably not that much more dangerous." Natural predators would be more numerous in a tree and flash floods could swamp a tunnel in a bank. Life was pretty precarious for little birds.

She thought of one little pardalote that had built in the exhaust pipe of an old tractor at home when she was a child. The tractor was sometimes not used for ages and just sat in the shed. One day, they started the tractor up and a startled, little black pardalote flew out. The smoke from the exhaust had covered it with black soot, and they had an unusually black pardalote for a few days.

There was a great big huntsman spider's web near the downpipe, strung across from the old shed to a branch of a peach tree that looked even older then the shed. The spider was at home and it was a massive spider, too. They were fascinating to watch from a nice, safe distance. The one thing Kendal really hated was when she walked or rode into one of the webs. She knew the spiders weren't dangerous, and she wasn't frightened of them, but she hated the creepy feeling of being entangled in a web and not knowing where the spider had landed.

A little day-dreaming and speculation helped Kendal feel more positive about the day ahead – positive enough to get herself ready for the week ahead. She folded up her work and went back to her bedroom to put it away and to collect her washing. She put on the first load and from the laundry she wandered into the kitchen to get a drink. Tom was in the kitchen and he greeted her, "Good morning, Kendal, how are you today?"

"And top of the world to you too, Tom."

"You're chirpy today again, my dear. Whatever happened to you last night? Something must have upset you."

The painful memory cut through Kendal's determination to be positive. The pain of being used was still too raw to even think about, much less discuss. She didn't answer but went to the cupboard and took out a glass. Ever observant, Tom didn't press for an answer and changed the subject. "You've been looking around the garden, I see," he commented.

Kendal was on firmer ground. She turned on the tap as she answered, "Yes Tom, there must have been a lovely garden out there once. Do you miss it? Do you ever play tennis?"

"Yes and no," Tom replied, folding the newspaper he'd been reading at the kitchen table. "It all belongs to what seems like another lifetime. I'm busy and happy here and don't often think about the old days."

She sipped her water and, looking at her glass and not at him, asked, "Do you mind me asking why you live alone here with Charles and why you don't get a housekeeper to help? I have a feeling you'd quite like someone here." She looked up. "Charles seems to tell you you can't have a woman here. But why do you let your bossy son tell you what you can and can't have in your own home?"

She saw his face tense, revealing a bit of pain around his eyes. Quickly and a bit embarrassed for prying, Kendal gave him an opportunity not to reply. "I'm sorry. It's none of my business. I can live with mystery and Charles will have his wish – I'll be away from here soon and you won't have an inquisitive female to worry about." She finished with her glass of water and put it in the sink.

Tom didn't look upset, though. "No, Kendal, you've asked me now and I do like to think about it all now and then. Most old people like to talk about the past, so you can humour an old man. You've said you're interested, so it's your own fault if I bore you."

Kendal moved over to a stool and sat on the edge of it facing Tom. "No, I won't be bored," she assured him. "I'd love to hear your story."

Tom's mood was reflective, and Kendal could tell he was envisioning something in the past. "Charles's mother died while he was still a little boy," Tom began. "She died in early pregnancy with our second child." He paused a moment and then continued. "While Nancy was alive we had what everyone dreams about, I guess, in a family life. Times weren't too bad on the land then, and we had a very happy life, plenty of help on the place. Nancy was a keen gardener and housekeeper and a good mother. I had time to help her and we had a lovely home and garden and played lots of tennis. Neighbours came for tennis parties and it was all as you were imagining out there." He took out his handkerchief and wiped his glasses. He kept them in his hand and looked at them not at her. "Perhaps I'm looking back with rose-coloured glasses, but Nancy and I were in love. We were young and the world was a wonderful place."

Kendal could see the old memories were bringing as much pain as comfort to him, so she quietly said, "Oh, I'm sorry. Don't go on if you'd rather not."

He put his glasses back on and looked straight at her again and said briskly, "You've got me started now, Miss, you'll hear my story out. Not long after Nancy died, I had a housekeeper here called Kathleen. She seemed such a friendly woman and she did so much for us both. Nothing seemed to be a trouble and she seemed to be genuinely fond of Charles. He was a bit prickly with her all along, you know, but I put that down to all the usual reasons one hears – like someone else instead of his mother being in his home. I genuinely thought Kathleen was good for us both." He stopped looking at her again and just stared out the window. Kendal didn't interrupt this time. Finally he turned towards her again and said, "Before long she started to hint it would be easier for Charles if she and I got married and she could really be his mother. She was a clever woman, she really convinced me that she loved us both."

He took out his handkerchief again and blew his nose. "I was still in shock a bit, I suppose. She kept saying it would be best for Charles and I believed her. Anyway, it didn't take very long after we were married for her to show her true colours. She began to neglect the house, pick on Charles and stopped being loving to me. We lived together in reasonable harmony for a while and everyone in the district was very kind and accepted her as my wife. She had thought it would be wonderful to be married to a station owner – a wealthy grazier, I suppose she thought – but she didn't really love either of us. She really only wanted money and what she thought of as position. Kathleen didn't realise life on the land was hard work. There's always the house and garden and not much social life or going out. So Kathleen started to agitate more and more to go away from here – to go to Brisbane and spend money, to be about and be seen."

Kendal was both fascinated and saddened by the story. The more she heard, the more she understood the strange household she'd found herself in.

Tom had continued his story. "Charles went to boarding school down in Sydney, near Nancy's parents, and my life here was very lonely. Times were not so good on the land, wool prices were down and Kathleen was always away spending money. It was the only thing she wanted. She was seeing other men in Brisbane and I was out here on my own, mostly. Charles came home on holidays. He liked it better when Kathleen wasn't at home – so we had a good time together during his school holidays when she wasn't here. After he left school, Charles decided he wouldn't make his life on the land. By this time, he really hated Kathleen and what she was doing to our life and the drain of capital out of the property.

"Strangely enough – or perhaps not so strange, considering Nancy's father – Charles seemed to be born with an entrepreneurial skill. Even when he was at school, he used to buy things and trade them. He watched the stock market like a hawk, and property values as well. He must have inherited this from Nancy's family – no-one in my family was like that. He spent a fair bit of time with Nancy's parents in Sydney when he had weekends and time off school. They wanted him down there and thought he was better off where he had relations close at hand. Charles always loved his grandfather and it was old Alan Carpenter, Nancy's father, who taught him about the stock market and was his mentor when Charles set up his own business. It had nothing to do with me."

Kendal interrupted. "Charles has his own business?" she inquired.

Tom nodded, his eyes twinkling a bit at how Kendal jumped at the mention of his son's name. "I'm getting to that, Kendal," he replied, but continued his story. "Mrs Carpenter, Nancy's mother, was a complaining woman with a large family who didn't like the fact that her darling youngest daughter, Nancy, had gone to the outback country in western Queensland. It was too far from civilisation as she knew it, and never lost an opportunity to tell Charles how unreasonable I'd been. She used to tell Charles it was my fault that his mother had died. Charles never told me this in so many words, but I knew it was going on. She never let a chance go by without telling me, either. Not that I saw much of any of them. We only keep in touch with one of Nancy's sisters, Penny."

The strange set-up at Carmody Plains was beginning to make sense to Kendal. "So," she said, "Charles doesn't actually live out here then all the time?"

Tom shook his head. "No, girlie, he only comes out now and then to organise shearing or something when I'm in trouble. He likes to get back to his roots, as he calls it, and I'm delighted to see him, but he doesn't really live here any more. He lives in the business world."

Still upset by Charles's treatment of her, Kendal focused her indignation on Tom's present plight. "But I still think it's a bit much for him to tell you that you can't have a housekeeper here," she charged. "It's still not his place to tell you what to do."

Tom smiled at Kendal's defence of him. "There's still a lot you don't know about us, Kendal. Carmody Plains is legally Charles's place. He owns it now. You see, Kathleen finally wanted out of our marriage altogether and demanded that I sell the property to give her half of the proceeds as a divorce settlement. I was heartsick about the whole thing. Actually, the stress of it all made me pretty crook for a long time. I've lived here all my life. My family has had the place for five generations and it was dreadful to think of parting with it. I don't think I could fit in anywhere else very well anymore. Anyway, Kathleen had me between a rock and a hard place. My lawyer told me the best thing I could do was sell Carmody Plains if and when I could get a good price. He said if I left it too long and Kathleen won, I wouldn't get as good a price. So, someone made me a good offer and I took it."

Tom was very hesitant and Kendal, sensing his pain, wanted to brighten him up. She said cheerfully, "But you're still here, and in good health. You must have bought the property back when times were better?"

Tom nodded. "You're half right. I am here, and I'm feeling fine, now. But I didn't buy the property back – I'd never have had the money. What happened was that Charles discovered Kathleen was putting me through the wringer, and he was the one who made an offer on Carmody Plains. He had to make the offer through a holding company he owns – because if Kathleen had known he was interested, she might have made more trouble – but he bought Carmody Plains so it could stay in the family. The result is that he owns the property, but I live here."

Kendal felt a little mollified. She appreciated Charles had put many thousands of dollars of his own money on the line, but still felt Charles's behaviour towards his father was dictatorial and unfair. "Well, I don't like to be too persistent, but if you live here, shouldn't you choose your own employees?"

Tom smiled good-naturedly. "You're determined to know the whole story, aren't you, girlie? Charles is a wonderful son and he's only trying to help me." He shook his head as if he couldn't believe there was still more to the story. "You see after we did get it all sorted out, I had a young man, Brad, and his girlfriend living together in the cottage. Heather, the girl was called, she used to come and do a bit of cooking and to clean and tidy up for me. That worked quite well for a while." He shook his head again and said, "You'd think you'd only read about this in the papers. But Heather got pregnant and Brad took off like a scared rabbit. So Heather decided to claim I was the father of the baby and wanted to slap a paternity suit on me."

Charles's objection to women on Carmody Plains – and his violent reaction to her presence that first night – was all starting to become clearer to Kendal. She shook her head at the crises Tom had been forced to endure. "Oh, Tom, what a rotten time you've had with women. So, what happened? Where's the baby?"

128

Tom sighed and then laughed ruefully to himself and looked out the window again. "Well, Brad had taken off because he was scared of the responsibility of being a father. But after a while, he changed his mind and decided he'd be proud to have a child and came back and married Heather. She was quite brazen about admitting she'd only named me because she thought there might be a bit of money in it." Tom looked at her again. "So all of that together, girlie, is why you see us as we are."

Kendal gave a rueful laugh. "It's certainly easier to understand what motivates Charles now, Tom. But you must be quite a strong person to still be so friendly to women, Tom, otherwise you wouldn't have me here, either!" She decided she needed another drink. She went to get her glass again and, as she filled it, said as nonchalantly as possible, "So, is that why Charles reacts so badly to me? Does he treat all women like that?"

Tom wasn't fooled by her feigned indifference. "Kendal, I suspect the real reason is that he's really quite attracted to you and so he's finding reasons to keep you at arm's length." He, too, went and got a glass and helped himself to a drink. "Mind you," he said, "I saw how he jumped to the wrong conclusions the first night you were here and I suspect the other things he's told me about you are just as imagined."

"What other things?" After Tom's disclosure that he considered his son attracted to her, Kendal's voice was sharper than she'd intended.

"He told me he first saw you when he stopped for petrol and a drink at Miles on your way out here, and that in a very short space of time you'd been all over some old man and then you walked right off with another young man instead of going on the bus." Tom quickened his pace to stop her interrupting when he saw her indignation rising. "He saw you again having a noisy party with yet another lot of young men at the Charleville Motel and then he thought you were busy seducing me as soon as you walked in here." Tom laughed, trying to lessen Kendal's obvious dismay. "You're an attractive girl, Kendal, but I think Charles is giving you too much credit. That's surely too many men to get entangled with in such a short space of time."

Anger and amazement made it hard for Kendal to get her words out. "Bloody hell, Tom, how could he! How could anyone believe such rubbish? I'll kill him!"

Tom set about pouring oil on troubled waters. "Don't get upset, Kendal, don't get too upset. Maybe I shouldn't have told you, but it might help you know what's bothering Charles."

Kendal banged her hand down on the bench in the kitchen. "Damn him! Why should I bother to explain it all to that bloody man? He'd never believe it anyway." She turned back to Tom, determined to make him know the truth. "I'm not promiscuous, Tom. He's misunderstood everything that's happened and I wasn't doing any harm in Charleville. I shared a room with Thea. You saw her when you met me in Juno with Bruce Thompson. I've never gone from man to man in my life!"

Tom was quick to reassure her. "You don't have to explain yourself to me, Kendal. I can trust my own judgment and you're quite a special young woman." Then he smiled. "Charles might think I've got a bad track record for making judgments about women, but I believe in you."

Then he leaned forward and said confidentially, "Actually, I think Charles is so impressed with you that he doesn't trust himself to stay away from you. So that's why he keeps having to find fault with you. He finds it necessary to think the worst."

Tom's last words extinguished Kendal's flare of temper. If anything, she felt a bit winded. Could Tom be right about Charles's feelings for her? She needed time to think, so she rose and put her glass in the sink. "You, at least, are very nice to me, Tom," she said. "I'd better go and get my clothes out of the washing machine or I'll have nothing to wear next week. Thanks for this heart to heart."

Tom didn't seem to realise what a shock all his confidences had been to Kendal. "I'm looking forward to meeting Rick, Kendal. Do you think he'll like it here with me?"

Kendal no longer thought of advising her brother not to come. Charles wasn't here all the time, so Carmody Plains did need a manager. He'd be OK here with Tom. Tom was a nice old bloke.

"He'll love it, Tom," she replied. "You're a really top bloke. You'll like him too. Kenrick's a good scout."

Kendal decided the best thing she could do was to get busy with her weekend jobs. First, she'd hang out her washing and, while it was drying, she'd go across and service her bike. So, she hung out her first load of washing and put on the next load. Then she walked quickly across the grass and onto the gravel that surrounded the sheds and garages.

She wheeled her working bike out from under the cover of the old slab barn and she heard someone moving about in the garage where Bill-Bob kept his gleaming machine. She smiled to herself. Men were really crazy about their vehicles and Bill-Bob was a great example of it. That road bike of his was always being overhauled. She wheeled hers towards the garage shed to get the tools and the oil she needed.

As she walked into the workshop, she said casually, "You still playing around with your baby, Bill-Bob? You'll polish that chrome right off it one day." She was not surprised there was no answer from him. She thought he was playing cagey, disdaining to answer her teasing. She found the oil she was looking for and turned around to face him, trying to think of a teasing comment smart enough to make him answer her.

But what she saw caught her words in her throat. "Bill-Bob!" she cried, running to the old man, who was slumped on the ground, grey-faced and breathing very heavily.

"What is it Bill-Bob?" she demanded frantically, as the old man struggled for breath. "Oh God, what is it? Is it your heart? What can I do? Have you got your spray?" She could see he was trying to talk and leaned closer to him.

"Spray... on my table..." he managed.

Kendal needed to make sure she had the right directions. "Your heart spray – you haven't got it with you?"

Bill-Bob shook his head.

"It's on the table in your quarters?"

As he nodded, Kendal pulled him up into a sitting position and leaned him against the wall. She'd heard it was better to sit up with heart problems.

"Stay there," she said. "Stay there and keep breathing. Don't worry, I'll get it. Hang on in there, Bill-Bob."

She ran out to her bike. Thank God she hadn't started to pull it down yet. She kicked it into life and took off faster than she'd ever ridden a bike.

"Hang in there, Bill-Bob. I'll go as fast as I can. Please God, keep him safe until I get back. Hang in there, Bill-Bob." Almost like a mantra, the same thoughts desperately played around Kendal's mind as she swerved full-tilt into the driveway of his quarters, and threw herself off the bike, leaving the engine running.

She pushed the door of his room open and looked into the spotlessly clean and pristine room. The little spray was quite obvious on the table, marked BB Carpenter.

In one motion, she picked it up, shoved it in her pocket, and raced back to the bike.

Still talking all the time to herself – and to Bill-Bob and to God – she raced back to the garage and inside. Bill-Bob was still alive but seemed barely aware of her presence. She sprayed under his tongue and propped him up again. When he began to breathe more easily and his colour gradually improved, she ran across to the house to call Tom.

Minutes later, Bill-Bob was well enough to refuse to let them call the Flying Doctor. Still sitting propped up against the wall, he glared at Tom and Kendal, and Charles, who'd joined them. "I've had these turns before, that's why I have the spray. I refuse to go anywhere. You can't move me without my permission now I can talk. Give over, I won't go."

Unconvinced but unwilling to upset him further, the best they could do was take him to lie down in his quarters. Kendal sat beside him. He told them to clear off and leave him alone. He made such a fuss that they reluctantly agreed to leave, if at least one of them could stay. He would only agree to have Kendal. Surprised, but happy that he'd at least been willing for someone to stay, Tom and Charles reluctantly left.

After a while of resting, Bill-Bob started to talk to her. "You know, it was the queerest thing," he said slowly. "While you were gone, my whole life flashed through my mind. Just like you hear about. All sorts of scenes from my whole life went through my mind. The really odd part was that you were there, Kendal. All the time you were there, every single scene you were there – and you had no right to be. Can you imagine it? There I was, a child with my sisters and brothers, and yet you were there standing by my side, all the time. What were you doing, Kendal? How did you get into my life so completely?"

"Goodness knows, Bill-Bob," Kendal said gently. "I'm just glad that you didn't die."

"Are you, Kendal? An old man like me, there's not much need for me to be alive any more."

His calm manner alarmed Kendal. "Don't say that, Bill-Bob. What a sad thing to say." She tried to change the mood. "I once

132

read that there is one sure test to see if there was still work for you to do in this life."

"Well, don't keep me in suspense," Bill-Bob demanded good-naturedly. "What is it?"

"If you're alive – there is," Kendal replied.

"Well, very clever," he acknowledged. "I'm probably – very probably – only alive because you kept me that way. I wonder what you need me to do, Kendal?"

She looked horrified. "Don't give me that responsibility, Bill-Bob." Then she smiled at him, "Just be yourself. You don't have to do anything remarkable."

No-one had ever known what Bill-Bob was thinking. He was a man who had kept to himself for so long and had fiercely protected his independence. But that afternoon, as he was recovering, he seemed to have changed altogether where Kendal was concerned.

Before she'd rushed down to get his spray, she'd never been to his quarters at all. Now, because he hadn't given her a flea in her ear, she was willing to stay, just to see he was OK and to see if there was anything he needed. In fact, he seemed happy for her to be there and certainly Tom and Charles were glad Bill-Bob would let someone stay. They'd urged Kendal to stay and look after him as long as he would let her.

Kendal found that he was really quite fascinating. Everyone had indicated Bill-Bob was obviously an educated man, but Kendal hadn't realised just how interesting he could be. It made all the more sense of the stories of his really close friendship with Ethel Alsop.

Tom had told her in the past that Bill-Bob only had two treasured possessions – his powerful motorbike and his equally exceptional radio. Everyone said he kept abreast of all the national and international news by radio, but she only knew this by repute. Despite her best attempts, Kendal had never really had a good talk to him. It had been a game with her to try to trick him into saying anything at all.

And now it was all different. It seemed their roles had reversed. Bill-Bob now asked her questions and drew out her opinions on a wide range of subjects. Kendal was amazed at his knowledge and interests, and equally surprised he wanted to talk to her. She didn't want to let him overtire himself, but rationalised that by staying and talking she was keeping him quiet and in one place.

Most things about the man surprised her. For one, why was such a well-educated man living almost a pauper's existence in outback Queensland? His living conditions were spartan, although spotless. The area outside his hut was bare earth, swept clean – a sight Kendal hadn't seen outside old houses since she was a little girl. Tom had told her before that he'd invited Bill-Bob to live at the homestead long ago, but that he wouldn't even consider it. So now she felt she had his confidence, Kendal dared asked him some questions, too.

"Why do you choose to live down here by yourself, Bill-Bob?" she started. "Why don't you live in the homestead with Tom? With only the two of you, it would be more friendly."

"I like it better here," was his quick retort.

"But it's so primitive. So bare. Why don't you have some comforts, paint the walls and grow some grass..."

"Hey, hey, hey," he interrupted. "Just let me decide how I want to live." For a few moments, it looked as if that was all the answer he was going to give her. Then, not looking at her but almost staring into space, he started to talk. "One of the great philosophers said true wealth is not needing anything. I decided I agreed absolutely. If one has clothing, food and shelter, all the rest are extras. I have my extras, too. A machine that will take me a long way in a very short time – should I decide to go anywhere, and I occasionally do – and I have another machine that lets me listen to anything I care to hear.

"Apart from that, what else do I need? That little library in Juno has all the books I can read – they can get me anything I ask for from Brisbane. I like to be clean and I like to be tidy. I can see the grass and the planted trees up at the homestead. Here I can just step out the door and I'm in the bush. I want nothing else from life than what I have."

Kendal was impressed, but still curious. "Well, you must admit it's unusual. Most other people want a lot more. Do you despise other people for wanting more?"

"No, not at all. Maybe the best I can say is that when I think about the way other people live, I actually feel sorry for them. Always wanting more and more. Always needing something. Always needing someone."

"What made you like you are, Bill-Bob?" Confident by his tone that he wouldn't mind more questions, Kendal voiced her opinion.

134

"There must be some reason why you feel so differently from everyone else."

"You think so, Kendal?" He looked at her searchingly for a moment. "You're right, of course. There's always a reason, isn't there? I've kept my thoughts to myself for so long now I'm not in the habit of sharing them. Actually, I've been thinking about a lot of things lately – and that might include talking to you."

He suddenly seemed to regret getting so confidential and said briskly, "Right now, though, girl, we'll have a cup of tea."

He started to get up to get it and Kendal pleaded, "Please lie down, Bill-Bob, and let me get it."

The old man was resolute. "Nope, I'd rather get up," he said. "Can't lie around all the time."

Thinking, 'God preserve us from independent old critters', Kendal merely urged him to sit on the verandah. "I'll put a chair out there and I'll get the tea. Don't make me feel useless."

Finally, Kendal convinced him she could find her way around his quarters. While she couldn't get him to lie down again or sit on a chair, he did at least sit on the steps. He liked to sit on the step and look out across the backwater of the dam. He took the tea and she put a plate near him with some dry cracker biscuits she'd found in a tin.

She took her tea and sat on the edge of the verandah, but he didn't talk much for a while and any attempts she made he turned aside. She wondered if he was regretting his previous burst of talk, or if he was thinking of his close call. To break the silence, she hopped down off the verandah and wandered over to a myall tree nearby and broke off a little branch. She idly pulled off the leaves, one by one. Finally she asked, "What's on your mind, Bill-Bob?"

He looked up at her and, with no preamble, said, "Kendal, how much affection do you really have for Charles?"

Embarrassment made Kendal burst out with laughter. "Hey, Bill-Bob, that one's hitting below the belt. You used to hardly ever talk – and now that you've started, you think you can dash right in and ask really personal questions? Spare my maiden blushes!"

But Bill-Bob wasn't laughing. "No, Kendal, actually I'm deadly serious now," he replied. "I've been watching the two of you, and for once in my life, I've decided to step in and try to influence others. This is something that means a lot to me."

Realising the old man was a bit embarrassed, too, made Kendal more embarrassed still. She was very fond of Bill-Bob, but she had no desire to drag out her feelings to look at them herself, much less discuss them with someone else.

She still hadn't decided what to say when he started to talk again.

"I'd hate to see the two of you upset each other and stay apart if it is only some silly misunderstanding between you," he said. "I know you both pretty well now and I'd like to see you get together. I've known Charles a long, long time and I know how he's been upset by quite a few women. I also know he's deeply in love with you, Kendal, but he's been hurt so many times in his life that he doesn't find it easy to let himself love. And to tell you the truth, you're the only woman around him that I'd be prepared to go to bat for."

Kendal stood still, with only her eyes moving as she looked questioningly at Bill-Bob and away. Her hands still held the denuded branch and she started to break off little pieces of the stem and drop them at her feet.

Bill-Bob started to talk again. "You've often hinted around that you'd like to hear my story and I'll tell you a bit now, lassie. It's got a bearing on what I'm asking you, and I've got my reasons for telling you now. I was young. I had plenty of money and there were plenty of girls who made it quite clear that they would be happy to help me spend it. There was no lack of friends and acquaintances in my life. I lived in the city with city folk, but I only had one idea in life – and that was to go bush. Go bush I did, and we hit one of those times that we all know so well. Bad seasons and bad prices. Things weren't all that bad for me personally, but my mother had never wanted me to go out west and she used to really rant at me that I'd made a bad mistake. Somehow, from her talk, all my friends got the idea that I'd lost all my money and my oh-so-willing companions became oh-so-busy elsewhere. I was still young, and at first I was badly hurt and confused. I was anxious to assure everyone that things weren't that bad – particularly one special girl. The more I talked, the more it only seemed to convince everyone that things were indeed really bad, and that one special girl I had thought of as my own made it very clear that I was no longer all that special to her."

Kendal had seemed to disappear from Bill-Bob's view, and she could tell he was talking almost as though it was all happening before him. She couldn't think of anything to say, and didn't want to stop the flow of his reminiscences.

"So I went back to the bush like many others, a sadder and wiser man. Various other things have happened to bring me where I am today." He looked up at her and changed his pace. "I'm not sorry, mind. I've had an interesting life. It probably seems isolated to you and to most people. But it's been pretty good, really. I'm naturally an introvert and I enjoy my own company. I listen to the radio and hear the news of the world and I listen and watch the people I meet. You'd never take me for a people-watcher, but because I don't talk a lot, I listen. And I could tell you a great deal about all the people around here. That's why I know about you and Charles."

Before Kendal could respond, Bill-Bob was away again in a time long gone. "I go away to Quilpie and I listen and watch there, and I also go back to Brisbane or Sydney at times, and I can tell you the fortunes of all my old friends and acquaintances. I know who has prospered and who has not, who has lived a life of private hell in a disastrous marriage that looked good in the beginning and who has found happiness. There are those who have conquered adversity and those who have been defeated by it. I've watched it all. It's not so hard to watch all this from afar." He paused. "And why am I telling you all this?"

Wondering herself at Bill-Bob's sudden flow of confidence, Kendal just nodded a bit.

"I'm fond of Charles and I've watched you carefully these last few weeks," Bill-Bob went on. "All I've experienced and noticed about you has pleased me. There is every chance that Charles will do as I did, so many years ago. He'll end up convincing himself he's better off on his own and denying himself the chance of a family life. Now if he didn't have the right girl, he would be better off – I believe that all right. But marriage, when it works out, is the best arrangement. Marriage and children, family life. I'm also sure that you are the right girl for Charles."

Shocked by his decisiveness, Kendal said nothing. But she wasn't prepared for his next declaration.

"I've decided now that that is why you saved my life today," Bill-Bob said. "There had to be a reason, and this is it. I was ready to die and all my life had been lived – but in every scene in my life, there you were, urging me to live. So now I'm alive and God alone knows how much longer I'll have. But I've decided that this extra time was specially granted so that I could help you and Charles."

He continued. "You love him. It's very obvious, but he hurts and confuses you. Everyone has their problems. He's been plagued by a lifetime of devious, scheming women and he doesn't understand your open, frank and loving ways. He suspects your motives when you're only being your exuberant self."

Bill-Bob was so close to the mark that Kendal could almost feel the prickle of tears in her eyes. She blinked, determined not to let her emotions show to the old man.

"I'm telling you to trust your feelings," Bill-Bob said. "I'm going to tell him it's time he used his brains and stopped thinking the world is populated by only treacherous females, and thank his lucky stars he's met you."

Kendal could hardly believe what she'd heard. Bill-Bob could see this and gently continued. "You didn't think I could talk so much did you?" He chuckled quietly. "I'm quite a philosopher at heart. So now I have all this sorted out, don't go willing me to live, Kendal, when I'm ready to die. Next time let me go."

Kendal had heard vaguely of near-death experiences, but she didn't know what to say.

Bill-Bob was pressing her, "Promise me to leave well enough alone in future, girl," he urged her. "I need your promise."

She didn't like this at all. Bill-Bob kept at her. He was determined to organise his own death the way he'd lived his life.

Reluctantly – and hoping the decision would never come down to her – Kendal gave the old man her promise. "I will, Bill-Bob," she said. "I hope I never have to, but I will."

Bill-Bob was satisfied and fell silent. Before long, Kendal had convinced him he needed an early night. She found him quite cooperative and got him ready for the night. She left him, reasonably certain he'd be quiet, and she went back to the homestead.

Thoughts of Bill-Bob's near-death, his announcements about Charles and herself, and even Tom's disclosures from the day, kept her quiet and introspective for the night. Tom and Charles didn't pry. They, for their part, were wondering how to get Bill-Bob to live closer to the house and safe from harm. It was a quiet night at Carmody Plains.

Chapter 12

She'd left Bill-Bob early, so Kendal had a long evening ahead of her. With plenty to think over, she sat down with her sewing again.

It was Kendal's habit to keep her hands busy while she thought. Not that she had the time or the inspiration to design anything, but it was the ideal time to finish off some garments she'd already started and machine sewn. The repetition of making tiny hand stitches was a good contemplative job.

As well as beautiful clothes, Kendal loved silk underwear and she often bought remnants of really attractive, expensive silks and made elegant garments for sale, and for herself or friends. Tiny pieces of underwear didn't take up much room in her suitcase and she never went anywhere without a few pieces of handwork in case she had time to sit and sew. Some people meditated, Kendal sewed. She found in it all the things she needed – a challenge, fun to do and soothing to her soul.

There was plenty to think about. For one, Bill-Bob had put her mind in a whirl. There were also Tom's comments, and the fact Rick's leg was finally on the mend and he was coming out soon. So she didn't have long before she'd have be leaving Carmody Plains.

Kendal wondered what her next move should be. When she was in Brisbane, she'd been happy enough to stay there. She loved her work with fashion and it would be exciting to see if she could make a living from it, or, dare she hope, do really well. Somehow, being out here and all that had happened and been said had unsettled her a lot. Part of her wanted to stay and see what eventuated. There was no way she'd ask Charles if she could stay at Carmody Plains, even after what Tom and Bill-Bob had said – or perhaps especially after what they'd said. Anyway, that would maybe interfere with Rick's job and she'd only come to Carmody Plains to safeguard that. Nevertheless, so much had happened since then and she had to try to work out how she felt herself. There was no harm in admitting to herself that she'd been very happy in lots of ways. She would love to live on a property again.

And then there was the big one, the attraction of Charles himself. Her relationship with him was very much in her mind most of the time. He had such a powerful effect on her that she found it impossible to believe it was all one-sided. She was quite sure now that the magnetism flowing between them had to be dynamically activated from both sides to be so strong. Both Tom and Bill-Bob obviously thought so, too. What did Charles think?

Perhaps the only trouble was his reluctance to admit to himself – let alone her – that he felt this way. She knew that she felt differently at times. Sometimes she was dying to confront him about their relationship and make him admit there was attraction there, while other times she felt it would be better to forget it and get as far away from him as possible.

"Maybe that's what he's thinking," she thought to herself. "Maybe he thinks that if he keeps his distance long enough, I'll be gone and he won't have to face it at all."

And, of course, there was that wretched other woman in his life. Tom didn't seem to know about her — or at least he must have made a point of leaving her out. Bill-Bob hadn't appeared to consider anyone else. But then again, Bill-Bob was a very sick old man, and Kendal couldn't be sure how much of what he'd said was fantasy and how much was considered thought.

Nagging in the back of her mind was the thought that she had a few of the pieces of the whole jigsaw of her relationship with Charles, but that she couldn't quite put them together. Besides, every time she thought of Charles ordering flowers for that woman, she just felt too wretched to examine it thoroughly.

At least her chat with Tom had helped her understand where the Porsche fitted in. She hadn't thought to ask Tom about it during their conversation, but she'd obviously seen the businessman Charles before his transformation to the countryman Charles. She made a mental note to ask Tom where the car was kept. It couldn't be like Cinderella's coach and turn into a pumpkin when Charles changed into a country boy, so it must be somewhere.

She sighed. There were too many questions about Charles and not enough answers. So she turned her thoughts to Thea and how her little friend from the bus would settle down in the west. She'd been speaking to Thea every now and then and it seemed Thea had found her niche at Kalanoa.

Every conversation with Thea seemed to reveal she was revelling in country life.

"I'm really becoming a bushie, Kendal," Thea had announced just recently. "At first the really muddy-coloured water was a bit of a shock, even after you warned me. But now I'm quite used to it. Apparently most people have muddy water from a dam or a creek. Do you have dirty water? I'm an old hand now. I know all the different taps in the kitchen – the one for the drinking water and the one for dam water, as well as the hot tap. Mum is a bit worried that it might ruin my clothes, but everyone else seems to manage all right and so can I. Miss Thompson is a lovely lady and she manages, so it must be all right. Bruce says I adjust very quickly."

It did sound as though Thea had been on a steep learning curve since she'd arrived. Kendal had heard all about the owl scaring Thea silly on that first night, but she was pleased to hear Thea relay how she was enjoying the bush sounds.

"The birds wake me up every morning," Thea had told her. "At first, I didn't like it much. All the quiet and stillness and then the sounds so loud – and Mum said perhaps I'd better get another job where everything isn't so strange and frightening – but I've come to love the bird calls and I try to see if I can tell which ones I can hear. In the mornings I get up really early and have a cup of tea in the kitchen with Bruce. He makes a cup of tea for his Aunt Bessie and takes it in to her, and then we sit in the kitchen and listen to the early morning sounds. He helps me to identify the different bird calls. We sometimes look up that *What Bird is That* book together. Of course, he's very busy and he doesn't always have time to talk for long in the morning. But it's nice when he does."

Bruce and his little girls had also been a hit with Thea.

"Bruce said we'd go into town soon," Thea had announced soon after she'd arrived at Kalanoa. "Bruce said the girls like me, that he's never seen them take to anyone so quickly. I love the little girls too, Kendal, they're so sweet. You know, Bruce said he'd teach me to drive soon, but that I'd better not think of going too far away on my own."

Kendal had thought then that there were nearly as many 'Bruce saids' as there had been 'my mother saids' on the bus coming out. She wondered if Thea had learned to drive yet. It would be interesting to watch what developed in that relationship between Thea and Bruce.

The next day was a real scorcher and by the afternoon it was getting steamy. There were heavy clouds and it started to feel sultry and oppressive. At times there were gusts of blustering wind that in the heat really did feel like blasts from a furnace.

Towards evening there was a stillness and a strange ominous light that made the countryside look a most unnatural green and almost fluorescent. Each tree stood burnished starkly and isolated in the glowing light. This was the beginning of a magnificent *son et lumiere* performance, orchestrated and choreographed by the master of the most spectacular effects, God himself.

At first, in the stillness, there were a few flickerings of lightning in the distance and hardly a sound. Gradually it built up more and more in all directions – the light flashes getting closer and closer and the accompanying clash of thunder growing from piano to forte.

The wind, as Ballet Master, started a small rustle in the trees, a ripple in the grass. Gradually it increased the tempo until there was a definite shiver through the trees and a shimmer on the grass. Finally, with increasing noisy passion in the eerie, flickering light, the grass and the trees and every movable object danced to its direction with reckless abandon.

But all these effects were wasted on this particular audience, who were tired and had work to do.

"Do you think there's anything in it or just another of those bloody dry storms?" one of the shearers asked.

"I don't know," was another's rejoinder. "Could be something if we're lucky."

"You can see a bit of a downpour here and there, not much about," Curly grumbled to Kendal. "Be lucky if you get under anything I'd reckon. Bloody dry bastard."

The strange light made it difficult for Donna to judge the wool properly, so by five o'clock the classer had closed the shed.

With the wind growing increasingly fierce, Charles asked Kendal to help him get the sheep branded so he could take them out.

"Then you can get up to the house and do the chores," he said. "Make sure the old man and Bill-Bob aren't out in this – it could be dangerous. There could be a bit of stuff blowing around and branches could fall off some of those old trees around the house."

He looked at her with concern. "And for Christ's sake, girl, watch yourself."

Kendal lost no time. She checked on Bill-Bob first, but Tom had been there before her and everything was fine. After a few words, she battled to do all the outside jobs.

There were plenty of extras this evening. The door had come open on the meat house and it was slamming wildly. *Bang! Bang! Bang!* She secured that. Some empty boxes usually stacked on the back verandah were blowing about the yard. She collected them and put them in the laundry.

Then it started to rain – just little pitter-patters blowing in gusts of wind. It was hard not to get excited and beg, 'come on rain, come on'. A frog joined the action and a deep *croak-croak* came from out the back near the kitchen somewhere. A higher pitched *knee-deep* came from along the verandah. It must have been in the garden bed along the side.

Was the rain getting a fraction heavier? If it was, it was still hardly enough to wet the ground. The air had been so dry and it was so hot that it was evaporating before it had time to soak in.

There were still plenty of jobs to do and as Kendal battled the wind she thought, "It'll probably be past before I even get this finished. Then I'll have wasted all this time, but just in case..."

She struggled on until she thought she had everything in control and nothing dangerous was blowing about. Then she hurried in out of the wind.

She had just gone inside and was taking her boots off when the phone rang. Tom answered it and Kendal couldn't help overhearing him. He was making soothing noises on the phone but with a touch of exasperation in his voice.

"Just take it easy, my girl, take it easy, no need to cry like that."

Kendal guessed it was Thea.

Tom went on. "These blustery storms aren't all that bad. Keep the children inside. Don't worry about the animals, love, just keep the children safe. No good taking risks with them. You'll be OK."

He looked thoroughly exasperated and then said quickly, "All right, settle down, girlie, settle down. I'll get Kendal for you."

Kendal sighed. She didn't like talking on the phone with lightning about. She always feared that lighting could strike the line and the electricity could be travel along the line and kill or injure anyone using the phone. God knows what these new phones did.

Were they better or worse? A bit reluctantly, she took the receiver from Tom.

"What is it, Thea?" she said, a bit abruptly. "I'm not keen to talk in a dry storm like this unless it is an emergency."

"It is Kendal, it is!" Thea was crying and the words were jumbled. "This awful storm and the worst thing is the geese are just going berserk. Instead of sitting down, they're rushing about with their babies all around their feet. They are going to walk all over them and kill all those baby goslings and I can't stop them." She sniffed and continued, "And the ganders go for me every time I go near them."

"Where's everyone else, for God's sake?" Kendal asked impatiently.

"They're all out." Thea was starting to calm down. "Miss Thompson and Clara went to town and Bruce and Sam are still out on the place somewhere. I was doing so well, I thought, and I've been so busy. I've done all the jobs and stopped things blowing about. The house is all closed up and dinner is well under way." She started to cry again. "But there is always something I can't handle. Kendal, I can't bear it knowing that those little babies are surely going to be trampled to death."

"Thea, I am sorry." Kendal tried to talk calmly to her. "I can't suggest anything and if you've got everything else done, you're doing a pretty good job. These storms can be scary – you can see for yourself even the animals go berserk a bit. Hang in there, you'll be OK."

"I thought you'd know what to do," Thea pleaded. "You always know everything. I'm the one that can't cope in an emergency."

"Come off it, Thea. If you've done most of the jobs and have the kids OK, you've done a mighty job and you'll just have to get used to the fact that no-one can do everything. Sorry, kiddo. There's nothing that I know of that you can do." Kendal hung up the phone.

Tom looked at her. "She's pretty hysterical, that girl. Are those kids safe with her?"

"From what I can tell, she's got everything in hand pretty well," Kendal replied.

They both winced as a flash of lighting struck nearby, accompanied by a particularly loud crack of thunder.

"Crikey, that was close!" Kendal laughed. Then she said thoughtfully, "Actually, Tom, she seems to have everything going well. She's not worried about herself. What she's really upset about is the geese are going berserk and she's scared the goslings are going to be trampled. That's the goose's fault, not hers. The stupid goose isn't sitting down with her babies under her, she's rampaging about. There's nothing Thea can do. The ganders won't let her anywhere near. They can be pretty vicious, those ganders."

"Is that what's worrying her?" Tom looked surprised.

"Yeah. Everything else seems to be OK. She's a perfectionist and thinks she has to do everything, but there's one thing she can't be. She's not a mother goose..." Kendal trailed off as Tom had stopped listening and was going back to the phone.

He dialled and Kendal wondered what he was doing. She was interested and quite unashamedly stayed to listen to what he might be going to say.

"Thea?" he began. "Tom Carmody here again. Are you having trouble with the mother goose and her goslings? Is that your trouble?" He listened.

"Well, get a broom. A straw broom and a wool pack or a heavy rain coat or something like that... yeah, and a big box or a carton. Doesn't matter exactly what, just something pretty heavy, but not too heavy so that it won't hurt the birds.

"Now take the broom and drive the ganders together. The goose shouldn't worry you too much. When you have them together, throw the coat, or whatever, over the ganders and quickly pick up as many goslings as you can and put them in the carton and take them inside. If you don't get them all before a gander gets out, don't worry, just bring what you've got in, get your broom and do it again."

He listened again.

"A blanket might be too light. The ganders might get out from under it pretty quickly. But see what you've got and do the best you can. You'll be OK, girlie, I think you just might do a pretty good job."

Kendal was most impressed with Tom's idea. She hadn't had a clue what to do but it seemed pretty obvious once she heard him say it.

Tom for his part was quite impressed with Thea.

"I thought she was just a silly hysterical kid ringing up because she was frightened of the storm," he said. "But she's OK. She listened and caught on pretty quick." He nodded, pleased. "She might be OK that one, after all."

"I think so too, Tom," Kendal said thoughtfully. "She's pretty new to all this and she's the sort who likes to really know what she's doing to be comfortable. But she's obviously a quick learner and willing to have a go, though. She'll probably cope pretty well as time goes on."

She grinned at him, "We'll make a bushie of her yet. Is there anything else you want me to do or can I have a bath now?"

"Most things are in hand here too, young lady," he replied. "I think I can hear Charles's bike coming, so you'd better hurry if you want the bathroom first."

Since his bad turn, Kendal often made time to go down to talk to Bill-Bob.

Now that she'd broken the sound barrier with him, he'd talk to her and she found he was a very interesting man indeed.

"People tell me you are quite an authority on the old aborigines, Bill-Bob," she said to him one day.

"People say anything," was Bill-Bob's characteristically short reply, but his eyes twinkled.

"Come now, Bill-Bob," Kendal wheedled. "That's the sort of answer you would have given me ages ago. Can't you just open up a bit more?"

"You're taking liberties, I think, my girl. Give you an inch and there's no holding you. You expect a fella to talk away like a threshing machine on any subject you choose."

Kendal didn't say anything but sat quietly, letting Bill-Bob grumble, hoping that he'd eventually run of steam and then just keep on talking. She knew her mark and before long he was cooperating.

"They're a fascinating lot, you know," Bill-Bob began slowly, fingering the handle of his tea mug. "Poor devils, they're caught between the devil and the deep blue sea now. Every time anyone does anything to help them, they only make it worse. It'd take a man with the wisdom of Solomon to ever solve the problem and there's not many of them about now."

They sat in silence for a while, and then he went on.

"There were so many different tribes. The coastal fellas had quite a different lifestyle from those out here. Might as well talk about the customs of the Scandinavians and the Mediterranean people as one." He thought for a while. "There's lots of people around here you could talk to if you're interested. I'm interested in the big picture, the overall, not the details. Just as an onlooker, girl. I've sat and listened and looked all my life, and watching the unfolding story of the indigenous people has been part of the picture. But, young John McMahon now, he's really interested in the details of their way of life, how they did things. Of course, there's no-one much to tell him any more. None of the old blokes are around and none of the young ones know anything much."

Kendal was startled at Bill-Bob's assertion. "Is that right? Aren't the young ones interested?"

"That's right," Bill-Bob nodded. "Hardly any of the young ones around even want to know the details about their old way of life."

She interrupted. "Come on, Bill-Bob, I'm not sure I can accept that. Give me an example of what you mean. You can't say something like that and then generalise."

"You're determined, aren't you?" He thought for a moment, and then went on. "Well, John has been trying to find out how the old people were able to get resin from spinifex for hafting their spearheads onto the shaft. He's read about it, but can't figure out how to get enough for the little blocks of resin the old fellas apparently carried about with them." She'd asked for details. Well, he'd give them to her. "The shaft was made from young mulga or gidgee and they put a groove in the end and they'd use the spinifex resin like glue to stick on the stone end. Then they wound sinews from a kangaroo or a wallaby to bind it in place. Sometimes they used lawyer vines or even human hair. Different tribes used slightly different techniques, according to local conditions. As I said, John's information comes from books, not people. No-one has been able to actually demonstrate how it was done."

She still wasn't convinced. "Has he asked around?"

Bill-Bob was exasperated. "Kendal, this is his abiding passion. He's obsessed with it. He travels fairly widely around every time he hears there's someone who might be able to show him. Most people know about boomerangs and didgeridoos, but not these other details."

"Well, fair enough," she said, struggling to adjust her ideas in the light of this information, "why do you think this is so?"

"They are like every other young person. They want to experience life – now – as it's happening. You know, fast cars and grog and getting on with life. I mean, think about it. How many young people do you know who are interested in their family tree? It's the old people who want to pursue things – usually after they'd ignored it all their lives and then suddenly they want to know everything and wish they'd listened when they were young."

He took a sip of his tea. "You know, there's one person around here who really does know something about it all, and that's old Sam from Kalanoa. He was almost brought up by an old aboriginal fellow, they tell me."

Kendal was fascinated. Everyone had always told her that Bill-Bob knew everything there was worth knowing. "Is that a fact?" she said to Bill-Bob, encouraging him on. "Tell me more."

"Well, it's a long story," Bill-Bob continued. "Sam practically grew up on Kalanoa and there was this old fellow out there. They were really close, those two."

"So, why doesn't John McMahon just talk to Sam about the old ways?" Kendal interrupted. "Surely Sam would be able to give him some good information."

Bill-Bob smiled at her. "You know, I heard once that there's always a simple answer to any complex problem – and it's wrong. Don't know who said it, but they were right. It certainly applies to the whole Murri problem and it applies to Sam and young John."

Kendal might have known there'd be complications.

"Sam and John's father, Fred, were boys together and they never hit it off. Sam had a problem – that's why his family sent him out here, out of the way, as a kid. He can't read, you know, and Fred never left him alone about it – teased him rotten. To tell the truth, Sam doesn't talk about his tribal knowledge at all, and if he ever did want to discuss it, it wouldn't be with a McMahon."

Kendal decided to make the most of Bill-Bob being in a talkative mood. "Will there be any trouble with native title around here?" she asked him.

"That you can bet on," the old man said. "Most people feel sorry for all the problems the original inhabitants of this land have had to suffer. Then add to that the fact that Australia wants to look good in the eyes of the world and look after its indigenous people. Plus, there's the fact that it's very easy to give away rights to someone else's property, just as long as it isn't your own land, of course. As long as the cities where most of the voters live aren't in trouble, then anything can happen. Start to think about that picture. There'll be terrible trouble out here unless we're very lucky."

Kendal appreciated Bill-Bob's strong feelings, but didn't understand the logic behind it. "But will it really matter to the graziers out here if a few of the Aborigines want to come out and hunt and fish?"

Bill-Bob was outraged. "Dammit, girl! That's a typically stupid comment. Have you really thought it through? How would it grab you if you were out mustering and suddenly heard shots around you? They don't hunt with spears any more, you know." Kendal blanched. Bill-Bob went on angrily "I can't believe you said that, girl! Don't you understand at all? What's to stop them actually coming out hunting and fishing now if they want to? Lots of them have arrangements on different properties."

He was ready to lecture her. "Just for argument's sake, let's say they do come out – as a right, not by arrangement. Apart from tragic accidents what happens if they leave the gates open and mix up the stock? Who sorts them out? Who pays for the labour? Let's say bulls get in with the heifers. Who pays for the heifers who die in calf? What if it rains when they're out there and they all get bogged on their way to town? Who fixes the roads they ruin? God knows we have enough trouble when we have a new young man on the place, much less unknown numbers going anywhere with no reference to each other."

He looked grumpy and tired. "You annoy me, just mouthing the mindless stuff that's said by people who don't understand and couldn't care less as long as it's not their lives or personal property affected," he said. "You'd better go and find something better do to than annoy an old man who should be resting."

Kendal took the cue that it was time to go. She was sorry she'd irritated Bill-Bob, but even more than that, she was concerned not to make him too tired, as well.

But a few days later, she managed to get Bill-Bob going on Aborigines again.

"There's plenty of people around here to talk about native title if you're really interested," he said to her. "For example, you'll get two very different stories from the Carmodys and from Tony next door. Tom, now, he likes all the facts, so he reads all about it and keeps up to date with Hansard."

Kendal couldn't help herself. She interrupted. "He reads Hansard? Whatever for?"

"For the same reason as anyone reads Hansard," Bill-Bob said. "Just because he lives out here doesn't mean he can't take an intelligent interest in his country. Actually, he can quote you precisely what people have said about this whole issue over the years."

Kendal was amazed. "I've never heard him talk about it at all."

"Don't suppose it comes up often in everyday conversation and Tom only talks about it when he's at a grazier's meeting or with someone who'll listen instead of just mouthing off. Now, take our next door neighbour, the good-looking Tony. He hates the blacks, as he calls them, and he won't listen to reason at all. No good getting into an argument with him. He and Tom have agreed to differ. You'll hear Tony go off at the pub, but never at Carmody Plains."

"I wonder if he'd talk to me," Kendal thought out loud.

Bill-Bob shrugged. "The pub's the place to go to hear him carry on," he said. "He's got plenty of mates there. There are lots of blokes who hate all the special treatment that Aborigines get. They feel that plenty of other people had it tough. After all, most of the early settlers didn't want to come. Take the MacFarlanes, now, Tony's great-grandparents. They were part of a group rounded up in Scotland, put on a boat and sent to Australia with practically nothing, virtually only the clothes they stood up in. This was the time they called the enclosures in Scotland, when all of the crofters were put off their land and sent out of the way. There were plenty of Irish sent over at the time of the potato famine and lots of them were political prisoners, too.

"They all had to start from scratch and work for years to put a bit of stuff together. Old MacFarlane decided to try his hand out bush and brought his family out here. His wife drove the dray, loaded up with the baby and what possessions they had by then. MacFarlane rode a horse to drove his few stock and his oldest son, who was only about seven or eight at the time, walked all the way behind the stock.

"Like a lot of others, they built a bit of a bark hut with a dirt floor – you can see the sort of thing at the Stockman's Hall of Fame. But they kept at it. Put up with unimaginable hardship and eventually built up a good place. The women taught their kids, grew their own vegetables to keep them healthy, milked cows or goats, kept chooks and did their own doctoring. Some women had to learn all this from scratch. Their old way of life was destroyed, but they didn't just sit around and watch their kids die because their way of life was changed. They had to organise their own water supply – no-one put in tanks and taps for them. No-one does even yet, for that matter. All the places have to organise their water themselves. This is self-help or perish country."

"Are you trying to tell me that everyone out here has had it hard?" Kendal asked.

Bill-Bob shook his head. "No, that's not the truth, either. It's a bit like life anywhere – it's always infinitely varying. Some came out with pots of dough and lost the lot. Others came out and prospered. Some came out poor and stayed poor, barely eking out an existence, while some came out poor and did very well. The ones who drew a block and had good seasons and good prices did fantastically well. Those who drew a block and had a run of rotten seasons and poor prices, or had too many floods and fires, might have slaved for years for virtually no reward at all. It's like all of life – you play the hand you're dealt as well as you can, but there's no guarantee in this life. But it's pretty certain that if you don't try, you won't get anywhere."

He was warming to his subject. "That's the problem with the Aborigines now," he told Kendal. "Everyone is telling them that they're disadvantaged and that the world owes them a living – and I reckon that's a sure fire recipe for disaster. You need a purpose in life and a sense of self-worth to succeed and be happy. Tell anyone that he's a poor, misunderstood soul and get him to sit around and wait for money from heaven, and he'll do what a lot of Aborigines do today – sit around and die of hopelessness. We need to give them a sense of purpose.

"All of this land rights business is crazy. If one tribe gets a claim on an area – and around here they're fighting with each other about who has the proper claim on most places – how can that help those who were dispossessed around Port Phillip, Sydney Harbour or Brisbane? Lots of Aborigines lived there and very few out here. Life was tough for them out here the same as it is for us, it didn't support many people. If they ever grant title here, it still leaves most of them dispossessed and how will that work? If they really want

151

land, the government's already allocated one point four billion dollars to buy significant land."

Kendal came in quickly. "But they want land that is special to them. Just the way I like to worship in a particular church."

Bill-Bob sighed. "That's what I said, significant land. But that's not all they're asking for. They're claiming huge areas, not just their sacred places. You can't tell me this can be sorted out easily. I'd just love to see them all have a chance to buy what land is of particular significance or as close to it as they can and let that be an end to the matter. To let people make claims anywhere, any time, is just too disruptive. How can that possibly work?"

Kendal realised she had a lot to learn about it all.

But the next day, her life took a startling change that drove all other thoughts far from her mind.

It started when Tony came over late one afternoon. The homesteads weren't all that far apart, considering the size of the properties, and Tony was fond of company. He was practically an honorary member of the household at Carmody Plains, and was always welcome to join them for a meal at night.

He was just arriving that evening when he saw Kendal coming down from the shed where she'd parked her bike for the night. He gunned the throttle a couple of times to make the bike roar and get her attention. She looked up, and when he was sure she'd seen him, he couldn't resist putting on a show. He opened up the throttle and pulled the bike onto its back wheel – showing off his trademark, flamboyant wheelie. It might have impressed Kendal, except he hit an old galvanised pipe that was no longer buried but lay across the top of the track. Tony felt the bike skid on the pipe and flung out his arms, but he lost control and his balance soon followed. He flew backwards, hitting his head on the ground with a thud, the bike falling on top of him.

Kendal saw it all happen, and was running over to lift the bike within seconds of the accident. Tony was lying on the ground, dazed, and his arm was bleeding badly. It looked to be a fairly small cut, but it was obviously pretty deep by the way the blood was pouring out. Kendal fumbled in her pockets to see what she could use to stem the flow. She ripped the plastic off a pack of tissues and folded them in half to make a pressure pack, and then bound it on tightly with her handkerchief. Luckily, it was one of Rick's big ones and not just a dainty, feminine one.

She was watching his arm carefully to make sure the pressure was stopping the bleeding when Tony started to come around. He hadn't been out cold, but was dazed and disoriented by the impact.

As his senses returned to normal, he realised what had happened. "Golly, that was close," he said ruefully. "It must have been quite a sight, the bike catapulting like that!" Then he noticed his arm, and that blood was splattered all over Kendal's arms and hands. He was already pale and clammy from the fall, but now he broke into a visible sweat.

"Oh my God, Kendal, is that my blood all over you?" He buried his head in his hands. "God, what a mess!" He turned away from her, berating himself. "You stupid, bloody, dangerous fool!" he said over and over.

For a moment Kendal didn't get it. She thought that it was some strange overreaction from the hit on his head. She listened to Tony and looked at her hands. There were plenty of cuts and scratches from her work and plenty of blood splattered over them. Surely he was overreacting? She remembered how dentists' assistants always wore gloves, and slowly, she started to freeze. A cold chill started at her feet and spread right up her body. Thoughts of the consequences of infected blood, of AIDS, tore through her mind.

Tony looked at her with his usually cheerful face contorted in anguish. "Oh God, Kendal, I'm so sorry. I'm HIV positive. You shouldn't have touched me. I'm not worth saving. I'm a social pariah." He went on vilifying himself, becoming more and more distraught.

Kendal was shocked – both for herself and at the depth of Tony's distress. She tried to pull herself together because she feared Tony in his distress would knock the padding off his arm and maybe blood would be all over the place again. She put her arms around him, partly to restrain him and partly to calm him down. "Tony, please Tony, don't carry on." It all seemed terribly surreal, except for the sick, sinking feeling Kendal felt in her stomach.

"I shouldn't be around other people," Tony said again desperately, struggling away from Kendal. "I'm a danger to everyone. I couldn't live with myself if I've infected you."

Kendal tried again to calm him. "Come on, Tony, come up to the house and we'll both clean up."

Tony vehemently shook his head. "No way. There's no way I'm going up there now. I'm not fit to be around decent people. I couldn't sit there and look Charles in the eye, knowing what I've done to you."

Despite her best efforts, Kendal sensed her voice become more tense as she fought off panic. "Come on, Tony. I need a wash and you do, too. There's no way we can tell if I've been infected and there's nothing we can do about it now, anyway." She looked at her hands. "I've only got a few small cuts and scratches."

"Yes, you go and wash," Tony agreed immediately. "I'll take off so I don't hold you up and you go and have a good wash. There's nothing else to do now." He picked up his bike, and as he did so he put back his head and let out a loud bellow of rage and frustration. It was a loud, primitive roar of anguish. Kendal had never heard such a sound before, and it frightened her with its intensity. Then his bike kicked over and he was gone.

Kendal's ineffectual words of "Tony, don't go" were drowned out by the noise of his departure. She watched him go for a second and then rushed inside to scrub herself down.

Later that night, she still felt as if she'd walked into a dream sequence in a film or a hologram, her body heavy and clumsy, and her mind not quite able to function properly with everything swirling around her.

Charles and Tom both noticed the change in her immediately and couldn't work out what was wrong. To all their questions, Kendal merely answered, "I'm all right – nothing's the matter". When she asked when the Flying Doctor was next holding a clinic, they were concerned. And when she still wouldn't say what was wrong, they decided it could be women's troubles and backed off.

By the greatest of luck, the clinic was only two days away. Charles decided he needed to go to Juno that day, too. He didn't want her to have to drive in and out on her own if there was something wrong.

On the other hand, Kendal desperately wanted to go by herself. She didn't want to have to hide her feelings from someone else all the time, particularly Charles. She wished she could confide her troubles in him. He was the epitome of the strong, silent male and she'd love to have his strength to lean upon. But how could she tell him Tony's secret, or her dread? And anyway, if she tried to tell him she thought she might have acquired HIV from Tony, how would he think she'd caught it? Oh, no. She could just see Charles putting two and two together and coming up with quite an answer.

Because there was so much she needed to know and because she couldn't talk to anyone, time was suspended and dragged on. Eventually, the days passed, and Kendal found herself in the car travelling to Juno with Charles. It was time to go to town, to a tiny little dot of civilisation in the middle of nowhere where she had an appointment with fate. Was she living with a death sentence or not? She wasn't even positive what had to happen. She thought it was a blood test straight away and one three months later, but she wasn't sure. Three months! It was a long time to wait for a verdict.

"Dear God, help me," she prayed on and off during the trip. "And help that damn silly Tony. He looks so well..." She wondered if she, too, faced Tony's future.

Charles wondered what was worrying her but when she only answered him abstractedly, he stopped trying to make her talk.

Finally, it was her turn to go in to see the doctor. It wasn't the usual doctor, she was told, but a fellow doing a locum. That was all right with her, because she'd never met the regular doctor and she thought all she needed was a blood test.

But when Sean Fowler, the young locum, asked her cheerfully, "Well, what can I do for you?", Kendal didn't know where to start. Hesitantly she eventually managed to tell her story.

Sean mildly mentioned the importance of wearing gloves when carrying out first aid and Kendal jumped on his comment bitterly. "That's all very well, but that doesn't help me now," she said. "Besides, what was I supposed to do? Walk inside to get a pair of gloves while Tony bled to death outside?"

Sean looked up with interest. "Who was it that you were helping?" he asked.

"Tony MacFarlane," she replied.

"Oh," was his only comment. Sean had been opening the packet of a new syringe and adjusting the needle, but now he stopped.

Kendal noticed his reaction and became even more frightened. Her face drained of colour and she felt herself begin to panic. What did he know?

Sean realised he had inadvertently frightened the lass even more. He was in a bind. She seemed such a nice girl and was so frightened. Did his medical ethics have to extend to keeping her in a state of panic unnecessarily? If this nice young kid knew the score, perhaps she could help Tony.

While Kendal agonised, Sean's training and common sense fought it out for supremacy. Finally, he decided to tell Kendal the truth.

"Kendal, do you know Tony's story?" he finally said.

She nodded. "Sort of," she said hesitantly.

His next words were reassuring. "The first thing I need to tell you is that there is practically no chance at all of you being infected. Sometimes when people are in a particular emotional state, they can imagine troubles for themselves that have no substance in reality."

Kendal interrupted, almost stammering in her relief. "W-what are you saying?"

Sean looked thoughtful. "This is in strict confidence, Kendal, so that you can best deal with the situation." He waited for her nod and her acknowledgement before continuing. "But I meant what I said, that you have no need to be concerned about your welfare. Tony MacFarlane has had a particularly traumatic experience. He came out of prison convinced he was HIV positive. What happened to make him feel this way we can only surmise. But whatever it was, it must have been extremely traumatic. Together with trauma, shock and the guilt from the car accident, it's left him completely irrational on this issue. He comes in here for test after test after test. They're always negative, but he's never reassured. A few months later, he comes back again."

He paused to allow Kendal time for the news to sink in. "Unless he's been putting himself at risk in the last few months – and because of his compulsive belief in his own contamination I am convinced he'd never do that – you are completely safe. This illness is just a figment of his imagination. A recurring nightmare, but imagined, nonetheless."

The news left Kendal dizzy with relief. After 48 hours of agony, she could hardly believe she had the all-clear. Yet she had to be sure, absolutely certain, so she asked Sean to go ahead and do an HIV test. She needed a negative test result to finally put the whole issue to rest. Sean happily complied, as it was the correct thing to do, although he still assured her the risk of her contracting HIV from Tony was so slight it couldn't even be measured.

156

Walking outside to meet Charles, Kendal could hardly believe her luck. She had expected to be living the life of a sleepwalker for three months while she waited for the final test. Now she felt as though she could see colours, hear sounds, feel the air on her skin... be part of life again, in fact.

Part of her, recalling her terror, understood how the fear of AIDS could cut Tony off from reality. Even now with what seemed like an all-clear, she still felt strangely under a shadow. No longer an opaque wall of terror; just a shade of shifting doubt. All the same, she was so light-headed with relief she was almost giggling.

Tony's plight occupied her thoughts for some days to come. When she felt she'd recovered from the fright, Kendal tried ringing South Pines to talk to Tony – he needed a friend. There was no answer.

Tom told her Tony took off without warning "every now and then".

"He's a law unto himself, is our Tony," Tom said. "I heard there was the blur of that black Porsche of his roaring through town on Tuesday – the day you went to the doctor, I think it was. That's all we'll see of him for a while, now."

Kendal nodded. So that was that. She was likely to be gone by the time he returned. She wondered what had called him away from his property.

Tom's answer had resolved another question for her, too. The black Porsche was Tony's, not Charles's after all. Charles must have been just having a turn at the wheel when they first saw each other at the roadhouse.

"How easy it is to get the wrong impression," Kendal murmured to herself.

Chapter 13

Kendal's last Saturday at Carmody Plains arrived and it was the night of the Quick Shear.

Still a bit fragile and battered by events, Kendal didn't feel much like going but she did want to have one night out with all of her shearing friends before she left. Perhaps a night out with lots of people about would help her get back to normal, she reasoned.

Sheila, Donna and Kendal walked into the hall together. It seemed to be ages since they'd been away from the station. There is no doubt that a long period of isolation gives the most ordinary gathering a sparkle and makes the most mundane outing exciting. Sheila was delighted with the occasion, the whole outback experience was great as far as she was concerned. She was dressed to the nines to make the most of the number of good-looking fellas around. Donna, for her part, was more down to earth. She'd spent the last few years of her life going out to the sheds and then back to town. Besides that, she was really interested to see how the Quick Shear was organised and how the local shearers, the ones she knew, would stand up to the outside competition.

As they looked around the hall, there were a lot of people about – some they knew and many that they didn't. There were quite a few of the fellows they knew from Carmody Plains. Charles and Tom were already there, and not surprisingly, Charles was already talking to Bruce. As soon as she saw Bruce there, Kendal looked around to see if she could see Thea. Sure enough, there she was with a group of older women halfway down the hall. She didn't appear to be absorbed in their conversation and spent more time looking around.

"I'm going over to see my friend from the bus, Thea," she said to Sheila and Donna, who were busy looking around. "She's new to all this and probably doesn't know anyone yet. I'll bring her back to meet you."

Thea was delighted to see Kendal and hugged her enthusiastically. "It's so good to see you," she exclaimed. "You said you were coming and I've been looking out for you."

Kendal returned her embrace warmly. They caught up for a few moments before Thea turned and introduced Kendal to Miss Thompson and her friend, Mrs Alsop.

"I'm so glad to meet you at last," Miss Thompson said. "Thea has spoken about you quite a bit. How are you enjoying Carmody Plains?"

The two ladies were easy to talk to and lots of people stopped to say a few words as they passed. Soon Kendal and Thea were quite busy meeting new people and chatting away.

People that Kendal knew were passing by too. Dan Flannigan nodded as he passed, scratching his beard as usual.

Ethel Alsop said, "I can't abide that great galump of a fellow. He's always dirty and scratching and," she rolled her eyes, "you just wouldn't know what was living in that beard."

Bessie Thompson laughed good-naturedly. "Come now, Ethel, you know it's Saturday. He would have had a bath tonight."

Ethel didn't look at all impressed. Thea didn't have any idea who he was or what Bessie meant, but Kendal was amused.

Their attention was taken from Dan when Tom Carmody came along with Sam Hastings, and the two men stopped to talk for a moment.

Bessie asked Tom and Sam if they were going to have a go at the Quick Shear. "You know, show the young ones how to do it?"

Tom just laughed. "No," he said, "our days are over for that sort of thing."

Sam had obviously put a few drinks under his belt already and was unusually talkative. "If it was horse sports now, I'd still give these young ones a run for their money," he boasted. "Once we all got out there of a weekend and rode our horses for sport. Now they don't ride at work and don't even have time to train their bloody horses."

He looked at Ethel and immediately said, "Pardon me, ladies." Then he was off again. "The sheep still have to be shorn but, so now they do this to amuse themselves. Bloody good night..." He caught himself again. "Pardon me ladies, it'll be a blood... a good night, yes, a good night. Yes, I reckon it'll be bloody good."

159

Poor Sam. The more he tried, the more he tripped himself up, much to Kendal's and Thea's great amusement. He obviously didn't want to swear in front of the ladies, but his tongue was a traitor under the influence of a few drinks. Before long, Tom decided to put an end to his misery and escorted him over to a group of men where Sam didn't need to watch his vocabulary.

Kendal lost track of all the people she was meeting, but two women interested her in particular because they both had daughters. Jean Johnson had a large family of boys and one girl, and Margery McMahon had a couple of quite young sons, plus two older children – a daughter, Wendy, and a son, John.

Jean told Kendal she was happy that Wendy was coming home from boarding school soon. Wendy apparently was all for staying at home and not going on to study further, but her mother thought it would be good for her to have training in something and not just come back to the property. Jean was interested in Thea's and Kendal's opinions.

Meanwhile, the Johnsons had a different problem. Their daughter, Sally, was working in Brisbane and they hardly ever saw her. They knew she'd become very interested in a man from the Sydney office of the firm – an auditor who came to Brisbane quite often – and they were quite worried Sally would marry and live even further away.

Kendal didn't feel that she had anything terribly constructive to say, but enjoyed hearing all this chatter about other girls and what they were doing and what they might do, after all the time she had spent with the men and listening to their affairs.

After a while Miss Thompson offered to keep an eye on Bruce's children, and encouraged Thea and Kendal to meet some other young people. So the two young women went off together and joined quite a large group of people around their age who were gathered together.

Sheila was having a ball. She said to her friends, "This is the place to be. The room's full of men and not many of us girls." There she pulled a face, "But I wish that Tony MacFarlane was here though, can't see him anywhere. I'd really like a dance to get close to that fella."

Donna laughed and said, "You and every other girl who's been around Juno. He's such a great bloke and soooo good looking. We were all sorry when he was taken out of circulation by Elspeth but all the single girls are getting hopeful again now. Some of the married ones aren't beyond making a play for him either!"

Kendal wondered how long it would be before Tony was back to normal. The main topic of conversation was the Quick Shear competition – who were the visiting guns and who had a chance locally. The newcomers were content to listen, watch and absorb the talk and atmosphere around them.

The bar was open and Thea and Kendal were soon plied with drinks.

Thea was very interested in the proceedings, and didn't seem to notice Kendal was a little quieter than usual. She told Kendal they hadn't had any shearing at Kalanoa yet, and so it was going to be a novelty to her. Thea was also keen to watch out for Bruce, who was going to have a go.

This news grabbed Kendal's attention. "Bruce?" she asked. "He's having a go?"

"He said he was," Thea replied.

Kendal was curious. "Is he any good?" she questioned further.

Thea nodded emphatically. "Of course he is," she said loyally. "He's pretty good at everything."

Kendal tried to hide a grin. "I might have known you'd say that," she thought to herself.

Donna, agreed with Thea. "She's right at that, he's pretty good," she put in. "He does a bit of shearing. Most of the young cockies do now, you know. All of them need money. Shearing makes for a good cash income." She remembered Sheila's main interest. "Tony MacFarlane doesn't – he flies his gyro, as you know, and makes extra money mustering, mostly." She thought of another one they knew. "Charles doesn't, either. He's away with his business too much." She looked around the crowd and pointed out a few of the fellows as she saw them. "Bruce does a lot, and all those Johnson boys do." She thought again. "Except Brendan doesn't in that family; he makes silver jewellery."

Kendal was amazed. "He does what?"

Donna laughed at her reaction. "He makes jewellery. Don't look so surprised – quite a few fellows do, you know. They're supposed to be quite good at welding and other techniques they need to do it. They have to be a bit artistic too, I guess."

She continued looking around the room, surveying the talent. "Getting back to the shearing, one of the Johnsons – Barry – is

161

really good. He'll probably be one of the close contenders. Actually, Curly will be hard to beat, too. But there are quite a few strangers here tonight who fancy themselves. We don't know much about them yet. These competitions are fairly new, but they're getting to be pretty popular. There's big money in it if you do OK, you know. Some fellas are starting to follow the competition already."

Stumpy went past and Donna caught his attention and asked, "Can you see that David Short bloke here that they're all talking about?"

"Yeah, he's over there." Stumpy scanned the room. "Or he was a moment ago. Yeah, there he is – the short, dark bloke in the navy singlet."

While Donna sized up the competition, Kendal was left to think over what Donna had said. Things had changed in the years since she'd lived out here. The implication was that no young men were left working on their properties full-time. But what was going to happen to the properties if only the bare essentials were done and no-one was there to attend to the regular maintenance? Until then, she hadn't really understood that people were so desperate to find some sort of cash income. Maybe Donna was exaggerating. She'd just watch a bit and see what was happening for herself.

Down the front of the hall, a big, burly fellow with a sprinkle of grey in his hair took the mike.

"All right, folks, let's get this show on the road. Can you all hear me?" From his mannerisms and speech, it was clear the MC was a shearer from way back.

"Well, welcome to the first ever Juno Quick Shear competition, and I'm sure at the end of the night you'll all agree that it won't be the last one," he boomed in a loud, confident voice. "I'm Joe Markwell and I'll just go through the rules for you here now. This is just a speed contest. The winner is simply the bloke who can shear his sheep in the fastest possible time. The only other rule is it has to be to an acceptable shed standard."

"And who's going to decide that?" shouted one of the larrikins in the front. "You?"

A few comments weren't going to put Joe off his task. "Don't worry about that, folks, we've got a team of three judges out the back. Our judges aren't here to worry how they get the wool off those sheep. Their only concern is the end result. We time them in here and then the judges will examine the sheep outside to see that

162

the sheep isn't cut around at all and that the wool is off to an acceptable shed standard."

He waved his hand over to a box with six big lights set in three rows of two. "See those lights over there? Well, there are three green lights and three red lights there. Each of the three judges awards a red or a green on each sheep. If he thinks the sheep is hurt in any way or that it isn't shorn to an acceptable shed standard he gives a red, otherwise he gives a green. Three greens, that's OK, but three reds and he's out. Two greens will get him through and two reds will see him out as well. So you see, the judges don't even have to watch the shearer in this competition. They just examine the sheep after it's shorn. Show shearing is different, but this here is Quick Shear, and that's what we're doing tonight."

Joe turned his attention to the competitors. "We count you in – three, two, one, go! – and off you go. When you've finished, you pull the rope to stop. Don't worry about the sheep – that's where it's very different from the sheds. We've got officials here who'll look after the sheep. Just pull that rope. You're timed from when you pull the rope to start to when you pull the rope to stop."

The rules over, Joe launched into a long list of local and big name sponsors. Pretty soon, the competitors were all wearing the same singlets, courtesy of a major sponsor.

First up for the night were the veterans and Joe kept up the patter as the first competitor walked forward. "Our first contestant is a local lad from way back," Joe began, and a big cheer drowned out his words. "Jacko Walker. He's been shearing around here since Adam was a boy. You ready, mate?"

Jacko nodded.

"He's ready!" Joe glanced across the room. "Time keepers ready, judges ready?" There was a wave from the door. "OK, folks, let's count him in. And get ready to cheer your local man. Three, two, one, GO!"

The crowd obliged and whistled and yelled, and Joe, the professional organiser, kept up the hype on the mike. "Go man, go! Give him a buzz! Get behind him, folks!"

Then he yelled at Jacko, "Leave the top knot – leave the top knot." Joe turned to the crowd, egging them on, "He's going well – he'll break the minute here." Then to Jacko again: "Pull the rope, man, pull the rope!"

Jacko was slow to pull the rope and lost a few seconds. The officials efficiently grabbed the sheep and passed it out the back to the judges. Jacko stood around, not quite sure what to do. The crowd was quiet for the moment, too, not sure what happened next.

Joe kept the patter up. "Holy smoke, what a ripper!" he enthused. "But wait for the official timekeeper!" A tall lank boy loped over to Joe. Joe raised the pitch a notch higher. "1 minute and 15 seconds! Well, he's set a good time for all you fellas. Now we just have to wait for the judges' decision."

Rowdy, from the team at Carmody Plains, came in from the back and went to work at the official light box. One green light! Two green lights! Three green lights!

"He's in!" Amid cheers and yells from everyone, Joe kept it going. "Next fellow up. Another local. Give the local a cheer, folks." The crowd obliged.

"Now you know the rules," he told the contestant, who was shuffling from foot to foot. "And don't forget to pull that rope. Right. Three, two, one, GO!"

Again the crowd urged the contestant on, with Joe keeping up his repartee. "He's a bit nervous, so take your time, mate. Take your time," he laughed, "but hurry up! Come on, mate, you're doing well."

Joe turned to the gathering. "We'll wait for the official time," he told them. "This old-timer's a beauty in the sheds, but he's a bit nervous here with all you folks watching him. Give him a cheer, folks!" He turned his attention to the lights again. "Now, how'd he go? Here we are – one green, two green, three green lights! There you go, mate, you're in!"

The next contestant was from Cunnamulla, according to Joe, a "gun shearer" called Nugget.

"Good thing Johnny Howard isn't here in Juno," he told the crowd. "He's put a ban on guns, and with all these shearing guns around tonight, we'd all be in big trouble." The crowd obligingly laughed. Thea hadn't heard the term 'gun shearer' before and she soon found out it meant a pretty good shearer - reserved for the best in the shed. But there was no way she, or anyone else hearing it for the first time, would ever forget.

Nugget seemed to live up to his reputation, clocking in at one minute, one second – and with three green lights.

Joe kept the pace going. "Bloody beautiful job and the fastest time yet tonight!"

The four girls were talking together again, having to listen carefully to hear one another over the din.

"Can Bruce really shear as quick as that?" Kendal asked.

Thea shrugged, "Goodness, I don't know. I guess he probably can."

Donna cut in. "It's a bit different from shed shearing. But if they've got time to have a good look and see what happens, they can see the difference well enough. I reckon it was a bit tough on Jacko, having to go first."

Tom Carmody and his friend Jack Johnson, who lived next door to Kalanoa, had come up behind them and Jack said, "Serve him right for being pushy and wanting to be first. He should have waited until he saw what was happening."

Kendal's attention was caught by an older man who was serving behind the bar. He was a fine-looking man, and quite exotic, with his silver-grey hair swept back. But mostly Kendal's attention was caught because he reminded her of someone. She'd noticed him earlier, and had been wondering occasionally why he looked familiar.

So she turned to Tom and asked, "Who is that man? He reminds me of someone."

Straight away, Sheila said, "Tony MacFarlane. I've been looking at him, too, and I reckon he looks like Tony."

Tom nodded. "That's right, Sheila. That's his uncle, Arry O'Tel."

"You're kidding!" Sheila was fascinated and was openly staring at the bar tender. "Is that really Harry O'Tel?"

Kendal was confused. "But I thought Harry O'Tel would be an Irish man," she said. "That man doesn't look the least bit Irish."

Tom laughed. "What's an Irishman look like?" he teased Kendal. "No, he's not Irish. It's quite simple, really. You called him Harry a moment ago. We don't just drop the h, his name is Ari. Short for Aristotle, really. His full name's Aristotle Hippocrates Coustropolus. He and his wife Maria and his sister Nana came here shortly after the war. They were related somehow to the other Greek hotel families out here, I think. Certainly the Corones families were good to them. Anyway, they arrived and no-one could get their tongues around their fancy Greek names."

Jack broke in, "Or was willing to try, you mean," he said wryly. "Soon they called him Ari, and that became Arry, and then he was Arry from the hotel, so it was a short step to Arry O'Tel. Everyone could say it, everyone knew who it was and it seemed to suit him somehow – so that's what he's been ever since."

Kendal wasn't satisfied. "But," she said, "if he is Greek, how is he Tony MacFarlane's uncle?"

"You ask a lot of questions, Kendal," Tom commented, but obliged her with the story. "Maria Coustropolus, Arry's sister, married Ian MacFarlane from South Pines. She was a very pretty girl – dark and exotic, but very shy. All the fellows were interested in her, but Ian was completely smitten. As soon as she arrived, he fell in love with her hook, line and sinker. Before long, it became obvious she really had eyes for no-one else but him, either. The courtship took a long time. Arry was very protective of his sister. But it was a foregone conclusion from the moment they set eyes on each other. They had a long, happy marriage, too. Their only real sadness was that they didn't have a large family. Apparently she had lots of trouble. Still, they were lucky. They finally had a little boy Antonio Hippocrates MacFarlane – Tony. Such a tragedy it all happened the way it did in the end."

"Yes – but then their happiness was a bit of a tragedy for Bessie Thompson," Jack reminded him. Thea pricked up her ears at the mention of Aunt Bessie.

Tom explained. "She and Ian MacFarlane had been going out together for years. They'd always been mates and during the war years, when he was away, she wrote to him and sent him parcels and even went to Brisbane a few times to see him when he was on leave. Everyone thought they'd get married straight after the war. But instead of that, he took one look at Maria Coustropolus, and he never thought of Bessie again, except as a good friend. I don't know which would be harder – living in the district like that and having to see the love of your life marry someone else, or going away."

"Why didn't she go away?" Sheila was drawn in by the tragic tale.

"It probably would have been better for her, but her parents were old and having a bit of trouble running Kalanoa," Jack answered. "During the war, they had two sons away fighting, so Bessie was their mainstay. There was another sister, but she lived in

Brisbane. That was Sam's mother. Eventually, Josh – Bruce's father – came home but Steve didn't make it. He was killed in New Guinea. Josh married a pretty little thing who was always feeling the heat and being sick, so they would have been in a right mess if Bessie hadn't stayed at home."

Kendal thought of all the people and all the stories. Finally she turned her attention back to the shearing, and couldn't believe the speed of the shearers. Joe kept saying, "Leave the top knot, leave the top knot" and kept telling the crowd the shearers could beat the minute – but there was no way that that was normal shearing. Kendal wanted to ask Donna if the trickier parts of the sheep were shorn first. But Donna was captivated and didn't want to chatter. She didn't want to miss a trick. Every single performance absolutely absorbed her. After all, it was her world, the shearing game. They would all be talking about each and every performance in the sheds for weeks to come.

Sheila's interest was directed more towards the men than the shearing. By now, she'd moved over to near the bar and a couple of fellows were around her, talking and laughing. A pert, vivacious girl, Sheila never had any shortage of men wanting to chat her up. Kendal knew she'd be wasting her time trying to nut out the details with her.

Thea was trying to follow what was going on but she had so little background to build upon that she didn't have any opinions to offer when Kendal asked. There was so much happening that was new for Thea that she couldn't take it all in. It didn't worry her, though. She was pleased just to be in among all the activity. After all, it was the first large gathering of people she'd been in since she'd come west. She didn't have any shortage of admirers, either. What she might have lacked in Sheila's teasing ways she made up for with prettiness and daintiness.

So Kendal decided to wander outside and see what was happening out there for herself. She looked around the hall. Those in the front were absorbed in the competition, while those at the back were more interested in the bar and catching up with friends. The ones in the middle were talking a bit and would stop and watch the shearing when something exciting happened or someone they knew was on.

Kendal found it easy to edge her way through the little groups of talkers, greeting a few as she went. Finally outside, her eyes took a few minutes to get used to the half-light after the brightly lit hall, but it gave her a chance to get an idea of what was happening with the judges. She saw some men would bring the sheep out from the hall, and the judges would look at it. Then it was put in a yard straight out from the door.

Along the side of the hall they had made a temporary yard, and it was full of sheep. They seemed to be taking them from there to go into the hall. So she moved across to the yard to take a closer look. And as she'd suspected, each sheep was shorn on the poll. The head around the ears and eyes completely clean shorn. "Makes sense," she thought, "the way the fellows are racing, they could endanger the sheep's eyes or ears."

Bruce Thompson saw her there and came over. "Lost interest in it all, Kendal?" he inquired.

Kendal shook her head emphatically and explained why she'd come outside. "I couldn't believe the times. They were so quick that I thought they'd have to be partly shorn before they started racing in there."

"Yeah, it's the only way to go if you think about it," Bruce agreed. "All the vulnerable bits are shorn the day before and that protects the sheep from any bloke getting careless or cruel, carried away racing. It makes for better spectator sport, too, really. When they're racing and getting them done in about a minute each, it makes pretty good watching."

Sensing her interest, Bruce invited her down to watch the judging. "There's actually not that much to see, but you'll get an idea of what's happening," he said.

Kendal was glad to go with him. She'd already noted Charles judging and she hadn't wanted to go over by herself and look as if she was interested in him or something. Heaven forbid.

They'd just reached the doorway when the two big double doors opened out and one of the officials brought out a sheep from the hall. Charles and the other two judges looked at it carefully and a fellow came around with a box. They each placed a marble in that box, and then put their other marble in another box.

"Well, what's happening here?" thought Kendal. "If they vote twice, how do they tell?"

"That's a check on us judges and all the officials," said Charles, as if reading her mind. He looked at her and smiled slightly. "The first box is the one taken inside and the lights are worked according

168

to the colours in that box. The other one is checked to see that the colours balance against the lights. That's to see that no-one puts two marbles in and votes twice either for or against someone." He excused himself as another newly-shorn sheep was hustled through the doors.

Leaving him to his judging, Kendal started to wander back to the hall. When Sheila and Donna had first mentioned the Quick Shear, she'd been a bit disappointed her only outing was going to be to a shearing competition. But it had been as good a night as any.

But the next morning, just when she thought things were quiet again, she had an urgent call from Thea.

"Oh Kendal, I just had to ring up," she wailed. "I just can't cope any more. I'm going home. I just need to talk to a friend and you're really my only friend out here."

Kendal interrupted, "For goodness' sake, Thea, what's wrong? You were so happy last night."

Thea sniffed. "I thought I was, too, even though I didn't really understand what was happening there. That's my trouble – I don't understand things and it's too much. Everything's gone wrong and I know I'll never get used to country living and so I'm going home as soon as I can so I don't get into any more trouble."

"What trouble?" Kendal was confused. "Bruce hasn't been unkind to you, has he?"

At the mention of Bruce's name, Thea became more teary. "Oh, no, Bruce is wonderful Kendal, just wonderful," she protested. "I keep doing the wrong thing and he's so good about it, but I know I'm just hopeless..." She broke off into sobs.

Kendal waited a moment and then inquired again. Finally, Thea told her.

"Well, yesterday I was watering the garden and the phone rang. They've got a lovely garden here but it has to be watered all the time because it's so hot out here and everything dries off so quickly if you don't keep..."

Kendal interrupted. "Yes, Thea, I know that. But what happened?"

"Well, this man Ken Jensen rang and Bruce was out and his Aunt Bessie was having a rest – she gets tired going out at night without taking a rest – and so I took the message. He said he wanted to look at some sheep tomorrow – I mean, today – and for Bruce to ring him back if it was not OK. Then after I hung up, Kirsty said she was hungry and could she have something to eat. It was just about smoko time so I gave the girls some milk and biscuits and thought I might take a cup of tea to Miss Thompson. We were all busy getting ready to go out."

Kendal was thoroughly confused by now. "Thea, what went wrong?" she demanded.

"Oh Kendal," her friend wailed, "I forgot about the hose! I left it on all night and this morning there was no water. You've no idea how awful it is to suddenly have no water. Then Ken Jensen arrived to look at the sheep and I hadn't told Bruce either. So he didn't have them in for inspection. I forgot and I feel so awful. Bruce was very understanding about it, but I could tell the man was angry."

Kendal was starting to get the picture. It can be devastating to find the household is without water because of your stupidity. Water is so precious and a hose left on can be a major disaster if the supply is limited. She knew she'd had it drilled into her at an early age that taps and water were the first priority and yet it was still easy to forget. She sympathised. And then to jeopardise Bruce's sale of sheep! For someone as unsure of herself as Thea, it must all have been pretty dreadful.

Thea went on, "And Kendal, this morning, early, there was a snake. Bruce was here and he was wonderful. The cat was watching something and Bruce got up to look and it was this huge snake. I wouldn't have known to see what the cat was doing. Bruce killed it so easily. But Kendal, what would have happened if I'd been out there with the little girls? I couldn't do that." She finished off with a sob in her voice. "I can't do anything right and I'm going to go home."

Kendal tried to reassure her, reminding her of how well she'd been doing. But Thea was resolute. "No Kendal, I can't stay. I'm going as soon as I can arrange it. That's another trouble about here – it's all so far away. I rang Mum, and she agrees I should come home."

Over a cuppa with Tom, Kendal discussed Thea's decision.

"You know, I thought she was really settling in," she commented. "What she doesn't understand is that we've all done things like that in our time, as silly as they are."

Tom agreed. "It seems to me she'd be a lot happier if she didn't think she had to rush back to her mother."

Their thoughts turned to Thea's job and what would happen to Bruce's little girls.

After a bit of a pause, Tom made a suggestion to Kendal. "What are your plans, Kendal?" he asked. "Maybe you could offer to go on over there and help them out. You're obviously happy with the life out here and you'd be pretty good with kids, wouldn't you?"

Kendal didn't dismiss the idea out of hand, but she was cautious. "You mean go over to Kalanoa when Rick comes out here? Bruce mightn't want me."

Tom scoffed at that. "Why not? You'd be just as good as anyone else – better, probably. You're clean, presentable, well-mannered – if I might say so – and I'd be willing to bet you could handle children and keep them safe and happy."

Life seemed to be full of sudden decisions and changes of direction for Kendal lately. This seemed like the perfect chance to stay out west. Bruce would need a hand, and it would give her a chance to stay around until she'd given her relationship with Charles a chance to work itself out. "It might just be the perfect way to stay close to him," she thought. Maybe it would be a very good idea to look after Kirsty and Carla Thompson.

Before long, it had all been sorted out. Bruce, who'd taken Thea to Quilpie almost immediately, jumped at the chance for Kendal to help out.

So, that was it. She'd be moving to Kalanoa within a few days.

Before she left, she did find time to go down to see Bill-Bob, leaving time for a decent talk. She wanted to say good-bye and talk about a few things, and also to have a chance to hear what he had to say about Tony.

She didn't want to give too much of all her concerns away, but she'd knew Bill-Bob would be just the person she could talk things over with and maybe get things clear in her mind about Tony. And when she mentioned Tony's name casually, she discovered she was right. Bill-Bob was already concerned about him.

"He worries me," Bill-Bob told her, "as much as I worry about anyone else. I do believe in minding my own business, but Tony seems to me to be someone with real problems. I hope he solves them, but I don't think he wants to. It's almost as though he's pushing himself to his limit, hoping that his recklessness will provide him with a way out."

Kendal couldn't help but be amazed at how astute Bill-Bob's observations were. He seemed to be spot-on to her.

What saddened her was that Bill-Bob didn't think Tony could be helped. "If people want help, you can talk to them," he maintained. "But if they're not looking for help, you can't force your ideas on them. Why should you? We each have to work out our own salvation."

Kendal thought that was a pretty slack way to go about things and told Bill-Bob so.

But the old man insisted that interfering was unprofitable and unwanted. "Goodness, girl," he said "it took a pretty close shave with death to force me to change my mind on that in your case. I still feel a bit funny about having interfered in your life. Nothing's happened yet to make me think I have the right or the responsibility to interfere in young Tony's life."

"Fair enough," Kendal accepted his view. She was grateful having just talked about Tony with someone who could see things below the surface. "I'm going to miss you, Bill-Bob. You're really one of a kind. There's not many other people about with your wisdom. You are a pretty bright boy – except for your eccentric ideas on how to live," she finished, teasingly.

"Come now, Kendal, my ideas aren't unique," Bill-Bob protested. "They've been held by thinking people all through the ages."

"Oh, go on Bill-Bob, don't give me that," she retaliated. "I believe that you're some sort of lovable old nut with queer ideas of your own."

"Not so young lady." Bill-Bob pretended to be a bit miffed. "I can quote any number of eminent thinkers. Epicurus, an ancient Greek philosopher, believed that 'Wealth consists not in having great possessions, but in having few wants'. Marcus Aurelius, who lived very simply for an Emperor, said, 'Very little is needed to make a happy life. It is all within yourself in your way of thinking'."

"Even Plato – and everyone knows Plato," he said, because he could see she was unimpressed with either Epicurus or Marcus Aurelius, "Plato said, 'Self conquest is the greatest of all victories'. They are the old thinkers and you don't even have to go into all the Stoics and the Spartans. Nothing has changed, you know – so if you want more modern thinkers..."

Kendal held up her hand in mock defeat. "Whoa, there, Bill-Bob, you've convinced me! Convinced me that you've thought about this and that you really know your philosophy but not that we should all live like you believe. Who else but you thinks about these things, much less follows them? Most people like their comforts too much."

"Most people are missing the real point of life," Bill-Bob countered.

"Bill-Bob, I don't want to argue with you," Kendal said seriously. "I'm happy to believe that you have reason to live as you do, but don't ask me to agree."

"You don't even want to discuss it, do you Kendal?" Bill-Bob observed mildly. "That's OK. As I've said, I don't try to inflict my ideas on other people. Most people are happy to believe like you that I'm just an eccentric old cove. Probably I am. Ethel Alsop, now, she's a beauty. She gets right in and gives me a good debate. She's always got an opinion and is just dying to give it. We can have some right old arguments – or spirited discussions, if you will – about most things."

Kendal smiled. "I'm glad you've got someone to talk to like that, Bill-Bob. Just don't get too deep with me. I love to talk to you but this is getting out of my depth. Simpler things are my speciality. You just look after yourself while I'm not here to keep an eye on you."

She put her hands on his shoulders for a moment and they looked at each other in silence for a moment. Then Kendal quickly gave him a hug before he could protest and left.

Now that she was poised to go, there was a certain dovetailing of arrangements to get everyone where they needed to be. Kalanoa was a lot more than a five-minute car trip away.

It was too difficult to fit it in with Bruce's arrangements. Besides, Charles was going into Charleville for a graziers' meeting, among a few other things, so it seemed a good idea that Charles would drive Kendal into Quilpie. Rick was driving out. He was staying with friends in Morven for the night on the way out and would come on to Quilpie the next morning. He could pick Kendal up in Quilpie and drop her off at Kalanoa before he went on to Carmody Plains. That way, she'd get a chance to do some shopping, have her hair trimmed and whatever, and catch up with Rick before they went off to their new jobs. That seemed a satisfactory arrangement all round.

Kendal was sad to say goodbye to Tom. He'd been a good friend to her and she'd enjoyed his company.

"Bye Tom, look after yourself now," she said. "I'm glad you're going to have Kenrick here to help you. Maybe I'll be able to come over fairly often to see you – if Charles doesn't think I've got evil intentions."

"Come off it now, Kendal," Tom lightly admonished. "Charles knows you aren't the designing woman he thought you were at first."

"Perhaps, Tom."

Chapter 14

Kendal was a prey to mixed feelings, leaving Carmody Plains. She was sad to be going away, but glad to be having a trip in the car with Charles. She was excited to be seeing Kenrick again, and wondering how much to tell him about the actual circumstances at Carmody Plains.

She knew she should let him form his own judgment on the situation, rather than tell him too much. Besides, she had too many emotions involved to give a rational account. Still, Rick would read something into that, too. He knew her well, and if she wasn't her usual talkative self, he'd be wondering why.

As they drove along, Kendal felt quite shy with Charles. Except for her trip to the doctor – and she didn't count that because she'd been too distracted then – it was the first time they'd been alone together since their day out riding on that memorable Saturday. There was so much left unsaid from that day, and so much that had been said by other people. Alone in the car with Charles, Kendal knew it was a perfect chance to try to sort things out, but for the life of her she didn't know where to start.

Her mind was busy with unspoken questions.

Did he go to Brisbane much?

Would he be out west often?

Why did he send flowers to that damned Penelope Carpenter?

But she said none of that.

Charles was a good driver. He drove fast, but carefully. They left early and there were still a few kangaroos about but before long there wasn't much chance of hitting a roo. Sun up and sun down are the times when kangaroos are really active and there is every reason to be extremely careful any time at night. Kendal knew from experience kangaroos were rare on the roads in broad daylight.

Finally she thought of a safe topic. "Kalanoa is an Aboriginal name, isn't it? Do you know what it means?"

"To tell you the truth, I don't," Charles replied, glancing at her for a second. "Never thought about it, really. I did try to learn a little bit about the language – or languages – when I was growing up, but there are lots of words I've no idea about."

"Me too," Kendal agreed. "We learned quite a bit, or thought we did, at one stage growing up, but after a while you take it all for granted. You need something in particular to take your interest to keep it up."

"There's enough names about to take them all for granted – Cunnamulla, Dirranbandi, Angellala, Bungeworagi," Charles suggested.

"Yeah, we'd find out what they all meant and then just as quickly forget."

"Lalla means water to the tribes around Mitchell I was told," Charles continued. "There are lots of places or creeks around there using that – Angellala, Mungallala, and lots of others. And 'dilla' is used a lot. Oolandilla, Dulbydilla."

"You don't have any Aboriginal names on Carmody Plains, Charles – any particular reason?" Kendal was starting to feel more relaxed as their conversation progressed.

"No, not really, Kendal. Dad's grandparents took up the land in the very early days. Most of it is plainland and I believe other people called it Carmody's Plains. Gradually it became Carmody Plains more formally. Some of our neighbours and, as you know, lots of people around, have used local names for things."

"Actually," said Kendal, "I know of quite a few quaint names that sound as though they come from the native tongue and don't. One of our paddocks was called Munya and everyone thought it was an Aboriginal word. What really happened was Dad was putting in some internal fencing and creating a new paddock when I was just learning to talk. I called cats Munya in an attempt to copy the meowing sound they made. It amused Dad, apparently, and since he needed a name at that time, he used it for the paddock. We all knew where it came from and it was only when one of our friends would ask 'What does it mean?' that we realised how it sounded to other people."

Charles smiled. He could imagine Kendal as a very cute youngster. Rather than comment, he changed the subject. "Can you reach the apples in the back? Pass me an apple from the box, will you?"

Kendal was happy to comply. She found she couldn't reach it very well and so she undid her seatbelt and started to turn around to get one.

Suddenly and at first quite silently, with no warning at all, the car started a life of its own. It shot right across the road at an angle of forty-five degrees into the table drain on the wrong side of the road. Charles, using all his concentration and driving skill, fought hard to regain control of the vehicle. Narrowly missing a deep gully in the side of the road which would certainly have flipped the car over, Charles finally managed to bring the car to a halt a few feet in front of a huge old gum tree.

With no seat belt on, Kendal had been thrown around and fallen forward, hitting her head on the windscreen.

Charles sighed and put his head forward, resting it on the steering wheel. He visibly shuddered at the thought of what might have happened if he couldn't have stopped the car before it hit the gum tree.

As he caught his breath, he looked across at Kendal, who hadn't said a word. Charles was instantly snapped out of his shock, because she was slumped forward, completely still, dazed from the bump and he could see blood on her forehead.

He reached over to her. "Kendal," he said, putting his hand on her shoulder, "Kendal, are you all right? Are you OK?" He lifted her head. She looked at him, her eyes blank. "Oh, my darling, what have I done to you?"

Kendal was confused. Her head didn't really hurt much, just felt thick and woolly. Through it, she could vaguely hear him talking, and figured she must really be knocked out to be hearing such things.

By this time, Charles had undone his seatbelt and moved across towards her. Putting his arms gently around her, he turned her towards him. He could see that the blood was from a little nick on her hairline. It bled freely but it wasn't much. "Kendal, darling, are you OK? Of all the stupid things to do, to let you take off your seat belt! I know you don't think much of me, but I think you're wonderful. I'll never forgive myself if you're hurt. Talk to me, Kendal – are you OK?"

Kendal was still a bit shaky, but, blinking a bit and taking a few deep breaths, was rapidly beginning to feel better. "Yes, Charles, I'm OK, I'm all right. I felt a bit funny for a moment or two, but I'm OK now."

At her words, he pulled her close and held her tight. Then he gently kissed her hair and then her forehead, quietly murmuring, "My darling, I'm so glad. I'm so glad you're all right."

His lips moved over her hair and traced little kisses down her cheek. Finally, his lips found hers and there was no more talk.

First the knock on the head, and now this? Kendal was completely dazed. She had no idea what was going through Charles's mind, but there was no way she was going to fight it. In fact, she wanted to be held tight and keep the feeling forever.

Nothing lasts forever. They slowly drew apart, looking at each other wonderingly.

Charles was the first to speak. "Wow... well, yes... you seem to be fine. I'd better check the car."

That broke the spell. Kendal asked, "What the hell happened? What made us shoot across the road like that? We didn't hit anything. I didn't hear a blow-out. What was it?"

"Damned if I know, Kendal. But if you're OK, I'll get out and have a look. You stay here."

Kendal wasn't going to play the invalid. They both got out. Charles, full of purpose, and Kendal, very unsteady but quite determined. They discovered the trouble at the same time. By the time Kendal had steadied herself and knew she was secure on her legs, and was looking at the tyres on her side, Charles had checked his side and was around beside her. There, the back tyre was neatly sliced right around.

"Look at that!", said Kendal, amazed. "That's not just a blow-out. What happened to that?"

For all of his years and kilometres of driving, Charles hadn't seen anything like it before either. He squatted down and examined it carefully. "Here it is," he said, "it's this piece of wire. It's wrapped around the wheel shaft and the end has just cut through the tyre like a knife. It must have gone straight into the tyre then, as the wheel rotated, sliced it around neatly and cleanly. No wonder we skewed across the road like that."

He grimaced as he stood up. "Weren't we lucky it happened here?" he commented. "We're just so lucky it didn't happen on a culvert or a built-up part of the road with a sharp drop on the other side. We'd have turned over for sure – and you without your seatbelt on, Kendal!"

Kendal put a hand on his arm. "Don't worry, Charles. It's all ended OK. I'm only a bit shaken, no real harm done. All we have to do is change the tyre and things will be back to normal. It could have been a whole lot worse." She smiled like her old self. "You've always got to expect the unexpected. Makes life more interesting."

There was a pause, and then Charles put his big hand over hers. "My life is usually pretty well ordered, Kendal. But somehow you have a knack of shattering my well-ordered existence. Is life always hectic around you? At least it's always interesting."

"Seems pretty normal to me," Kendal replied, relishing the feeling of his hand on hers. "I know I love life and I'm not afraid of the unexpected. I like to grab the moment."

Charles looked thoughtful. Carefully, as though wanting to choose the right words, he said, "Maybe I've put all my love of adventure into my business deals and been too careful in my private life. If I team up with you a bit more, Kendal, I know you'll put more excitement into my life. You enjoy everything – even the simplest things – and somehow there's never a dull moment around you."

They both smiled. Then Charles moved away to start changing the tyre.

While he did – and, experienced bush driver that he was, he even had an extra spare tyre in the back – Kendal watched. She couldn't believe what had happened in the last few minutes. Before the accident, they were struggling to keep the conversation impersonal. The fright had broken Charles's resolve, and he had acknowledged his true feelings to himself as much as to Kendal.

They set off confidently once more, the atmosphere in the car relaxed. Kendal even felt brave enough to say casually, "Who is Penelope Carpenter?"

"Penny's my aunt," Charles replied at once, looking at Kendal a bit curiously. "She is the only woman I've ever had any time for – until I got to know you, of course." They both grinned. "She's my mother's sister and she's another one like you who loves life and isn't afraid of getting into things. Funny you should ask about her – only the other day she had a special dinner in Sydney to mark thirty years of working for St Stephen's hospital. And I do mean working. She was no grand lady who stood back and watched the others. That's why they had the dinner. I was sorry I couldn't go, but I couldn't leave Dad to organise shearing on his own with only a jillaroo and old Bill-Bob now, could I?"

179

Kendal was still composing herself when Charles asked, "What made you ask about her? Was Dad talking about her?"

Kendal made a quick decision to tell the truth and clear the air. "Charles, I owe you an apology, I'm afraid. The night after we'd been... out riding together, I overhead you ordering flowers for her." She glanced at Charles, but she couldn't read his expression. "I didn't know she was your aunt. I was so hurt, all I thought about was that you were sending flowers to another woman. I was jealous. So, that's why I treated you so coldly that night."

Light was dawning on Charles's face. "Uh-oh, now I see. So that's why you behaved like that. Well, I owe you an apology, too," he said. "I thought you were just being a tease and leading me on and then putting me back in my place. I guess we've got a lot to learn about being together."

"Now isn't that the truth," Kendal agreed.

They passed the rest of the trip talking away quite comfortably.

When they got to Quilpie they both had plenty of jobs to do and were busy. Charles had arranged for them to stay with friends of his who lived a few miles out of Quilpie.

Jim and Hazel were a bright young couple and they had a friendly welcome for Charles and Kendal when they got there. Another couple were also coming for dinner – a new agent in the town, Tony Short, and his wife, Vivien.

Altogether it was an enchanted evening for Kendal. Her good clothes hadn't had much of an airing since she'd been at Carmody Plains and it was wonderful to dress carefully for dinner with friends. She'd been to the hairdresser and so she'd splurged and had her hair swept up and styled. After Charles's declaration of love, she was really sparkling with happiness.

The conversation was witty and interesting at dinner and Kendal couldn't remember when she'd enjoyed herself more. Had she still been walking on eggs with Charles, she was sure she wouldn't have been able to relax and enjoy herself. As it was, she had that extra glow that comes when Eros is in charge. She and Charles exchanged glances all night. He was no longer a stranger and the room wasn't crowded – but they couldn't keep their eyes off each other. Sometimes it was a shared joke, sometimes she'd catch a glance of concern from him and sometimes just a moment when their eyes met and expressed their newly-acknowledged love for each other.

Their hosts were actually delighted to see Charles so obviously infatuated with a girl at last. Jim and Hazel were no exception to the rule that married people love to pair off their single friends. They'd commented earlier that night before Charles and Kendal arrived that they hoped Charles would one day settle down. They knew him well enough to know his deep distrust of women. Little did they know they'd be seeing an all-new Charles that night, who could relax, enjoy himself and actually flirt.

As soon as Tony and Vivien left, Jim and Hazel sent them to sit on the front verandah. They wouldn't hear of them helping to clean up.

"You two go and sit on the front verandah," Hazel insisted. "You haven't got much more time together, with Kendal going to Kalanoa and Charles back to Brisbane soon. Anyway we work so well together as a team now, we're pretty professional. You'd only get in the way."

Charles and Kendal took them at their word and drifted off together. Charles's first action was to take the braiding and the clips out of Kendal's hair. "This looks wonderful but I've been wanting to run my fingers through your hair since the first moment I saw you standing by yourself at that damn roadhouse in Miles." He gently loosened her hair and buried his face in it. Then he slid his hands up the back of her shoulders and into her hair, and gently turned her face up to his and kissed her. Leaving little light kisses all over her face, he murmured, "You are completely adorable, Kendal. You are so alive and so lovely and so soft."

Kendal felt as though she'd melt on the spot. She could listen to his gentle voice whispering her praises all night. Then he was kissing her lips gently, reassuringly. She'd been accepting his caresses, loving being loved, but slowly she surrendered to the whirlpool of sensations and responded more and more. Her lips, her tongue, her whole body became part of the passionate encounter.

It seemed a cliche, but Kendal felt as though the world had stood still for them. There were no more questions, no more doubts – just she and Charles together in a perfect blending of body and soul. Eventually, they came back to reality and stood close together, wrapped in each other's arms.

"You're quite sure you're all right, darling, after that terrible knock today?" Charles asked, untangling one arm to gently brush her forehead where the tiny scratch was.

"Charles, I'm not sure of anything at all, much less if I'm all right, after a kiss like that." She paused and put her fingers up to stroke his face. "There are so many questions that should be asked and answered and you've just managed to make them disappear completely. I'm perfectly all right while we're together like this. I feel I know you love me so completely."

"Well, I'll just have to try to convince you that I'll always be in love with you," was Charles's response before kissing her again.

The next morning Kendal was still walking on air. She and Charles said their goodbyes in private before they set off for town. They had arranged for Kendal to meet Rick at nine o'clock at the post office, and he arrived only minutes after them. Kendal was always up front and she threw her arms around him and hugged him enthusiastically. When he didn't return it as thoroughly as she might have hoped, she realised that since he was meeting his new boss for the first time, he'd rather she was less exuberant. He didn't know she was practically bursting with happiness.

Trying hard to be her most decorous, she introduced Rick to Charles and heard their polite acknowledgments of each other. The men's conversation was typical.

"Had a good trip out?"

"Yeah, pretty good thanks."

"Leg quite OK now, then?"

"Good as new."

"Keeping dry."

"Yeah, but it was pretty green around Roma coming out. The Downs aren't too bad either."

Soon Charles was ready to take off for Charleville, and he and Kendal said a suitable public goodbye. Charles farewelled Rick, saying, "I'll see you back at Carmody Plains in a few days." Then his eyes met Kendal's, and they smiled at each other, and he was gone.

Kendal felt bereft as she watched him go, but the spring of happiness still bubbled within her. It was all so new, this expression of love from Charles. She tried valiantly to stop thinking of him and to be as enthusiastic about her brother as she might normally have been. She plied him with questions.

"How is Mum? Is she still being a pink lady at the hospital? How is that working out?"

"Yes, she's fine and I think she really enjoys her life as a volunteer at the hospital. She sent you out a parcel, Sis." Rick looked at her carefully. "She's been a bit worried about you. She would like you to have gone home, not just started another job out here. You haven't said much, but what you have said has been pretty contradictory. What's been the matter with you?"

"Nothing's the matter with me, Rick," Kendal was quick to reassure. "Charles is a bit difficult to get to know and there have been times I wasn't sure about him. But I'm very sure about him now. I think he's wonderful."

Rick looked unimpressed. "What's there to be sure about? You women are funny creatures. You make a personal issue about everything."

Kendal felt a bit badly done by with that remark. Charles had definitely been the changeable one, but there was no way she was going to tell Rick about that – particularly because she wanted Rick and Charles to like each other. It was bad enough some of her vacillations had reached her mum and Rick in Brisbane.

Her mind wandered off onto thoughts of Charles for a moment and when she tuned in again Rick was saying, "I am really grateful to you, Sis, for coming out. Something else may have turned up, but this job seems tailor-made for me. What actually has Charles got to do with it all? Is he likely to take over and leave me without a job?"

"I wondered about that for a while too, but, no, you're right, Rick. He's got a business in Brisbane, some sort of computer business I think it is. Unless things change dramatically, he won't be coming out here to live permanently." She wondered to herself what implications that could have for her, but commanded herself to stop daydreaming and went on. "In the meantime, what they need is someone reliable who can learn the run of the place and take the responsibility off Tom's shoulders. You know, keep the place going for them all. You'll be ideal. I'd love to have told you all this on the phone, but I didn't want to be overheard telling you all their personal details."

She hesitated, and then decided to tell Rick a bit more. "At times I wondered whether Charles might be going to come out here to live, and at times I even wondered if I thought he'd be OK to work for. I'm sure now that things are pretty perfect, as right for you as you will be for them."

Rick shrugged. "Trust a woman to make a big issue of a fairly straightforward proposition. I was told six or seven weeks ago that that was the situation. Why did you have to do all that soul-searching to decide whether it was all right or not?"

Kendal figured it wasn't worth trying to explain things. "Forget it, brother dear. Just be glad it's all turned out OK."

The siblings talked for a bit more, with Kendal outlining her plans for Kalanoa.

Rick was a bit mystified. "Well, you've got me beat, but if that's what you want, go for it. Mum's a bit surprised, and a bit disappointed too, I think, that you're not coming home. She'll be happy, though, as long as she knows you're really happy. We weren't sure about how you were going for a while."

"No wonder," Kendal thought. She'd certainly been through a few traumas one way or another in the last six weeks. Her family couldn't help picking up the vibes.

Chapter 15

Kendal found settling in at Kalanoa quite easy. It was a very different household from the bachelor establishment at Carmody Plains but not all that different from her own early life. She'd lived in a family situation, too, with children, love, animals, gardens and lots of cooking. The girls were good little people on the whole and the family seemed to enjoy each other's company. Actually, it seemed as if the children quite missed Thea, but they accepted Kendal well.

She was usually up early in the morning sharing tea with Bruce in the kitchen, just as Thea had described. But instead of a cosy chat about the birds and the bush, Bruce's thoughts usually turned to Thea.

Most mornings, he'd go on and on at length. Kendal quickly realised he didn't find Thea's timid ways irritating – rather, it was quite the reverse. He was obviously attracted to the pretty, ethereal woman. From Bruce's perspective, everything Thea had done was wonderful. She was so sweet and decorative and vulnerable, and Bruce wanted to look after her and smooth her way.

"No wonder she'd been frightened," Bruce said, shaking his head. "She was wonderful the way she coped with all the strange sounds of the bush and all the inconveniences like the creek water and no shops." Apparently even the animals had fallen under her charm.

"A girl like you, Kendal, born and bred in the bush – well, all this is natural for you. But Thea had only been in the city before and it is just incredible how well she fitted in. She always managed to do a good job and never stopped trying to get things right. She's a determined little thing when she gets going." He paused, then looked a bit sheepish. "I'm going to go down to see her. Maybe take my little girls down for a holiday."

"I'm sure Thea would love that," Kendal said, and left it at that.

It was funny how different people reacted to others, she thought. Bruce was nice enough, but he didn't stir her emotions the way that Charles did. Yet it seemed Thea and Bruce had really hit it off.

Miss Thompson, his Aunt Bessie, was a darling, too. She was a plump, pleasant, person, with clear blue eyes, who still wore an apron in the kitchen – no jeans and T-shirt for her. Miss Thompson obviously loved and enjoyed the little girls, but they made her very tired if she was with them for too long, so she was happy to have Kendal about. Together they arranged the day. They shared most of the household jobs and Kendal was working at finishing off the correspondence preschool Kirsty was doing.

It was getting on to the end of the year, and Bruce had already made arrangements for Kirsty to start Year One with the School of Distance Education the next year. She was excited about starting school like any other little girl, and she didn't realise how different it was going to be from most school children in the world. It wasn't a novelty for Kendal, either, because she'd started school the same way, only it was called School of the Air in her day. Even though most of the equipment was different, she'd experienced isolated education in much the same way as she was preparing for Kirsty.

The play box from the preschool had lots of activities, and Carla loved taking part in these as well as Kirsty. The girls also had lots of animals around the property that they helped to look after and played with. Bruce, like all country men, had his working dogs and the children had a lovely golden labrador as a pet, called Chloe. They weren't allowed to pat the working dogs much, but Chloe lived in the house yard and was always there to play with.

They also had the chooks in the fowl yard. Black hens, these were let out at about three o'clock each afternoon and then at about five or six o'clock were fed and put back in. Each child had her own little bucket for collecting eggs. They loved collecting the eggs and were normally very careful carrying them in. They also had bantams, ducks and geese, and a turkey or two. They had two cats, Tom Kitten and Pinkle Purr. Somebody had obviously read Beatrix Potter in that family. Tom Kitten was a lively little cat and loved the children, but Pinkle Purr was an old lady and wouldn't tolerate any nonsense. The girls had learned this the hard way long ago, so they gave their pet all the respect she demanded. There were also a few pigs in a sty who ate scraps and were fed grain. They were fed each evening and the girls loved to go down there, but they were only allowed to go with one of the adults. They also had ponies to ride and that was one of Kendal's favourite jobs, to ride with the girls.

Altogether they were two lively little girls enjoying life, always talking and asking questions. They had a habit of telling long, involved stories and it took all of Kendal's concentration to follow their stories and make the right replies.

It was such a different life from the time she'd spent at Carmody Plains. There, she'd worked with men and she'd lived the outdoor life of a jillaroo. At Kalanoa, she wasn't needed as much in the paddocks; she had mostly domestic jobs. With the house, the animals and the children, there was plenty to do, and she was pleased she decided to help Bruce out.

She felt as though she was helping Kirsty and Carla enjoy a normal childhood, too. They seemed to cope well with the fact that Diana – their mother and Bruce's ex-wife – had left them. It would be good for them if Bruce could marry again. It would have to be someone who understood their life, though. A bad second marriage would be worse that no second marriage. In the meantime, although they'd had had a succession of people to mind them, they did have the stability of a loving, kind father in Bruce and a doting great aunt in Bessie Thompson.

Charles only went back to Carmody Plains for a few days after Rick had started at the property, before flying to Brisbane and on to Sydney on business. He'd rung her a couple of times from home and from Brisbane, and once from Sydney, and wrote to her at least twice a week. So there was a letter from him every mail day and there was always one from her for the mailman to take back. Letters between Thea and Bruce came and went quite regularly, too.

So far, there had been no talk of Charles coming out west again for a visit and he didn't mention his business plans to her, except in passing. Somehow there was always plenty to say to each other without that.

She was often on the phone to Rick and twice she'd visited. It was good to keep in touch with him and to have news of Tom and Bill-Bob. Sometimes if she rang and Rick wasn't in, Tom would answer the phone and they'd talk for quite a while anyway. She did like Tom, he was a great person. Bill-Bob didn't come to the phone, of course. She really missed her talks with him.

187

Rick was fitting into Carmody Plans as well as Kendal thought he would. She was glad he was there to look after her two old friends. She was also glad for Charles's sake that there was someone reliable there. It took a lot of worry off his shoulders.

She'd also tried ringing Tony a few times. He didn't answer, and for quite a while there was no news of him. Then, finally, she heard he was home again. Rick got along well with Tony. As far as Kendal could gather, Tony hadn't started any of his high-spirited tricks with Rick – but she thought that would just be a matter of time. She hoped Tony was all right. Poor old Tony – weighed down with such trauma under all that bravado. Kendal would have loved to have helped him, but couldn't think of anything to do that would help him. She didn't see him either, now that she wasn't just next door any more.

Rick himself was very happy. He liked both Tom and Bill-Bob, and told Kendal the two men were helping him in every way. It was no surprise when he told her that he found that Tom talked a lot, while Bill-Bob hardly said anything at all. "The best thing," he told her, "is to be in a place where all the vehicles and equipment are in such great order. It's really wonderful, Sis, to be working on a property where no-one's let anything get run down because they didn't have time to do improvements."

She was happy to let her brother rave on. She was glad to hear he was happy and she liked to hear about her friends. The only thing she didn't like was when Rick got started on her.

"I don't know what you were on about, Kendal," Rick told her. "Charles is a beaut bloke. I only had a few days with him before he left, and a few phone calls since, but he's excellent. He knows what he wants from me. Told me straight. He was clear and concise. There's nothing wishy-washy or changeable about him. I don't think I've ever worked for a better fellow."

Of course, Kendal was delighted to hear Charles's praises sung, but she didn't like the implication that she'd been an empty-headed female. Her wretched brother insisted on making these veiled, sexist remarks, and she didn't, nor couldn't, explain why she'd been in two minds over Charles for so long. She knew Tom and Bill-Bob would be loyal to her and Charles and wouldn't mention a word about their relationship – if, in fact, they knew anything. The only way Rick would find out about Charles was if the shearing team gossiped about them.

Meanwhile, Kendal kept the spoken admission of love from Charles to herself. She felt it was too precious and too personal to share with anyone else yet – not even with her mother, who regularly asked if there was someone special on the scene. In her most honest moments, Kendal admitted to herself she had a little fear it wouldn't last, that it would prove to be a fleeting, ephemeral thing. But most of the time, she didn't allow herself to think about that.

One thing that pleased Kendal was that while she was at Carmody Plains one weekend, she and Kenrick found the chance to sit down with Tom and talk to him about native title.

Kenrick was really interested because he hoped to get an idea of what people felt in this area. It had been a pretty fiery issue where he'd been before. Kendal, for her part, had been keen to hear him talk about it ever since Bill-Bob had told her that Tom had been following what it was all about.

Tom, as promised, did have all sorts of papers and facts and figures available. The first point he made was that it was all very complicated.

"There are so many different situations and conditions in widely different areas," he told them. "It is going to be almost impossible to have any hope of sorting it all out to everyone's satisfaction."

Kenrick asked him, "Can you tell us what is the situation in this area? On Carmody Plains?"

Tom showed them the copies of actual claims that included his property. There were four of them by four different groups of people. He said this was a common problem now that ambit claims had been accepted.

"Claim after claim is being made on land where sometimes no-one has ever seen the claimants," he explained. "To make matters more complicated, several tribes are making competing claims over the same area and they are generally quarrelling among themselves."

He explained that although it was reported and widely believed that the native title claimants only wanted access to the land to hunt and fish, the claims were practically identical and stated:

The claimants are entitled as against the whole world, to the possession, occupation, use and enjoyment of the whole country within the area of application, including
land
waters

189

artesian, sub artesian and other underground waters
flora
fauna

and that their people continue to maintain the connection held by their ancestors for thousands of years over the area of land claimed.

He produced maps showing that it was even worse in some places in Western Australia, particularly around the gold fields of Kalgoorlie and Coolgardie. "In some places, there are as many as fourteen different groups all claiming that they alone have lived on, hunted, fished and walked through that area," he said.

It wasn't hard for Kendal and Rick to see that this naturally had the effect of putting the different claimants against each other as well as the bewildered pastoralists against the claimants.

Tom went on, "It's all very, very sad and difficult to resolve. If the aboriginal claimants decided to get together and share there might be some answers, but they are having big disputes."

Kenrick asked, "Are many of these claims finalised yet?"

Tom turned up some other papers relating to hearings. "Very few claims have been heard yet," he told them. "One claim has been heard in Mitchell." He showed them copies of these original claims. The Gungarri people had claimed the Balonne, Booringa, Bungil, Murweh, Paroo and Warra Shires. "But see here," he pointed to the papers, "the Bidjara people have also claimed the Booringa, Bungil, Murweh and Paroo Shires, as well as eight other shires further to the north which clash with other claims, not the Gungarri."

He told them that when the Native Title Tribunal was to hear the case, some aboriginal objectors maintained there was no such tribe as the Gungarri tribe. There was a certain amount about it in all the local papers. He produced some cuttings.

"Well, who was right?" asked Rick.

Tom said he had no other knowledge about the details of it all. He didn't know if the Gungarri people had a bona fide claim, were bona fide people or where they lived. He only knew what was reported. At the hearing, they had apparently withdrawn most of their claim except to land around the Mitchell area.

"But the way the law stands they can reinstate their claim anywhere, any time they like," Tom explained.

"What's the aboriginal position about all this, Tom?" Rick questioned.

Tom wasn't coming into that. "You'll have to speak to an Aborigine if you really want to hear the native side of native title," he told them.

What he did say, though, was that as far as he could see, there were as many different attitudes on the aboriginal side as on the pastoralist side. He knew there were some quite genuine native claims and that there were some ambit claims, out for whatever was going.

He had copies of a letter written to the editor of a Western Australian paper by a native of the Kimberleys saying he wished the whole "Aboriginal industry" would go away, and that the average native bloke felt that the whole thing was built up by lawyers wanting money and leaders wanting a platform and bleeding hearts wanting a cause. Tom said he knew a few people of aboriginal blood who felt exactly like this, too, but he had no way of knowing what numbers of people felt which way.

"It's a hard decision," he said. "Naturally, anyone would want whatever they could get, but most of them don't want to be singled out for special treatment." But he said, as far as he could see, most of the indigenous people he knew wanted to be counted as normal people living in our society, not as someone needing special laws and handouts that separated them from the mainstream community. They wanted to be treated with dignity and respect, not as some cause to be fought for.

The laws discriminating for them were causing them as much hassle as the laws discriminating against them. There should be no place for laws based on race at all.

There were other issues, too, and Tom had all the documentation to show them – claims overriding freehold, claims on the seas and how politicians had taken a different stand on the issue in what they said in Parliament as the years went by. They stayed up talking about it all, far into the night.

There was another couple living at Kalanoa, Clara and Sam Hastings. Kendal met them pretty soon after she arrived because they were both very much part of daily life. Before long, she liked them as much as everyone else did. Both Sam and Clara were quiet and reticent at first, but then proved very interesting to talk to as

Kendal started to get to know them. Still, being private and quite shy people, they wouldn't say much in a crowd. Although the night at the Quick Shear when Kendal had met Sam after he'd had a few drinks, he'd certainly had plenty to say that night! That was an exception.

From what she could gather, Sam was some sort of relation to the Thompsons, although all his other immediate family now lived in the city. He had come out to Kalanoa when he was a lad during the war, and stayed there all his life. Clara was a Quilpie girl, whose father had been a shearer.

Kendal quickly discovered that Sam was an absolute joy to talk to. When he was by himself, she could usually coax him into talking. In the right circumstances, he'd launch into a long, funny story, usually against himself. Everyone had been fearful a while ago, for Sam had cancer, but now he seemed to have it beaten. He was due to go back for more treatment, but they were hopeful that after that it would then be under control.

Since Kalanoa was close to Juno, Bessie was very involved in the activities around the centre and had a lot of friends. She loved the CWA meetings, and her cooking and handcraft skills were renowned.

Clara, too, loved the meetings. Her specialty was making sweets and she entered in all the cooking competitions and stalls that the CWA arranged. Some of the women entered their cooking at the Quilpie Flower Show and even as far away as Charleville. Bessie loved to compete sometimes and, Kendal gathered, another keen competitor was Daisy Flannigan. Daisy's speciality was elaborate afternoon tea cakes but she was also a dab hand at preserves and pickles. Just the mention of Daisy's name was enough to get Bessie prickly. For some reason, she just couldn't abide the woman. Kendal had the feeling the antipathy went way back in history, but all Bessie would say was that she found Daisy slap-happy and unreliable.

Sometimes Kendal went with the two women to meetings in town and when she did, the two girls came along to play with any other children who turned up. If they were busy at home, Kendal stayed put and kept the household going while the two older ladies enjoyed their outing. Either way, Kendal was pretty content. Life was very busy but it was down to earth and real somehow. There was nothing artificial about it at all.

She sometimes wondered if she and Charles would end up with a household like this, if they did actually get together. It would be wonderful to make Carmody Plains a family home again. Kendal didn't know if Charles wanted to settle in the bush, or if his business interests were too demanding. If anyone could set up a telecommuting centre for working from the bush, it would be Charles with all of his computer know-how. Maybe they'd need to be in the city so he could have his business interests close at hand.

She caught herself thinking the word 'they'. It seemed pretty obvious to her that she'd faced the fact that she loved Charles and wanted to be with him always. Anywhere. She thought she'd rather live out here, but she didn't mind as long as she was with him.

One hot afternoon, Kendal looked longingly at a photo of people surfing at the Gold Coast that was on the kitchen calendar. She was cleaning up in the kitchen after Kirsty and Carla and Aunt Bessie had gone to have a rest.

When Sam came in with some vegetables out of his garden, Kendal said all the right things about the vegetables and then motioned to the calendar. "Look at that, will you? Doesn't it look great? On a hot day like this I wonder what I'm doing out here in the heat when I could be in the surf."

"That might be what you'd say, Kendal," Sam countered, "but I'd rather be here. None of that for me."

"Go on. You don't know what you're missing," Kendal replied.

"Don't I, now," Sam challenged. "That's where you'd be wrong. Gawd Almighty, I've been swimming in that there surf alright and there's no way you'd find me silly enough to do it twice."

Kendal could sense a story. She was right.

"Years ago – a good fifteen years ago, I reckon – Clara and I were silly enough to go down to the big smoke for a break. She decided we was gettin' old and needed a break like, she said. It was a silly place to go. Nothing to do. Clara quite liked it, though. I was going into this pub one morning to have a drink. I liked a drink or two then, y'know. Same as now, really. Well, who did I bloody well see on the street but Bill-Bob. You know, Bill-Bob from Carmody Plains. I said, 'Well stone the crows, fancy meeting you here!'

"Well, we had a bit of a yarn and he said, 'Well, I'm goin' in for a swim. You comin', Sam?'

"'Gawd no', I said.

"So Bill-Bob tells me I'm a silly bugger and that I can spend all day in the pub back home and I should try something different. I try to tell him I can't swim, but Bill-Bob tells me I don't have to swim, I just have to get in the water and get wet."

Kendal leaned up against the kitchen cabinet, pleased Sam was comfortable enough with her to use his normal language.

Sam went on, "Anyway, Bill-Bob nagged and nagged, and to shut him up, I thought I may as well have a go at it. I had all the gear, y'know. Clara had bought it. Pair of shorts and a lairy shirt. Even had a fancy towel.

"So, we crossed the road past all the bloody cars, and walked through a park with even more cars everywhere and down to the sand. There was a stretch of calm water that all the little kids were in, and then there was a sand bank behind that, and then a bit further out than even that were waves that were fair crashing against the sand. And, strike me, Bill-Bob tells me that's where he wants to go swimming.

" 'What the hell for?' I ask him, because, you know, I can't swim. And Bill-Bob tells me that it's the only way to swim in the surf properly, that the calm water was just like wading in a creek back home."

Sam shook his head ruefully. "I was younger than I am now and still a bit silly then, I reckon, Kendal. So I let him con me into wading through that first bit of water and we got to the far patch of sand that was high and dry out of the water. A bit of water washed over it now and then from one of them really big waves, but it seemed a fair place to stand.

"Bill-Bob raced into all those waves with all the other blokes. They'd go out and float around and then get in front of a wave and come crashing in on it. Looked like you'd have to be born in it to do that, to me. No way I was going out into those waves. But y'know, for a while I thought it wasn't too bad standing out there watching it all.

"Now and then Bill-Bob would come right into where I was standing. He'd shake the water off himself and push the hair out of his face and say, 'This is the life, eh Sam?', before rushing in again, and now and again I'd even think, 'Yeah, this is the life'."

He paused for effect, and Kendal knew a twist in the tale was coming.

"I was standing there for a while, and the water was starting to cover the sand more and more. It was only coming in slow-like, mind. Sometimes it was a bit deeper when a wave came in. Anyway, after a while the water was up to my ankles, and then up to my knees. It seemed to me to be a pretty good way to get used to the surf.

"Bill-Bob was still rushing at the waves, and finally he rode one in, right to me. 'That was a beauty', he told me. 'Right to the sand'. Then he looked around, a bit puzzled, and asked where everyone was.

"Well, I thought I knew my way around the beach alright. I'd been down a day or two, so I told him. I said, 'Mr Whippy came onto the beach and rang a big bell and they've all gone to buy an ice-cream'.

"At that, Bill-Bob yelled, 'Christ! A shark!' and he dived into that channel of water between us and the beach and swam for dear life away from me."

Kendal chuckled at the image.

Sam continued, "Of course, the water was too deep for me to follow him by wading back to the beach now, and even after an hour or so of standing on the edge I still couldn't swim, you know.

"So, there I was, just me and the shark in the ocean.

"Lucky for me, after a minute or two Bill-Bob remembered I couldn't swim. He turned around and swam back, grabbed my arm and half-drowned me as he pulled me back with him. I felt like I'd swallowed half the ocean by the time I got to shore, and when we got to the beach, I gave myself a shake like I'd seen the swimmers do and pushed the wet hair out of my eyes and told him, 'You stupid bastard!'"

Sam looked solemn. "You know, I ain't ever goin' back on a beach as long as I live. This life is good enough for me out here. That stupid Bill-Bob, well, he does go to the beach now and then, but I'm not that stupid. Clara, now, she wouldn't mind going again, and she can – but not with me."

Kendal was really tickled with this story. Sam was so serious and it was so funny, listening to his droll way of talking. "Mr Whippy came onto the beach and they've all gone out to buy an ice cream," she repeated, still chuckling.

Sam wasn't offended. He knew the story would amuse her.

"Didn't you know about the shark bell, Sam?"

Sam shrugged. "No, no-one tells you these things. I'd never been on the beach before, but I'd seen Mr Whippy."

Later in the week, when no-one else was around, Sam relayed another top story against himself. This time, it was about when he had to take a mob of sheep to Cannon Hill in Brisbane. It was before road trains were used out west, and so he had to take them on the railway.

"Well, we had this here mob and Ian MacFarlane – you know Tony's father from South Pines – he had a mob, too. We had a fair few between us. Well, we drove them normal like to Quilpie with horses and then we were going to put them on the train.

"Our sheep were off shears but the MacFarlane sheep were in full wool like, and just before we got them into Quilpie it rained – a good two or three inches it was. Well, when we got in there, strike me if the agent tells us there's no bloody train drover. Only a few hours 'til they left and they couldn't get nobody.

"So the long and the short of it was they told me I'd have to take them. There wasn't any choice. The sheep weren't used to being fed in yards and there was nowhere else to put them except on the train. Besides, I was silly enough to try anything. Anyway, by now those bloody full wool sheep of MacFarlane's were wet through and had trouble standing up. So I spent all day and all night going through them time after time, you know, standing them up as best I could."

Sam shook his head at the memory. "Well, finally we gets to Chinchilla at some unearthly hour, like two or three in the morning, and the train stops on a side line. I said to this bloke, 'What are youse doing? You're not taking any carriages off?' And he assures me, 'No mate, you're right'.

"I never had much sleep, you know, and now they was stopped I figured the sheep would be right for a while. So I thought I'd have twenty winks or so in one of the empty carriages. I had twenty winks, all right! I woke up just on daylight. Here I am in just this one carriage and the sheep are gorn! All I could say to myself was 'Holy hell'. The agent had arranged for another bloke to pick me up in Brisbane at a quarter to eleven. 'Oh my gawd', I thought, 'I'll never get out to the sale and the sheep are gone'."

Kendal loved to hear Sam's tales. He had such a way of painting a picture with his words.

Sam went on. "Anyway, I'd seen some bloke darting around and I asked him about my mob of sheep, but he reckoned he didn't know nothing about it. But he thought it could have gone through with the train about twenty to five. I told him it was a whole train full of my sheep, and his only suggestion was that I catch a fast diesel at about a quarter to eight."

He paused and explained to Kendal, "This is when the diesel first came out. But you can just imagine me. All I had was my swag and a sheep hook. Anyway, here comes the fast diesel train and I hops on and I gets to Brisbane and then I can't find the flamin' joint.

"So I thought I'd get a taxi. The driver tells me, 'Mate, it's around here somewhere' and drops me off, but you know, I can't read. So I couldn't work out where I was. I didn't see nothin' I knew.

"So I got another taxi and thought he might take me to the right place. We went round and round when, dash me, I saw a bloke who used to be an agent at home. Peter Jenkins, his name was. So I made the taxi driver stop – he was glad to get rid of me, I reckon – and yelled out to Pete.

"Pete walked over to me and said, 'There's a gentleman waiting for you', and, dash me, here was the agent I was meant to meet. All I could think of was how was I to tell him I'd lost the train? I didn't want him to think I was too much of a dill so I just says 'G'day, mate'.

"So, anyway, we gets out there and, you know, I had this yellow bloody shirt on, a real bright lemon yellow colour. Clara had bought it for me and sent it in my swag. I was the only person there at this turn-out with a yellow shirt. All the others had blue or green or grey or something like that.

"We had a cup of tea and then they start bidding away. I'm not paying too much attention like. I couldn't follow the bidding too well and then I heard this man point to me and say, 'The fella in the yellow shirt's got the last bid'. I just thought to meself, 'That B must have forgotten who I was'. I'd only just met him, y'know, just an hour or so before. I didn't know what to say. I wasn't game to cough or do any damn thing. Looking down at me boots, I thought, 'Oh my Gawd. I've brought all these damn sheep all the way down here and now I've got to take them home'. Luckily, someone else bids and he took that bid and the sheep went to them.

"So, the auction's over and the next thing he says to me is that we'll go and have some dinner. So we're eating, and I tell him that

I thought he was going to knock the sheep down to me. He just smiled, and said, 'You've got to get a bid from somewhere!'

"When it came to paying me for this train droving, I thought I'd better be honest and tell them I lost the train at Chinchilla. You know, they just laughed and laughed. I told them that up 'til then I'd done all I could to keep them up, and I asked them if there'd been any problems. They told me there were ten or twenty dead. I nearly had a heart attack on the spot, but they reckoned that it wasn't a bad number for wet, full wool sheep. The same number would have died in the paddock. I don't know about that but, by crikey, imagine losing a whole train load of sheep."

He shook his head, finishing his story with, "Give me horses any time. I can manage horses. I'm not too bad with them."

Kendal had already heard about Sam and his horse skills. She'd heard Charles and Tony talk about him and it was usually to do with horses or horse sports. Sam was always modest about his achievements, but Bruce had told her how Sam had helped nearly all the young ones in the district with their riding and coached them all for polocrosse. They'd all had a wonderful time, he said, and for most of it they could thank Sam.

Chapter 16

The weekend was coming up and Bruce offered Kendal the use of the old ute to go over to see Rick again at Carmody Plains. She jumped at the chance. She enjoyed getting over there when she could and was glad Bruce had offered. She didn't like to ask for a vehicle too often.

It was arranged she would go soon after lunch next Friday. She could finish the preschool work in the morning and then go over early so there'd be plenty of daylight if she had trouble – and she'd be there before any roo trouble as well.

Just on lunch time that Friday, Tony called from South Pines to Rick at Carmody Plains on the two-way.

"That bull you've been looking for is in my yards," he said. "I brought a mob in and I've drafted him off. I'm taking mine out now. Your fellow will be OK here for a day or so. I've got a bit of hay I can throw in the yard for him and I'll put him in the yard with water."

"Thanks, mate," Rick replied. "Should be no worries. I'll see how the day goes. I should be able to make it this arvo."

Rick got Bill-Bob to give him a hand getting the crate onto the back of the truck. He wanted to get over and back fairly quickly, he said, because Kendal was coming over.

Bill-Bob offered to go instead. "I'm no good any longer for a long day's mustering but I should be able to go next door and back in the truck."

So Bill-Bob headed for South Pines while Kendal was driving to Carmody Plains. Bill-Bob enjoyed the drive over to South Pines. He'd quite often been over in the years he'd been at Carmody Plains and he was always interested to see how the country was looking. The rain that had been around had been patchy all right – some places looked pretty good and then others were very light on. The storms hadn't gone very far.

He arrived at the yards at South Pines and there was the bull. He seemed a bit restless, probably from being in the yards by himself. Bill-Bob hadn't brought a whip or anything, so he thought he'd have a look around and see if he could find anything to prod him with – a good strong stick or a piece of poly pipe would do, he reckoned. But there was nothing about.

The house yard wasn't far away. Bill-Bob knew Tony was pretty obsessive about not letting anyone into his garden, but he felt a bit fed up with Tony's insistence on sentiment and decided enough was enough. He wanted a drink and didn't fancy sharing the trough with the restless bull, and he'd surely find something in there to help him handle the animal. So in he went.

The garden tap he found was connected to a dripper line and he ended up going into the laundry. He got himself a drink, and looking around, he found an old mop that would be just the job for poking the old bull. Then, going out from this door, he saw the garden from a different angle and he suddenly understood why Tony was so obsessive about his privacy.

"You mad bastard," he thought, as comprehension dawned. No wonder Tony had wanted to keep everyone away. He really was a different person since he'd come out of prison, and this was all part of it. "You silly goat," he muttered. "There's no future in this, Tony m'lad, no future at all."

Tony was again on the two-way. This time, he was calling urgently, "South Pines to Carmody Plains, South Pines to Carmody Plains. Come on the line, someone, won't you? For Christ's sake, someone answer! South Pines to Carmody Plains!"

Within seconds, there was an answer. "Carmody Plains, Tom here. What's your problem, Tony?"

"Tom, old Bill-Bob's here and he's had an attack. I can't find his spray on him anywhere. Can you see if you can get it and get over here ASAP?"

"Roger, Tony," Tom responded immediately. "We'll see what we can find here."

Kendal and Rick had heard the conversation through their receivers and Kendal called through, "I'm pretty sure I know where he keeps a spare, Tom. I'll get it and go over at once. You coming?"

"No," Tom said. "I'll stay here. You and Rick go over and you can let me know anything by radio. If Tony has any trouble with getting the flying doctor or anything, I'll be able to call from here."

Kendal quickly found Bill-Bob's spare spray and, like the last time, started praying flat out. It was hard not to mutter, "Hold on, Bill-Bob, hold on." But she remembered her promise to him and tried her hardest to pray, "Keep him safe, Lord, keep him safe. Whatever is the best for Bill-Bob. If it is his time to go, please make it peaceful. Bill-Bob, you old devil, go if you must. I won't try to keep you if you are to go. Go with God if you have to." Her promise got easier as she went along, and although tears were streaming down her face, she felt strangely at peace. The panic had lifted and the tension was gone, and she felt a lot calmer knowing God had the situation in hand.

"Don't be too upset, Sis," Rick said as they sped towards South Pines. Seeing her sitting so still with her face wet with tears, he was concerned for her. She'd raced into the hut for the spray, but since she'd been in the car, she was so quiet he thought she'd collapse. "Bill-Bob will be OK," he said reassuringly. "He's had these turns before."

Kendal was now quite sure that Bill-Bob indeed was all right. She had a strange, unreal feeling of peace and calm. But whether Bill-Bob was OK because he'd survived the attack, or because he'd gone to God, she wasn't sure. Whatever it was, she had to be glad for him. She felt almost as if Bill-Bob was there with her, somehow. She couldn't stop the tears flowing – nor did she try, because she barely noticed them. They were part of her release.

The trip over was time suspended. The two homesteads were not very far apart and Kendal remembered her talks with Bill-Bob about Einstein's theory of relativity and how relative time was. This trip was neither short nor long. It just was. When they got there, it was Rick who was shocked to find that Bill-Bob was dead and Kendal who was quite calm. Something had definitely happened on the trip over. She would think it through later. Now she had to help Tony and Rick do whatever was necessary. Tony, too, was quite distraught.

It was just as well that Kendal was able to be calm, because there was a great deal that needed to be done. Bill-Bob's death caused great distress to Tom, even though he knew it had been on the cards for ages now. "It's still always a shock to lose an old mate,"

Tom kept saying. "He's been living here for so long he's just like one of the family."

It was quite late when Kendal thought to ring Ethel Alsop and let her know about her friend's death. It would be unkind to let her hear it through the grapevine, and not direct from the people who had found him. Whatever their relationship was, they were very good friends and she deserved to be told first. It felt very sad and unreal to actually have to say the words, "Bill-Bob is dead".

She didn't feel like doing it. It had to be done and Rick didn't know about Mrs Alsop and she did. She steeled herself and went to the phone. She glanced at the clock. It was late. The phone only rang a few times before it was answered with a terse, "Are you aware of the time?" No hello, no salutation. It floored Kendal for a moment and she just answered, "Yes, um..."

"Well then, what's the emergency?" the voice demanded.

Kendal knew she was talking to Ethel Alsop all right. This was just as people had described her. She gathered her thoughts. It was hard to find the right words, but eventually she managed to break the news as gently as she could. But what gentle way is there to give such awful news?

Mrs Alsop suddenly sounded quite old and tired as she said, "Oh, no..."

Kendal wished desperately that there was someone there with her. Then she heard the old lady say, "Oh well. It was quick. As he wished. He got his heart's desire – but it's tough on the rest of us." Then slowly, "Thank you, Kendal. Good night..." She hung up. There was obviously no more Mrs Alsop had to say and no questions she needed to ask straight away.

Charles was lucky enough to be able to book a flight out on the Monday and everyone was counting on him to start to get things in order. Little did they know that by the time he'd get there, he'd be needed more than anyone could possibly have imagined.

The first shock was when they started to sort things out, to try to find Bill-Bob's family and next-of-kin. No-one had ever gone through his papers or belongings in his room while he was alive, of course, but naturally they had to go through them now he was dead. They did so on Saturday morning with Sandy, the police constable.

What they discovered shocked Tom almost more than the death of his friend the day before. The papers showed that Bill-Bob, the

202

loner from Carmody Plains, was really Robert Alan Carpenter, Tom's own brother-in-law. Tom's wonderful wife, Nancy – grown more wonderful when seen through the rose-coloured glasses of the years since her passing – was the little sister of this man who had come to them as a passing itinerant. They'd always thought he'd only stayed because somehow the place suited him, but now they had his diary, they found he'd made a point of coming to find his sister's family. She was the only other member of his family who had even thought of anything but an urban life, and he'd always felt closer to her than the others. He wanted a country life and was happy to make it his life's work to keep an eye on her family, especially her child. He felt one of the family and he felt like the uncle he was to Charles. That he hadn't told the others was beside the point to him, apparently.

Tom, who was a man who liked to yarn and in fact needed to talk, couldn't understand it. He couldn't understand someone keeping that sort of information to himself. Quite shattered by the situation, he really needed someone to lean on and needed Charles to come home. He begged Sandy to wait until Charles arrived before they contacted Alan Carpenter in Sydney. He just didn't feel he could stand the strain of talking to Alan on his own. Even if the police made the contact, Alan Carpenter would surely want to talk to them. Charles knew his grandfather well and it would be easier on them all if he were there.

Tom missed his friend and yet it was more. This was such a strange circumstance that it left him feeling disoriented. It also made the loss of his wife somehow fresh again and more poignant after all these years. He wasn't sure if he felt hurt and betrayed by Bill-Bob's not telling him who he really was or just shocked. He needed someone who had been with him all the years to talk it over, and discuss things again and again. So many things to go over that had happened over the years. He felt he needed Charles's help to put these new facts into perspective.

Kendal perhaps understood Bill-Bob's reasoning more than anyone else. As a newcomer, she could see it more clearly than those who had lived with him for so long. Her long talks with him in the last few weeks also helped her to know the man. She thought, after all the hurts he had suffered earlier in life, he wanted to be accepted at Carmody Plains for who he was, and not for his family ties. It wasn't as if he'd set out to confuse the issue – it was just the way it was. Because over the years he'd become Bill-Bob the shed hand, instead of Robert Alan Carpenter from Sydney, no-one had ever thought to connect him with the man who'd taken off from his Sydney home years ago. Certainly Tom, coping with his own grief and caring for his young son, was not likely to give more than a passing thought to the coincidence of Bill-Bob's surname. Since Bill-Bob had never admitted a family tie, none was considered.

As the years passed, Bill-Bob was accepted on his own terms, just as he'd wished. He was known as someone who'd been about for ages, who was undemanding, a good worker, great with machinery and willing to help out in any way. There were enough other people about who didn't talk much about their past for it not to be noticeable, especially Bill-Bob who rarely talked about anything much. He listened more than he talked and never about himself.

Naturally enough, Bill-Bob's secret caused a great deal of talk in the district and was the chief topic of conversation at the pub and in all the homesteads around. Any death in a small district is always discussed at length. When a community is small, death is felt by all. But this fact – that he was really a member of the Carmody family and no-one knew all that time – was a nine-day wonder. Every aspect of the situation, real and imaginary, was discussed at length.

Of course, the nature of the relationship between Ethel Alsop and Bill-Bob came under the district microscope again, as well. In fact, Bill-Bob's death gave everyone such a rich treasure trove of gossip that it even pushed the topic of weather out of the conversation for a while.

For her part, Ethel Alsop talked very little and grieved very deeply. He'd been a good friend to her and good friends are rare. No-one else besides the two of them really knew exactly what their relationship was – even though most people in the district were sure they did know.

Kendal, too, missed him badly. She grieved, and at the same time wondered about the strange experience she'd had on the day of his death. There was a lot she didn't understand. Bill-Bob's spray, the one he promised Kendal he'd always keep with him, was missing. The spray Kendal had grabbed from his room was his back-up one. So where was the original one? They'd all accepted Tony's account of no spray without a worry – after all Bill-Bob had left it behind so often in the past – but there were a few little things making her uneasy. She consoled herself. After all, her feeling of uneasiness was probably because she felt guilty because she hadn't prayed for Bill-Bob to live. She kept telling herself that after a death everyone feels guilty they hadn't been loving or caring enough. Besides, who was she to feel that her prayers would have made a difference, anyway, to what God had decided was best for Bill-Bob?

Bruce and Aunt Bessie urged Kendal to stay at Carmody Plains for a few days. She was the only woman there and she felt it was important to be with all three – Tom, Charles and Rick – at the moment. Besides, she knew the run of the place, and Charles and Tom were really busy with all the arrangements. First, they had to get in touch with Bill-Bob's father, Charles's grandfather. Then there were arrangements for the funeral, of whether to go to Sydney or Quilpie or bury him at Carmody Plains to be worked out between them all.

On the Sunday afternoon, Kendal really felt like getting away for a bit and she decided she'd enjoy a ride to blow a flew clouds away. She caught and saddled Dancer. She didn't deliberately choose to go towards South Pines but Tony was never far from her thoughts. She was over in the paddock joining Tony's when she saw him in his gyrocopter. He used it a lot on his place to check bores and fences and other jobs. But today he seemed to be just playing around.

"The silly fool of a fellow," she thought as she saw him clowning. "One day he'll really hurt himself badly." He was going along pretty close to the ground and then darting up and skimming the tops of the low scrub. At times he was almost among the tree tops and she thought he'd have an accident if he wasn't careful. She remembered the first day she'd mustered with him, when he'd landed with leaves all over the wheels and even a small branch in his mouth. Always such a dare devil. But today he was going overboard. She watched as he took the craft up high, higher than she'd ever seen him fly. Higher, in fact, than she thought a small craft could safely go.

Then, suddenly, the tail went up with the rotors and the craft flew into a frenzy. It flipped over and seemed to come straight down, right into the ground in the middle of a stony outcrop. It crashed into the boulders. The light machine smashed up. It all happened so quickly.

"Oh, God!" breathed Kendal. "This can't be happening!" Her dash to the fence and to open and shut the gate seemed to be in slow motion. Every movement seemed heavy and slow. She paused only to tie Dancer up securely – she didn't want to be out there with no way to go to get help. Before she reached the gyro she knew that it was hopeless.

Sick with apprehension, Kendal made herself approach the wreckage to make sure. She couldn't go back to the house to raise the alarm without trying to help. There was nothing she could do.

She sat beside the wreckage of the little machine and the twisted, shattered body of this utterly charming and handsome man, Tony, and wept. He was so lovely. So good-looking, so dynamic, such fun, and now he was not there. There was just twisted meat in the wreckage. Tony had disappeared.

Kendal was shaking. Before this weekend she'd never seen a dead person before. Now this weekend two people had died, one after the other and both dear friends she'd come to know well.

Finally, she made herself stand. She didn't want to leave, but she knew she'd have to get help. She thought to try the two-way in the gyrocopter, but wasn't surprised to find it was smashed beyond use. She knew she'd have to pull herself together and go back to the house. She had to get help and let others decide what had to be done. Thank God Charles was arriving tomorrow. She badly needed the comfort of the strong, sensible man.

Charles proved even more necessary to her over the next few days. Despite his own grief over losing Bill-Bob, and Tony, his lifelong friend, he was a rock of strength for both Kendal and his father.

At first, Kendal had to face the fuss of reporting what she'd seen to the police. It seemed the questions about what happened, how the gyro went out of control and what went wrong would never end.

Then there was even more fuss. Constable Sandy and Charles went to Tony's house, and it was then that startling details of Tony's story came to life. There in the garden – this garden that everyone had thought Tony kept in sacred memory of his parents – was a large crop of marijuana. Packed in between the other plants were these illegal bushes. It was a bombshell to everyone.

Of course, there had always been curiosity about where Tony had found his spending money. After all, there was no money to be made on station properties these days. Some thought Tony had been left money by a distant relative, but opal mining had been widely thought to be a very possible explanation of his wealth. It was a sensible explanation, because it was a well-known fact that miners kept information about their finds to themselves to stop intruders. So a number of people in the district had decided Tony must have had a mine that had produced some pretty good stones and that he'd kept it a secret to stop poachers. Arry O'Tel could never be drawn to discuss his nephew's extravagances.

Now the police knew the answer to Tony's wealth for sure, they were interested in who else knew about – or even involved with – his illegal scheme. Charles Carmody was a close friend of Tony MacFarlane, had independent wealth and travelled to the cities a lot. The police soon made him the object of their close scrutiny.

Kendal found herself with a particular problem. She was not at all sure that the two deaths were unrelated. What if Bill-Bob had found out about Tony's garden that day he was over there and Tony had had a hand in Bill-Bob's death? She couldn't believe that he'd actually bludgeon him to death, but what if he shouted and yelled at him and pushed him in with the agitated bull? Then pulled him out when he collapsed and had deliberately not given him his heart spray? What if it was after then that he panicked and called the others? Or cold-bloodedly called the others when he was sure Bill-Bob was dead?

While everyone reeled at the tragedy of the dual deaths, Kendal found herself with a particular problem. She could voice it to no-one – after all, no-one knew of Tony's secret fear of AIDS except her. But what if? What if Tony had killed himself? He was already depressed and on edge before Bill-Bob's death, and it could have been enough to send him over the edge. Was this the quick, painless release Tony had wanted?

The only person she really wanted to talk to about all of her questions was Bill-Bob, and he wasn't there any longer. He would have helped her sort it all out, make sure of the information and cut out the hysteria. She couldn't talk it over with Tom, who was too shocked and upset himself. Charles had his own problems to deal with, both his grief and now the police investigation.

So Kendal was forced to think over the possibilities in her own head. There was no way she could solve these problems. She was learning that life presents these conundrums, and that one just has to learn to live with them.

There are lots of suicides in the bush these days. And lots of accidents.

Chapter 17

It was a very sad Christmas for all of them that year. Life goes on and most people already had arrangements made, so they just got on with it. However, it was a subdued holiday for everyone who had known the two men, and that included the whole of Juno and its district.

Not many arrangements were cancelled because of the tragedies. Bruce had been going to take the children for a visit to Brisbane to stay with his mother for Christmas and he went ahead with those plans. Her house was in a retirement village and was very small. They were crowded so it gave him a good excuse to go to the coast often to visit Thea, who was living there with her mother again.

Kendal and her mother had arranged long ago, before she'd even set out for Carmody Plains in the early spring, that they would spend Christmas in Tasmania with family. Charles felt it was really necessary for him to go to Carmody Plains to be with his father, so Kendal and Charles were going in opposite directions.

On the other hand, the McMahons had family coming out to stay, and they, as usual, included their friends in their arrangements so that no-one would spend Christmas on their own. Everyone went through all the motions of doing all the usual things to celebrate and to honour the occasion, but the joy of Christmas was not as light-hearted as usual and everyone was more aware of the fragility of life.

Before long, Christmas had come and gone, New Year was celebrated, and Kendal was back at Kalanoa. Not that things were exactly back to normal. Things could never be the same again, but life had to go on. Tom and Rick were together at Carmody Plains. Charles was again in Brisbane, finally clear of the police after his lawyer fully disclosed Charles's earnings, bank accounts and business transactions for the past five years. The stress had taken a significant toll on Charles, who had been forced to both grieve and defend himself against the allegations.

Meanwhile, Kendal kept busy with her usual jobs to take her mind off the double tragedy. Doing run-of-the-mill jobs always helps put life on an even keel, and Kendal found keeping busy was the best balm for the terrible shock she'd had.

One day at smoko, Bessie said to Bruce and Kendal, "Did you know that Sally Johnson is engaged?"

"Is she?" Bruce commented. "That will be an excuse for a few good parties. Who's the fella?"

"Aiden Carmichael, he's an accountant from Sydney," was her reply.

Kendal remembered that Sally's mother had told her at the Quick Shear that she was worried her daughter would marry and move further away.

"Will we be seeing the young man, I wonder?" Bruce continued.

Bessie nodded. "Yes, Margery McMahon was just on the phone and they are going to have a party for them sometime around Easter. They haven't been able to fix which day yet because no-one is sure when her fiance will be able to come up – but he's going to make arrangements to come out and meet Sally's family sometime then."

"Well, he'll meet all her friends, too." Bruce turned to Kendal. "That will be a good chance for you to get out, too, Kendal. You need to get out a bit. It's good to have something to look forward to."

Not much later Miss Thompson said to Kendal, "Well, they're definitely going ahead with the party for Sally and Aiden. We're to take a salad and a sweet. It's a while off yet, so I'll have to write it on the calendar. What do you think we should take?"

They were soon into a deep discussion about the advantages of different dishes. Kendal was quite familiar with country parties where the whole household went out together, from the youngest children to the grandparents. Each family was usually asked to bring some of the food – the only practical way to cater for the large crowd that resulted from such an arrangement when there just isn't enough room to store such a great quantity of food adequately or enough money to buy it.

It was bound to be a fairly big party. Most of the families around Juno had known Sally all of her life. Everyone had seen her grow up from a baby, watched her go off to school, then to a job in the city, and now coming home prior to being married and starting a new life once more. Everyone would want to wish her well, so the party would probably end up being anything up to a hundred adults and half as many children as well.

Not long after this, Bruce walked into the kitchen after taking a phone call. He announced to Bessie and Kendal, who were working there, that a cricket match would be held the next Saturday. "It's the local east and west match. How do you feel about that, Aunt Bessie? Feel like fronting up to that?"

"No, not me, Bruce," she replied. "It's a bit of a long day out in the heat if I go in with you. I'm not as interested as I used to be to sit around in the heat all day. I'll give it a miss, thanks." She turned to Kendal. "What about you, Kendal? Do you feel like going? I'll look after the little girls here and you can have an outing without them. Do you good to get out."

Kendal thought about the cricket. She didn't really feel like going out – or being enthusiastic about anything, really. Politely, she declined, "No thanks, I'll stay here too."

The older lady gave her a thoughtful look. Later, when Bruce was out working and the girls were busy elsewhere, Bessie sought out Kendal. "What's all this about not going to cricket?" she wanted to know.

Kendal shrugged. "Honestly, Miss T, I just don't feel like going out."

Bessie was firm. "Well, I think it's necessary for you to motivate yourself and go."

"You don't want to go either!" Kendal protested.

Bessie would not be moved. "That's quite different. I'm old now and, besides, I'm coping with life quite well. You're young and you should go out more. To tell the truth, I think you're really suffering from shock and depression. It's quite natural after being there when two people you've been working with have died. That's a big enough shock for anyone. But I can tell you, girl, that's what life is like. Everything goes along smoothly, and then out of the blue, things go wrong and you get a rough patch. In this case, things went very wrong. So many dreadful things happening one after the other. The only way to cope is to carry on."

210

Kendal was a bit indignant. "I am carrying on. Aren't I doing all I should be doing here?"

"Yes, dear, I'm not faulting your work," Bessie reassured her. "You are doing all right but you've lost your sparkle. You're a young girl in my household and I feel responsible for you. I think you should make the effort and go out, meet people. Does your brother play cricket? He might get a game." They talked for quite a while and Kendal could see that it was probably very good advice she was getting.

Finally she agreed. "Thanks, Miss T, I'll try. I usually enjoy watching cricket. Dad used to play when we were kids and Rick played at school. I often went along to cheer him on." She turned to the other woman. "Do you think that he'll be asked to play too? He used to be pretty good, he made the First XI."

"I must admit I didn't think about Kenrick when I was talking to Bill," Bruce said later when Bessie mentioned Kendal's comment. "Of course, I didn't know if he'd be available. I'll be talking to Bill again later, so I'll let him know there's another player in the district. Tom Carmody never used to miss a match once but he doesn't always come any more. He used to score most of the time after he stopped playing himself. I'll tell Bill to remember Carmody Plains."

Later, when talking to Rick on the phone, Kendal discovered he'd been asked to play. Apparently, as well as being a bit of fun, it was going to be a farewell match for Jacko, who'd been a top wicket keeper and district cricketer for years.

Kendal remembered there had been a Jacko in the shearing team at Carmody Plains and that he'd opened the Quick Shear competition, too. Kendal wondered if he was the cricketer, as well.

She soon discovered the east and west match referred to whether the player lived east or west of the river. Kalanoa was on the west of the main channel, but Carmody Plains was on the east, so Kendal knew she'd be barracking for the eastern team.

On the Saturday morning of the big match, Kendal and Bruce set off early. Bruce, who was playing, was in long white trousers and a creamy coloured polo shirt, plus a white towelling hat. Kendal, on the other hand, had tried her best to take Miss Thompson's advice and had dressed up a bit. She was still dressed quite casually, but she agreed dressing up had lifted her spirits. Her hair was pulled up in a knob on the top of her head and covered with a shady hat. For the first time in ages, she felt pretty good about how she looked. Feminine but practically dressed for a day at the cricket, she went with Bruce towards the shed where the main activity was centred.

It was a typical country setting. The players were mostly in some sort of white for the game but not all, and there were a few onlookers and they were in everything from working jeans, to shorts, singlets and T-shirts.

A few dogs and a number of children ran around and it all looked pretty confused. Kendal knew that, come ten o'clock, things would start like any other cricket match. She slowly started to walk over to the shed and spotted Kenrick coming towards her.

"G'day Sis, how're you going?" He gave her a big hug and then held her out at arms' length, studying her carefully. "You don't look too bad. I was getting worried about you."

His concern was almost her undoing. For a moment she felt like leaning on his shoulder and crying her heart out. He'd let her, she knew, and that's why she was so tempted to collapse her control and have a good cry. It would get her nowhere and just knowing he was there for support should make her stronger, not weaker.

So she just sniffed a bit and smiled weakly and said, "Well, thanks for the backhanded compliment. Anyway, how are you, and how are things at Carmody Plains?"

He was glad she was coping, and said readily, "Tom is bearing up OK. I talked him into coming in and seeing people today, and I think that'll be good for him. He'll come by later. I'm not sure why he didn't come with me, but he said he'd come along later in the afternoon." He looked at her carefully again. "Heard from Charles?"

She was aware of Rick's scrutiny and didn't want to admit that she was hearing from Charles very regularly indeed. In fact, since he'd returned to Brisbane after Bill-Bob and Tony's deaths, he'd talked to her quite a few times on the phone and continued to write often. He seemed to gain some comfort from being able to talk to Kendal about Tony and Bill-Bob – something he couldn't really do with Tom, who'd been badly winded by the whole tragedy.

Despite their growing relationship, Kendal still felt it was fairly new and fragile, and something she still wanted to hold pretty close to her heart. She knew the fact that there was a relationship with Charles was pretty obvious, but she didn't even want Rick to know just how involved she was or how much she cared. So she simply answered her brother, "Now and then. When are you expecting him home?"

"I haven't heard anything definite, but from the way he's talking I think he'll be out soon," Rick replied.

That was the impression Kendal had, too, but she hadn't wanted to reveal that to Rick. Charles hadn't given her any dates, just a promise that he had to finalise business and then he'd be out as soon as he could.

As they joined the others under the shed, people smiled and everyone greeted everyone else with, "G'day" or "Hello there". Some people she recognised and some seemed to be strangers. Before she got too far, some of the shearing team she'd met at Carmody Plains saw her and called out to her. Jacko, who was the man of the moment and was definitely one of the men she'd met before, asked, "Is this your brother, Kendal? Come and meet the other fellows."

There were only a few women and girls around, but Kendal knew from experience that more would probably come later in the day when it was time to break for lunch, or even later at afternoon tea.

Someone called out, "Anyone willing to score?" No-one rushed him. "Come on now," the man called again, "we need a scorer."

Kendal moved over to Bruce and said, "I can score if I'm not taking someone's usual job."

"Great!" he said enthusiastically. "We often have trouble getting someone to score if old Tom's not around. No-one else has taken over the job on a regular basis and I gather that he's not coming in until later. Not a lot of people really like to score."

By agreeing to score, Kendal knew she'd have to be glued to the game and not spend her time talking with the other spectators, but she figured it was better to be part of the action and to keep her mind busy. This way she'd be fully occupied and have to keep her mind on the job. There'd be no time to sit around and mope.

Jason Rogers was the umpire. He usually was. He was an old fellow who'd worked around the district for most of his sixty odd years. He was a real identity, a dry old stick who never drank, never swore and took the game very seriously needed. You'd think every game they'd played was an international one-day game at the MCG, at least. He spent a lot of time umpiring for the matches and was not impressed with any clowning around. The only trouble was that he wasn't as sure-sighted as he'd always been, but it was an equal handicap to both sides so everyone usually accepted him happily enough.

The team from the west won the toss and decided to bat.

Kendal was surprised to see Jacko, who was supposed to be padding up, getting stuck into a couple of stubbies. It was still so early in the day, and she was a bit disappointed. It wouldn't be much of a match if he got on the grog this early.

Rick, getting ready to field, saw her look doubtfully at Jacko and said quietly, "Relax, Kendal. They tell me Jacko always needs a couple of stubbies to start his game. His hands shake, they say, without a few under his belt, and with them aboard he's as steady as a rock."

Kendal decided she'd reserve her judgment. Before long, they were all in place. Red and Curly were the opening batsmen. Sandy was opening bowler and he sent down a beauty. Red was taking strike and he handled it well. The second ball really started the action. Sandy bowled a great ball that clipped the bat and moved away towards the slips, a good metre wide of the keeper.

Jacko dived to the side and pulled it out of the air. Full of glee, he shouted, "Howzat?"

The man who made the first catch always got a carton of beer and Jacko was sure the prize was his.

But the umpire declared, "Not out."

Jacko threw his hands out in such an impassioned plea that his gloves flew off onto the ground around him. He stamped about and shouted, "You stupid, blind old fool. Can't you see anything? Are you deaf as well?" He ranted and raved and Jason just stared at him. Red held his ground. Jacko picked up his gloves, yelling at Jason as he went, "If your parents ever get married, I for one won't be coming to the wedding!"

He finally settled down behind the wickets. Sandy continued to bowl well and there was one more controversial decision. A yorker swung around across the wickets. But Jason again said not out.

Finally Sandy sent one down that caught Curly completely unprepared, taking out his stumps. This time Sandy shouted, "Howzat!"

Nearby Kendal heard someone muttering dryly, "Now, that one must have been close, mustn't it?"

214

Not long after, Kendal winced when Rick dropped a catch. She had been hoping he would distinguish himself. She was glad to hear that everyone yelled at him in the same way as they would have if he'd been one of the regulars. If anyone dropped a catch, it was traditional that they shouted a jug of beer for the team at the pub after the match. Cries of "That'll cost you a jug!" had come from all around.

The game settled down.

A little group of blokes just behind her were telling yarns. Arry O'Tel was a star performer. Kendal had heard he was a great raconteur and she tried to catch what was said. He was certainly amusing his audience. There were regular great shouts of laughter. Now and then she could hear clearly and she realised that what she'd heard about Arry being racist was also true. Other people topped his stories and words like boong and gin were being thrown around. She couldn't hear it all, but she caught enough to know they were pretty rough. She'd heard that sort of thing often enough in her life and she knew how carried away they could get. She didn't know people well enough to know who might have some Murri blood and who didn't. She hoped there was no-one within earshot who did. The raucous, laughing group certainly didn't care who heard them.

She wished they'd go away so she wasn't so distracted. She was glad she was scoring and was not able to protest. Her conscience was clear. She hoped that wasn't being a moral coward but she thought it was useless to protest anyway when the group were all urging each other on like that. One-to-one she'd have her say, but with a group like that she knew she'd be wasting her breath. They weren't going to talk rationally. Just cheap laughs was what they were interested in.

She would have liked to have had a talk to Tony to see if she could have understood his attitude and tried to find some common ground. "Well, that won't happen now," she thought.

She raised her hand to acknowledge the umpire signalling a wide.

At lunch time they had a little farewell for Jacko. Speeches were made, covering many old occasions of their time as a cricket team. Kendal was surprised to hear Bruce have his say. Maybe it was the beer talking.

"One match I remember was when we went to Charleville and played Colts on the Turf Oval," Bruce began, wiping his mouth.

"Turf wickets are obviously meant to be closer to the coast, because the cracks in the wicket would have taken Tony Greig's hand, let alone his keys." There were appreciative laughs all round from those who remembered seeing Tony Greig on TV using his keys to measure cracks in Test wickets. "Anyway, Jacko here won the toss and put us in. Fifteen overs and thirty-two runs later it was all over, batsmen and wickets went everywhere while the wicket weaved its magic." Bruce took another swig of his can of beer and continued. "'Well, we'll win this one easy enough', we thought," he took another swig, "but when our score reached twenty-four our last batsman was out and our tails were between our legs. It just goes to show that it's not over until the fat lady sings. You can't be sure of anything in cricket."

Curly remembered one of their greatest matches against Toompine in Quilpie. "They scored two hundred and thirty off their forty overs and then it was our turn," he told the gathering. "Off to a great start with me and Barney opening, and we were fifty without a loss. Then a few quick wickets put the pressure back on us. Jacko here then got going and a fine hundred from him put us back in the picture. The heat was taking its toll on the fielding side and a few dropped catches let us sneak in with only a few balls to spare."

And so the speeches went on, remembering the good times and the bad. They'd all had a few beers, except Jason, of course. But the event wouldn't have been complete until he'd said a few words as well. Jacko replied and then they got on with the job of having their lunch.

Kendal was free to move around and talk to people, and she realised she knew most of the people around. She was interested in the women talking to Dan Flannigan. The short, fat one, she guessed, must be his Daisy. There was no doubt that whatever beauty Daisy had once had was no longer visible to the naked eye. After all, it's hard to be beautiful with sunken cheeks and conspicuous gaps in your smile from a couple of missing teeth. Her hair, grey and thin, had resisted heroic efforts to curl it successfully. The young girl with them, now, she was different. Her hair was thick and lustrous and curled softly around her shoulders – with or without artifice it was impossible to tell. It certainly made an attractive frame for a truly beautiful face. She was obviously pregnant and she was one of those women whom pregnancy

216

becomes. She was standing next to an awkward-looking tall, gangly youth, who had long, lank hair and was barely past the pimple stage. Dan and Daisy were beaming at them, clearly delighted with them both. The youth looked a little sulky and resentful, while the girl looked radiant.

Kendal was talking to Dan before lunch was over. The usually quiet Dan was ecstatic. He couldn't wait for Kendal to meet his Daisy and his daughter, Lily. Lily, he told her importantly, was going to be married and have a baby. He, Dan, was going to be a grandfather.

Daisy was as quiet as Dan usually was. She smiled a rather toothless but genuine smile that lit her eyes. Kendal had a fleeting glimpse of a likeness to the splendid girl who was their daughter. Lily was a picture and quite composed. The youth – her fiance, Jim – looked a little simple. Maybe he was just stunned. Whether it was at his luck to have such a beautiful girl as his bride, or because he was being pressured into a marriage he had no wish to make, Kendal had no way to tell. Together, they made an interesting group.

She also saw the legendary Mrs Alsop and some of her family. Her nephew, John McMahon, was playing in Rick's team. She remembered briefly meeting Margery at the Quick Shear, and she was also introduced to Joe, her husband, and their two young sons, Lex and Mark, who were running around. Joe also pointed out their daughter, Wendy. Kendal was interested to note that she was the girl with soft, lovely, big eyes who was talking to Rick.

Much to Kendal's disappointment, Mrs Alsop didn't say anything remarkable while she was in earshot. It was a blow, because Kendal had come to expect from what she'd heard that the indomitable Mrs Alsop dropped cutting remarks every time she opened her mouth. Instead, she appeared to be a quiet, pleasant, elderly woman. However, from all that had been said, Kendal knew that Mrs Alsop would be grieving the loss of Bill-Bob, and wouldn't necessarily be her sparkling best. In fact, Kendal thought it quite brave of Mrs Alsop to face a crowd after her recent loss.

Red's team was fielding after lunch and Curly was down to open the bowling. Jason went out to umpire. But before he took his place, Curly quietly put one of the empty beer cans into his pocket. He made a great show of cleaning the ball on his trousers as he looked over the placing of the field and finally indicated he was satisfied and he carefully measured out his run. He bowled a normal first ball, but then discreetly changed the ball for the beer can, and made his run up and bowled the beer can. Its flight was different from the ball, of course, but his aim was true and he completely bowled the batsman, taking his centre wicket. Red appealed vigorously to the umpire. The batsman hadn't really known what had happened, but his wicket was down and he started to walk.

Jason was incensed. "Bloomin', fool bowler," he yelled. "Bloomin' well should know better! The batsman is NOT out!"

Those players close to the wicket knew what was happening and shouted their opinions to stir Jason up more. "Go on, it's a fair ball – took the wicket clean as a whistle," they yelled. Those further away couldn't make out what all the fuss was about. But the joke gradually passed around the field and out to the spectators and it added colour to the day.

As the afternoon wore on, the air was hot and still. Not surprisingly, when the captains called for drinks, they players happily left the field for the shade. The men drank freely from one of the many polyurethane cold containers that had been brought in for just this purpose. Children had been clamouring all day for drinks but one container was always kept just for the team. The men drank beer even more freely. Bruce came over and had a word and joked about the bowling. Rick sat beside her while he finished his drink and looked at the score pad. "You OK, Sis?" he asked, wanting to make sure she was holding up all right.

Kendal smiled, touched by his concern. "Fine, thanks," she replied.

Curly came across to Kendal to look over her shoulder to see the score. She gave him a bit of cheek about his second ball and he just grinned. Looking up and seeing one of the local girls with a camera taking a photo of her boyfriend, Curly immediately began to clown around and putting his arms around Kendal. "Hey, over here!" he called. "Take the photo of the prettiest scorer we've had for many a year! Take her photo as she kisses Curly, to congratulate the best bowler on the field today!"

Kendal joined in the spirit of the moment, laughing and playing up to him. She kissed him coquettishly on the cheek with her arms around his neck. Then something caught her attention and she glanced past the photographer to see two tall figures walking towards the shed.

One was Tom, and the other was Charles! Kendal was thrilled to see Charles unexpectedly, and then realised that instead of joining in the good-natured laughter and encouragement the crowd around her were showing, Charles was clearly not impressed.

Kendal remembered him cracking up when she was clowning around with much the same crowd after shearing at Carmody Plains. He looked pretty ready to explode again and she pushed Curly away and made it clear to him that the game was over and she wanted out. She desperately needed to get to Charles to explain it all before they were both upset by his misunderstanding. Heaven knows, they both were pretty vulnerable and still needed all the support they could give each other.

The fooling around Kendal cleared as quickly as it had started. The couple with the camera were organising someone else to take their photo together and everyone's attention had drifted elsewhere. There was now a clear path through the onlookers, but Kendal didn't go.

Charles hadn't exploded. His look of rage had been replaced by one of blank indifference. One moment he was there, and the next he was gone. He'd spoken a word to his father, Tom, who had been beside him, then he'd turned on his heel and walked away. He didn't actually appear to hurry, but his tall figure disappeared in a second.

To the others, if they'd even noticed, it was an event of no significance. No-one else had any inkling of what the fooling had done to Kendal and she was left standing, wanting to go after Charles but quite sure his car would be gone before she got near him. It just looked as if he'd come to drop his father off and not intended to stay. She knew he'd intended to stay, though.

Tom Carmody was now slowly walking over to the group by himself and was being greeted by several players with calls of "G'day Tom". One of the players gestured towards Kendal, saying, "Someone else is doing the scoring today. Reckon the scorer is on your side, but. Pity Charles couldn't stay. We haven't seen him at the cricket for a while."

Hurt and confused, Kendal hardly heard the remarks all around her.

Then the captain of the west team called them all back to the field, "Can't spend all day standing around, you blokes. Back to work."

As the others all sorted themselves out – the players to the field and the spectators to the seats – Kendal took her place. For a moment, Tom came and stood behind Kendal, patted her on the shoulder and then walked away without saying a word.

Kendal was glad she had to concentrate and didn't have time to indulge her feelings. She was touched at Tom's understanding, but it was Charles's understanding she needed, not Tom's. She knew just from Tom's touch that he thought the whole fiasco was a pity. But why couldn't Charles trust her and love her enough to know it was all a game? Surely he couldn't believe that she'd really be kissing someone else, publicly, when he must know that he was the only person she loved? Why did he have to come at just that moment? Any other time all day and there would have been no misunderstanding. There was definitely a jinx on their relationship. Kendal's mind was turbulent. If she'd felt depressed and heavy before, it was twice as bad now.

Luckily, the work she was doing was automatic but needed her full concentration. Upset as she was, she could cope with her job. One ball bowled, one mark on the pad. Six balls accounted for each and every over. Six little marks routinely recorded. Simple and like clockwork, but requiring her complete attention. No-one expected her to make light conversation and by the end of the game she had herself well in hand and appeared to be her normal self.

A few days after the cricket weekend with no word from Charles, Kendal decided to tell Bruce that she wasn't going to stay at Kalanoa. She'd had enough.

Her dismay over the cricket incident had turned to frustration and anger. She was now quite sure she couldn't cope with Charles's lack of trust. There was no doubt that she was deeply in love with Charles, but she also felt that there was no way he was ever going to really let himself love her. Kendal always prided herself on being a realist and a practical lady, so she figured she'd be better off a long way away from the area. She'd stayed so that she might see Charles – now she wanted to go so that she wouldn't.

She told Bruce she wanted to go.

Bruce was upset at her announcement. "Oh, no, Kendal, do you think you could stay for a few more months?" he pleaded. "I really need you to stay a bit longer. If there's no reason you have to leave immediately, then please stay a while."

Kendal hadn't told Bruce why she wanted to go, of course, only that she didn't feel she wanted to stay for too long and she thought they'd better look for someone who'd stay through the year. She was firm. "No, I really do want to go and I'd like you to start looking for someone else – I really won't stay for very much longer."

Bruce's reply was curious. "Kendal, you have no idea how badly I need you to stay right now. I think things are working out for me right now, with any luck. But you've got to give me time to make my luck work out."

He'd piqued her interest. "What are you on about, Bruce?"

"You're a good scout, Kendal. If I'm going to get you to stay, I'd better take you into my confidence. I'm hoping that I might be able to talk Thea into coming out here again. Permanently. As my wife."

As Kendal squealed, Bruce continued. "She's been a bit frightened of all the differences in our way of life, but she'll be OK. I know she'll be OK. She's strong underneath, you know. The girls love her and so does Aunt Bessie, and Thea's such a gentle, lovely girl. I don't want her to come out to work again. Feeling the way I do, it just wouldn't be proper for me to have her here. We do have to live with Aunt Bessie, you know. But I don't want the girls to have someone else to have to get used to in the meantime."

He ran his fingers through his hair. "They're used to you and are happy with you and Aunt Bessie, and they don't need another change in their lives right now. I'm sure that in a little while I'll get Thea to realise that she does want to live with me and the girls. She'll cope beautifully once she gets used to it. It won't be strange forever."

Kendal gave in immediately. Bruce and his aunt were old-fashioned and caring and she felt she had to help them. She couldn't take the job because it suited her and then not be fair and stay a while if Bruce needed her. So she relented. "OK, Bruce, of course I'll stay for a while. I wish you all the luck in the world. I agree Thea is a dear and I'll keep things rolling here for a while. But Bruce, I'm not staying for ages and ages. If Thea needs a whole lot more time, you'll have to get someone else." She put her hand on his arm and grinned. "Go for it, fella."

She walked away with a big grin on her face. She thought Bruce and Thea had been corresponding fairly regularly, the way Bruce searched the mail every mail day for an envelope with Thea's distinctive handwriting. Kendal just wished that Charles was as keen about her as Bruce was about Thea. But Bruce thought Thea was some sort of goddess and he'd put his pretty little love up on some sort of pedestal. In Bruce's eyes, Thea could do no wrong.

But in Charles's eyes, Kendal thought dismally, she was some sort of Circe. A dangerous siren luring men to their doom, or something. Oh yes, she was the practical one. She could ride, muster, cook and keep her head in an emergency – but Charles clearly thought she was leading some sort of double life. Maybe he'd put the wonderful attraction between them down to some sort of dangerous illusion. Certainly, he'd made it clear he thought she couldn't be trusted.

"Damn him, damn him to hell!" Kendal fumed. He'd only make them both miserable if he couldn't trust her. She would get on with her life without him.

Chapter 18

For all her preoccupation with her own life, Kendal began to notice that Bessie's behaviour was definitely becoming a bit odd. The elderly lady seemed to be constantly in a state of ceaseless activity, almost in a frenzy of preparation. Preparing for what? Their days were busy enough as it was, and for a woman in her seventies, Bessie always kept up a spanking pace of work. But lately, she seemed to be driven by a compulsion to get more and more done. Whenever they'd sit down for smoko, she'd talk for a moment, but before long she'd jump up and get to work again.

Kendal asked Bruce if he'd noticed anything. He said he thought his aunt had always kept busy.

One day, something happened to convince Kendal it wasn't her imagination. Bessie had made some jam and was quite pleased with her efforts after it was all bottled. There was nothing different about that – but Kendal was staggered when she heard her telephone Daisy Flannigan and offer to swap some tomato jam for some pickles. For Bessie to ask Daisy Flannigan for anything was definitely out of character. Something was up.

Kendal tried to be nonchalant. "What's eating you?" she asked. "You seem to want to have the whole place perfect – yesterday. And you're like a squirrel putting his nuts away for the winter. Looking at recipes, freezing more than normal? What's up?"

Bessie tried to fob her off. "Nothing, Kendal, nothing at all," she said lightly. "Good heavens, girl, I'm always busy – you know that."

Kendal persisted. "There's a difference, Miss T. You're just different somehow. The place has always been clean and tidy, but lately it's becoming an obsession with you."

"No, no, you're just imagining it," Bessie said.

"Well, if you would tell me what you want to do, maybe I could help you," Kendal offered.

"There's nothing to do," Bessie said.

Over the next few days Kendal could feel the elderly lady eying her speculatively. She always seemed to have a purpose in her looks and Kendal began to feel a bit like Hansel or Gretel being sized up by the old witch. She was more sure, more than ever, that something was going on and she tried to be extra helpful, but couldn't think what else to do.

Finally, Bessie spoke to her. "You can keep a secret can't you, Kendal?"

"Of course," Kendal replied.

Her elderly friend persisted, "No, this is serious, really serious to me. If I felt I could really trust you I'd tell you about it".

Kendal laughed, "Goodness, my lips are sealed!"

Instantly, Bessie looked offended. "Don't play the smart aleck with me, young woman!"

Kendal was contrite. "I'm sorry, I didn't mean that to sound pert. I'd love to know what's eating you and to help. I'll never tell a soul, I promise."

It took a bit more cajoling to convince her, but Bessie was obviously dying to confide in someone, even though she was reluctant to put it all into words. "Well, it's a long story in a way, so be quiet and just listen until I explain it all."

Kendal stifled any impulse to be flippant in case she frightened her off again because by now she was truly curious.

The elderly lady leaned forward and said, conspiratorially, "The crux of the matter is, I've got a plan to organise Bruce to marry Thea. And then maybe I can go away for a long holiday. Do my own thing, as they say."

Kendal couldn't believe her ears. This was the last thing she had expected, and although she didn't say a word, her wide eyes spoke volumes.

"Maybe it doesn't look like that with all the cleaning and working I've been doing, but it's all part of my plan," Bessie continued.

Kendal had visions of Bessie taking off for a world tour, leaving freezers full of food and a sparkling house behind her. "But you can't ever cook enough or clean enough to last for very long, especially not out here," she commented.

Bessie just looked at her. "I told you to be quiet and listen. That's not my plan at all. My main plan is that I intend to get Bruce married off to Thea."

Kendal dutifully stayed quiet but again she couldn't hide her incredulous look.

"Yes, I know cleaning up and cooking won't make any difference to Bruce and Thea," Bessie continued. "But, my dear, it would make a tremendous difference to her mother."

Comprehension dawned in Kendal's eyes as Bessie went on. "Thea is very, very influenced by her mother – as no doubt you know, Kendal – and it's my plan to ask her mother out here as well as Thea some time in the autumn, probably Easter, and let her see what a fantastic life it is out here. So peaceful, so easy. We all just breeze along and watch the sheep grow their wool. That's what everyone thinks we do, isn't it?"

Kendal was stunned at the plan. "How do you think you'll do that?" she asked. "Thea has been working here and she knows how busy it all is. She was overcome with how hard it is. That's why she left."

Bessie nodded. "Yes, Kendal, Thea knows that. But Mrs Moreton doesn't. Thea will be too busy being glad to be back to point out how different it can be – and, anyway, her mother won't believe her. She'll see with her own eyes how easy, how charming, it all is."

Kendal just couldn't comprehend what she was hearing.

Bessie Thompson just gently smiled at her. "Come on, Kendal. I've lived a life time out here and I know what my friends think of it. We all go flat out getting things ready, clearing the decks so that we can spend a few days with our friends without being too tied down with work while they're here. You take them fishing or visiting, go out for picnics, show them School of the Air working, feed them over and over and a dozen other things. When they leave you're behind with everything, you're exhausted and have to go flat out again to catch up. And then when you meet them afterwards, they say what a wonderful life you lead. No work, all pleasure and parties. What a laugh!

"Well, this time I'm going to cash in on it. For the first time ever I'm going to do this deliberately. Before I've just tried to clear the decks to enable me to spend time with visitors, just to be able to enjoy having them to stay. This time I intend to give an impression – in fact, I'm working flat out to create an impression, that just isn't true. And I'm not the least bit sorry or guilty. Thea knows it a bit more truly and she's the one I want to live out here. I just want her mother to think it's a lovely life her daughter will be leading. She's the one I want to con."

Kendal thought the plan was brilliant and brave. "Well, you've floored me," she said. "I'm speechless. I didn't think you'd do something like that."

"Well, tut-tut and fiddle-dee-dee," was the quick retort. "Bruce needs a wife and the children need a mother. Besides, if he isn't married again and the children don't have a mother figure, Diana might be able to make a case to take them away if she ever changes her mind. I'd do anything to stop them going to live with her. She's a selfish, self-centred, vain woman with no thought for anyone but herself. They need better than that."

Kendal thought Bessie had touched on the crux of the matter. The elderly lady was desperately concerned about the little girls' future.

"Besides," Bessie was saying, "he loves Thea. I'm sure of that and I'm practically positive she loves him and she'd be a good wife for him when she settles down and feels confident with this life. She is a great girl, really, and very kind and loving. She's shy, but she'll mature. It doesn't matter at all what her mother thinks, except to her, and if I do it well – and if you keep your side of the bargain – she'll never know she was conned."

She took off her apron and hung it on the hook where she kept it and turned back to Kendal. "And to be quite honest, I'd like to see Bruce married and someone else take the responsibility for running this house. I'm getting to be an old lady now and there are other things I want to do. Not all the time. I don't think I could leave out here altogether, but I do want to get away for more of the summer. I want to visit old friends and I want to see things I've heard about all my life but never seen. I've never been to Tasmania. I've never seen snow and I've never seen a real red and gold autumn."

Kendal was in shock. She'd never have guessed any of the things she was hearing. She had thought Bessie Thompson was as much wedded to the land and the great outback as Bill-Bob had been. Hesitantly she said, "Well, what exactly are your plans and what do you want me to do? Have you got definite plans?"

"Oh yes indeed," Bessie nodded. "Very detailed plans in my mind and now I'll try to tell you all about them and get them moving along. It has to be autumn. The only time of the year you can count on to be decent out here. Summer, of course, is out. No

226

amount of subterfuge can soften a summer out here sufficiently. They can be survived only by a true believer or someone with no options. Winter can be pretty good, but the nights are really cold for people from the coast. Spring is no good at all, either. Too windy, too many dust storms in any sort of dry year – and most years are – too changeable the weather. No, autumn through to early winter – that's the time visitors think that we all just complain about nothing. Days get a bit hot and people think that's what heat is. Mornings can be a bit chilly and someone thinks that's what a cold winter morning's like. They can think they've felt it all when it's the only time of the year that you can count on it being mild."

Kendal shook her head. "You amaze me, Bessie. You sound so cynical and I thought you loved your life out here."

"I do, Kendal dear, I do." She looked a bit thoughtful and amended that. "I did." Then she went on, "I guess I still do but I am a bit cynical of what other people think of our life out here. I also really want to expand my life a little before I die. I'm getting on and I want to see other things as well as this life. Don't get me wrong – this is a good way to live. One has to be tough and prepared for hard work, but it's real. So many people go camping or rough it or do a little bit of hard work and think it's natural, and think they are seeing real life. For some reason it makes me mad. They make their life so artificial. They buy their milk in a carton, it's homogenised and pasteurised and most of them truly don't know it comes from a cow. They swoon at the thought of killing a cow or a sheep or a chicken, but they'll buy their meat cut up and wrapped up in meal-size-pieces in plastic. They wouldn't have a clue what real food is. They keep their houses the same temperature all the year round practically, bland. That's what it is, bland."

She paused a bit. "But that doesn't stop me from wanting to relax in some of their luxury myself – for a while at least. To have things a bit easier, even if that means it's a bit less real. I'm not the only one, Kendal. A lot of women out here want to get away for a bit. There's a letter from one of my old school friends I can show you. She's been married and has lived on the land for all her married life until a year or two ago when she moved to Brisbane. She sent me this letter last Christmas and I kept it. I get it out and think about it sometimes. I don't think I'll move, but I do want to get away now and then. I do want it a bit easier for a while. And to travel. I'd love to travel."

She fussed about and then produced a letter. Kendal took the letter and read.

Dear Bessie,

What a wonderful year I have been privileged to enjoy. I firmly believe that life is a gift, not a right, and I am so grateful to my God for all His many blessings.

I am as happy as a bird (I won't say king!) in my little unit where in winter I have the sun on my balcony until after 2pm; and in summer I bask in cool river breezes (well, for 95% of the time). Such bliss after thirty-eight western summers.

I enjoy heaps of live music and theatre on a wide and varied scale on a weekly basis. There's a ferry next door to Southbank and my bus (opposite) takes me direct to the performing arts complex and the art gallery. There's a great bus service. I keep abreast of the latest movies (of my choice) and find the public library all-embracing and helpful. I am so warmly enveloped in love by the delightful Salvation Army folk – they're my weekly shot of spiritual power. They just shine and I keep hoping a bit of it may rub off on to me. But I remain an Anglican still!

After seventeen months I still can't believe all these options – so dear to my heart and real food for my spirit – are mine. I can't seem to lose the feeling that I'm on holiday! I am able to be of some help to the family. I babysit my grandchildren sometimes and I can be called upon when necessary. Sandra is doing postgraduate work and she often needs a bit of peace and quiet. With all my children with degrees, I am quite left behind, but I've enrolled in U3A for next year, so there!

I pray this wonderfully joyous season will bring peace and good health to you and yours and may God look kindly on you in the New Year.

With fond memories,
Elaine.

Kendal was amazed. She said slowly, "Well, I think I understand. She seems happy enough."

Bessie said prosaically, "The gilt will wear off the gingerbread eventually, but I'm sure Elaine will never really miss the dust, the flies and the heat."

She was delighted to have an accomplice for her scheme and she was more than happy to rope Kendal in and tell her about her ideas and preparations. Together, they kept carrying out Bessie's plans.

Kendal was still very interested in native title. By this time, she felt she knew quite a bit about it. Certainly enough not to ask about hunting and fishing rights on Kalanoa.

Sam had been willing to talk about it at times, and she always found it interesting. She couldn't remember all his colourful phrases, but she felt she had a pretty good idea about his attitude.

When she got him talking about his old friend, Charlie, he summed it up. "Charlie never stopped being a real Aborigine. He remembered all the old Dreamtime stories and the old ways, but he put on our clothes and he put on working for a living. These fellas today are too soft. They want the good things of civilisation but they don't want what goes to get it. They would, you know, if only we could get it through to them."

Sam had a definite philosophy about life: "A man's got to stand on his own feet to feel a man. This sittin' around bludgin' is no good to no-one."

Kendal thought over the other things he'd said. It seemed that Sam felt that most of the land right claims were a con to get more money. He told her that they had places all over the country and they didn't run them properly. He thought sitting around in town had ruined them. What they needed was pride in achievement. The places they had been given hadn't given them that. They just ignored them and stayed in town drinking. He told her white people had destroyed the old native way of life – but most of the original white people didn't choose to come here, either.

"Now the Aborigines have got to decide," he told Kendal. "Do they want to join us in civilisation and accept things as they are, or buy a place – they have over a billion to do that – and go back to hunting and fishing and their old ways? There is no half way. If they accept things as they are, they have to accept things as they are. They can't accept all the schooling, health treatment, housing, welfare and so on, and then say they want land rights over most of the state, as well."

Sam's love for them was obvious. He told her that they were great people who knew what they were on about and laughed and played and lived off the land. They were generous and shared everything they had. But it wasn't a way of life that taught them to be provident and careful and to save for a rainy day.

What were his words? Kendal remembered. "After all, how long does a dead kangaroo last?" Sam had said. "The one who kills it has to share to be a good fella with his mates and he's safe knowing whoever kills next week will share with him then."

He went on about how that was all right in a tribal situation. They probably had their own way of dealing with anyone who was a bludger and didn't pull their weight. "That isn't the way in our society," he'd said. "We have to work and save for a rainy day and that is the only way for so many people all living in a big society. It may not be better, but that's how it is. Communism was all about sharing, and that didn't work."

One day Kendal discussed with Bessie what Sam had said.

And Bessie agreed. "We have to find a way to help, and lots of handouts destroy their initiative and are no better than trying to assassinate them. The so-called stolen generation was started as a genuine attempt to help, and see how tragic that was in some cases."

Kendal told her one of Sam's comments, 'This land right thing is another stuff-up of an idea'.

Bessie laughed and said that on the whole she agreed. "It will help a few, no doubt, and put some unreal expectations in the hearts of others." She shook her head. "No amount given to you helps. A helping hand is OK for a short time, but the real effort has to come from the individual. A sense of achievement, a sense of self-worth – they are the only things worth having. You can help someone towards that, but you can't give it to them. Giving anyone something unearned only kills their initiative and makes them feel bad in the end."

Clara and Sam came in and were soon involved in the conversation.

Clara was forthright. "We will never please some of the noisy ones. Their only job is to ask for more and more. They will always ask for more, or they haven't got a job to do."

Bessie said, "It's a pity they can't see their job as being a leader, to lead others to a more productive life."

Sam thought about it. "There are stacks who do that, you know. But to be useful, it's a little bit here and a little bit there, and that doesn't get into the news, so we don't know about it. The people who want to help have to get out there and help, not tell others

230

what they should do. They can teach people to grow their own vegetables and grow their own fruit trees, instead of belly-aching about no proper food."

Bessie said, "I know plenty of dignified Murri people who are real achievers, but they go about doing their own jobs and we never read about them in the papers." Sadly, she said, "We always hear more about the rabble-rousers."

Sam called an end to his part in the discussion. He said they'd only come in to get a few things and they'd better get off home and get on with their own jobs. He and Clara went out and Kendal and Bessie were left in the kitchen.

Kendal was surprised to see that Bessie was quite upset. "This whole subject distresses you doesn't it?" Kendal asked.

"Oh yes, more than I can say, really," Bessie replied.

"Why so much? You must have seen a lot of sad things in your life. Why is this so much worse?"

"Well, Kendal, I wondered that myself for a while. I think it is because so much trust has been broken. We all know the weather can be chaotic – floods, drought, bushfires. We know people can be changeable and difficult." Here she paused and said almost incredulously, "This is the government of our land. These are the laws and the rules of our life.

"We've been here a long time. Our great-grandparents first bought this land and each generation since has had their problems and struggles. We thought we belonged here. By the laws of this country we had legally bought this land. If we fulfilled the conditions of the lease, the land was ours for the term of the lease. We could sell it or pass it on to the next generation and the conditions of the lease would hold. This has been the case for nearly one hundred and fifty years. The first land laws in Queensland were passed after separation in 1859. In all the years in between, no-one has ever questioned the right to land you had bought.

"Now, in the 1990s, everything has changed. Even after Mabo in 1993, we were assured that there would be no native title claim on pastoral leases. In 1996, claims were accepted by the Native Title Tribunal. How can we have faith in our government? How can we believe anything we're told any more?"

Kendal could see the pain of this went really deep with Bessie. She was just going to suggest getting a cup of tea when Bessie went on, "Some of my Murri friends are upset by all this, too. They want to live their lives accepted by the people around them. Every time native title comes up, or someone apologises for the stolen generation, or one of their people demands the right to eat an echidna – and it gets into the paper – they know that the public think they are being singled out for special treatment and resent it. Most of them don't want race to be an issue. They want their families to be normal, average, members of the community – not someone wanting special consideration."

She was very earnest and trying to get Kendal to understand this point of view. "Every case of special consideration means that someone gets annoyed about it and it's just that much harder for the aboriginal children to get jobs as an everyday Australian. Once they are seen as someone different, well, employers see there's plenty of people about and that it's better to employ someone who won't get the customers offside. Oh yes, Kendal, I'm very upset about all this, from everyone's point of view."

Kendal now had the chance to suggest they have a cup of tea. It was all very interesting, but she didn't want to upset Bessie any more.

Life wasn't all sitting around and talking. There was always work to be done. One of the big jobs due to be carried out – and one Bessie definitely wouldn't show Mrs Moreton – was the butchering of a beast to fill up their rapidly depleting freezers.

Over the years, Bessie and her good friend Ethel Alsop had developed a habit of putting the meat away together. Ethel and Bessie had been friends all their lives. They'd lived in the district around Juno for all that time and had seen so much. Babies together in the twenties, young girls in the depression years, young women in the war years. They both lost their young men as a result of the war. Ethel had been married and lost her husband in the fighting, while Bessie had waited for her man, and lost him to a newcomer after the war. Each had struggled on to make a life of their own on the land ever since.

Bessie appreciated Ethel's help every time Kalanoa killed a beast. Some people hate handling raw meat, and Bessie was one of them. It was a reasonably common practice for friends who did not have large families to share a beast. Bruce's father had been a good butcher and had taught Bruce well, so they killed their own beast one time and then killed one for Ethel the next, and they shared the meat each time. Ethel was one who loved the job of cutting it up and putting it away. Bessie hated it and only did it because it simply had to be done.

Since Ethel had sold her place, Bessie and Bruce suggested they stick to their old arrangement. If Ethel came out and helped Bessie, she could have all the meat she wanted. She had no working men to feed now, and the little bit she ate would hardly affect the time the beast lasted for them. Ethel was not one to accept charity and she accepted the meat, but more than paid for it with cakes and jam and vegetables all through the year.

So when the beast was killed and had been hung for long enough, they arranged a day when Ethel came over. The deep freezers would have been emptied and defrosted if necessary, and the long, hideous job to Bessie – and the very satisfying job to Ethel – began. From long experience, they knew precisely what to do with each cut. Each one got on with her job with no great decisions to be made. Occasionally one or the other would say, "I'd like the round cut into steaks this time," or "I'd like more roasts than usual. I seemed to use them quickly last time". Ethel had more use for steak than before because it was such an easy meal for one.

The loss of Bill-Bob was still a very raw wound in Ethel's life. It affected everything she did. For one, she wouldn't ever want so many roasts again. She had usually cooked a roast each Saturday night for Bill-Bob, but now she would have no regular guests. Her nephew and his family often visited, and other people came and went, but there was no-one to cook for on a regular basis.

She might snap out her opinions often enough, but she'd made a point of never complaining. Working alongside her old friend, though, was an ideal time for confidences.

"I miss him, Bessie. He was a good companion," Ethel said, wiping her eyes. "He always had an opinion on everything that happened. It made everything so interesting knowing I'd have Bill-Bob to talk it over with on the weekend." She considered what she was saying. "Talking with you is comfortable because we are so alike and we think the same way about so many things. But talking to him was exciting because he always saw things differently from me and we could have a really lively discussion."

Bessie found it hard to imagine the two of them. Bill-Bob had always kept to himself and hardly spoke in a crowd. Her old friend Ethel was so terse and outspoken at times, she thought she would have reduced Bill-Bob to utter silence. She'd realised that this couldn't have been case for them to have stayed such close companions for so long, but she'd been like everyone else and didn't know exactly what was the strong attraction between them. Now, was she getting the picture of intellectual stimulation? She didn't want to intrude, but she was hoping Ethel would go on. It would do her good to talk.

"What did you discuss?" Bessie asked gently.

"Anything and everything," was the reply. "He was always interested in the whole bit. He had an intense interest in all that went on in life. He had an opinion about everything." She smiled to herself, thinking over past conversations. "He was cynical and distrusted most people. Disappointment in early life made him that way and he always said not much happened to change his mind about that, either."

Bessie couldn't help herself. "Did you know he was Nancy Carmody's brother?" she asked curiously.

"Yes. He didn't tell me until after I'd known him for a long, long time. Until we'd got to the stage of discussing practically everything. That's one thing we had quite heated discussions about. I thought he should tell Tom or Charles. He was adamant that he would not."

"Did you ever think of precipitating things for him? Telling them yourself?"

Ethel was incredulous. "Are you quite mad?"

Bessie could see she'd made a serious mistake. "You're right, of course. I agree with you, you couldn't have done that. I often feel like giving things a little push in the directions I'd like them to go, but probably not with Bill-Bob."

"No. Definitely not with Bill-Bob." Ethel put down her knife and moved over to wash her hands. "I wouldn't have dreamed of interfering in his personal life and, what's more, I would have lost a very dear friend if I had." She looked at her friend before collecting a pile of stew meat to cut up. "To have lost him because of lack of trust would have been infinitely worse than to have lost him like this."

Bessie could see she'd upset Ethel and didn't say anything else for a while. She had cut each topside into four pieces and she put two in the box for Ethel and took six of them down to her own deep freeze.

After a while, Bruce came in from the paddocks. Kendal and the children joined them and they all stopped for a cup of tea.

Bruce offered to give the women a hand for a couple of hours, but Bessie declined – although she usually would have jumped at the chance – hoping Ethel would continue to talk.

After smoko, when the others had gone and they were on their own again, Ethel suddenly said, "Did you know he's left me a lot of money?"

Bessie was staggered. "Who? Bill-Bob?" Questions raced through her mind at the thought of it.

Ethel said, quite matter of fact, "Yes, I got a letter from his solicitor only a little while ago. He said he wanted me to go to Sydney to see him and I told him I'd do no such thing." She had stopped working now and was just sitting talking to her friend. "I thought it would be a little bit of money or a memento or something, when the solicitor rang, but finally he convinced me there's a lot of money involved."

"Well!" said Bessie, stunned. "Goodness gracious me!"

They both sat in silence for a while and then Bessie asked the obvious question. "So, what are you going to do? Doesn't this change things for you?"

Ethel shook her head. "Not at all. It would have if it had happened while I had the place." She stopped for a while. "Actually, probably not. He wrote a letter to me about that. The solicitor sent me that, too. He said he was sorry not to give it to me when I thought I needed it, but he didn't like seeing me defeat myself trying to make the property pay. He said it would all disappear into the pockets of creditors and the governments and I'd be left with my white elephant. Besides, the government will still get a fair share because now I can live on Bill-Bob's money and I won't get a pension any more, so they will save on that."

Bessie was shocked. "Goodness me, Ethel, don't you want to spend it?"

"What on?" she shot back. "There's nothing I want." She was silent for a moment and then she admitted, "The only thing I'd like to do is travel and, quite frankly, I'm too scared to go off and do that by myself. I'd like to ask you to come with me, but you're still tied to your white elephant."

Kirsty had come into the kitchen to get some tissues for the school room. She looked from one to the other. Her eyes widened in delight.

"Aunt Bessie, do you have a white elephant?"

Bessie thought quickly. Was her property so sacred? Was it really a white elephant – impressive, perhaps, but unproductive and costly? Obviously, that's how Bill-Bob saw it.

"No, darling," she told the little girl. "Mrs Alsop was just teasing me. Pretending. I don't have anywhere to put a white elephant."

But Kirsty was so fascinated with the idea of a white elephant it effectively stopped their conversation in its tracks.

Chapter 19

One evening a few days later the phone rang for Kendal. It was Charles. He was full of apologies. "Darling, can you possibly forgive me?" he asked. He said he knew he was at fault, and that he had to learn not to jump to hasty conclusions. He had an idea. A way of making up for his behaviour, but more importantly, a way for them to spend time together. He asked Kendal if she'd come to Brisbane for a weekend to see him.

Kendal had lots of reasons for refusing. She'd already decided to have nothing more to do with him. It was just too painful to handle his changeable ways. In fact, she had lots of reasons for not flying to Brisbane to meet him, but Charles was entirely persuasive. She protested it was too expensive – and Charles told her he intended to pay for his sins and meet all expenses. So she argued she wasn't due for time off. Charles maintained she'd often been working weekends and he knew the Thompsons would be happy for her to have time off. She was tempted, and his charm clinched the deal. His deep voice was sending chills down her back. She told him she'd definitely be staying with her mother.

"Oh... of course," he said, disappointedly.

It took a few phone calls to actually set a date and a time for this trip. Charles had a pretty full programme but he bent over backwards to fit in with her. Whenever she could come, he'd clear the weekend. By the time it was all arranged, Kendal was rapt. And her fears about taking unearned leave were proven false. Both Aunt Bessie and Bruce were delighted with the idea, and they'd been urging her to accept Charles's offer. Her mother, of course, was also excited her daughter was coming home for a visit.

Flight West had a plane service that came out from Brisbane to Mt Isa twice a week. From Charleville to Mt Isa, it did what everyone called the milk run, stopping at numerous little towns on the way. Juno was one of these stops. It was a wonderful communication with civilisation but very expensive, so hardly any of the locals used the service except in emergencies. Still, it was wonderful to have it there in case. Oil people, opal buyers, and government workers used the service regularly, for which the locals were grateful. That way, it kept the service going for when they needed it.

The flight schedule seemed to be made to order for Kendal. The plane came up from Brisbane on Monday, and back on Tuesday. Up again on Thursday, and then back on Friday.

She asked Bruce if she could have the two extra days to go Friday and come back on Monday. Bessie suggested, and Bruce backed her up, that Kendal go on the Tuesday and come back the next Monday to enjoy a real break.

"If Charles is busy some of the time," Aunt Bessie decided, "it'll give you time to spend with your mother and go shopping with your friends."

Charles, of course, was at the airport to meet her and embraced her for a long time as soon as she stepped through the arrivals' door. Kendal felt weak at the knees just to be with him. She could hardly contain her delight at the prospect of a week with him.

Driving away from the airport, they discussed how they'd spend their time together. He had plenty of suggestions. He had a few business appointments on Wednesday and Thursday that he couldn't change, but every night was theirs.

They went straight to her mother's home and dropped off her case, but her mother was out because it was her day to help at the hospital. Kendal and Charles spent the day and half the night wandering around the city and catching up, and came home so late that Kendal didn't catch up with her mother until the next morning. Charles had suggested they spend that night quietly on their own and on Wednesday night join some friends of his and go to the Spanish restaurant at Southbank. On Thursday, he'd thought of getting some tickets to the Lyric Theatre.

Kendal was floating on air for the whole week. She loved the theatre but had hardly ever been, and of course since she'd been in the bush there had been no possibility. She spent ages going through her wardrobe in a flurry of preparation, trying to find which were the prettiest, the most sophisticated and the most flattering outfits in her wardrobe.

For the theatre, she decided she just had to get something new. For dinner with friends, she thought she could find something in her wardrobe, but she was determined to look special for the next night. Something that didn't look as if she was trying too hard, and yet something that looked as if it were natural for her to be sophisticated, elegant and poised. She wanted to be all things to this extraordinary man. She knew he had a history of escorting only the most elegant women and she felt she had lots of images of herself in dirty working clothes, covered in dust and flies, to blot out if she wanted to start to compete with them.

She raced out shopping on Thursday morning. She tried on lots of clothes but in the end she bought some fabulous material and decided to design herself a stunning dress. It only took her a couple of hours to make a dress and somehow it felt more like her. She did her hair and her hands, her fingernails and her toenails, she tried on all her wraps and some of her mother's and when she finally emerged she certainly had achieved most of her goals. She thought she at least looked her best, but was that enough?

Her mother, Andrea MacKenzie, thought it was more than enough. She thought her daughter looked superb. By now, Andrea couldn't miss how consumed Kendal was with Charles. Certainly, Kendal's letters and phone calls had blown a bit hot and cold about this dominant Charles. Today there was no missing Kendal's complete preoccupation with Charles and what Charles thought and felt, and what Charles might think and feel.

Andrea was glad for her daughter that she had found such love but she hoped and prayed that this man would be worthy of her daughter's devotion and that he wouldn't break her heart. She was comforted at least that Kenrick had sent such good reports of him as well, but she would be glad to meet him tonight to start making her own judgment of this man who seemed to be playing such a big part in her daughter's life.

When Charles came to collect Kendal for the evening, there was no mistaking that he thought she looked superb, too. Andrea was charmed with Charles, as she had every reason to be. Kendal had never seen him dressed formally for an evening out and she was not disappointed. He looked distinguished in a beautifully tailored suit and well chosen tie, and all those little things that old fashioned mothers look for, like well polished shoes, neat hair and clean fingernails. And apart from all that, although he was always regarded as a reserved man, he had an assured dignified manner and there was no lack of quiet charm. He was no callow youth to be overcome at meeting his date's mother and he was relaxed enough for Andrea to catch a glimpse of the very real person behind the polish and she was impressed.

So Kendal floated out of the house and down the steps on her way to her evening, enchanted with Charles and feeling her mother's approval and glad of it, even though she was a woman and no longer a child.

They were early and had plenty of time. Charles had booked their table at the Lyre Bird Restaurant. She'd seen people having meals there through the elegant glass walls but hadn't ever been inside before. Of course, Kendal in her enthusiastic manner was delighted with everything. The food was delicious, the service good, the company incomparable. Actually, she probably wouldn't have noticed if the food or the service hadn't been all that good, because the company and the ambiance was enough in itself. After months of down to earth living, and the few weeks with Charles which had included cleaning dirty troughs, dressing fly-blown sheep and riding a bumpy motorbike over pretty rough country, she felt as if she was in fairy land. Life had been pretty tough lately. But here she was feeling her best, well-dressed and smartly groomed in such a charming setting with a wonderful man who was behaving like a polished and ardent suitor. It was like a dream. If he'd been a shining knight on a white horse, she couldn't have been more enchanted. She felt like pinching herself to see that she was really awake and not dreaming it all. This was not the time to examine her doubts, nor the time to be sensible. No-one else had ever set her alight the way Charles did and having him actively romancing her like this was incredible. If she was asleep, she didn't want to wake up.

She bubbled with enthusiasm and pleasure and Charles was charmed. One of the things he loved most about Kendal was her frank appreciation of life. He'd seen her handle trouble and no-one could have failed to appreciate her practical good sense in an emergency. But he loved the way she lived each moment to the full. He thought she was breathtakingly lovely tonight. She would have been even without her sparkle; her vibrant hair, interesting face, and full, curvy figure were attractive enough, but it was the way she lit them up from inside that made her outstanding.

Kendal enjoyed herself and her pleasure was obvious all night. She delighted in walking up the steps of the Performing Arts Complex, feeling like a princess. Charles bought a programme and ordered drinks for the interval and they went out onto the overbridge across the street and watched the lights of the city reflected in the water of the river.

Feeling bad she hadn't asked how Charles's work was going, she inquired.

But Charles put a finger to her lips. "Don't let's talk about any of that tonight, darling. Let's keep this time special."

Kendal was content to do that, and kissed his finger instead.

On Friday they went to Noosa for the day and met up with friends of hers who lived there. By their reactions and their whispered asides, Kendal knew they were terribly impressed with Charles. They met friends again for lunch on Saturday and enjoyed themselves at the Breakfast Creek Hotel, but afterwards Charles took her home so she could spend what was left of the afternoon and the evening with her mother. That one act told Kendal that Charles could be thoughtful, as well as passionate.

Sunday was their last day together and Charles asked Kendal to choose how they should spend their time. Kendal, true to her word, had every moment planned.

They went first to St John's Cathedral. Kendal really enjoyed the cathedral and she hadn't worked out yet whether Charles liked it, too, or was only falling in with her idea. She had always had a strong faith and loved the feeling of worship with a crowd of people in the hallowed atmosphere. She hadn't had much of that lately. She also loved the building and the music and the whole spectacle of worship there. She wasn't sure if it really brought her closer to God, but it did make Him seem closer

After the service, they walked down the hill to the riverside markets. They had lunch there and Charles bought her a tiny silver fairy charm that she'd seen and loved. She felt it symbolised the magic of their time together. Charles thought how he'd known girls to be less enthusiastic about much more expensive gifts.

They slowly made their way through the whole length of the markets down to the botanical gardens. They sat on the grass very closely entwined to watch the concert. Charles was definitely more interested in Kendal than the music and, strangely enough, Kendal

241

would never have been able to tell anyone about the performance, either.

As they passed the kiosk, they bought ice cream cones and walked hand in hand down the path to the ferry. Charles couldn't believe his luck. Most of the girls he'd ever taken out had needed money spent on them all the time to be so happy. No-one else he knew would have ever suggested such a quiet day. Kendal couldn't believe her luck, either. Most of the men she'd been out with would have suggested she spend the day watching them play sport – or watch someone else play his favourite sport. Of course, Kendal was hoping to watch him play polocrosse and cricket one day, but she was impressed that he was willing to enjoy a day like this with her.

They caught the ferry to Southbank and had their dinner quietly at another of the many eating places there. Kendal watched the little ferries coming and going and impulsively suggested they take the ferry to New Farm Park and back again. Charles thought that sounded all right, too. He wasn't going to object to sitting close to Kendal for an hour or so. In fact, it would probably offer better chances for getting close than most places.

The ferry was nearly empty and the river was beautiful. Charles and Kendal had the top deck of the old ferry to themselves as they glided past the beautifully-lit Kangaroo Point cliffs, with the lights of the city and the trees of the gardens on the other. They floated past the yachts at their moorings and under the Story Bridge and on to the quieter reaches of the river. Charles had heard a night cruise on the River Seine was one of the most romantic events in the world, but he thought it had nothing on the Brisbane River ferry on a Sunday night with Kendal for romantic atmosphere. Maybe one day they would go to Paris together and compare.

Chapter 20

Not long after, Kendal was singing as she tidied the school room one Thursday morning. She was going to Carmody Plains for the weekend because Charles was coming home. Her beloved Charles, she mused. He looked so assured and debonair and yet he was so vulnerable and easily hurt. She felt she knew him so well, but her love at times was a two-edged sword. It gave her so much joy, but there was always an edge of tension when he wasn't there with her. If only Charles could overcome his life-long distrust of women and Kendal could overcome the jinx that put her in the wrong all the time. Admittedly, not a thing had spoilt their wonderful time in Brisbane or since then. Did she dare to hope their troubles were over?

She was packing up the school box to be returned and couldn't find the two big jigsaw puzzles. "Keep your mind on the job, Kendal," she told herself sternly. She really had to get it all together so she could send it off in the post tomorrow.

Bruce and his aunt were sitting in the breezeway listening to the radio. The forecast on the country hour was good for rain in the far south-west. It had been raining well in Alice Springs and the low was travelling east out of the Northern Territory and into Queensland, bringing good falls all the way.

Bruce was buoyant. "It really looks as if we might be lucky this time."

Bessie was more cautious, "Sometimes the weather map makes it look as if we can't miss and still it stays fine and clear."

But Bruce maintained, "I think we're right this time. It's getting pretty muggy and it just feels like rain."

As Kendal walked out of the schoolroom, Bessie said, "You might have a wet weekend, Kendal. If it really comes in, you'd probably be better not to go to Carmody Plains – you could get caught in the wet."

Kendal's heart sank. "Oh no," she thought. "This can't be the moment that the west finally gets its wish for rain."

The signs of rain kept coming and Kendal could hardly believe her feeling of disappointment. A lifetime in the bush and always wanting rain – and now, because she had plans of her own, the rain was a nuisance and not a joy.

Yet everything about rain is exciting, from the strange light to the smell, the sound and the feel of the air.

Harsh dryness is a part of life, a constant, in the far outback. So when the wind starts to blow off the rain, the moist air has a different quality that is tangible. Sometimes it's strong and gusty when it's blowing off a storm, and sometimes soft and gentle as the wet just creeps in.

As the first rain falls onto dry ground, the smell is strong and pungent. It's like no other aroma on earth. Animals can smell water from a distance when humans have no perception of it at all, but everyone can catch the wonderful smell of the first rain on really dry earth. There is no mistaking it.

In the bush, rain usually feels as though it is soaking directly into the human body as well as into the soil. People of the outback identify with the land and every drop of rain revitalises their bodies and souls as it revitalises the ground beneath them.

Bruce was watching every movement of every cloud all after-noon. As the clouds built up he went out on the verandah or right out on the lawn to have a better look. "It's building up out in the north," he commented to Kendal and Bessie. "That's a good sign, we always get good rain from the north. It's turning around a bit – look at that big black cloud coming in from the south-east! Remember, Aunt Bessie, we had four inches from rain that came in that way about six years ago?"

Excitedly, he called to his girls. "Come out and have a look, kids, I think there's rain coming. I think we'd better get all the outside jobs done early so that we can sit and enjoy the rain as it comes."

Every few minutes on that Thursday afternoon, Bruce had a different observation to make about their chances of getting a good fall of rain. Kendal had grown up with her Dad like that, watching every cloud and tracking its progress over the sky.

In fact, you could divide the world into two camps out here as the rain clouds build up. Some watch every change in the sky, constantly assessing and reassessing their chances of a fall, while some bury their heads in case it's all a false alarm. God knows there are enough of those. Her mother belonged to the second group of people, those who busied themselves with lots of other jobs and tried not to think about the rain because they didn't like to hope too much and then have to put up with the disappointment if it didn't eventuate.

"I can't bear to watch the clouds," Andrea used to say. "I just can't enjoy it until we have a couple of inches of rain, right there in the rain gauge, puddles in the garden and water in the tanks. Then I can relax and enjoy it. All the hoping in the world won't make the rain come out of those clouds if it isn't going to." So she used to get extra busy with something to keep her mind off the tantalising clouds.

Kendal was more like her father and usually she would be out there with Bruce rejoicing as the clouds built up and despairing when it looked as though it might pass over without wetting them.

Looking up at the dark clouds, Bruce threw his hands in the air and shouted, "Send her down, Hughie!"

Aunt Bessie tut-tutted, "I've had a lifetime of listening to that expression and I still don't really approve. It sounds pagan to me!"

Kendal listened to all the excitement and comments, and thought that usually she'd be out there with him and probably shocking the elderly lady, too.

But today she was wishing the rain just might go away for a few days. She couldn't believe the rains would hit the very weekend she'd planned to spend with Charles. She was terribly tempted just to jump in the ute and head to Carmody Plains, but she knew that would be foolish. Common sense and fair play made her stay. If it rained heavily, she'd be stuck at Carmody Plains until next week and would be no use to Bessie or Bruce. Besides, the boggy roads would stop Charles getting home.

She thought how strange it was to be in love, and how everything else and all other plans fade into insignificance in your mind. Being with Charles was the one thing that was important to her and she was having to try very hard not to be really rotten company to everyone around her in her disappointment.

As it was, she tried to pretend she didn't mind staying for the weekend as long as they all had rain. She tried to pretend that she was just as excited as she should be with rain coming. And she was trying to pretend she wasn't cross and disagreeable.

The children's excitement got on her nerves and that never happened any other time. She loved the little girls and had a good time with them. They had let the chooks out for only a little while and were putting them back to feed them early. The fowls were difficult and ran around squawking as they felt the thunder in the air. Thank goodness there were no goslings to worry about tonight. The children were hurrying and accidents began to happen. Carla dropped an egg too quickly into the bucket on top of the others she had collected and it landed with an audible *crack*.

"Oh, be careful, Carla," Kendal snapped before she could help herself. She felt a real heel when she saw big tears well up in Carla's eyes. The girls were disappointed enough when an egg broke. She quickly put her arms around her and gave her a hug and apologised. "Sorry kiddo, I know you didn't mean to break it. It's all the excitement of the storm coming. We'll both be more careful."

Moments later, Kirsty was skipping along and swinging her bucket of eggs. And sure enough, she fell over. Once again Kendal felt irritated and annoyed but she had herself in hand by now and she picked her up and cuddled her too. "Come on now, it's not the end of the world. It's just this good old storm. It's making us all excited. The whole fowl yard's in a flurry and a flutter, and so are we. Take my hand now and we'll go inside very carefully. I'll put a band-aid on your knee."

Kendal knew that the promise of a band-aid usually worked like a magic charm and she wasn't disappointed. She went on talking to them. "We'll take out all the eggs that aren't broken and wash them and put them away. You'll find there aren't many broken, really, and all the messy bits we'll put in some milk for Tom Kitten and Pinkle Purr. They'll like that."

That was accepted as a very good idea. Carla started looking carefully over her fingers and hands and legs to see if she could find a tiny scratch where she might claim a band-aid was needed, too.

It was getting dark quickly and the clouds were getting so heavy. The dogs were all put in a sheltered spot and fed early, as were the pigs. The horses were restless, galloping about. They were out in the paddock, so they were all right. The little lambs were put in the old stable and given their milk early. One by one all the jobs were done before the first big drops of rain came down.

When they did, the noise on the iron roof was loud – almost like bullets hitting – and the little girls were shouting and dancing with glee. Then they were constantly going in and out in the wet. They were having a ball. They put up umbrellas and went for a walk in the rain. Then, when the rain stopped for a bit, they danced in the puddles.

Kendal brought them in for a warm bath when she thought they might be getting cold. She was pleased the girls were excited about the rain and enjoying the unexpected treat. Kendal had met some children who were scared of it, because it was so unfamiliar. Bruce was almost as excited as the children and Aunt Bessie's eyes were bright and she was obviously happy. Kendal felt a bit like the spectre at the feast and tried hard to join in.

It had months in which to rain and now it would be goodness knows how long before the roads were open again. If it had waited just a little longer, she and Charles would have been together at Carmody Plains and it wouldn't have been her fault if she couldn't get back. Now he'd probably stay in Quilpie – or Juno at a pinch – and she'd be stuck here. In fact, if he'd been watching the weather reports, he may not have even left Brisbane. She didn't even know how long he was to stay up this trip. Maybe there would be something he had to go back for before he'd even seen her.

She did love him so, but she still wasn't really sure it was wise. Love wasn't what she'd expected, with all of this tension, pain and uncertainty.

She knew he wasn't unfaithful. She knew he loved her with his whole heart. But she felt he might always be suspicious, wondering if her intentions were true. He might always be looking closely to see that she was not doing the wrong thing. There was so much joy in her love for him – but she couldn't erase her memory of how he'd rejected her so painfully, so unnecessarily, so often.

Surely he'd realise that she couldn't leave in this weather. He would know that. If the rain really set in as it had been forecast, she couldn't leave Kalanoa. Bruce would have to think of the stock and the channels and Bessie couldn't be expected to look after all the house animals and the children in the wet. You could hardly expect Sam and Clara to take over. She was the logical choice. No, she was the one to don gum boots and a drizabone coat and paddle about in the wet doing the domestic jobs to leave Bruce free to think about the property at large.

Kendal hadn't done as good a job of pretending as she thought. Bessie noticed she was downhearted.

"In all the excitement I forgot you were going to Carmody Plains this weekend, Kendal," she said. "I suppose you're sorry you won't be seeing Charles."

Kendal thought sorry was putting it mildly, but all she said was, "Yes, I am a bit."

Bessie was philosophical. "Yes, it is a pity for you, dear, but you've got a whole lifetime ahead of you with Charles. He's probably just as pleased to see the rain as we are."

"Of course he will be, Miss T, who wouldn't be? We need it badly enough." Kendal knew that if she was sure of Charles's commitment, she wouldn't mind so much. She thought that if she was with him she could make him sure she was all he wanted her to be. As it was, there had been so many times he'd misunderstood her actions, she felt she was living with a ticking time bomb while they were apart. And therein lay her problem. If he really loved her, would he always think the worst?

By bedtime everything had settled down to reasonable normality. The children had enjoyed all their excitement but were ready for sleep at last. They'd seen all their animals attended to and they'd seen, heard and felt the rain before their baths. So now they were happy to go to bed with the sound of the frogs croaking and the rain drumming on the roof. Their father took them to bed, read them a story and heard their prayers.

Meanwhile, Kendal helped Bessie to clean up the kitchen. Once or twice, she thought she caught a shadow of pain cross the elderly lady's face.

"Are you OK?" she asked solicitously.

"Yes, of course, my dear," Bessie replied. "I occasionally get a slight nagging pain in my side."

"Are you sure you're OK?" Kendal repeated.

The old lady said sharply, "I said I was, didn't I?"

Although unconvinced, Kendal knew there wasn't much more she could do. "Well, if you're OK, I think I'll turn in early," she said. "Everything's done now, isn't it?"

"Yes, Kendal dear, we'll all sleep well with the sound of the rain on the roof. Sweet dreams to you. You can dream of that young man of yours. You'd better turn out the light as you go."

Kendal turned out the lights and slowly made her way to her bedroom. She didn't really want to go straight to sleep. She just wanted to get away on her own so she didn't have to choose her words and to be able to think her own thoughts. As usual, she got out her sewing while she was thinking things over.

She seldom wore frilly clothes, but loved feminine laces and frills in the beautiful and elaborate underwear she made. When she'd lived in Brisbane she'd sold it commercially, but now she hoped her collection could become her trousseau. At the moment she was adding a deep frill of chantilly lace to the top of a heavy silk nightie. The frill of lace was to go around the edge of the opera top with fine rouleau straps across the shoulders. She had it all tacked in place to her satisfaction and decided to try it on to make sure it was sitting the way she wanted when it was worn, before she sewed it down securely.

It felt wonderful as she slipped it on over her head and, looking in the mirror, she was quite pleased. She didn't really see herself as she was only looking at how the lace sat on the silk. But the chemise managed to outline her figure in no uncertain manner. The silk, cut on the bias, was sensuous and alluring, hinting at what it had hidden. Kendal had washed her face and brushed out her hair and in this beautiful garment she was, with no artifice, a stunning woman.

Time had passed more quickly than she thought and it was quite late when she heard someone walking down the passage. It had to be Bessie, but Kendal could hear the walk was irregular and quite unlike her usual gait. Kendal put her head out the door and was shocked at the elderly lady's pale face. "Miss T, are you all right?"

Bessie sat down carefully on the couch in the hall and said quietly, "I have this nagging pain in my side. I get it occasionally. Just be a good soul and run and get me two aspirin."

With no thought to how she was dressed, Kendal went straight to the kitchen. By the time Kendal returned with the aspirin, Bessie was almost writhing in what seemed to be dreadful pain. Kendal didn't have any idea of what could be wrong and she certainly didn't want to handle this on her own. Putting the glass of water and tablets down on the table, she rushed along to Bruce's room.

"For God's sake, Bruce, come quickly. Something dreadful has happened to your aunt."

Bruce didn't take long to appear and when he took one look at the situation asked, "Do you know what it is?"

Kendal shook her head.

"Well," he continued, "I'll pick her up and put her on her bed, you go and call the Flying Doctor straight away."

Kendal rushed into the office and turned on the transceiver and pushed the emergency call button. The minute that she had to hold the button for seemed like an eternity. She could hear the rain falling down outside and only hoped there was something in the medical chest that could help.

"This is VJJ Charleville," the radio crackled to life. "Would the station who pressed the emergency call button please identify themselves?"

Kendal could hardly hear Charleville because the weather was hampering conditions. In a loud voice, Kendal replied, "This is 8XY Kalanoa. I need the doctor."

Ian at the Flying Doctor base could sense the distress in Kendal's voice. Conditions were poor and he had trouble hearing her. Within minutes, Ian had Dr Ross and Kendal linked up.

"8XY Kalanoa. It's Dr Ross speaking, what seems to be the problem?"

Kendal was relieved to be finally talking to the doctor. "8XY to VJJ. Hello Dr Ross, it's Kendal speaking. It's Bessie Thompson. She is in dreadful pain, over."

"8XY, could you slow down and repeat your statement?"

Kendal was becoming exasperated with the conditions as she retold the statement to the doctor. Poor Dr Ross still could only make out a garbled version and had to get the base manager to relay the statement. Ian suggested to the doctor that he come down to the base and use the base radio, rather than face extra interference over the phone.

"8XY, Dr Ross will be with you in a few minutes. Due to the poor radio conditions he's having to drive down to the base to talk with you. Will you please standby?"

For Kendal, those minutes dragged by. Bruce came in and stood by the radio. Kendal looked up. "You heard?" she asked.

"Yup," he replied. Then he said, "You seem to be handling this OK. You keep in touch here, and I'll go find some candles and get

250

a torch. Otherwise, we'll be in a hell of a mess if there's a power blackout in this storm."

Kendal felt she had time to go back to Aunt Bessie's room to check on her, even though she wasn't really sure what to check. She hoped they would get the doctor clearly soon. Bessie was lying quite still on the bed in pain looking extremely pale and very sweaty.

"It's all right, Miss T, we're talking to the doctor," Kendal said with an assurance she didn't feel.

The elderly lady bravely told Kendal she was sure the pain would pass as it always had before, although she'd never had an attack quite like this one.

Dr Ross was soon at the base radio control room. "8XY, this is Ross speaking, go ahead please."

Kendal left Bessie's bedside and rushed to answer the radio. "8XY. Hello Dr Ross, over."

"8XY, what seems to be the problem, back?"

"Dr Ross, it's Bruce's aunt, Bessie Thompson. She is in terrible pain and she is all pale and sweaty, over."

"OK then. Where exactly is this pain, back?"

"It's in the right side of the back, over."

"Does the pain radiate anywhere else, back?"

"Dr Ross, I don't know. I'll go and find out, over."

Kendal returned quite quickly and told Dr Ross the pain started in her back and radiated down to the lower front, making her feel extremely nauseated.

"Right, is this pain constant or coming and going, back?"

Again Kendal had to go down to Bessie's room to ask her the question. She returned to report, "Dr Ross, the pain comes and goes, over."

"Okay, Kendal, I want you to ask Miss Thompson did this pain come on suddenly, or was it of gradual onset. Before you go off do you have a medical chest, back?"

"Yes, Dr Ross, it's right here by the radio, over."

"Good, I want you to get the thermometer from the top tray and take Miss Thompson's temperature. I also want you to take her pulse. Do you know how to do that, back?"

"Sure, I'll be right back."

While they were waiting for Kendal to report back, Ross and Ian discussed the rainfalls of the properties in the area. This time, the rain had appeared to be very widespread with most stations reporting between three to five inches of rain. From the satellite pictures, it looked like more rain was still to come.

"8XY to VJJ."

"Go ahead Kendal, back."

"Bessie's temperature is 36 and her pulse is 110. The pain was of sudden onset, over."

"Thank you, Kendal, I have a few more questions. Is Miss Thompson passing urine OK, can she see any blood in her urine, and are her bowel motions normal. Have you received all that, back?"

"Yes, Dr Ross, Bruce was writing them down and has gone to ask his aunt, over."

The airwaves were still very crackly and Ross waited patiently for Kendal to return to her transceiver.

"8XY to VJJ," she radioed.

"Go ahead Kendal, back."

"Miss Thompson says she has no trouble passing her urine and she can't see any blood, her motions are normal, over."

"Kendal, this sounds to me like it is most likely renal colic or a kidney stone," Dr Ross told her. "I will need to know Miss Thompson's age and her weight, back."

"Standby please, Dr Ross." A few moments later, Kendal returned. "8XY to VJJ. She is seventy-five years old and weighs fifty-five kilograms, over."

"I want you to give an intramuscular injection. Can you give an intramuscular injection, back?"

Kendal was suddenly a bit worried, although still calm. "No, Doc, I've never had to give one to a person before, although I've given plenty to the animals, over."

Dr Ross spoke clearly and slowly. "The most appropriate site for an intramuscular injection is to divide the thigh between hip and knee into three equal portions. Choose the middle third and on the outside of that third give the injection the full length of the needle. Did you get that, back?"

"Yes Doc. I divide the leg into three and then give the injection in the... top third, over," Kendal stumbled.

"No, I repeat divide the thigh between hip and knee into three equal portions; choose the MIDDLE, I repeat, the MIDDLE third and on the outside of the middle third give the injection the full length of the needle, back."

This time Kendal had scribbled it down. "Okay, Doc, I divide the leg between the hip and knee into three parts and give it in the outside middle third, over."

Next were the medication instructions. "Right. Draw up the complete ampoule of number nine seven, repeat nine seven, which is Stematil twelve point five milligrams, and one three seven which is Pethidine one hundred milligrams. Give the contents of the syringe into the outer aspect of the middle third of the thigh after first swabbing the site down with number two zero seven, repeat two zero seven. Did you get that, back?"

Kendal read back her notes. "Yes, Doc, I will draw up drug number nine seven and drug number one three seven into the syringe and swab the site with number two zero seven, over."

"That is correct; now go ahead and give it, back."

Finding the drugs in the medicine chest, Kendal immediately got back on the radio. "Doc, drug number one three seven is out of date, over."

"When did it expire, back?"

"It went out of date one month ago, over."

"There is usually quite a considerable safety factor in the expiry date of these drugs and I think we could quite safely go ahead and use it. Have you any further questions, back?"

"No doctor, over."

"Then go ahead and give the injection, back." Kendal went to Bessie and Bruce stayed on at the radio.

"What is the state of your strip, back?" Dr Ross inquired.

"Doc, Bruce here. We've had three inches of rain on it and it's still raining, over."

"There's obviously no hope of us picking up your aunt, so we can only hope the injection will settle her down. In the meantime, I want her to push fluids. Is she taking any other medications, back?"

"No Doc, as fit as a fiddle, usually, over."

"So I want her to push fluids to this extent. When she goes to bed after the injection, she should take a litre jug of water, she should not go to sleep till she has drunk it. When she wakes up to pass her urine, she should refill the jug with water and not go to sleep till she has drunk that and keep repeating the process until you get back to me on the seven forty-five am medical session in the morning. Of course, if you have any more problems tonight, you should get straight back to me. Any more questions?"

"No," Bruce replied. "Thank you, Dr Ross. Thanks for your help, over."

"Righto then, cheers for now."

Ian got back on the radio then. "8XY, Ian here. Is that all for now, back?"

Bruce answered, "Yes, thanks Ian, all OK."

"OK, then cheers for now."

Bruce went to get the jug of water and a tumbler, and then went back to his aunt's room. He told her what the doctor had said and asked how the injection had gone. Eventually, they had her settled down.

Bruce had been upset and quite white with strain while he'd been attending to his aunt and now that the danger was passed Kendal could see that he was almost exhausted. He felt his responsibility for all of them very keenly. She couldn't see herself but she thought she must look a bit risque. A little of the tacked-on lace had caught and was hanging loose and her hair was tousled, but she felt fine. At least Aunt Bessie seemed as if she was going to be all right.

They went out together to the breezeway. Kendal went across to Bruce and pushed him down on the couch gently, saying, "Cheer up, Bruce. It's OK. She'll be all right now. You just stay here and I'll get you a whisky. You look all in and I don't need another patient just now."

She thought about how she looked. "I'll just slip into my room and change before I get that drink," she said.

Bruce might have been a bit worried about his aunt, but he still had a sense of humour. "Oh, what a pity," he smiled. "I was quite enjoying the scenery."

Kendal laughed. "Behave yourself, Bruce, or I'll tell Thea."

"She'd never believe you," he retorted.

"Well, I'll tell Charles," she laughed. Then she added ruefully, "I'm afraid he would believe me."

She went to her room to change. As she sorted out some clothes, she became aware of the noise around her. The heavy rain had stopped and there were little, soft, gentle raindrops. The sound of the rain on the roof and that of the water swishing in the gutters and gurgling in the downpipe was quite musical, but there was a great cacophony of sound from the frogs and the toads.

Most of these creatures burrow into the ground and stay there for years and years while it's dry and then, when there is enough rain so the ground is soft, they come out in their hundreds of thousands.

It starts with just a few. They know it's time and, one by one, the little creatures hop outside and before long their throats puff out like huge balloons and signal their availability with all their might. Their numbers grow and grow until there is such a noise it's impossible to believe. You couldn't possibly imagine it if you haven't heard it. *Croak-croak, rebbit-rebbit, knee-deep* – high and low, every sound that's ever been heard to describe the mating call of an amphibian, and so many that haven't. Dozens and dozens, so that it's quite indescribable.

The numbers swell until there are thousands, all puffed up, bellowing in chorus. Each male tries to outdo his rivals. The usually dry, arid water courses become alive. Thousands of inland amphibians in a huge mating chorus, all desperate to attract a female and complete the mating ritual of their life cycle.

The sound grows and grows in crescendo until it's quite deafening, and stays that way for a few days. It then gradually recedes, and is not heard again until the next big wet.

The night wasn't cold, really, but Kendal found she was glad to have warmer clothes on. Just a skivvy and long pants kept the damp chill out. She came out of her room and said, "I love that sound. You know you've had really good rain when that gets going." She yawned and stretched. "It's been quite a night. You go to bed as soon as we have a drink and I'll hang around and keep an eye on Aunt Bessie. You know, top up her water and that sort of thing. I'll catch up with a sleep-in a bit in the morning."

Just then, the dogs started to bark and they both looked up.

"What's worrying them?" Bruce wondered. "You wouldn't think there'd be anything about on a night like this." He went out to the door and looked out. "Can't see a thing out there," he started to say, and then he said, "Oh yes, I can. That's not lightning. There's a light flashing out there. I think it must be someone walking with a flashlight."

Kendal went to the screen to look out, too. It wasn't long before a figure could be seen in the dark. At first it was just a shape and then Bruce said dryly, "G'day, Charles. What took you so long? We've just been sitting around here waiting for you."

255

"Well," Charles replied, equally dryly, "I came as quickly as I could. I got held up a bit, you see. Had a few minor troubles. The road's a bit wet."

Kendal just couldn't believe her good luck. Her eyes lit up and she just glowed with pleasure. She was just so pleased to see Charles, especially after having written off the chance of seeing him that weekend. And just so pleased that he'd bothered to walk so far in the pouring rain and the heavy mud to see her. And delighted that her own personal jinx had seemed to be looking the other way. If that jinx had been on duty, Charles might have found her looking quite risque in a satin nightie with lace hanging loose, her hair dishevelled and drinking whisky with Bruce.

But she bade the negative thoughts to stop. Charles had walked all this way in the rain and mud for her. She couldn't imagine a clearer demonstration of his love for her.

As Charles sat on the edge of the verandah and took off his boots and long drizabone coat, Bruce kept up the conversation. "Bloody beautiful rain, does it go far in?"

Charles dutifully answered, "Started the other side of Quilpie."

When he stood up, although his clothes were almost as wet and muddy as his coat had been, it was obvious that that didn't matter to Kendal.

As Kendal and Charles moved towards each other, Bruce muttered to himself, "Well, that's the end of any conversation here. I might as well talk to myself from now on, I expect. A fellow was going to be waited on and looked after, too. So, now I'll just have to go and get myself a whisky."

Chapter 21

Easter was arriving and Bessie Thompson was feeling a great deal better. She was spoiling herself, taking a quiet moment to sit in the shade on the verandah and look over the garden. Mentally going over all the plans, she felt she deserved a few quiet moments. Her plan of campaign was working out quite well. A few moments to rest and to savour the quiet and indeed, to feel a bit smug, were in order.

Of course, there was no guarantee all would go well but she felt reasonably sure she'd done everything she possibly could to ensure their success. She was a pragmatist at heart. She did all she could and then she just put her trust in luck. She had lived through enough summers to know that there was always a possibility of unexpected complications. They'd just sit back now and enjoy the weekend. If nothing came of it, she'd done her best.

She had thought at first that her attack of renal colic would completely sabotage her efforts. It was absolutely appalling while it lasted but it hadn't really had any long term effects after all.

The garden had needed quite a lot of care after she'd come back from a check-up in hospital in Charleville. Everything grows like Topsy after rain. She always felt the rain and the heat made the plants think their prayers had been answered, that they were living in a tropical climate and they were growing a rush of soft foliage. Then, when the moisture goes and the harsh dry heat returns, the lush growth can't be sustained and the plant has to harden up again. It takes a lot of water and a pretty experienced gardener to help it look its best, to say nothing of having to deal with all the weeds and grasses that grow in the wrong place after rain.

But by now she was really pleased. It had been a challenge and a lot of work for all of them. Bruce and Kendal had worked with a will, and Sam and Clara had come down often to help to get it all in order because she was having visitors. Only Kendal knew she had an ulterior motive. Bruce was driven by his own straight-forward desire just to have things looking good for Thea and her mother. Sam and Clara were used to everyone putting their best foot forward to keep things going well at any time.

So tons of extra work had been done in the garden and it looked a picture. Green and shady and a few spots of bright colour – all watered up and mulched and trimmed so that they'd have a minimum to do over the next few days. The house was as clean as it could possibly be. After the widespread rain, the dust wasn't its usual problem and the visitors should arrive to a fairly clean house. Every inch had been washed and cleaned and dusted and polished and maybe it would even stay clean for a day or two.

Bessie had planned her menus over and over and was pretty sure she could cope fairly well whatever emergencies occurred. It wasn't even all so hard now they had deep freezers. Before 240V power, it used to be a bit hard to keep enough food prepared ahead. Probably as long as she lived she would keep a fruit cake and lamingtons on hand because they kept pretty well in an airtight tin without other special care - but there was no longer a need to develop this habit.

She still had butter rubbed through flour and packed in plastic packets to make scones, rock cakes or tea cakes at a moment's notice. She didn't like the commercial taste to cake mixes – and besides, the habit stuck.

There were plenty of pickles and chutneys and home-made cordials. Plenty of cakes and biscuits in the tins and plenty of the makings waiting. Tomatoes, lettuce and other salad vegetables were in the garden. The hens were laying. She was lucky there. They usually went off a bit in the late autumn – the only time of year that they ever ran out of eggs – but they wouldn't run out this weekend. Bessie was sure of that.

Yes, all in all, Bessie was pretty sure she was ready. Bruce had gone in now to pick the visitors up from the plane.

Bessie was glad the plane service was there for Thea and Mrs Moreton. Mrs Moreton might be put off by the long, long drive. After the rain, the country wouldn't look too harsh, either. It was well worth the extravagance of a gift of an air ticket for her to see how easily her daughter could keep in touch with civilisation when necessary.

She had planned this Easter with the thoroughness of an army general preparing a military campaign. Hopefully they had enough activities planned to keep things interesting and not too much to be tiring. Luckily, there was plenty going on in the district so they didn't even have to think of anything out of the ordinary. People who never went fishing at any other time of the year enjoyed it at Easter. It had become a bit of a tradition for everyone to try to catch their own fish for Good Friday. So, the young ones could fish if they wanted to. Mrs Moreton and she could relax.

On Saturday, there was the party for Sally Johnson. Sunday could be just celebrating Easter at home and Monday there was a church service and she'd asked a few of her close friends – not a big party, but people who would probably interest Mrs Moreton – to come over after that. "Yes," she thought, "that will keep them busy without being too hectic."

As it was the Thursday before Easter, Kendal's last job was tidying up the school room and finishing up in there. Kirsty and Carla had gone with Bruce. Before they left, she'd made sure their room and the school room were tidy and now she just finished the sweeping and dusting to have it clean for the holidays.

She dropped down in a chair beside Bessie. "Feeling satisfied with your preparations, Miss T?" she asked.

"Yes, Kendal, I'm as ready as I'll ever be," Bessie replied. "I'm looking forward to meeting Mrs Moreton and to seeing Thea again. Although I've tried hard to be clean and tidy and do a few extra little things..."

"Now that's an understatement for you," thought Kendal.

Bessie was continuing. "It's just like visitors at any time. I always get a buzz to have visitors. I'm really looking forward to having a house full of people and there's plenty of things happening. It'll be fun." She gave a laugh. "And as you know, I hope they like it too." She looked around her. "It's a lovely place, Kendal. I know I want to get away, but only for a while. When I sit here and can relax and enjoy it, I wouldn't want to swap it for anywhere else on earth." She took her glasses off and polished them. "Let's just hope some value comes back into our primary production and we can afford to stay here."

Before long, the car pulled up. There was a great deal of greeting and talking. The little girls wanted to show Thea everything at once and Bessie took Barbara Moreton under her ample wing.

"Come along, Mrs Moreton, I'll show you your room and you can freshen up if you want to while we get some smoko ready." She turned to Thea. "Kendal is in your old room, Thea, but I've put you and your mother in the guest wing. Bruce will put your things in your room and you can catch up with them later."

Smoko was properly set out on the table on the verandah. It was, really, afternoon tea. Kendal's mother always made the distinction of smoko when they used mugs at the kitchen table or on their laps in the shade somewhere, and afternoon tea when she used her good china and they sat at the table. If anything, life had become more informal as the years went by and most people usually used mugs all the time. Most women enjoyed the chance to use good cups and plates occasionally, although most of the men didn't really like it at all.

But today, it was definitely to be good cups and saucers at the table on the verandah. It was still hot enough in the middle of the day and early afternoons to make it pleasant out there. The evenings were closing in and could be quite nippy, but, for the moment, it was quite lovely in the shade looking out at the garden.

Mrs Moreton was quite taken with the lovely, old, wooden house that wandered about all over the place with nooks and crannies filled with greenery. What Mrs Moreton didn't know was that the house, built to survive the long, hot, dusty summers, was a nightmare to keep clean during summer and absolutely freezing in the short, dusty winter. But she was quite right. It had a wonderful charm for a visitor who didn't have to struggle with housekeeping in the hostile elements.

The weather did its bit to further Bessie's plans. It was absolutely perfect autumn weather – quite cool in the evenings and early mornings, and warm as the sun rose in the sky before getting really warm at midday. Aided by the cooler weather, the night skies were starting to be their absolute best, their deep, black, velvety depths scattered with millions of sparkling lights.

This is what Bessie had bargained on and she wasn't disappointed. The weather was made to order.

They had their cups of tea and everyone had a look around the garden and saw the animals and talked about the weather and the flight out. Then the visitors were left to unpack and change if they wished. The family bathed and changed for dinner. Mrs Moreton and Bessie were soon getting on well together and adopted the informality of Christian names. A foregone conclusion with young people, but a bit more tricky with older ones. Sam and Clara were going fishing on that Maundy Thursday, and they had promised Kirsty and Carla that they could come, too. Bessie had thought that the five of them – Bessie and Barbara, Kendal, Bruce and Thea – would all have an early tea at Kalanoa. After tea, the younger ones could join Charles and Rick and some other friends fishing. They were all starting to notice that if Rick had anything to do with it, the McMahons would definitely be members of the party, too. Well, Wendy anyway. Bessie and Barbara would stay at home, unless Barbara would particularly like to go? Barbara voted for a quiet evening talking to Bessie.

Kendal would normally have gone to Carmody Plains for Easter, but she'd offered to stay to help keep things running smoothly at Kalanoa. Bessie and Bruce had been so understanding when she'd wanted time with Charles and now she could repay a bit. An extra pair of hands really helps keep things in order. The discoloured water causes a lot of extra work in the bathroom. Every drop left behind evaporates and leaves behind a dirty, little mark and every splash a dirty, big mark. Meanwhile, spiders can pop up anywhere. They can weave a chair to the table after you leave dinner at night and before breakfast in the morning. The geckos, which run about all over the walls, leave their calling cards. To keep a house anything like well groomed is a pretty constant job. Kendal was used to it and knew she could be helpful backing up Bessie's plans this weekend.

On Friday, Bessie planned to have the fish the others had caught and hot cross buns from a recipe she'd used all her life. The days of having to make her own bread had long since passed and she seldom bothered any more, but she like to honour Good Friday with its own special food.

They had planned to drive Barbara around the place a bit to see some of the stock and interesting places on the property. Sam had a bit of an opal mine he worked now and then, and that was always an attraction for visitors. He never took any of the locals there, but he was happy to show it to visitors like these, who could never find their way there again unaided.

While they were driving around in the morning, Bruce saw that some cattle had knocked down a gate around one of the watering points and were going through to the wrong paddock. After lunch, he decided to move them back where they should be. The four women were still in the kitchen talking as they finished clearing up after the meal when the two-way crackled into life.

"Mobile to base, mobile to base. You there, Kendal or Thea?"

Kendal was closest to the handset and picked it up. "Yes, Bruce."

"Would one of you bring me out some two-stroke oil? It's in the engine room. There's a new container in a box, but there should be one we've been using in a container on an old drum. The oil I want is a dark red. Castrol Super TT. You shouldn't be able to miss it."

Thea was making signs to Kendal that she'd like to go. "Righto, Bruce, Thea will be coming out." She passed the hand piece to Thea, who asked, "Which vehicle will I bring out, Bruce?"

"The Hilux is outside the shed, bring that. Over."

"And where are you?"

"I'm following the road to Box Flat. Come straight along you can't miss me."

Mrs Moreton was amazed at her daughter, and terribly proud. As Thea headed to the vehicle, she leaned over to Bessie and said, "It's amazing how everyone expects to help around here. My Thea seems so capable and competent."

Thea went out to the Hilux. Bruce was still supplementing feed in a couple of paddocks where the response of the grass was slow. He used the Hilux for this job and an old forty-four gallon drum that had been used for topping up the molasses was pulled over the tail gate a little bit. One of the bags of meat meal was finished and a full one was lying just on the tail gate too. Thea gave them a push but they didn't budge. They were certainly a bit heavy for her to shift. She didn't want to admit she needed help and she thought they'd also be too heavy to move around as she drove.

So, leaving the tail gate down, off she went. The road was really rough because Bruce had put a few banks across the road to stop the water rushing down the road and washing it out when it rained. A track went off to the side around those banks and it was quite easy to manoeuvre around them. Thea was glad she wasn't driving a car, but the Hilux had plenty of clearance.

Bruce hadn't gone too far along and was pleased to see her.

"That's my girl. Thanks, love", he said as he took the container of oil. He topped up the oil in his bike and gave her back the container. "I was hoping you'd come but I thought maybe you wouldn't like to leave your mother again when you haven't even been here twenty-four hours yet."

Thea smiled.

Bruce tentatively put out his arms to her and she shyly moved closer. He put his arms around her gently but she flinched and drew back sharply. He dropped his arms as soon as she moved and wondered where he'd gone wrong. She was rubbing her face. He glanced down and realised his two-way receiver was in his top pocket. It was hard and sharp and the aerial stood straight up and had poked her in the face. The sunglasses that he wore to protect his eyes from both sun and insects couldn't have helped the passionate moment either. He needed practice. He obviously hadn't done this for a while.

Bruce swore under his breath. Thea giggled a bit. He hastily took off his glasses and pulled the two-way out of his pocket and, no longer tentative, took her firmly in his arms and kissed her soundly. She responded equally enthusiastically and there were no other distractions strong enough to break the spell for some time.

As she drove back, she was savouring the feeling of being out in the paddocks – and with Bruce – again. It really was a wonderful life out here. She was still feeling competent and at peace when she stopped to open the gate. She drove through and went around to close it. From the back of the vehicle she noticed that the big drum from the back wasn't there. She'd lost it. She went into panic mode.

"Oh God, I'm an idiot!" she told herself. She should have got Kendal to help her. "I can't do anything right out here!"

She reached into the cabin and picked up the hand piece of the two-way. She spoke into it. "Bruce? Bruce?" It was dead. What would she do now? "Don't panic, go slowly and think," she told herself. "The engine's on, so what else needs to be checked?" She turned the volume dial and it clicked on.

With some relief in her voice, she spoke again. "Bruce, are you there, Bruce?"

A moment's pause and then, "Yes Thea, what is it?"

"Bruce, the Hilux had a forty-four gallon drum on it when I left the house and now it's gone. It's fallen off somewhere. What do you want me to do? Drive back and look for it? Come back to you?"

"Don't worry about it, Thea. We'll pick it up later." Bruce's voice was reassuring. "That's not a problem. It won't matter." His voice became affectionate and personal. "Thanks for bringing out the oil." His gentle tone almost caressed Thea, and she melted at the sound. Her panic had evaporated at the sound of his voice.

The conversation had clearly reached the ladies, who were now sitting on the verandah, just near the two-way in the house. The affection and concern reached them, too. Bessie was delighted. The way she saw it, Bruce was just too preoccupied with his visitors to have checked his bike properly before he took off. That's why he needed the oil. Thea had left the tail gate of the Hilux down, inviting trouble. Altogether, it was a thoroughly badly organised incident. But she was hoping Barbara Moreton wouldn't have the faintest idea of these far from ideal circumstances, and would simply view it as her daughter being able to calmly cope with emergencies in this wild, bush life.

The next day they were all bustling about getting ready to go out to Sally's engagement party. Their contribution for the food had been prepared and their present of towels, which Kendal had embroidered with the couple's initials, was wrapped and ready.

There was a bit of garden watering and quite a few other odd jobs to be done before they left. Not least, the little girls had to make their nests for the Easter Bunny to deliver their eggs the next morning, just in case they were late getting back and they were too tired to enjoy doing it then. They were all really busy but it gave Barbara time to walk in the garden and appreciate the quiet beauty and the serenity of the place.

The party was about thirty minutes away and they set out at ten-thirty to be there at eleven. Most of the district would be there, and Kendal was glad that she could spend most of the day with Charles. They took two vehicles because Bessie and Barbara would probably come home late in the afternoon, but Bruce, Thea, and Kendal would very likely stay late into the next morning with other younger guests. Sam and Clara would make their own arrangements and do whatever suited them.

It was a beautiful day for a party and the house and garden at Avonlea were picturesque. Several big trees stood over freshly-mown grass, making a gracious car park.

Joe McMahon and his little boys greeted them at the gate. The children all immediately went off together to have a look at some puppies, but Joe ushered the adults into the attractively laid-out garden that was scattered with chairs and tables under ornamental trees. The guest of honour, Sally, and their hostess, Margery McMahon, were together in the garden, so they said their hellos and introduced Barbara Moreton. Others were arriving all the time so they quickly moved on and took the food they had brought over to the table set up for that purpose, and then joined a group of friends where most of the guests were gathered.

Wendy and John McMahon and all the Johnson boys were acting as friendly hosts seeing that people were comfortable. Bruce was very careful to see that his guests had drinks and stayed to chat to people as they were first introduced to Barbara and Thea. Bruce and Bessie, of course, knew nearly everyone, because most of the guests were from their own district. The only strangers were a few friends of Aiden, Sally's fiance.

Thea and Bruce moved away to talk to others. Meanwhile, Charles had arrived and had quickly gravitated to Kendal's side. They quietly moved away to be by themselves for a while.

Before long, Barbara was sitting down and talking to a group of Bessie's friends, chatting about local affairs. One of them said he was having trouble with his two-way and Barbara said how wonderful she thought they were. "I'd only seen them before on security men in the city," she said, "I didn't know how useful they could be for ordinary people. I heard Bruce using it at Kalanoa yesterday and I can see now that they are such a good idea."

"We've all had them for so long now that we take them for granted," Ethel Alsop told her, "and we only notice them when things go wrong. They are wretched things when you're wanting someone and they are out of range – or they've turned the radio off for some reason."

Another lady joined in. "Do you remember when they first came into use? The men used to ride all over the place and call up. 'Station mobile to station base, do you read me; station mobile to station base'. No matter what you were doing – making bread, washing the floor, bathing the baby – you had to wash your hands, put the mop down, or wrap the baby in a towel and rush to the receiver and say 'Yes, station base to station mobile'. And then they'd say, 'Oh, good. Can you hear me from here?' And we'd have to reply, 'Yes, I can hear you fine'. It was all right the first few times, but it quickly lost its charm."

Ethel agreed. "Yes, they did need to get an idea of the range of the things, and where there were dead spots, but, oh dear, it was wearing on the patience."

Bessie laughed. "The only person I ever heard of who really got their own back was you, Ethel."

"Me!" Ethel was surprised. "What did I do?"

"You might have forgotten about it now, but I was most impressed," Bessie told her. "I was getting extremely frustrated. When I heard your story, I just loved the thought that someone at least had got their own back.

"Well, as I remember hearing, it was one day when John had been calling you up to get his range over and over again as they all did, when he was out mustering sheep. You were thoroughly sick of this, as we all became, on many, many occasions. But you could see the yards from your house. You bided your time and when he was in at the yards and really busy and having a bit of trouble with the sheep, you called 'Curlew base to Curlew mobile, Curlew base to Curlew mobile'. John had to let the gate go because he needed both hands to get out his transmitter."

Bessie paused long enough to explain to Barbara, "We didn't have the clip-on ones then, that they wear on their shirts now."

Bessie continued with her story. "He called back breathlessly, the sheep going everywhere, 'Yes, receiving you.' Ethel simply asked him, 'Having a bit of trouble with the sheep, John?' Just with that, she added to his trouble enormously. What sweet revenge! I was never able to set something up so well."

"Trust our Ethel to organise that," someone said. Most of them agreed that if anyone could find a way to put a fellow in his place, it would be Ethel.

The women's talk turned from old technology to the new, wondering if mobile phone coverage was going to ever work properly in the far west.

"Actually, I believe you can get some sort now, but at a colossal price," one lady in the group commented. "Do you know anyone with one? The normal ones don't work west of Roma."

Most of the women in the group were older women, who had started their married lives with very few amenities at all. They had wooden floors because, without vacuum cleaners, it was impossible to get the dirt out of carpets. The boards were either bare and mopped at least every second day to keep them decent, or polished, and that was a mammoth job without an electric polisher. Thirty-two volt power, if any, and a kerosene fridge which was a luxury compared to an old charcoal safe. Back then, they used Mother Potts irons.

Ethel told the group she thought her steam and dry iron was her biggest luxury, while another woman voted for the automatic washing machine. One woman noted that she'd lived thirty years of her married life before she'd had air conditioning, while her daughter had waited ten and the young girl on the property next door wouldn't get married until her new home had an air conditioner installed.

"Well, one thing I would hate to be without – and it has no modern technology at all – is my 410 Shot Gun," another in the group noted. "I can keep my distance from a snake and still kill it!"

"Yes," Bessie agreed, "I'd hate not to have a 410. What do you use, Ethel?"

"I like my .22," she replied.

Bessie was surprised. "A .22? You'd have to be pretty accurate to be able to use that!"

"Well, I use rat shot."

Bessie shook her head. "All the same, that's a much smaller spread than the 410. I wouldn't like a .22, even with rat shot."

"Well, I seem to get them," Ethel said simply. "It does me."

Barbara could hardly believe her ears. Here was this group of well-dressed, quietly-spoken women, some reaching their elderly years, sitting around discussing what sort of guns they used to kill snakes! Her friends discussed the price of eggs at the supermarket.

Bessie saw the look on Barbara's face and wondered, ruefully, if the conversation was going to ruin all her plans.

Worse was to come. Barbara had something she wanted to ask the ladies about. "You're all such nice people," she started. "You wouldn't be trying to stop the poor Aborigines from hunting and fishing on their own land, would you?"

The ladies all looked at each other. Where would they start to explain? How could they tell someone who knew so little, about the complications involved?

Ethel started to say, "There's quite a bit more to it", when Bessie jumped up and said, "I think Joe wants us to move across to the speeches. There'll be a toast. Does anyone need their glass topped up?" She couldn't get them moving quickly enough.

Everyone was called together almost as she spoke.

"Saved by the bell!" Bessie thought, relieved. Nothing set some people off more than native title. She didn't want them to get into a controversial discussion.

There were a few speeches and toasts wishing the engaged couple every happiness. Aiden, Sally's fiance, was new to everyone but his short, sincere speech in reply gained him friends. Sally spoke, too, because she had a few things to say to all these friends she'd known all her life. Joe McMahon had said how sorry they were to be losing Sally from the district and that they hoped they might see her reasonably regularly when she came back to visit her family. He then said meaningfully, glancing at Thea and Kendal, that perhaps the district might balance up the exchange of one maiden going to the city by gaining two maidens in return. There were plenty of friendly smiles at that, while the girls blushed and exchanged shy glances.

Seeing everyone all gathered together, Mrs Moreton was absolutely amazed at the number of guests. There were babies and toddlers and people of every age right up to and including grandparents. It was like a huge family party.

She was standing quietly with Bessie while they were waiting for lunch, and they could hear snatches of conversation going on all around them. Right behind them Tom Carmody was talking with Joe McMahon. They couldn't help overhearing these men discussing cattle prices.

"Dave Johnson just told me he sold weaners for 350 bucks a head!" Tom told Joe.

"What sort of age would they be, Tom?" Joe asked. "Six months?"

"Well, they'd have to be six. Where are we... January, February... April... maybe eight months. He probably calved early."

"Must have had some scale about them, Tom, for that sort of money." Joe's tone was impressed.

"That's the thing I'd like to do now," Tom said, "with the feed lots wanting to buy more home-bred cattle. I'd like to try to tie it up so we know we've got a guaranteed market for our cattle. As long as the money is pretty reasonable."

"It'd be damn good to have some sort of guarantee today," Joe was vehement now. "Do you think the future of feed lots is OK? They look pretty shaky as well."

They moved away but then they heard Brendan Johnson talking to Rick and that conversation came through clearly for a moment or two.

"We had a bit of a funny time the other night," Brendan was saying. "I was out pig chasing with Barry and Joe. We had my old dog, Blue. You don't know my old dog – but he's been a great pig dog in his time. Well, he bailed this pig up. A great, big, mean-looking boar it was, with huge tusks. Blue rushed in and grabbed him by the ear, but he wasn't up to it any more with such a mean, old bastard. It turned on Blue and carved him up, made a real mess of him, and then came straight at us. We scattered. There were only a couple of small scrubby trees there and Barry skinned up one and Joe up the other. I was hot on their heels, but they both had forks and there was no room for me. I jumped up and grabbed the limb just under Joe and pulled my legs up as high as I could just as the pig rushed at me. But then – *crack!* – the bloody branch gave way and I fell in a heap on the ground. Gawd, it was close!"

"Did he turn on you?" Rick was enthralled. "Did one of the others have their sights on him by then?"

"No, no need for any of that," Brendan said. "He just kept on running in the direction he was headed. We all laughed our heads off. Gawd, we laughed."

Bessie wondered how Barbara found all this talk. It was normal enough, but how would it sound to a city woman? Would she want her daughter living among it all?

In every other way, the party progressed most satisfactorily from Bessie's point of view. The food was delicious and plentiful, the company bright and talkative and the surroundings altogether as pleasant as you could possibly wish. She hoped Sally and Aiden were enjoying it as much as she was.

It didn't seem to be long after lunch when they noticed the time and saw it was nearly four o'clock. No one could believe it was so late and that the time had gone so quickly. They hadn't long finished drinking their tea and coffee that followed the meal.

Obviously, quite a few other people had noticed the time too and were deciding it was time to go. Here and there people were starting to collect their belongings. There was a definite bustle of movement and Bessie Thompson thought it was time for her to take Barbara home. A few hours out with strangers is enough, however friendly they are.

The younger ones all decided to stay. They would very likely party on until the early hours of the morning. Anyone else who wanted to stay would be welcome, of course, but unless there was a special reason to want to stay, most of the not-so-young found it easier to enjoy the company and the outing and then go home.

By the time they'd said their goodbyes and collected their things it was well after four, so it was going to be late enough before they were back at Kalanoa. Kirsty and Carla went with them so that Bruce and Thea could stay as long as they liked with their friends. Together they did the outside jobs and checked the nests were all right for the Easter Bunny and had an easy tea, because no-one was really hungry after the huge lunch. Bessie turned on the TV news and they watched a show or two after that. Barbara said she had had a very pleasant day. Bessie could see her plans were working well.

Chapter 22

Easter Sunday was a quiet day for everyone except the little girls. They were terribly excited to discover the eggs in their hats under their beds. Bessie had pretty boxes of eggs and chocolates to give to Thea, Kendal and Barbara and everyone had some little gift for everyone else. These were received with pleasure, but nothing like the excitement of Kirsty and Carla. They just loved it all – a Peter Rabbit each from Aunt Bessie, who didn't believe in too many chocolates for children, and pretty Easter mugs which Thea and her mother had bought.

Bruce noticed that there was nothing from Diana, not even a phone call to the girls, and he hoped the girls hadn't been expecting anything. Most of their expectations centred around the Easter Bunny and he hadn't let them down.

They made special meals for Easter. For breakfast they had pink and green boiled eggs, boiled with food colouring in the water. It didn't take much effort, but it was a huge success with the children. For some reason they weren't so popular with the young adults who had partied on the night before.

Dinner was set up in the dining room with all the trimmings of a celebration. Bessie Thompson was from the era when every dinner was properly set. She had gone along with the modern trend of informality, mostly by necessity rather than choice, but she insisted that they do things in style for special occasions and holidays. She insisted the children at least had to know that proper dinners existed and special occasions were celebrated. So they cooked a special meal and put it all on silver dishes and served at the table. Carla and Kirsty had helped to decorate the table with flowers and tiny Easter eggs, and were pleased with their efforts.

Not conscious of it as a challenge but because it was what she knew and valued, Bessie was still earnestly trying to give the children in her household satisfying experiences from the culture into which she was born. All too soon she feared it might be swept away by change.

Her generation was the last to be brought up to cling to gracious living. Years ago, women had come out to the bush with no comforts at all – just constant, bone-tiring work in a hard, hot climate. Most of them treasured certain pieces of pretty china, lace cloths and a few pieces of special family silver so that they would not have to live in a world consisting entirely of harsh reality. They carted water in buckets to grow a few favourite flowers and they made their sons and daughters learn a certain amount of poetry and good prose, to read their Bibles and to say their prayers.

Bessie was thankful she wouldn't have the responsibility of deciding what was needed in the future. "Hopefully, Bruce will have Thea to help him sort out what's appropriate for their time," she mused. Bessie's blood still ran cold when she thought of Diana ever having control of the girls again. She would never put herself out to teach the children anything. She hoped that if Bruce married Thea, it would put the prospect of Diana ever having the children safely out of contention. Until then, Bessie proceeded to enjoy every comfortable ritual from her own childhood with these great-nieces of hers.

On Monday morning they went in to church in Juno. It was a pretty normal sort of church service for them, but when Bessie thought of it through the eyes of a visitor, she decided perhaps it wasn't really a run of the mill church service. They didn't have regular services so when a minister or priest of almost any denomination came, anyone turned up. There was always a completely ecumenical congregation and it was the focus of a good social outing.

Bessie's job was to take in flowers. The whole household were involved and they all enjoyed picking and arranging the flowers in baskets and vases. They had quite a few and so did many others, so the hall was really dressed for an Easter service.

The priest was the Anglican priest from Quilpie and he had a visitor with him, Father Watson. Jim Watson was on a sentimental trip around the district. He had been one of the Bush Brothers who had looked after the west many years ago. He was a tall, thin, old man with quite white hair, but there were one or two who remembered him as a vigorous, lanky young man with black hair who had travelled around so many years ago. Bessie and Ethel were two of these and they had quite a yarn to him.

As usual, there was a lot of talk and movement as they all got ready for the service. Sometimes a new visiting parson could get quite upset at the convivial atmosphere – but the old hands were used to it and certainly no-one had cause for complaint once the service started.

They were a bit late starting. A christening had been arranged for Daisy and Dan Flannigan's grandchild – Lily and Jim's baby, Rosie – and so far the christening party had failed to appear. While they were waiting, Ethel Alsop sat down at the organ. Father Watson, or Brother Watson as Bessie still thought of him, was standing near her and said quietly to her, "I see Ethel Alsop is going to play for us. Is she still as sharp as she used to be?"

"Well, er, yes, I suppose so," said Bessie, not quite sure how to answer him.

"Well, I remember my very first service here in Juno," Father Watson continued. "I was pretty young then, and learning the ways of the bush. I arrived out here and it must have been a busy time and communications weren't good or maybe people didn't know the service was on. The long and the short of it was that Ethel was the only one who turned up. I dithered about a bit and wondered what to do. We waited quite a while and when it was obvious no-one else was coming, I asked her diffidently if we thought we should have a service with just the two of us.

"She answered, 'If I was feeding the cows, and one night only one cow came up, I'd feed her'. I took the message from that, and decided I'd better put my best food forward and gave her a full communion service. I'd prepared a sermon naturally, so I gave her that and all. In the end I was quite satisfied with what I'd done."

Bessie smiled at him and said, "Well, it probably was the best thing to do. I'm sure Ethel appreciated it. Imagine your remembering it after all these years!"

He answered her, "I'd remember it for twice as many years if I lived that long. Do you know what her last few words to me were that night?" He paused, his eyes twinkling. 'But I wouldn't have given her the whole bale of hay!'"

"Oh, Ethel!" Bessie thought, but she couldn't help laughing just the same. No wonder he'd remembered Ethel and his first trip to Juno. Their eyes brimmed with laughter. Bessie moved over to see that Barbara had someone to speak to. Father Watson moved to another group of people.

Eventually the christening party arrived, with Dan, as the grandfather, acting very much as the head of the family. Very importantly, he ushered in Lily and Jim.

Dan himself was resplendent in a brightly patterned shirt, that met over fresh, clean, purple trousers. It was Sunday, after all. Daisy was dressed in a tight, purple satin dress. Most of the assembled congregation recognised these quite exotic outfits as the ones that had first appeared for Lily's wedding.

Lily herself was in a pale pink suit with a matching soft hat and looked simply beautiful. As usual, Jim was still tall and resentful.

The *piece de resistance* was baby Rosie. She was to be baptised Rose Emily, but they all knew her fondly as Rosie. Like her mother, she was dressed in pink but she was a bright pink mass of frills and lace. She was continually passed from one to the other and was cuddled and kissed and constantly having her frock adjusted. They were all obviously so proud and pleased with her.

Chairs had been left in the front for them near the font and they took a while to straggle in and take their places. Except when it was their turn to cuddle the baby, they were all a bit harassed looking. They were all explaining at once and to everyone that they were late because they couldn't find the baby's bottle. They were sorry to keep everyone waiting.

The priest moved to the front of the altar and said, "The Lord be with you". The congregation answered, "And also with you". To his words, "Christ is Risen", came the joyful reply, "He is risen indeed", and the service started.

It was a beautiful service. The priest took them through the age-old ritual and this congregation of such diverse Christian faith joined in worship.

Little Rosie was baptised. This part of the service was the most informal. All the children came out and crowded around and watched every move that was made. Bessie wondered whether the family really appreciated the extent of the promises they were making on the child's behalf, but she knew they were really sincere in their desire to express their joy at her birth and to give their thanks to God for her life. Dan was an absolutely devoted grandfather. He was pleased and proud, and actually he had fortified himself for the service rather well.

Rosie started out such a good baby, quite content to be the centre of attention. She obviously enjoyed having all her family clucking around her. After a while she became fairly restless and fretful. Finally, she started to cry.

"There's no bottle – she's probably hungry, poor little mite," Bessie thought.

Rosie's parents and their immediate family and friends were starting to get really embarrassed. When the rest of the congregation were going up for communion, Grandfather Dan took her down to one of the chairs at the back. He was jiggling her about and bouncing her up and down. Her nappy worked loose and, with her stylish, frilly pink pants, was slowly sliding down further and further. The more he bounced her, the more they slid. Those in the congregation who were close were getting a bit worried, but were trying to attend to the service, keep the eyes away and mind their own business. When Dan kept bouncing the baby, the baby's frilly pants kept slipping and the inevitable happened.

The baby wet – and worse – all over his lap. He just didn't know what to do. He just sat staring at her, holding her out quite still now and at arms length muttering, "G-g-good on you, Rosie, g-good on you." Everyone else around him seemed paralysed, too. No-one made a move.

Ethel Alsop, from her position in the front, had seen it all happen. She quietly but quickly left the keyboard and walked down the aisle left between the chairs. As she passed Kendal, she whispered, "Come along with me".

As they reached Dan, he was just starting to get his wits back. "Sh-sh-shit," he said.

"Exactly," said Ethel, taking little Rosie from him and giving her to a bemused Kendal.

"Take her to the washroom and clean her up," Ethel told her quietly. "You'll find a towel in there."

Then she turned to Dan. "Get up you gormless goon," she hissed in his ear, as she made a quick wipe of the floor, "go across to the pub. When Arry O'Tel comes, he can give you a change of clothes. I'll clean this up properly later." Then, quite calmly, she quietly made her way back to the makeshift organ and started playing softly until the end of communion.

Kendal remembered Dan's opinion of Ethel Alsop and laughed to herself as she took the baby away to clean her up. She wasn't very dirty – mostly her grandfather had suffered. A hand towel was probably all she'd need until she could get a clean nappy from the baby's mother.

In its own way, it had been quite a memorable outing.

By the time the luncheon guests had assembled at Kalanoa, Barbara was pleased to find that she knew quite a few of them.

She remembered her hostess from Saturday, Margery McMahon, and of course her husband, Joe. She thought she could also recognise most of the family of the young guest of honour, Sally. She certainly knew her Mum and Dad, Jean and Jack, but she wasn't sure that she'd be able to place all their young sons. One she did remember was Brendan, who'd made the lovely necklaces she'd seen his mother and sister wear.

Then there was that tall, quite distinguished-looking fellow, Tom, and his son, Charles, who was so like him in features. What was their surname? She couldn't remember. They were both good-looking people but a bit remote for her, especially Charles. He obviously had an interest in Thea's friend, Kendal. He was a distinguished enough fellow but Barbara thought she liked Thea's choice much better. Bruce was much more friendly and companionable, she thought, much easier to get along with. She didn't realise that she felt her own position less threatened by the milder mannered man than by his more dynamic and forceful friend. Bessie never knew it, but she couldn't have done a wiser thing than to present that contrast.

Barbara went on looking around at the assembled crowd. Kendal's brother, Rick, she recognised, too. She had noticed that he spent a good deal of his time talking to that little girl with the straight brown hair who had such great big eyes. Barbara thought that her name might be Wendy and that she seemed to be some sort of relation of the McMahons. Then there was that sharp-tongued Ethel Alsop. She wasn't sure she liked Ethel all that much, but most of the others seemed to like her very much indeed. To the quietly-spoken Barbara, Ethel seemed a bit abrupt.

So there were plenty of people that Barbara remembered and she was starting to feel quite interested in them all.

What she didn't know was that she had an interview with Ethel ahead of her.

Bessie would have been less than pleased, too, if she had realised that Ethel couldn't contain herself and had resolved to make sure

276

Barbara went home a little more aware of what was involved in the native title debate.

After lunch was over, Ethel invited Barbara to do a tour of the garden which was as good a way as any to get her on her own and have a chance to talk to her.

Ethel knew Barbara lived on the Gold Coast so she put to her an imaginary case to illustrate for her the impact of native title. "Just suppose you live on the beach front and some aboriginal families wanted access to the beach through your yard," she began.

Barbara tried to explain where she lived, but Ethel insisted she was only painting a picture to illustrate her point.

Ethel continued. "In this imaginary case, you have a house near the beach and the native title claim you're told about is just about access. People want to come through your yard, in the front gate and out the back gate to the beach. Where's the problem? The mothers bring their children through your yard and out to the beach. Don't be selfish and try to stop this – after all, once the whole beach and all the foreshore and the seas belonged to them. Of course, the fathers would have to be able to come through, too, with all their fishing gear, and their friends. That's their right, to hunt and fish. Why should it worry you when you go to hang your washing on the line that anyone at all could be going through your property? After all, the Archbishop of Perth, media personnel and lots of other friends of the Aborigines visited a property in Western Australia and were really distressed that the graziers thought only Aborigines should have the right of access. These people thought graziers should let Aborigines bring their friends, too."

Barbara tried to say a few words but, as managing a woman as she was, she was no match for Ethel when Ethel had a mind to it.

Ethel now rammed home the point. "Now we have established that no-one on the coast would mind giving Aborigines native title rights to their land – even it if does mean not knowing who might be in your garden at any time."

Barbara tried to indicate that she thought people would mind.

Ethel overruled her. "Why should you mind? Everyone says we graziers shouldn't mind. We're not even supposed to have reason to be afraid. Bessie and the children are often in the house at Kalanoa on their own and the whole world thinks that they are selfish to stop anyone coming on to their place. After all, it could be a serious group of people looking for some sacred places. Could be a mob of drunks with alcohol and guns. They're not to mind, why should you?"

By now, Barbara was speechless. She didn't know what to say.

Ethel went on. "That's not the full story either," she told Barbara. "When you get the agreement about the native title in the mail, it doesn't actually say 'right to access to hunt and fish', it says, 'the claimants are entitled as against the whole world to the possession, occupation, use and enjoyment of the whole of the country within the area of application'. You see a really earnest, gentle-faced Aborigine on TV telling the interviewer – with the whole world to see – that he doesn't really want exclusive possession, he only wants access rights. You look at him and believe him – but would you, in your right mind, sign the piece of paper? He might honestly believe that's all he wants but why did his lawyers put those words in? Who might execute the full wording of the claim in one year, two years or ten years' time? The legal profession would laugh in your face if you try to tell them that it didn't mean exactly what it said when it was put to the test."

Ethel was winding down. "Can you see that scenario, Barbara? How will you feel if the native title debate escalates to being extended to be a held as stronger than freehold title and tribes start to claim coastal lands and the seas for themselves?"

Barbara, a little in awe of Ethel's outburst, admitted that she could see the whole situation in a different light.

Ethel was pleased with herself, but hoped Bessie didn't ever know about their conversation. She knew Bessie wanted Barbara to be really happy with her trip out to the bush and that her plans hadn't included thrashing out contentious subjects. But Ethel couldn't have stood by and not tried to get her to see what was involved more clearly.

After all, Barbara brought the subject up. Ethel would never have forced it upon her if she hadn't wanted to know – or so Ethel told herself.

Bessie never did find out. Actually, Barbara wasn't all that upset about it all. She was actually glad to think that she knew a bit more and it certainly gave her something to consider. She wouldn't let Ethel know that she was interested, of course, but she would think about it.

So what Bessie didn't know didn't worry her, and she was very pleased with the way everything went.

By the time the plane went on Tuesday, Bessie was pretty sure that Barbara wouldn't be working against them – even if she wasn't actually working to promote the match.

She was in a contemplative mood and thought things over as she had a cup of tea quietly by herself when they had all left. She was very happy with the way the weekend had gone.

Her mind wandering to other subjects, she thought of the three boys she'd watched grow up – Bruce and his friends, Charles and Tony.

Their early lives had seemed to hold so much promise and then, bit by bit, things turned sour for each one of them. Now there were only two of them who would continue on. Tony had lost the battle. This country had a history of making or breaking men, and whatever the exact circumstances, there was no doubt it had broken Tony. A little help at the right time might have made all the difference to him and the country might not have lost a most effective operator and a damn good citizen. Now, God bless his soul, he was dead and they were all the poorer for it.

Charles was obviously still keeping his options open. He was lucky that he had options. His interest in business put him in a different position from the average man on the land. "Would he settle for life on the land, or go for life in the city?" Bessie thought to herself. "How long could he keep some kind of mix?" He seemed to be ready to make one commitment at least, she decided, feeling satisfied. If ever a man was in love, she would bet that Charles was in love with Kendal. He couldn't go wrong there, she was a splendid girl and had a lot to offer. She would make a good addition to the district if they did settle here, but where would they decide to live?

Then Bessie's thoughts turned to Bruce and Thea. This was one couple she felt would certainly stay in the bush for as long as they possibly could. Thea was shy and tentative, but she was tough underneath. As well as that, she was loving and kind and would make a great little wife and mother. Bessie was glad that there was at least one young couple she was pretty sure would commit themselves to this way of life.

For over two hundred years, pastoral living had kept families going in Australia. Bessie prayed it would continue into the twenty-first century. She knew anything could happen. There'd been plenty of dry gullies to cross and plenty to come, but she was glad to see someone was going to try to keep things flowing. As she sat there, she had a vision of the pageant of life, of the past flowing through to the future. A few people stood out in the parade, but most were just ordinary people who did their best in whatever way they could – struggling through the bad times, praying for the good and trying to keep things going. After all, who knows what will happen in five or ten years' time?

Bessie hoped Thea and Bruce, this young couple for whom she felt most responsible, would prosper. Otherwise she might be guilty of what was now jokingly described as the latest form of child abuse – leaving the family farm to the children. She laughed ruefully to herself and pulled herself out of her reverie.

The tea was cold, the garden badly needed a drink, the kitchen needed a sweep, life was waiting and she had jobs to do.

"Sitting around here won't buy the baby a bonnet," she muttered to herself. She took her cup out to the kitchen, swept the floor, put on her hat and went out into the garden.

Chapter 23

It was only a matter of weeks later that Bruce found a quiet moment to speak to his aunt.

"Aunt Bessie," he said hesitantly, "Thea and I have decided we want to get married."

Bessie was jubilant. At last! All of her plotting and planning had paid off. She barely realised Bruce was still saying, "How will that affect you?"

To herself, she thought, "How will that affect me? Jubilation! Sing praises to the Lord!", but to her nephew she replied, "Bruce, my dear, I'm delighted for you. I really did think Thea was the girl for you and I've seen that the little girls love her, too. It will be a wonderful thing for you all."

"But are you sure you won't mind?" Bruce seemed oddly anxious. "It will mean another woman in the house again. You never did enjoy having Diana here."

"This will be an entirely different matter, Bruce," Bessie assured him. "Diana never really fitted in. You loved her, I know that, and you were blinded by your romantic ideals. She was never suited at all to our way of life. She thought that the life of a woman in the bush was a privileged, pampered existence. Nothing I could say before you were married would change her mind. She thought I was jealous and didn't want another woman on the place. Well, we all saw how well she survived life out here. This couldn't be more different. Thea doesn't know a lot about it either yet, but her attitude is so different. She isn't in it for some romantic ideal that doesn't exist anymore – if it ever did. Thea loves you, not the mistaken idea of a rich landholder. I wish you two every happiness."

Kendal soon was told, of course, and she was genuinely pleased for him and for Thea, too, and the little girls and even Bessie. Not least Bessie. It would be a really good match and great for everyone involved. She couldn't help grinning to herself and could hardly wait to get Bessie Thompson on her own.

"Well, you pulled it off you old schemer," she said when they were finally alone.

"Well, you were included," Bessie said. "Joy oh joy, and do you know Bruce was hesitant to tell me? He thought I'd be jealous. Jealous! When I'm so delighted!"

The letters. The talk. The whole house was full of excitement about the engagement. The ring, when were they getting the ring? When would be the best time for the wedding? How big a wedding would it be? Everyone in the district was delighted for them and wished them well. Where would it be? Out here or at the coast? Everyone who visited Kalanoa was immediately caught up in the talk. A church or a wedding celebrant? Could it be in a church now Bruce was a divorced man? Everyone was interested. Everyone that is, except Charles.

Charles was obviously completely and utterly disinterested in all this talk and fuss about the wedding. He didn't say much that Kendal ever heard against the wedding or the match, but it was impossible for her not to miss his extreme indifference, not to mention antagonism.

He said all that was proper to Bruce. His manner was perfectly correct and Bruce, in his own glow of happiness, noticed nothing amiss. But Kendal, tuned into Charles's feelings the way she was, couldn't help wondering if they would ever be in such a blissful state themselves. He seemed so terribly uncomfortable with it all.

Of course, before long Thea came out to visit Kalanoa. Naturally, some of the young ones of the district came over at the weekend. Rick and Charles were among them, and Tom – who wasn't a spring chicken any more but the younger ones didn't want to leave him at home on his own – came, too. John and Wendy came out from Juno station, as well as the Johnson boys from next door. By the time everyone arrived, there was quite a little group of them gathered.

They were all having tea on the verandah and the talk kept coming around to the wedding.

Charles, hoping to get the group on another tack, said, "The garden looks pretty good still. Surely it won't be long before the first frost touches it, though. You're lucky to be on the river here, it keeps the frost away."

The others were more interested in the plans for the wedding, and the talk quickly swung back again.

"Will you wait long before your wedding?" Rick asked. "You've not been engaged long."

They discussed the various reasons for and against long engagements, and the particular issues that they were considering.

"Are the little girls going to be flower girls?" Wendy asked.

Carla and Kirsty, who weren't going to be left out of any gathering and had joined the group, giggled. Thea had asked them when she had arrived at Kalanoa this time, and they were thrilled. Not that they really understood what was happening, but they were delighted to be part of all the fuss.

The conversation came around to the engagement ring, and Thea shyly showed everyone her ring. It was a pretty pink stone surrounded by diamonds. They were all most impressed.

Charles hadn't said much for a while, and seemed to be deep in thought. Bruce turned to him and asked, "What do you think, old fellow?"

"I think that you really ought to cut that mistletoe out of that big tree," he answered. There was surprised silence and then Charles, unaware or unwilling to acknowledge he had changed the subject, continued, "It really is a beautiful tree and that mistletoe will kill it before too long."

Everyone adjusted their thoughts and considered the tree. Bessie said, "You're right, you know. We were talking about that only the other day."

Bruce agreed. "Yes, we were talking about it just before Thea and Mrs Moreton came up to stay. Somehow I keep putting it off. I'll have to make sure I get to it. It's such a feature of the garden and Thea loves the trees, don't you, darling?" He turned to her, "I wouldn't want to lose that one in particular before you actually come here to live."

"I'm sure there's no imminent danger of that," said Charles, "but you'll have to get onto it."

"Well, we haven't quite decided when the best time to have the wedding..." Bruce began.

"I think it's time for me to go," said Charles. "You coming to see me off, Kendal? I brought over a couple of books we were talking about the other day – they're in the car."

As they were going out to the car, Kendal asked, "Didn't you like her ring?"

"Don't you bloody start," Charles said impatiently. "I've had as much talk about weddings and all the fancy trimmings as I can stand."

"What's your problem? Aren't you happy for them, Charles? Don't you want them to be married?" Kendal wasn't surprised at his attitude, because she'd been watching him closely, but she wanted to know his reasoning.

"Of course I want them to be married, if that's what they want," he replied. "Bless them. Every happiness to them. I just don't want them to talk about weddings every time I go near there. It might be of abiding interest to them, but it sure as hell doesn't interest me all that much."

Kendal was dismayed. It wasn't much of an attitude from the man she wanted to marry. Where had all the romance gone that he'd shown in Brisbane?

Bruce wanted the wedding as soon as possible. Once he was sure he had his aunt's approval and that she wasn't upset, he saw no reason to wait. Mrs Moreton, however, didn't see any need to rush. She wanted to get every last moment of pain and pleasure out of the whole experience. She was delighted that her daughter was to marry the man she loved, but she was strangely sad to be losing her daughter. She would never really have her to live at home again. However, she was enjoying the thought of Thea's wedding, but not yet – there was no rush.

Thea was caught in the middle of all of this. She wanted to get married as soon as possible, but she wanted her mother to be happy and she thought all the preparations were very important.

Bessie just wanted to keep everyone happy and on track so that it certainly did take place. She could wait. She'd waited for many things in her life and there was no rush for this. When Ethel Alsop came over they discussed it all again from every possible angle.

Kendal listened to all sides of the story. She was happy for Bruce and Thea. They were both great people. She could listen to the talk coming from all sides quite happily. The only problem was that it seemed to annoy Charles so intensely.

Whenever he was visiting, it obviously irritated him that the talk consistently slid back to the wedding. Kendal hoped the others didn't notice it as much as she did. They all found the topic so absorbing themselves that they didn't seem to notice, but Kendal – who would have loved to have been discussing the same subject herself with Charles – couldn't help notice his irritation. In fact, he was quite blunt and rude about it when they were on their own.

"That's it," he told her on more than one occasion. "That's enough talk about the wedding. Not one more word about clothes or dresses or flowers or weddings if you want me to stay sane. How can they go on and on about such a perfectly idiotic subject every single moment of the time? If you value my sanity, don't mention it again."

Kendal was discouraged. Far from encouraging Charles to think of weddings, it was obviously putting him off. Lucky Bruce. Lucky Thea.

Time doesn't stand still and gradually the talk about weddings was starting to be taken over, but not completely replaced, by talk about the Juno Gymkhana which they had every year to raise money for the Flying Doctor.

This function was getting pretty important. It was not as famous as the Birdsville Races but it was becoming quite famous in its own way and had its place on the tourist calender and it attracted hundreds of visitors.

Although it was called a gymkhana, horse sports no longer dominated the program. The name Juno Gymkhana had become known and it had a good swing to it, and that was the name, no matter what they put on the programme. The first changes they'd made was that footraces and motorbikes had come in. Then, gradually, other things were added, like crafts, flowers and paintings. It had become almost a mini version of a local show. This year, following the success of the Quick Shear, they had added a shearing competition. As it was the one big event for the Flying Doctor in this particular area, anything and everything that would bring the crowd and raise money was added. They all had to cook and plan to cater for the crowd.

Bessie's job this year was to be the official hostess. It was to be a much bigger job than she had anticipated when she'd accepted. This year, every politician who had the slightest excuse to be there wanted to come. With all the political upheaval about One Nation, all the pollies were busy waving the flag in the rural areas and all the locals were keen to get a chance to meet them and speak their mind. Everyone had burning issues to discuss – the sale of Telstra, cotton growing on the Cooper, native title, the GST and national parks, as well as the various other things that individuals around had strong feelings about. You never really knew what could rouse strong feelings in some people. Of course, everyone tried to be as good to the politicians as possible, too. After all, you never know who might be in a position to help when the district needed something.

It wasn't going to be a hard job for Bessie. Everyone was being very busy being helpful and as amiable as possible. Most of the political visitors were flying in and flying out with very tight schedules. Most arrived throughout the morning and were all assembled in time for lunch. Nearly everyone was there, and it was all organised by a team of workers, although some came and went as their areas of responsibility demanded. There were plenty of people to talk to the guests and Bessie had very little to do except to keep a eye on things and be ready to step in if anything demanded it.

There were stalls and bars all over the place selling drinks and sandwiches, cups of tea and cakes and whatever else anyone thought would sell. But there was a special afternoon tea arranged in the CWA rooms for the visitors to have with the gymkhana president and other officials before they left. Evening came in early in the winter and most of the pollies had to get away. It was thought if they gave them lunch as it fitted in and then a formal afternoon tea before they left with maybe a few drinks, that was all that was necessary as official hospitality.

Bessie's biggest cross to bear was that she had to work with the ones she didn't like as well as those she did. She was less than pleased but quite resigned to the fact that Daisy was in charge of the actual afternoon tea. They had worked for a great many functions in their time and they hardly ever saw eye to eye about things. It was Daisy's joy to organise special events like the afternoon tea. She had her own set of cups and saucers which she particularly valued. Privately Bessie thought they were garish and quite hideous, but Daisy had been proudly producing them for special occasions for many years and wasn't likely to change right now.

Before the big day, while they were all making mountains of sandwiches to help with catering at the gymkhana, both Kendal and Thea had asked Aunt Bessie if there was anything they could do to help her with her job.

"No, thank you," she said. "I should be all right. You just do whatever jobs you've been assigned. After you've finished, come over to the CWA Rooms. If you finish in time you can help me if there are any last minute jobs at the end of the afternoon."

The committee had asked Kendal to help with the foot races and particularly the children's events. She was glad to find Sheila, the cook she'd met at the Quick Shear, was in the district again and that they were working together. She enjoyed catching up with her. Thea was assigned to the crafts and helping Margery McMahon with the organising of the hall and all the exhibits. Clara was in the hall, too. Sam was with the horse sports. Bruce was over the other side helping organising the shearing. Tom was in charge of the bar for the day and had a team of helpers. Charles had made sure he would be available to be there with his dad.

Bessie checked all of her areas of responsibility quite early in the day. She went to the CWA room. Daisy had it all set up, cups in place, tea and coffee and sugar, milk in an esky, plenty of cakes and scones donated and Daisy's own cooking, covered but ready, in pride of place. The urn was full and Bessie knew better than to check what time Daisy was going to start that. She would take offence if she was too closely organised and she'd done it often enough to be able to judge the correct time. It was her one big job for the day and she took pride in doing it well. She was resplendent in the purple dress. It was covered with a big grey cardigan in the morning and with her ugh boots, its glory was somewhat diminished – but both the boots and the cardigan were shed as the day warmed.

They had no special program for the special visitors. It wouldn't do to miss anything and have the people involved in the particular section feel overlooked. So the visitors moved about with various officials with Bessie just keeping a quite eye on all that was happening. They turned up at the various children's races on time, watched the shearing, and looked through the hall with all the flowers and cooking and art.

At each stopping point there was always someone who wanted to have their say. This was their chance to speak directly to and question a person who normally was just a face on TV, and most people weren't about to miss it. In fact, a lot of people had quite a lot they wanted to ask, tell, demand or just go on about. The locals, and quite a few of the visiting crowd for that matter, were making the most of their opportunity.

Bessie had an unofficial timetable in her head of what time there was to spend where. As the afternoon wore on, they were starting to lag behind. By the time they reached the hall to look at the exhibits and displays there, she knew they wouldn't get to the afternoon tea at the time she'd arranged with Daisy. She left them all doing their thing and slipped away to let Daisy know they'd be a bit late. Daisy wasn't pleased. She'd gone to a lot of trouble and didn't like to be kept waiting. She made it plain that she felt a bit slighted and didn't hesitate to tell Bessie what she thought of the organisation when no-one had considered all the time she'd put into getting everything ready. But Bessie had no time for prima donna behaviour from Daisy.

"Oh, tut-tut and fiddle-dee-dee," she said, while Daisy complained. "They're not doing this deliberately. They can't help being late, they don't even know what a splendid afternoon tea you have waiting. They are just being polite to all the people who are wanting to talk to them and show them around. They'll get here all right, but just a little late." She started to smooth Daisy's ruffled feathers. "It's worth putting ourselves out a bit, Daisy. You never know who might be able to help us get better roads or better TV."

Charles had brought glasses and bottles from the bar and was setting up for a few drinks, and that part was going OK. Bessie went back to the hall to shepherd her flock on their way.

Everyone was really on their best behaviour. With all the different parties involved and different political affiliations, they were doing a splendid job of getting along and responding with bland replies to quite cantankerous questions. They were saying all the right things and taking such an interest in everything and everyone. It was a time-consuming exercise.

Just as she had nearly all the group rounded up and poised to go in to tea, another interruption occurred. Bessie could see the talk could go on for a few more minutes, so she slipped away to tell Daisy they really were on their way. When she arrived at the doorway, she couldn't believe her eyes.

There was no Daisy, no garish tea set, no set table. There were a few women sitting around looking vaguely uncomfortable. Thea and Kendal were standing at the back of the room.

Bessie said, "What's happened?"

"Well," one of the ladies said, "Daisy was getting more and more put out. Then she finally flipped and said 'They're not going to mess me about anymore. I never go nowhere and I can always watch a video'. She packed up her cups and saucers and put her cakes back in some tins, pulled the cloths off the table and carried it all away."

"Well, don't just stand there!" said Bessie, exasperated. "We've got a crowd of officials arriving any minute and we've got to at least give them a cup of tea!"

She turned to the local ladies. "If any of you can get any cups or mugs from home, go and get them as fast as you can. Kendal, go across to Ethel Alsop and tell her that I need her. Get all the cups and mugs she can give you."

Kendal said diffidently, "I just won a plastic picnic set in the governess's race, you can use that."

"Good," said Bessie, "We might need that, too. Thea, you go back to the display in the hall and see Margery McMahon. Ask her if you can take a cloth or two off one of those tables in the hall. No-one will miss them at this time. And see Mrs Johnson and ask if she can bring a bowl of flowers. I put one in for competition and there are probably one or two others, too, that we can put on the table. If you see Clara, ask her to come if she possibly can. She's good value."

She turned to the others around her. "There will be things to eat in those packets. Maybe one of you could go over and see if we can have some of the cooking they were going to auction. This is a good cause after all. Who's looking after that today?"

So Bessie was able to get them all organised to cope. Thea was wide-eyed with wonder and concern. Kendal didn't dare show she thought it was really quite funny. She estimated that Bessie Thompson wouldn't begin to see the joke for a couple of weeks at least.

Eventually, tea was taken. They all had a round or two of drinks and before long it was all over.

Bruce arrived just as the officials were going off. Thea couldn't wait to tell him all that had happened. "You'll never believed what happened here!" she told him in amazement. "All those important people coming and Daisy Flannigan just walked out on the afternoon tea!"

Charles could see the funny side of it with Kendal. While Bessie was trying to get organised they'd hardly dared look at each other in case they laughed, but with it all over they delighted in telling Bruce the joke. They were really enjoying themselves when Thea said, "I don't know how you can think it's so funny. I think it's a dreadful thing to have happened. Just imagine if something like that happened at our wedding, Bruce. We'll definitely get married at the coast. We can't get married out here."

Bruce immediately stopped laughing and put his arm around Thea, assuring her that they'd make sure such a thing didn't happen to their special day.

Charles had stopped laughing, too. Grimly he said to Kendal, "Come on, we'd better go. You'd better give me a hand. I've got a few boxes and things to take out to the car."

As soon as they were out of earshot he exploded, "I knew it! I knew it! She was sure to get around to that damned wedding sooner or later – and sooner it was. She just can't keep off the subject! I've never met anyone so completely besotted with a wedding."

Kendal tried to let it all wash over her. "Let him rave on," she thought. "Don't rise to the defence and he'll get over it all the sooner."

As they collected cartons and things, she let her thoughts wander and attended with only half her mind. She didn't really listen to him at all – it had been a busy day.

They reached their vehicle and Charles put down his gear and came around to her side to open the door. Or so Kendal thought. But he took her things and put them down and leaned his hand against the door. His manner was completely changed.

He looked at her, and Kendal thought he had a strange look on his face. "Bill-Bob was right, you know," he said gently. "A fellow should really take his advice."

Kendal was confused. What was coming now? "How did we get onto Bill-Bob?" she asked, with questions in her eyes.

He looked straight back into her eyes and said hesitantly, "It seems a best thing a fellow can do. He should get married – if a fellow is lucky enough to know a girl like you, of course. How about you? Would you like to be married? To me, of course?"

Kendal didn't answer. She was too amazed at the sudden change in the course of the conversation. Then, slowly, she said, "Come again?"

Charles had earlier lost his bravado and now he lost his offhanded way. He was deadly earnest. His feelings were deep, but raw, and his words stumbled out.

"I'd even be willing to go through all that fuss for you, Kendal. God knows how a fellow could stand it, but I'd do it for you. Be

290

merciful and make it quick. How quick could it be? Can you make it soon? You will marry me, won't you? How soon will you marry me?"

At first she'd been a bit dazed by Charles's change of attitude. And then she started to feel more and more overwhelmed with happiness. She started to realise that Charles really did mean it. He was actually proposing to her – even wanting to set a date. Charles, who was so sure of himself in every other way but had never managed to stick to a relationship, wanted to marry her.

She smiled. "I think I could just about do that," she told him. "I'm pretty good at arranging things, darling. I bet I could even arrange it so you'd hardly know it was happening. You'd have to go through it on the day, of course."

"Bless you, Kendal." Charles's relief was obvious. "I should have known I could count on you. To think I almost let their fussing about put me off. But I'd even have all the fuss if it was the only way I could have you."

Kendal was charmed. For Charles, this was the ultimate sacrifice. "You've been thinking about this, then?" she asked playfully.

"Oh no, not much at all," he replied nonchalantly, and then he smiled. "Not more than twenty-three hours in the day." He kissed her thoroughly and added, "Thinking about it? I hardly think about anything else."

He started to kiss her again and they didn't talk about much at all for quite a while.

Finally they drew apart. He reached into his pocket and then took her hand in his. He slipped a ring on her finger. Kendal just stood there. She couldn't speak.

"Do you like it?" Charles asked anxiously. "It was my mother's." He took her silence for rejection. "We can get another one if you don't like it."

Kendal stared at the old-fashioned diamond ring on her finger. She thought it was the most beautiful thing she'd ever seen. She found her voice. With stars in her eyes, she assured him it was perfect. "What a wonderful, wonderful thing to do. Your own mother's ring!" She was just overwhelmed and went on and on. She realised she was gushing, but she was just so excited.

Charles was delighted with her reaction. He'd been prey to all sorts of fears.

Kendal had come down to earth a bit and asked curiously, "What was it that Bill-Bob said to start all of this?"

Charles smiled with a twinkle in his eyes and asked, "You really want to know?" The stress of the proposal out of the way, he was back to his old confident self. He was excited and relieved, playful at the moment – rather than romantic. Too much emotion was a strain.

Kendal nodded. She should have been warned by the mischief in eyes, but she walked straight into it.

"Well, when he was in one of his 'do as I say, not as I do', moods, he said to me that every man should have a wife."

At this, Charles broke off, took Kendal in his arms and kissed her again quite thoroughly. Then he stood back and prepared to duck for cover as he teased, "Because, after all, there are some things you just can't blame on the government!"